"So scandalous . . . this one kept me entertained."

—*Jane* magazine

"A light year's leap beyond chick lit."

—*Pittsburgh Tribune-Review*

" . . . tackling edgier and darker questions."

—*USA Today*

THE BOOSTER

A Novel

Jennifer Solow

WASHINGTON SQUARE PRESS
New York   London   Toronto   Sydney

Washington Square Press
A Division of Simon & Schuster, Inc.
1230 Avenue of the Americas
New York, NY 10020

First Washington Square Press trade paperback edition July 2007

WASHINGTON SQUARE PRESS and colophon are registered trademarks of
Simon & Schuster, Inc.

For information about special discounts for bulk purchases,
please contact Simon & Schuster Special Sales:
1-800-456-6798 or business@simonandschuster.com.

Designed by Karolina Harris

Manufactured in the United States of America

The Library of Congress has cataloged the Atria Books hardcover edition as follows:
Solow, Jennifer.
The booster: a novel / Jennifer Solow
p. cm.
1. Unemployed women workers—Fiction. 2. Loss (Psychology)—Fiction. 3. New York
(N.Y.)—Fiction. 4. Shoplifting—Fiction. 5. Unemployed—Fiction. I. Title.
PS3619.O4375B66 2006
813'6—dc22   2005053627

ISBN-13: 978-0-7432-8183-6

ISBN-13: 978-0-7432-8184-3 (Pbk)

TO TOMMY

JILLIAN SIEGEL likes to shoplift at least once a day. It is not a crime as she sees it; it is her birthright.

Her spoils needn't be as tall as a Louboutin boot or as wide as an Hermès scarf; often the tiniest trifle will do. Just the act of closing a fist and releasing it again into a pocket, feeling the blush of her cheek as the fresh treasure is absorbed, knowing the thing, the coveted thing, is now owned and cherished, is enough.

In general, she is a shopper. Deliberate colors like tobacco and pale lavender make her happy. She runs her finger along the folds, occasionally selecting one above the rest for more generous attention: a close hold, a caress on the cheek, a fondling of the nub, a sizing up in the mirror.

Stores are restful, tidy places for her. Six or seven items placed on an up-lit counter, quiet and articulate, each one folded then folded again infinitely throughout the day by handsome women in black uniform; a measured array of consecrated goods placed precisely so as not to touch one another. The faintest smells of cement and coffee beans at Comme des Garçons, the smoky wood planks and jasmine blossoms hovering in the air at Azzedine Alaia, or the patent leather, bubblegum smell at Betsey Johnson replenish the soul.

To make an acquisition, by purse or pocket, is to bring home the experience.

There was once a time when Jillian did not need to shop, much less steal, to get her fix. When fine camel-hair coats, fluffy fur muffs, and new Mary Janes just appeared at the foot of her bed. When her wardrobe, like that of a princess, bloomed perpetually—a rainbow of new delights on hangers she wasn't even big enough to reach. This endless bounty was not, for her, simply a material one; it was the backdrop of an enchanted world. One filled with magic—the true kind of magic that animates Christmas windows, makes the sun sparkle through the clouds, and, on some mornings, makes entire stretches of Park Avenue smell like hot chocolate.

But then one day, as if by some foul patch of weather, the wind came in and blew it all away—the sun and the moon and the joy that once made everything bright.

And now, a thousand pages later, these provisions, the mislaid pieces of her heart, the silky squares of material, the soft pleats of embroidered cloth, are scattered throughout the universe, longing to be amassed again by their rightful owner.

It is not a crime as she sees it; it is the eternal job of a patient practitioner.

Certainly once a day is not too much.

* * *

1

"I DON'T understand why you don't come, Jill." Alex Wald is yelling loud enough from the loft bedroom upstairs for Jillian to hear him clearly in the bathroom below. "Ever."

"Have you seen my Ativan?" Jillian is rushing through her apartment opening things and closing them again. Her bare, pedicured feet shuffle across the wood floor of her 940-square-foot "loftlike" apartment on Twelfth Street. "There was that small bottle in the medicine cabinet with a peeling label and then the other one in the zipper thingy in my pocketbook." The floor is like the rest of the apartment, decent enough, big enough, good enough for now. It's a fine holding spot until she can get a real apartment—at least 1,500 square feet—a place where she could one day serve dinner parties or keep fluffy guest towels in a spare closet.

How many times can two people have the same conversation, she wonders as she rushes from the closet to the bathroom and back again. It's not like *coming* is the easiest thing in the world to do; it's not as if you can just order it up, like a dry Ketel One martini with extra olives, and *poof*, there it is, perfectly chilled and waiting for you to take a sip.

Jillian is wearing only a pair of Cosabella thong underwear. A spot of Alex's fresh ejaculate wets the middle of the sixteen-dollar sliver of material. It's just the thing she was worried about when he woke her up early, pressing his hard-on into the middle of her back. Not that she doesn't love to feel the weight of him rolling on top of her, she does—the fleeting moment of safety beneath him, the salty taste of his shoulder as her mouth lingers there, the way his body provides sanctuary for hers, if only for a second. She does love all that, it's just that she doesn't love *all that* less than seventy-seven minutes before the biggest presentation of her life.

"I know I have another Ativan." She holds her breasts, one in each hand like beanbags, as she darts from room to room.

"I am not the keeper of the pharmaceuticals, Jill." Alex rolls back underneath the comforter—a thousand-thread count, extra primaloft Vermont goose down—the softest she could find at Bed Bath & Beyond on Sixth.

"Shit." Jillian opens the empty prescription bottle from the side pocket of her purse. "Shit. Great. Perfect."

"You don't need a tranquilizer. You'll do great today, Bubb."

"Goddamn it." Jillian pulls the sticky cotton material out from its crevice. "I can't even wear this underwear now." She wiggles her thong down to the floor, hurls it in the direction of the laundry basket, and dashes into her closet: a second bedroom in her apartment converted with shelves, bins, and wire racks.

"You don't even want me to make you come, Jilly. I mean, I think most girls would at least *want* to."

She marches up the spiral staircase to the bedroom clutching a linen shirt underneath her armpit and pointing a toothbrush with the other hand. "Yogis don't have orgasms, Alex. They save up their chi." Jillian's never told him that she hasn't had an actual orgasm with another person in the room, unless you count Sharon Levy at Timberwood sleepover camp, and she's never told him that she really *does* want to, that she really does try to get there—she tries to reach the point of no return, but then it just all falls completely apart.

"You're not a yogi." Alex reaches out for her hand and nibbles on her fingertips. His eyes are clear and sweet, and the sunburn he got two weeks ago in South America has faded to a soft patina. "And you have enough chi to choke a horse."

"This isn't a problem for you because you don't actually have to *go* to work today and make the presentation of your life—a presentation to people who just stare at you because they haven't had their double espresso yet and they can't actually propel messages from one side of their brain to the other. . . ."

"Oh yeah. My job is really easy."

"And I have absolutely nothing to wear and *now* I need to stop at McKay's." Jillian's nerve endings feel as if they're about to burst. Alex should know this about her by now.

"You say that like it's my fault you're out of Ativan. Like it's always my fault." Alex puts a pillow over his head and presses down hard. "You're the pill popper." His words are muffled through nineteen ounces of Vermont goose feathers.

"I'm not a *pill popper.*" Jillian shoves the toothbrush into her mouth and brushes. She talks through it. "I have a prescription for exactly eight pills. Eight one-half-milligram pills last me, I don't know, months!" The toothpaste begins to foam around her mouth. "I would think a pill popper would need more than eight pills."

"Why don't you wear that black suit with the bow hickeys on the sides?" Alex squeezes along the shaft of his penis, pushing the remainder of semen out into a droplet at the tip. He rubs the white ball into his chest and turns over toward the pillow.

"Jesus. That's my bed!"

Some things should just be done in private, Jillian thinks, with a tissue, or at least when no one else is staring right at them preparing for a big presentation. Alex, she recalls, will pee off the side of a dive boat. He knows nothing of personal boundaries. "Those are my good sheets."

She races back down the tight spiral staircase into the bathroom and spits into the sink. "Plus the black suit makes me look like an anesthesiologist."

"Just wear what makes you comfortable."

"What's that supposed to mean?"

Jillian wonders why she's even asking him—Alex buys everything from the REI catalog. Not that he doesn't look great in his old Patagonias and Carhartts; he always looks great in an I-don't-care-how-I-look kind of way. The worn cotton of his collar and the hole in the armpit of his old cashmere sweater always make her heart skip a beat. Sometimes Jillian wishes she could be like him—a carefree, hole-in-the-armpit photographer, roaming the wild one week a month with only stubborn sherpas to contend with and not big presentations to caffeine-deprived bosses.

Jillian rifles through her hangers, pulling things off one by one: the patent leather vest is too much of a dominatrix thing; the Donna Karan suit is trying too hard; the gray pinstriped vest and skirt are okay, if she were going to a meeting at Goldman Sachs instead of an advertising agency, the floral Liberty button-down looks like it was an impulse purchase from the Harrods shop at Heathrow Airport (which it was), and the black Daryl K is too down-market.

"And besides, orgasms are overrated," she yells back from downstairs as she zips up a beige suede skirt along her hip. "I don't need to have an orgasm to enjoy myself. I just really, really like, you know, the fuck itself." The beige skirt seems too short. Dorkish even. She remembers when it was her favorite thing—the Miss Sixty skirt—completely over now. "You generally seem to be fine with that."

Finally, after seventeen minutes and a floor strewn with the discards of her closet, Jillian settles on the Armani pinstriped pleated pants, slim at the waist, wider at the ankle. It's an elegant pant that elongates the leg, making it appear as if the line goes on forever. These minuscule vertical lines that look golden from just a foot away add butter and warmth to the otherwise crisp angle. She tops the pant with the white Vandevorst work shirt—a classic enough garment with long French cuffs and a well-cut neckline but a surprisingly improper peekaboo slit down the back between the shoulder blades. A sliver of skin shows through as the capricious twists and turns of the day unfold. And finishing the whole thing off, at the base of the sweeping leg, a small triangle of maroon leather emerges, the tidy toe of a fierce Louboutin high heel—neither as vulnerable as a sandal nor as relentless as a boot. The pointy glimpse of color and texture is the ideal juxtaposition to the pinstripes and white cotton—a classic combo. The result, Jillian thinks, is a kind of masculine-feminine look, perfect for her height, appropriate for the occasion, mature, a touch groovy without being overtly so, smart, tasteful, and pulled together.

She can present well in this outfit. She is sure of it.

She walks back up the staircase balancing on the balls of her feet, careful not to put too much weight on her spiny heels. "Does this look okay?" She hesitantly stands in front of the bed.

"You look wonderful, Jilly. Like a double espresso."

Jillian exhales. For as little as Alex knows about clothes, his opinion can always make or break her confidence.

He sits up and moves away from her just an inch. "How about a memory picture?"

Jillian puts both hands on her hips and smiles widely. "Cheese."

Camera-less, he holds his hands up in a square in front of his face and blinks both eyes at her. He has a million of these shots of Jillian: standing on the Brooklyn Bridge, posing beside a pug in the park, trying on wigs at Patricia Field's, buying bialys at Kossar's. He taps his temple with his finger. "Good one." Alex pulls her into bed with him and kisses her head.

"What's on your agenda this morning?" Jillian relaxes into his arms for the moment.

"My agenda, my beautiful girl"—he carefully smoothes down her eyebrows—"is that I need to go to B&H and get a new adapter ring for the camera. Mine broke in Honduras."

Jillian looks at her watch. "You gotta be out by nine, though." She pulls herself up and straightens her shirt. "Yolanda's coming—thank God."

"Yolanda can make the bed with me in it." Alex curls around the pillow. "It's a cruel world out there, Siegel. I'm staying right here."

"Please don't freak out Yolanda. You know her position on the whole premarital relations thing."

"She's just jealous."

Jillian leans over and inhales his puppy dog breath and cool laundry smells. "I'll miss you too tonight, Allie."

"Tell your mother my ass is still recovering from the last time I saw her."

"Lois loves to squeeze. What can I say?" She reaches out for a kiss, one that doesn't disturb lipstick, or makeup, or the general look whatsoever. Alex manages to press his lips against hers anyway.

"And tell them I think you're the greatest, smartest, cutest associate creative director in New York City. With the nicest onion this side of Fourteenth." Alex grabs a chunk of her rear end.

"I will."

"Good luck." Alex brushes her hair back with his hands. "I'll see you after the deed is done."

"Thanks, Bubb."

"Sure, Bubb."

"I love you."

"I love you too."

Jillian walks into the foyer of McKay's Drugs at precisely eight thirty-one A.M. She still has twenty-nine minutes, which should be plenty: ten minutes of waiting and nineteen for the calming effect of the pill to take hold. She picks up a small tube of Hurley's Grapefruit & Mint lip balm on the way to the pharmacy in the back. Hurley's has great packaging, and the lip balm with its tasteful olive and saffron encasement is no exception. Her heart quickens at the luscious sight of it. Instinctively she pulls off the cap and smooths a layer of the tender ointment across her lips. The sweet cooling oils seep in through her skin, adding flavor to her tongue and chilling her skin. Goose bumps emerge down her arms the way they always do when she holds a dear prize like this in her palm.

It is mine. It is mine. It is mine. She is careful to remember the mantra.

She envelops the lip balm entirely in her hand and slips it into her suit pocket. It is a relief just to know it is there now—that it is hers forever.

She counts out the timing as she waits in line; the numbers alone impart a sense of calm: if the prescription gets filled in less than thirteen minutes, she'll have enough time to take a half a milligram under her tongue, stride quickly up Park while the pill melts into her bloodstream, and still be in Billy Baum's office, lightly sedated, with one minute to spare. The timing is good.

Absentmindedly she rubs along the length of her nose, gripping the bridge between her thumb and forefinger. She draws down along the tip, then makes the journey over the hook, pulling it up just a bit and back down again. It is not so tall as a mountain or as wide as a bus—but it is there and, as some have commented, often gets there before she does.

From the cheekbones up she could be Irish or Italian or even Spanish, but the true origin of her face—part Polish, part Russian, part Czech, and part German—is betrayed by this protuberance. Larger and more obtrusive than one would expect on such a refined landscape, the thing has been left in its natural state despite four consultations with Park Avenue specialist Dr. Adam Blumenthal. Jillian always believed that keeping this particular blemish intact set her apart from her mother, so she held on to it like a talisman over the years.

"I understand why men would want to look at you, darling." Lois Siegel said to her daughter Jillian when she just was fourteen. *"You're a beautiful girl. And Lord knows you're growing bosoms."* Jillian looked down at the twin volcanoes waiting to erupt. *"It was cute when you were younger, but, let's face it, no man is going to want to reproduce with that nose."*

Lois Siegel walked her daughter over to the mirror. *"It's not painful at all; you're asleep the whole time. And then you wake up and it's all perfect. Look at me." Lois kissed her daughter gently on the cheek.*

The pharmacy line is short, only four people ahead of her, so Jillian sits in the chair patiently waiting for her number to be announced and going over the presentation in her head. She's got to remember not to talk too fast. She always talks too fast when she presents. It's like some sort of time warp thing happens that causes the words to tumble from her mouth full speed ahead and she can't remember how the sentence she started was supposed to end so she just ends it in an arbitrary way that makes no sense whatsoever and people look at her like they wish it was time to check their cell phone messages or order their Cubano sandwiches from the Coffee Shop.

"Thirty-eight," yells the girl behind the counter—a pregnant girl named MELVA, with blatant hair extensions, an overly large nose stud, and a flat red smock covering her pendulous breasts.

It's eight forty-eight, and Melva has the bottle in hand.

Jillian writes her initials on the line, officially refusing the consultation from the pharmacist, and signs her name on the credit card slip—a grand swirling *J*, a cascading *S*, and barely anything recognizable in between. She reaches out for the prescription.

"I can't read that," Melva broadcasts, clutching Jillian's medication away and dangling her mouth open, revealing to God and the world the wad of purple gum perched between her teeth and tongue. "I'm gonna need to see your license."

"I come in here all the time. You can't read that?" She fumbles through her pocketbook and thrusts her arm elbow deep into its depths. *Oy. This thing is such a mess. Maybe one of those little baguette pocketbooks would stay neater. Maybe pink suede.* "Why can't you read that?"

"I'm gonna need to see your license."

"Shit." The contents of her behemoth bag tumble onto the counter like a cornucopia of stolen secrets: bitter flecks of tobacco; travel-size hair gel; a free sample of perfume inside a little card; tea tree oil breath drops; a swollen, open tampon; a bursting Filofax; and a bunched up pair of black thigh highs flood the surface in front of Melva's bulging belly. "Goddamn it." A MAC eye shadow, Patina Frost, falls to the floor and cracks into a thousand tiny crystals. "Shit."

Jillian looks back at the growing line behind her. A man with a coiffed mustache rocks back and forth and audibly exhales. One woman with a china doll haircut and red reading glasses fans herself with a magazine subscription card. Melva waits sucking gum bubbles into her mouth and popping them. Jillian works to keep her body cool and undisturbed (relaxed eyes, arched eyebrow, calm slouch) despite her mounting angst. Without at least eight minutes for the Ativan to kick in, the whole morning will be ruined. She could also use a mint.

And a new Patina Frost.

And a pink suede baguette pocketbook.

"Here. Here it is. I found it." She pulls out the license from the side pocket, the place where she usually keeps it but never looks. "It was right here," she curls her hair behind her ear and shrugs her shoulders to the group. They stare blankly at her. "It's a really big purse," she adds.

Jillian hands it over to Melva, who glances at it briefly and deems it accurate enough to turn over the booty. Jillian opens the bottle and gobbles down the pill right there at the counter. Nibbles it in half, then works both halves under her tongue, finding solace in the saccharin sweetness of the melting pieces. And, as she only has six minutes to make it to Billy's office, she pops in a second dose. Six minutes will definitely be enough to dissolve a full milligram of Ativan. Having the peak-effects kick in midmeeting, after all the small talk is out of the way, might actually be perfect timing.

"Thank you for shopping at McKay's." Melva pops another bubble.

2

"IS BILLY in yet, Grace?" Jillian asks the receptionist of Bomb Advertising Agency Incorporated. At least twenty years older than the average Bomb employee, Grace sits in the center of the long glossy counter that extends nearly the entire length in front of the elevators. The table (and Grace) is a genteel barrier between the stark waiting area in the front and the frenetic inner workings of the advertising agency itself.

"One second, doll." Grace puts a finger up. She smiles and holds up a toy shih tzu doggie from behind her desk. She waves hello to Jillian with the toy paw. "Bomb Incorporated. Hold please." Thin-lipped, pale-skinned and blonde, Grace is nearly as white and presentable as the surface she sits behind. "Bomb Incorporated. Hold please. Bomb Incorporated. Hold please." Grace winks at Jillian, the headset framing her face. "I think he is, doll. Mandy's at her desk, she would know. Bomb Incorporated. Hold please."

Grace has been there forever, since Jillian's very first interview at the agency. Jillian remembers walking in that first time with her black portfolio hanging off her arm—nervous to meet Billy Baum, the man she'd wanted to work for since college. During her forty-minute wait for the legendary ad executive,

Grace smiled, brewed her a cup of Earl Grey, and made Jillian feel welcome.

When she finally did meet the man, he was shorter and younger than she expected. And instead of leafing through her work, and grilling her on her past experience, he asked her candidly what she thought of his new open-seating plan—common tables of six or seven people in the center of the space instead of private desks or offices. She was frank with him, maybe more so than one should be in an interview, and told him that the open space was too open.

"The more public you ask people to be, the more privacy you need to give them," she said confidently, repeating one of her uncle's favorite aphorisms. "Ultimately people make all their big decisions in private, Mr. Baum." She suggested that the people who worked at the open tables should still have ways to screen themselves off from one another and sketched out an eye-level panel that could be placed beside or in front of every worker. Billy took the sketch, nodded, and called his architect while she was still standing beside him. Jillian left that day—hired, her portfolio unopened. Jillian sometimes wonders if she'd have gotten the job if he never asked her that question.

Jillian walks down the long corridor toward Billy's office in the back corner. A brick wall runs the entire length of one side. Oversized windows punctuate the center of each glass-enclosed office. The windows sit low, nearly to the floor, as if the whole floor was added recently to another much larger space not used for this purpose at all. Bomb's decor is more industrial chic than fancy. All the telltale signs of a young, hot shop are here: the exposed wood beams, the open studio, the campy collection of 1960s and '70s lunchboxes mounted one after another on the wall, the small mountain of neon orange beanbag chairs piled up in the corner, an open box of last night's pizza on the counter.

Clients come to Bomb for Billy's unconventional approach to advertising. Usually after a lackluster stint with a conservative shop uptown, they seek out the turbocharged momentum that Bomb and Billy Baum are famous for. They mop their brows, loosen their Hermès ties, and direct their Town Car chauffeurs downtown to the brash office and its irreverent maestro. They hope to introduce, or, more accurately, their lives *depend on* introducing their new product with a bang. Or more often, dusting off their tired old brand and making it fresh and relevant again for the modern young consumer.

Down the hall, a few doors before Billy's office, a war room is set up for the Loevner's Department Store pitch. It's actually the agency's smaller conference room usurped for the duration of the project. Usually Bomb's war rooms are in smaller spaces—the unused office next to Production, the hallway across from the bathrooms, or, in some cases, just a wall for hanging up the work. But the Loevner's Department Store account, which includes the hundred or so Loevner's affiliates around the world, is the biggest the agency has ever pitched. The media spend alone is enormous. Sacrificing prime space seemed warranted.

Jillian walks in to pick up her presentation. There are old coffees on the table, half a turkey sandwich, and the remnants of Billy's chewed but never lit cigar hanging off the edge of the table. Jillian can see his bite marks on the soggy end. Her stack of black boards rests against the side wall alongside the other six campaigns. The temptation to look at everyone else's ideas (especially Brandon Pietro's) is huge, but she doesn't want to distract herself immediately before she presents. Plus Brandon's idea is bound to be indiscernible without Brandon himself there to present it—a target in the middle of the page, a stick figure standing upside-down, the cover of *People* magazine with an *X* marked over it. Brandon's ideas are always esoteric, yet Billy falls for his charismatic presentations every time.

A new exhibit is up on the easel—a black board labeled TARGET AUDIENCE, with pictures of sophisticated women torn out of catalogs tacked to it. Jillian thinks about how the target photos are way off. They'll eventually figure it all out after the planners do their weeks of consumer research, but she knows it all by heart already. The Loevner's customer has always been sophisticated, sure, but a kind of left-wing sophisticate who boldly mixes patterns and designers. She might go to Noodle Town for a bowl of four-dollar soup wearing a thousand-dollar jacket and jeans and a vintage cocktail ring. This is what the store has always been about. The Loevner's woman is riskier, more fabulous, more off center. These photos are too uptown and conventional—too suburban.

Jillian jots down *"Loevner's target audience way off"* on a Post-it and stuffs it in her pocket.

She walks deeper into the war room to a dark spot in the corner next to the empty chart. Hanging a bit below eye level is a Xerox copy of the old Loevner's ad. The image is classic—as supremely sophisticated and modern as it was when it was taken, over twenty years ago.

Three "models" punctuate the space of the black-and-white photo. On the left, the haughty actress Brianna Terrell pulls back the skirt of her Balenciaga gown, her arms enveloped to just above the elbow in matching gloves. The folds of her duchesse satin dress are accentuated by the dramatic chiaroscuro lighting, which skims the top of each graceful curve and darkens it on the opposite side. Her eyebrows are dark and pointy, and the mole under her eye mars her otherwise perfect symmetry. She seems frozen in the world's most elegant pose, poised to step toward the center, off balance, like a butterfly about to flutter away.

In the middle, wearing an impeccable tuxedo, the flamboyant Loevner's spokesman, the owner himself. He's a delicious foil to the tall and comely actress: a Truman Capote to her Babe Paley. Even then, his face had more personality than most; his round head, his suntanned skin, his barrel chest, generous belly, and his easy smile warm the image—making it real and human. On his cheek, as it is in every ad in the series, the lipstick residue of a brilliant kiss. Perhaps from Ms. Terrell? Perhaps from another fan? The iconography is provocative but never, not in a hundred images, completely explained.

And finally, set back a few feet and to the right, away from the other two, sits the mysterious little girl. Perched atop a white piano, she has the unaffected slouch of any bored seven-year-old—overly dressed and asked to pose for a picture. She is not smiling. She is not, like the actress, trying to look her best. It is, at first glance, easy to think she doesn't belong there. That she's merely an accessory to the real action. But the eyes, the round, haunting eyes of a woman five times her age, draw you in. In these two pitch-black marble-sized spots on the page the viewer realizes it is she who deserves the attention.

Above all three, in the spindly Didot typeface favored by magazines like *Vogue* and *Bazaar*, the curious faux-French headline that captured the imagination of an entire city for over three decades:

Je t'adore Loevner's!

Someone has drawn red stars and written across the image in red:

THIS WAS LOEVNER'S!!

Jillian tucks the black boards underneath her arm and smooths her hair behind her ears as she approaches Billy's executive assistant, Mandy Mandel. Mandy's chest seems to have a life of its own. It bulges out in front of her—balancing atop Billy's Day Planner.

"Is Billy in yet?" she asks the young secretary.

Mandy's listening to headphones and cutting out images of women from a stack of catalogs, presumably on assignment from Billy. Mandy is, as far as Billy's concerned, the resident expert on the pulse of the young New York woman. "Billy's in the little boys' room. You wanna wait in there?"

"I'm a few minutes late." Jillian feels the Ativan about to smooth out the edges.

"It's fine, hun. He's been in there for half an hour," Mandy whispers. "He took the *Times*," she adds privately. "Catch your breath."

Jillian walks into Billy's office and takes a moment to settle. After two years of working there, the place still makes her anxious. His office is in its usual condition—hastily purchased designer furniture draped with the advertising debris of the past five years: a cardboard cutout of a basketball player perched on its side, now wearing a bra and plaid boxer shorts; a case of David's Surefire Ale (the brainchild of one of Billy's buddies from Brooklyn); a blow-up basketball with a Xerox of Billy's face taped to it; a Star Wars lunchbox (a gift from a wannabe employee); various photos of Billy with semicelebrities and politicians; a dartboard with Billy's face superimposed on it; a white easel in the corner with the words LOEVNER'S BRAND EQUITY and four big red question marks on top. And four thousand used black boards balanced atop every possible surface with long-dead advertising ideas glued to them.

Jillian takes a seat in the low leather chair and adjusts her slacks. She's sure Billy won't appreciate the thought put into this outfit. Billy Baum, founder, CEO, and executive creative director of Bomb Advertising Agency Incorporated, does not think about these things the way Jillian does. Instead, the Brooklyn-born Baum focuses his efforts more narrowly—on cowboy boots: horned-back alligator cowboy boots from Billy Martin's that he merrily places on his desk, right over left, so that his entire body is eclipsed by the foreshortened soles of these well-shined waffle stompers. In this position, across from Billy's endangered footwear, it is not difficult to find oneself diminished and intimidated. This, Jillian guesses, is the only stylistic strategy with which Billy concerns himself.

Jillian looks up at the framed photo on Billy's wall of the smiling, newly promoted Brandon Pietro on the cover of last year's *Ad Age:*

PIETRO'S CAMPAIGN FOR SUREFIRE ALE WINS BIG AT BOMB!

She wonders what they'd write in *Adweek* or, better yet, what might show up in the *New York Times:*

SIEGEL SAVES THE DAY! BOMB WINS LOEVNER'S PITCH!

She should be smiling for her picture too, yes definitely, casually smiling, and maybe with her arms crossed in front like Brandon, or maybe sideways, hand on hip, slimming at the waist. She could wear something eye-catching, maybe even a touch controversial— a provocatively low neckline under a smart Prada jacket or a whimsical Vivienne Westwood or something effortless and sophisticated like a McQueen tweed or a Vuitton bouclé something.

She pulls the lip balm out of her pocket, rolls a minty layer over her lips, and reviews the day again just to keep her focus. *Talk slowly. Talk slowly.*

"No one takes a dump like me? Right, Mand?" Billy smiles and swats his *New York Times* against his hand, his blue and yellow cowboy boots clumping heavily on the wood floor.

"You're the king, Billy." Mandy hands him his double espresso without looking up. He slides the door shut behind him as he walks into the room. The sound of it—the metal pulling along the groove—always makes Jillian uneasy. She is glad her easy smile has taken over. Billy walks over to his desk and takes a minute to rummage through some papers.

Billy yells to his secretary loud enough to pierce the closed glass door. "Mandel, don't let me forget to call Craig Allen." He shuffles through a pile of mail left on his chair. "Why do all these guys from Chicago always have two first names? Craig. Allen. Paul. Roger. What is that shit, Siegel?" He looks vaguely in Jillian's direction. "There's coin in it if you give me a good answer." Billy pulls out a twenty from his wad of cash and flips it out at Jillian. He lets out a short hyena laugh.

Jillian shrugs her shoulders. She's never been good at Billy's games.

"Shit." Billy stuffs the bill back in his pocket and buzzes Mandy from his phone. "Ask Pietro why those Chicago guys all have two first names."

"Okay, Billy." Jillian hears Mandy's nasal voice from behind the glass door. Jillian crosses her legs the other way around and inconspicuously checks herself for armpit sweat.

"So," Billy turns his attention her way, "if it isn't the infamous Jillian Siegel." Billy places his cowboy boots on his desk, right over left, and takes a sip of his coffee. "Goddamn it." He spills a dribble down the front of his shirt and wipes at it with a piece of paper. "Mandy!"

"Here ya go, Billy." Mandy enters the room on cue with a stack of paper towels. "Brandon said something about needing two first names when you have a little *putz*." Mandy measures an inch out with her thumb and forefinger and shrugs her shoulders.

Billy lets out another laugh and hands her the twenty as she leaves.

"So"—Billy blots the stain below his collar—"how is Jillian Siegel?"

"I'm good, Billy." Jillian knows there's a more clever answer to this question, a bit of the old crackerjack repartee that delights Billy so much, a waggish answer that Brandon Pietro would have at his fingertips, one she will think of later, probably in the little girls' room with the *New York Times.*

"Good. Good." He shuffles some more papers around. "You know Loevner's will be our biggest account."

"I do, Billy. And I feel like I really have a unique perspective to offer the agency on the campaign."

"You've heard the rumors that they're gonna have a big management change over there. Craig Allen is retiring to his golfing or fly-fishing or whatever those *goyisha* all do in the twilight years. Palm Springs. Whatever. We'll need to step up to the plate. We could be reporting to somebody much worse. Probably another one of the board's Chicago suits."

"Yes, sure. I did hear something like that." She did not, in fact, hear that. She never hears anything.

"Good. Good." Billy shuffles through another pile of paper. "Okay." He puts the papers back down on his desk and moves his Gold Pencil Award on top of the pile for emphasis. "Lemme have it."

"So." Jillian holds the boards on her lap. She smiles and takes a deep breath. "Shopping at Loevner's is really all about the *experi-ence* . . ." She drags out the word to stress its importance. It sounds good. She's doing great so far. This is exactly the first sentence she practiced. ". . . even more than the clothes."

"Right. Right." Billy seems engaged—interested already.

"People who shop there, I mean women who shop there, because most of the customers are, of course, women, and these are the kind of women who lunch at Noodle Town in really, really expensive jackets with jeans and vintage jewelry and these women—"

"Mandy!" Billy yells to his assistant.

"Yes, Billy?" Mandy Mandel pokes her head in the office.

"Call Levinson. Ask him when the fuck he's gonna pay me back for the tickets."

"Sure, Billy." Mandy answers Billy's usual barrage of demands with her unique brand of disregard, attentiveness, and feigned submission. It is this sort of symbiotic relationship with employees that keeps Billy's corporate wheel well greased—the sort of relationship that Jillian never perfected.

"Those were courtside fucking tickets."

"I know, Billy."

"Better yet, get him on the phone. I need to talk to him."

"Sure, Billy."

"Now, Mandel!"

"Sure, Billy."

"Where were we?" Billy takes another sip of espresso.

"We weren't really much of anywhere, Billy." Jillian cracks the tightness out of her thumb. She takes another deep breath. "So these women really want to be *seduced* by the in-store experience." She thought of that word yesterday and is glad she did.

"Right. Right." He's still with her. Sexy words always bring him back into the room.

"So . . ." Jillian flips up the first board. It is a stick figure drawing of the Loevner's two old doorman, Pierre and Gerhardt, tipping their top hats to a lady stick figure as she leaves the store. The headline reads:

"Thank you for shopping at Loevner's!"

"It's a doorman campaign?"

Jillian is not sure if Billy's question is good, bad, or rhetorical, but he is still listening after thirty seconds, which is unusual for him. "Well, not *exactly.*" Jillian hedges her bets.

"I get it. It's like these two old guys are the spokesmen for the store. We could give them names. Something really crazy." He's excited, on a roll.

"Pierre and Gerhardt are their names," Jillian mumbles. She's feeling thrown off course. Billy's talking about doormen, but that's not really the point. "Well, but, it's sort of—"

"Right. Pierre and Gerhardt. Now *that's* funny." Billy is chuckling to himself. "The doorman campaign!"

"It's not just about doormen, Billy." Jillian flips up the second board. On it is a drawing of a scarf display. But instead of a conventional store display, the brilliantly hued scarves are hanging from a live tree planted in the Loevner's foyer.

The headline reads:

"Loevner's is spectacular!"

Jillian continues, "It's about the ambience, the atmosphere." Desperately she flips the boards up from her lap one by one, each illustrating a new detail from the department store experience and a headline that defines it. "It's not just about doormen, Billy; it's about everything! It's about the people at Loevner's and they way they do things, which is not just the same way every store does it, I mean it's not; it's a really, *really* special place, really, and if you're the kind of person, I mean the kind of woman who shops there then . . . then . . . you're fine with. I mean great with. With those things."

The sentence has tumbled out chaotically and Jillian is out of

breath. The whole idea seemed amazingly brilliant to her just minutes ago. It actually seemed like she was onto something. But now,
saying it out loud to Billy, none of these thoughts seem connected
in any discernible way. Her campaign is made up of *thoughts*—good
thoughts even, but strung together loosely if at all, and certainly
not, as Billy calls it, the Big Bomb Idea™. She wants to throw up.
She should have never turned over the second board.

Billy glances down at his watch. He picks up the phone and
yells into the distance. "Mandy!"

"Yes, Billy?

"You got Levinson?"

"One second, Billy."

He lowers his voice and looks back at Jillian. His eyes don't
make it above her clavicles. "I think it's time . . ." Billy looks at
the phone, as if he's forgotten why he's holding it. "Mandy!"

"Hold on, Billy."

"I think it's time—"

"I got him, Billy." Mandy yells back with excitement. "Line
one."

"I think it's time we parted ways." The words spill quickly out
of his mouth like gravel from a dump truck. "We're looking for
someone with the big idea and frankly, Siegel, that's just not you.
Where's 'Apple 1984'? Where's 'Nike, Just Do It'? Where's the
BBI™? I just don't see it here."

Billy holds his hand over the receiver.

"Bomb is like an organism. It either accepts you or rejects
you." Billy pushes line one. "Levinson, you asshole!" Billy puts a
hand back on the receiver and looks vaguely in Jillian's direction.
"You can say you resigned." Billy takes another sip of coffee and
turns his chair to face the window. "Is that how you thank me for
courtside tickets, douche bag?"

Jillian sits in the low designer chair. The weight of her back is
heavy against the leather. Her smile is stuck to her face. Her
French cuffs feel suddenly claustrophobic. A sizzling heat travels

up her body to her neck and cheeks. She wants to grab Billy's coffee and pour it on his face or on her own, or splash the scorching liquid across his desk. She wants a hydrant of coffee and a fire hose; she wants to spray the place down, the white walls, the pony-skin chairs, the designer furniture, the dead black boards.

"Did you need something, Siegel?" Billy looks up from his call and sees Jillian still sitting there in exactly the same place. She gets up and turns and walks out the door. A scream works up from her belly but does not fire off; instead, her muscles simply move her out of the office.

She will hold it together. She will not expose herself to these people. She will leave before they know. She will never, ever, ever see any of them again and never, ever, ever talk to any of them again. She will walk confidently (slight smile, long strides, upright posture) to her office.

"G'morning. Morning. Hey. Morning." She will keep it all together for another three minutes, until she can grab her address book, the old photo of Bingo and Alain at Café Borgia, the Polaroid of Alex in Costa Rica, her paprika pashmina, and the bamboo pencil holder from Chinatown. She will leave the new plant she bought last week. It's dead already anyway.

"I need you to look at the Ambience layouts, Jill."

"You're on a conference call with Lanky at ten."

"Are you going to the Color-Correct today after the briefing?"

The various citizens of Bomb Incorporated seem to split and multiply in front of her. Their foul mitosis makes her dizzy. Brandon Pietro walks into the Loevner's war room balancing a bagel atop a cup of coffee. Brandon, like Billy, also wears cowboy boots that clap along the floor. The rest of the pitch team is already in there, laughing and hurling wads of paper in the air. Brandon shuts the door with his foot, quieting the noises from the room.

"Yes. Sure. Okay. Yeah. I'll be right there." Jillian grabs her things and walks calmly to the elevator door. She presses the button and waits.

"I'm so sorry, Jill." Grace looks at her with soft eyes and a tilted blonde head. "I heard." She holds up the stuffed doggie again and moves its head. "Mr. Jiggies will miss you too." The elevator door opens, and Jillian escapes inside. She stands quietly in the middle of the crowded space and holds on as the waves of nausea move through her. Her calf cramps into a knotted ball.

Instead of down, she is taken up, hoisted toward the sky and one by one, floor by floor, people exit into their various foyers. Can they tell, she wonders, can they tell she is no longer one of them, no longer a real person?

Jillian's eyes chase the space for an inch of relief—some free air, a blank, empty spot of wall. The people stand there, belonging perfectly in this small ascending world—they in their coordinated suits and appropriate leather accessories—staring at the lit numbers, rifling through their pocketbooks. They do anything to avoid linking eyes with one another.

Jillian wishes she were alone in a Town Car, encased in metal and glass.

The last man gets off on twenty-one. He is skinny and purposeful and doesn't look back as he enters into his bustling, wood-paneled world. The doors close, and the car shifts downward. She leans her whole body against the wall, the muscles and skeleton finally giving in to the emptiness. With a loud ding, the elevator opens again on her floor. The doors, like eyelids, blink open onto the bright horizon and then close again. Two girls—familiar, Bomb interns perhaps—wrestle their way through the doors just before they close. They gossip with each other, clutching their designer wallets to pay for cappuccinos and toasted bagels at the deli downstairs.

Her phone buzzes from the bottom of her bag. Maybe it's Alex calling to get the scoop. Jillian barely manages to pull her vibrating cell phone out of her pocketbook. "Hi. It's me." Her words come out in their usual singsong, despite her depressed state.

"Hello, Miss Siegel. It's Yolanda Plazas." The signal's weak in the elevator and the words, barely audible. The accent, however, is unmistakable.

"Yolanda, I can't really talk right now." The saliva is thick in her mouth. She struggles to form the words correctly. "I'm in an elevator." The two interns try to keep their eyes off Jillian and her overly loud conversation.

"Miss Siegel, I no find a check today."

"Yolanda? I can't hear you. Where are you?" Jillian watches as the numbers creep lower and lower toward the ground floor.

"Yes. It's me, Yolanda Plazas. I no find a check today."

"I put a check on the counter for you." She straightens up and clutches the phone tight to her ear, hoping to hear the words better. She holds the phone outward in hopes of a better signal a few inches to the left. "Is Alex still there? Yolanda?"

"I no have a check last week."

"I told you, Yolanda, I would put a check on the counter for you for *both* weeks, *this* week and *last* week. Which I did. Right on the counter. Where I usually put my keys and mail and other things. I'm sure I did." Jillian is not sure, never sure, of these kinds of things, but *sounding* sure is as important as being it.

"I look on the counter. I no find it."

"Christ." Jillian grips the phone with her chin and rummages through her purse.

"What?"

"Nothing, Yolanda. What time is it? Where are you?"

"In Grand Station."

"You left already? You left and didn't do any cleaning?" Jillian remembers the rejected outfits strewn about the floor and the general disarray of the last seven days without a housekeeper.

"I go to my next job."

"Wait. Wait. Yolanda, please don't go. It's Shabbat-at-Bingo's tonight. A family tradition. The Jewish holiday. At my uncle Bingo's." The elevator stops, seemingly on every floor. New people enter, all holding on to their coffee money and trying desperately not to stare at the girl on her cell phone. "He's very sick, Yolanda, you know that, and my entire family will be there." Jillian is now pacing the small space. "Yolanda, please, *please* don't leave. Please. I need some clean clothes for tonight." Jillian is crowded into the back of the elevator. The freshly straightened hair at the back of happy coworkers' heads grazes her face. "Christ."

"What?" The sounds of Grand Central Station drown out Yolanda's words.

"Can you come back downtown, Yolanda? Can you just stay there? Just stay right there. Don't move one inch. I'll come and get you." Jillian holds the phone tightly under her chin like a violin as she pleads with the housekeeper.

"I no hear you, Miss Siegel."

"What?"

"I gotta go, Miss Siegel."

"Please don't leave, Yolanda. Please." Jillian watches as the elevator nearly reaches the ground. "I'll pay for your cab. Anything"

"I think it's more better you find someone else to clean your apartment."

"Oh God, Yolanda. Please, don't leave me. I got a promotion today. I'll give you a raise. I have a new, very important job. Have you heard of the Loevner's Department Store chain, Yolanda? Please, please, please stay. Please come back!" The people in the elevator turn and stare.

"Sorry, Miss Siegel. There's my train."

"*No!!*" Jillian holds the phone down beside her. None of the muscles in her body work; they simply release and the device drops to the floor. The elevator doors open into the ground floor, and the people release in a gush into the light.

A girl picks up the phone and hands it to Jillian.

"Thanks." She takes the phone and claps it shut.

"Are you okay?"

"Yeah." She tries to stand tall and brush her hair back into something respectable. "Yeah. I'm okay."

3

JILLIAN hurls the wad of keys onto the counter in her kitchen. The metallic sound sends a chill up her spine. It is before noon on Friday. The light streams in through the blinds in an unfamiliar sixty-degree stripe across the floor. Even the air is different. People shouldn't be at their apartment at this hour. It's depressing. The only people home before noon on a Friday afternoon are housewives and the "self-employed" who pad around their studio apartments sipping Cup-a-Soup in their old socks and college sweatpants.

The sunlight reflects off a photograph hanging on the wall that Alex took of her when they first met. The "Cigarette Picture," Alex calls it, because it was taken back when Jillian still smoked and the swirl emanating from the Marlboro Light between her fingers frames her body provocatively. The white stripe of sunlight across the wall seems to slice the photo in half—obliterating her face from view.

The message light on her machine reads "0" but she pushes the button anyway, just to be sure. The synthetic voice hands down the ruling, "You have," the voice pauses to calculate the results, "zero messages."

Zero messages! Nothing. She hasn't checked her messages since last night before dinner.

She opens the refrigerator, looks in and closes it. No messages? As far as the machine's concerned, she's been gone since yesterday. Things have *happened*. Not even an annoying message from Lois. Or the official HR call from Bomb about COBRA benefits and vacation pay and all the things they invent to make it seem as if you have parting gifts coming to you on your way out the door.

The two-week-old hydrangea sitting in a stew of water is a blatant reminder that Yolanda is definitely gone. Which means the dry cleaning is not picked up, the toothbrush is still on the counter, the dirty sheets are still crumpled on the bed, the thong is still dangling off the doorknob, the half-eaten croissant is still in the sink, and, as expected, there are thirteen outfits still scattered throughout the closet and on the bedroom and bathroom floors. She plucks the half croissant from the sink, and, stuffs it into her mouth.

Zero messages?

Maybe the machine is broken. Answering machines break all the time. She dials her home number from her cell phone and listens to the mismatched double ringing, one phone in each ear: "Hi, it's Jill. Leave me a message. . . ."

"Testing, testing. This is Jill testing my machine, testing, testing." The sound of her voice on the machine echoes back, disturbingly hopeful. She hangs up the phone and watches as the message light changes from zero to one—one message from herself, lingering in the guts of her properly working machine.

Jillian opens the cupboard over the stove, hoping for a few crackers to munch on, maybe a PowerBar, but it's empty. She wanders through the war zone of her apartment and into her closet. She pushes around what remains hanging. It is the dregs of the dregs. No inspiration in sight.

My God, she needs new clothes. What was she thinking? There is nothing in here for tonight. Nothing. Sure, there's the slinky silk charmeuse slip dress that can be paired with a cardigan and heels for a Paris in the '20s thing, and there's the white Courrèges which, with hoop earrings, looks kind of modern Barbarella, and then there's scads of low riders with boy waistbands and pencil skirts and minis, surfer cords and yoga pants, but there's nothing appropriately classy yet lightly coquettish for the evening. Nothing.

Where are the black capris? Where are the cashmere sweater sets? Where is the black tea-length coat and matching cocktail dress? The Audrey look was a complete bust, and the Audrey look would be perfect for tonight. Actually, her whole wardrobe should be Audrey—everyone knows Audrey is good for any occasion.

Why can't she just decide who she is and commit to it? She gets sidetracked by chunky platforms or maroon fur collars—sometimes even by silver loafers! She gets diverted from the mission, by these, the odds and ends of her closet that do nothing at all for her. They hang there, tags still attached, bringing down the rest of the clothes, and now she has nothing to wear.

Jillian needs something to turn the day around. She opens the refrigerator again, hoping for a little sweet to have materialized. It has not. She opens the cupboard to the side of the stove. An open box of Near East Rice Pilaf and vegetable bouillon cubes float around in the dark space. She walks the length of her apartment then walks it again. Her sound of her footsteps bounces off the ceiling.

She can't go to Shabbat-at-Bingo's like this—desperate, hopeless, *rejected.*

She needs to hold it together. This is what she does. She holds it all together with the miscellany of her toolbox: new clothes, new perfumes, new salves and ointments, new polishes and sprays, new hangers, new tweezers, new hair ornaments, new *anythings* to brighten the moment and give her a reason to be.

For tonight she needs help, a compass rose to point her away from the morning and toward the evening. It doesn't have to be big; it just has to be something. With her big suede purse still around her shoulder, she scoops up her keys and makes her way to the little shop around the corner.

Through the window she is surprised to see that La Petite Coquette is full. In the middle of the day! A man in for a look-see; a woman about the same age as Jillian looking desperate, as if she too is seeking sanctuary in lingerie; and another woman overloaded with shopping bags cram the undersized lavender-scented shop.

It looks like Christmas inside—shimmery, hopeful, and filled with goodies. She's so eager to go in that she nearly forgets her mantra. She inhales a deep breath to compose herself. *It is mine. It is mine. It is mine.*

La Petite Coquette sells primarily expensive underthings, but occasionally items like soft sweaters, airy drawstring pants, and silky scarves make their way onto the racks. Last year she bought a wildly expensive Deborah Marquit leopard bra and matching low-rise hipsters, so the way she sees it, she been a good and loyal customer of the store.

She wanders by a row of corsets and past the undershirts and panties, toward the back by the bras. Her heart picks up the pace, the pulsing palpable below her blouse.

One bra in particular catches her eye—tiny eyelet straps, piercingly white, demicups. Her fingers trace the edges. Not perfect under a T-shirt—too bumpy, but impeccable under a jacket, clean—the tiniest scallop edge framing the décolletage. Lovely. 34B. Close enough. Double seamed. Flawless. Custom-made closure. Heartbreaking.

She glides it off the satin hanger and lets it drop to the counter. It must weigh less than an ounce! Her breath pounds out in heaves. Her teeth chatter; droplets of sweat trickle down her side, sending out a rank perfume; her nipples harden. She swallows a mouthful of saliva, the gulp of it echoing in her head. A quick slide off with a nimble hand and *poof* . . . it is gone. Engulfed by a cavernous pocketbook.

On a normal day this trinket would be enough. She would go home and build a new world around this tiny but poignant acquisition. But today there's a larger hole to satisfy. She meanders around to another spot and smiles at the young salesgirl. "Hello." "Hello." "How are you?" "Fine." "Fine." Jillian lowers her eyes, using the thinnest drape of eyelid to protect her from the world.

It occurs to her for a moment to run. To pull out the flawless 34B white eyelet demicup and hand it to the young salesgirl and say, "I'm sorry, I'm sorry, I didn't want to take this from you, I didn't mean to. I didn't mean to take it from you." It occurs to her to run away from La Petite Coquette with nothing crammed into her purse or her pocket and to be whole once again, innocent, a regular person once again—but she can't; she can't because she is not, and she has not been, for as long as she can remember, free or clean or whole or beautiful, or a regular person.

Three scarves drape over a counter: one red, one teal, and one burnt orange. The flossy surface of the fine material tickles her fingertips. These tiny filaments, hundreds and thousands of them to the inch, rise up from the weave and flirt with all who approach. She smooths her moist palm lightly along the surface then brings her hand up to her face to smell the musky fragrance. She imagines it folded in her drawer or resting against her skin tonight. The desperate longing seeps from her stomach into her bloodstream fueling her bravado. With a sharp exhale and a nimble wave and scoop, it is home.

The hole is filling up, but empties itself almost as quickly. Another smooth walk around, she is panting invisibly, nearly vomiting. Her left hand trembles in her pocket. *It is mine. It is mine.* It is mine. Another smile and nod to the pretty salesgirl and two pairs of stockings, size unknown, are added to the goodie bag. *I'm sorry, I'm sorry.* "Thanks." She gestures and adds a blasé smile. She escapes, nearly falls, out the front door and into the street.

Out of breath, sour sweat pouring down her wrists, she stumbles home to throw up and change.

4

"LOIS, *you* are a cunt." Marshall Pollack, Lois's "long-term male companion," as the girls at the Concordia Club call him, waits for the elevator in Bingo's building. He tilts his head back and squints at his lady friend through thick reading glasses. Marshall Pollack uses the C-word like most people eat chocolate—he breaks off a square and chews it with a satisfied smile on his face.

"I was only saying, Marshall, that if we were going to the Liebermans'—and it's fine if we do—then we should try and come home from the club earlier," Lois retorts, putting on an extra coat of lipstick. Lois Siegel is in her Shabbat fur, a tight brown mink from Bergdorf's with a fat leather belt and a large *LS* monogram on the left inside pocket.

"Elaine and Benny will live if we're a little late." Marshall pushes the Up button a second and third time. He has insisted, on numerous occasions, that this works.

"An hour is not a little late, Marshall. Fifteen minutes is a little late. An hour is . . . *rude*," Lois says as the gleaming doors part.

"I'm just saying, they'll live."

"Hi, Marsh." Jillian slithers in just before the doors close and plants a red kiss on his shiny head.

"Hi, honey." Marshall polishes his bifocals with a silk square from his pocket.

"It's nice of you to show up to Shabbat-at-Bingo's, Jilly." Lois rasps in her cigarette voice, kissing her daughter's cheek then wiping the lipstick away with her thumb.

"Nice to see you too, Mother."

The floor numbers go up: 4, 5, 6.

"Marshall just called me a jackass." Lois looks at the surrounding mirrors and lifts her hair just an inch.

"I called you a cunt, Lois."

"Either way, it was not a pleasant thing for a man to say on Shabbat."

"I'll save it for Tu Bish'vat," Marshall Pollack mumbles to himself.

This is the sort of familial banter Jillian has come to expect. She doesn't even hear it anymore. Or if she does, she buries it deep into a lump in her stomach that feeds and multiplies but never erupts or, according to an article she read in *Marie Claire*, might someday metastasize into cervical, breast, or stomach cancer or possibly an inoperable bleeding ulcer.

"Where is your gorgeous boy, Jilly?" Lois pulls out a hankie from her pocketbook. "He has the most delicious *tush*, darling." Lois squeezes down on her hanky. "Doesn't he have the most gorgeous *tush*, Marshall?"

"I didn't want to subject him to your butt pinching tonight, Mother."

"Oh God, please." Lois blows her well-hewn nose into the material. "Darling," she says as folds the hankie into a tight square, "you need to hang on to that boy."

Lois raises one arched eyebrow in Jillian's direction—the well-articulated gesture that says the words from mother to daughter that do not get spoken by the mouth. The sharp shrug of forehead and lid, which, if it could speak, would say, "*You need to hang on to boys before they leave, darling. And they do leave, Jilly, two weeks and three days before their daughters are born. They leave, as you well know, and you must not sit around and stew about it. You must not let them know that a woman's life just ends because they decide to up and leave. So you, of all people, need to hang on to that boy . . . better than you hung on to your father."*

Jillian looks at her mother's reddened, allergic nose. It's so meticulously manufactured: equal on both sides, the once-generous curvature scooped out into a concave slope in the center, two odd flat parts at the tip with a delineated symmetrical flare on either side. Jillian can feel the tension build up inside her like a wiry trap being set, ready to snap at any moment and break the tiny neck of an animal curious enough to come in. She wonders if that was what her father felt before he left.

"You know, Jilly," Lois checks her lipstick in the mirrored surface, "Bing was turned down for the electrical implant. He's not a good *candidate*, whatever that means. He's not doing very well, honey." Lois rubs a trail of lipstick off her teeth with her knuckle.

"I know, Lois. You think I don't know?" Jillian does not have room for this today; her capacity for grief has been reached.

She shouldn't have come.

"I know you know, honey. I'm was just saying he wasn't a good candidate for the implant, that's all." Lois tightens the belt on her coat.

"Jill knows. I know. Everyone on the East Side knows. Leave her alone, Lois." Marshall looks up at the numbers as he speaks.

"It's just that Jilly and Bing—"

"I know already, okay?" Jillian is thankful she decided to take a Zoloft from her sample pack before she left her apartment.

"That's a nice scarf, Jilly, honey." Lois picks invisible fuzz off her daughter's chest. "Burnt orange is not the best color in the whole wide world on you, but you're such a gorgeous girl. Who needs perfect color, right, Marshall?"

"Whatever. Who cares about color? She's a beautiful girl."

"A beautiful girl who could find something to wear other than dungarees that show off half her *toe-kas* on Shabbat."

"It's *tokhes*, Mother." Jillian accentuates the Yiddish syllables. "You're not a Presbyterian. You can pronounce *tokhes*." (German

Jews, according to Lois, cannot pronounce Yiddish words and eat gefilte fish only out of the privacy of their own refrigerators.)

"*Tokhes.*" Marshall pronounces the word to himself.

The elevator doors open into Bingo's dramatic foyer, a great rotunda with sculptures of various sizes scattered throughout. His "pied-à-terre" (as he preferred to call it, as if it was some weekend getaway spot in Paris or Milan) on Ninety-second and Park—stylistically stuck somewhere in the Eisenhower years: hard horizontal furniture, once-fluffy flokati rugs, and the deep intrinsic smell of long-ago cigars—is both sumptuous and depressing. Overflowing martinis, sharp heels of fashion editors, the long tubular ashes of cigarettes tapped gaily, and the occasional remnants of those who could not hold their liquor have all left their indelible marks on the vast plains of Bingo's New York showplace.

Lois, as usual, is the first to step out of the elevator. She smiles generously, both arms outstretched to the room. Jillian follows behind, her serotonin reuptake comfortably inhibited, with Marshall bringing up the rear.

"Belle, your pork smells divine." Lois hands the housekeeper her prickly mink. "You simply can't get a good pork in Sardinia."

"Hi, Belly Belle." Jillian kisses her old friend on the forehead. Just the sweet, powdery smell of Belle makes Jillian want to curl up, drink hot cocoa, and watch a Gene Tierney movie.

"How are you, child?" Belle extends a pink palm to her cheek. Her curly gold wig rests high on her head, the small frizzy undergrowth lightly visible beneath.

"I'm chicken salad, Belle, chicken salad." She crouches down a few inches to give Belle a hug.

"Chicken shit or chicken salad?" Bingo emerges, a walker pushed out in front of him, his fine silk smoking jacket tied high around his waist. The words that would have boomed from his grand diaphragm now merely wiggle out of the corners of his mouth.

Once the debonair older brother, Bingo seems two decades older than his sixty-nine years tonight; he's gaunt where he should be plump, swollen where he should be thin. His left eye is smaller than his right and doesn't focus on anything in particular.

"My God, you two, with your little greeting. Can't you for once say hello without the chicken you-know-what?" Lois kisses her brother on the cheek and wipes away the residue. "Bing, darling, Sardinia was fabulous. You would have simply adored Cala di Volpe." Lois embraces his chin and kisses the side of her big brother's face. "Hello, my darling," she adds up close.

"Bingo!" Marshall's greeting sounds like he's just won the Friday-night round.

"Marshall." Bingo nods a hello to his quasi-brother-in-law, the man who's stuck around in his sister's life a good two decades longer than anyone was betting on.

"Hello. Hello, *meshpucha.*" Benjamin Fishbaum, the Park Avenue attorney, emerges from the hallway behind Bingo. "Don't mind me, don't mind me, I was just leaving." Lovingly referred to as "Uncle Fish," Benjamin has known Jillian's family for more than forty years. He has served as their legal counsel, loyal confidant, and, possibly because of his liberal use of Yiddish, spiritual guide. He is putting on his overcoat and snapping his briefcase shut.

"Benjamin, darling!" Lois greets him warmly. "What are you doing here? Bing didn't tell anyone you were going to be here."

Benjamin Fishbaum wipes his ample nose on his hankie and glances quickly at Bingo. "Oy, it's a whole *magillah,* my darling *nudje.* No one needs to be bothered with such a *bizel* on the Sabbath." He wraps his palm under Jillian's chin and squeezes. "They grow up so fast, don't they, Bingo?"

"Please stay for dinner, Fish." Jillian is glad to see him and, as usual, thankful for the distraction he provides.

"Oh, my darlings, you don't need another *meshuggener* at the table tonight." Benjamin Fishbaum wraps a fine cashmere scarf around his neck and blows kisses as he lumbers toward the doorway. "Shabbat shalom, good people."

"You too, Fish." Jillian blows a kiss as the old man leaves the apartment. She then looks at her uncle curiously, wondering why both men seem to be keeping a secret.

"Can I . . . ," Bingo smiles pleasantly enough to the group as the front door shuts, "get anyone a drink?" He takes another breath to finish his thought. "Honeydew?"

"I'm pouring a double, Bing." Jillian helps herself to the crystal decanter of scotch on the sideboard. She stares at the wallpaper in front of her, suddenly sorry she came. The sight of her uncle, the remnants of him, is nearly unbearable.

"One of *those* days, honeydew?" The words spatter out from his lungs.

"One of those days." She doesn't want look him in the eye.

"Why don't you go and freshen up." Bingo's hairpiece looks strange on his head. It emphasizes all that is no longer right with him. "Go on, honeydew."

Running out of oxygen, Jillian slips out of the foyer and into Bingo's luxe powder room, just past the small Balthus painting in the hall. A needlepoint hangs on the door, *Misery Loves Company!*, in black letters with a yellow owl to the left of the phrase. She holds the door shut behind her, leans on it with all her weight, and gasps for air.

Bingo always sends Jillian away to "freshen up" when Lois is around. A moment *"dans la toilette"* as Bingo has said upon more than one occasion, "gives a girl the chance to catch her breath and prepare for battle." But the quick escape to the powder room is usually interpreted by Jillian as a time to assess and contemplate the contents of the medicine cabinet. And "freshening up" has always been a popular pastime for her in Bingo's powder room.

She surveys the cabinet's options: hydrocodone, Xanax, Dexedrine, Lorazepam, Claritin, Zantac, Klonopin, and an unnamed bottle of yellow and blue capsules in an easy-to-open container. Her choice is based entirely on proximity. The unidentifiable two-toned jewels, which are supposed to be TAKEN WITH FOOD OR MILK and NOT COMBINED WITH ALCOHOL and whose prescription has expired eight years prior, slide easily down her throat. As long as she AVOIDS EXCESSIVE EXPOSURE TO DIRECT SUNLIGHT and DOES NOT OPERATE HEAVY MACHINERY, she should be fine.

She studies herself in the mirror, closing her left eye, then her right, then her left again. She finds a moment of relief in this simple exercise. Her right eye is slightly narrower and tilts inward. Her left is wide and open. It gives the sensation that one side of her face is naïve and good, the other side, angry and mistrustful. Harmonious together, but separately—each side seems unfamiliar and dissonant. She imagines the two new faces that would be created by doubling each half and wonders which of them she would rather be.

After twenty-nine years of service, her skin is beginning to hold on to its injuries rather than recover from them. The minuscule patch of brown on the bridge of her nose is slightly larger than a freckle. There is one beginning to form between her eyebrows as well—the remnants of a second-degree sunburn on Lake Mead more than a dozen years ago. Maybe she should start using sunscreen for real or buy a cowboy hat for summer.

Sprinkled lightly with freckles, the nose itself appears darker than the rest of her face—both size and color distinguishing it. She tries to imagine her mother's face with this nose, the original proboscis—not cut and shaped into that sharply faceted gem. She rubs hard at the splash of freckles as if they might release up and peel away.

The new additions to the powder room—the handicapped toilet seat, the metal bar along the length of the bathtub, and the jumbo box of adult diapers—invade the sanctity of this oasis. She closes her eyes and inhales the odors: once aromatic and elegant, now dusty and decaying, the mutated smells of her childhood make her stomach clench in on itself.

A black hair sprouts from beneath her chin like a splinter. She picks at it with her fingernail and wipes the red dot away with the back of her hand. These little black hairs never grow beyond a millimeter. They are plucked and pulled or clipped or ripped off and remain one of her many carefully guarded secrets. A dormant pimple rests below her temple, the irritable hill barely visible to the naked eye. She squeezes it upward then blots at it with a tea towel soaked in hot water and lemon-shaped guest soap.

Her fingers move downward—self-propelled now and out of breath, she peels her sweater up, revealing the white eyelet lace-covered mounds. The misbegotten undergarment is so pretty and fresh. It feels as if it belongs on someone else.

Another morsel of the unnamed medication finds its way from the cabinet to beneath her tongue.

The delicate bra strap rolls easily off her shoulder, revealing the swell above the areola. A faint scar traces in a circle around the pink. She squeezes her nipple, looking down at the land-scape—a tiny topographical map with minuscule mountains and tributaries. There is less sensation in it than there used to be—only a numb prickle remains. She follows the silvery white line down the center of her breast to the swooping cut mark beneath the entire fold. It's been ten years since she gave in to her mother and these incisions were made, since the superfluous material was discarded, leaving perfect B cups in their place. She holds the breast from underneath, lifting it up and down then squeezing it hard, in search of feeling. Her grief for what was has faded, like the scars—still there, but barely visible, washed away by time.

She lowers her back down the length of the door and runs her fingers through the shag carpet, yanking at the bits of yarn with all her muscle. Her face reconfigures into the shape of a scream, but nothing comes out.

All is not well for Jillian Siegel, if the truth be told. She has been *rejected from the organism* and her eyes are not symmetrical and there is a box of adult diapers next to Bingo's toilet and she has no messages and no one cares enough to call, even though she was gone the entire day! Loevner's is gone forever, and burnt orange is not the best color in the whole wide world on her.

Jillian rests her cheek against the scratchy rug and breathes in the dusty fibers.

"Jilly, honey, Belle's done a little souvlaki thing you simply *must* try." Lois Siegel enunciates over a loud knock on the bathroom door. "Jillian? Honey? I hope you're not vomiting in there." Jillian rolls her sweater back down and gets up from the floor. She shuts off the light and stands in the darkness holding the doorknob.

It is, for one brief moment, quiet.

"How many times do we have to hear the same goddamn thing, Marshall?" Lois says through a sip of scotch.

The Siegel family banter is audible from four rooms away.

Marshall removes his reading glasses. "I've never told Bingo that one."

"Not tonight you haven't, darling." Lois straightens out her tailored jacket. Jillian appears in the doorway. "You're *schvitzing*, honey." Lois opens her pocketbook and pulls out a lozenge.

"I know, just leave it."

"Are you getting sick, honey?"

"I was running around all day."

"Take a zinc. It's lemon-lime."

"I'm okay, Mother."

"Zinc is fabulous, honey. You should always have a zinc on hand just in case. It's always smart to carry some zinc." Lois twists open the lozenge and pops it onto her own tongue.

The family consumes their cocktails in the library—a small room teeming with monstrous art books, the only television in the apartment, a collection of antique Chinese snuff boxes, and an old photograph of Bingo and his late partner Alain Crawford in the Hamptons, the only photograph of the two men together still left in the apartment. This is Bingo's version of a family room. It is relatively relaxed, and its configuration encourages the more intimate of party chitchat.

"So, Jillian—what's the *hot* news in advertising nowadays?" Lois uses the word *hot* as if she invented it. "Of course, we're all following the big pitch for the old place." She prefers to call Loevner's "the old place" rather than speak the actual name out loud. Even when Bingo still owned the store, Lois called it the "old place." According to Lois, admitting when things are truly magnificent is gauche. ("Oh, this old dress? These old shoes? That old place?")

"Oh," Jillian says, trying to send her synapses the message to say something sensible. "There's a lot of stuff going on right now." The weight of the latest round of medication settles into a consistent hum. None of the words have much meaning anymore. It is the grating buzz of an empty brain—slightly irritating, but nothing compared to the alternative. "You know, the pitch and everything and all. You know." Jillian swirls her scotch around in the glass and watches it settle.

"Oh, darling, I almost forgot to tell you. Linda's daughter sold a screenplay in Hollywood! Isn't that fabulous?"

"Suki Friedman sold a screenplay?" The image of catching her friend from Spence in her tennis whites giving Bear Bouchez a blow job in the Concordia clubhouse will be forever etched in her brain. The thought that thirteen years later she sold a screenplay is both unbelievably annoying and entirely predictable, what with her double-handed technique and all.

"Linda says that IBM sold it for six figures."

"You mean ICM sold Suki Friedman's screenplay for six figures?"

"That's what Linda said. You should give Suki a call, darling. I mean, networking with successful people never hurt anyone."

"Well, isn't that *grrreat* for Suki Friedman." Jillian makes no attempt to hide her insincerity. Once her best friend, Suki

Friedman was not one of her favorite people in the world.

"Don't sell yourself short, darling. The big pitch at the Bomb, I would think that's very *hot* too right now."

"A nine-figure account. Call ICM." Jillian averts her eyes.

"My God! You see, Bing? I told you." Lois takes a gulp of her scotch and raises the glass to her brother. "You should have listened to your lawyer, Bingo. You should have listened to Benjamin. And now you've heard it here, straight from the horse's mouth." Lois nods at Jillian.

Bingo's face is frozen in a cockeyed smile. "That's good news, honeydew." His words shake out.

"I guess." Jillian looks into her drink.

"Benjamin knows these things, Bing." Lois applies a fresh coat of lipstick. "You should have listened to him."

"Dinner is ready in the dining room." Belle's West Indies accent refreshes the room. The family follows the smells of Belle's home cooking into the next venue. Marshall puts a light hand on Bingo's back, guiding him along with his walker.

Bingo's dining room is, as usual, set to perfection: crab fork next to the salad fork, next to the dinner fork, over the folded napkin, next to the plate, underneath the smaller plate, underneath the green plate, next to the sharp knife, next to the less sharp knife, next to the big spoon, next to the small spoon, behind the red-wine glass, next to the white-wine glass, next to the water glass filled with eight ounces of water, four ice cubes, and a sliver of seeded lemon. The madcap decor—the grand patterns, ornate dishes, swirling paisleys, florals, and stripes are enough to fill a room ten times its size. But here the mix teeters precariously on bombardment without actually ever falling off the edge.

Marshall helps Bingo into his chair and puts the walker by the door.

The room immediately fills with a cacophony of clanking

utensils and simple chitchat. Belle places a dainty plate of shrimp salad in front of each family member. The tiny pink shrimp shimmer beneath a gelatinous heap of dressing.

Marshall Pollack raises his scotch. "We'd like to give thanks today on this night." The room quiets as he continues the usual blessing. "For our *health*," Marshall pronounces the word in a decidedly Yiddish way, gurgling the *h* out from behind his epiglottis and staring at his companion, "and for our *happiness*." The family members hold their glasses up and await a sign that he's finished.

"Shabbat shalom."

"Shabbat shalom." The members of the family raise their leftmost forks in unison and begin to skewer two or three of the small briny bodies and bring them to their mouths. Bingo smiles at his food, his neck stiff and reaching outward like a strange oversized bird. His head shakes to a song no one else hears.

"Belle, this is fabulous!" Lois removes the dressing from the salad in brusque forkfuls. "What do you call it?"

"It's just shrimp, Ms. Siegel." Belle wipes her hands on a dish towel. "Shrimp with dressing."

"Well, it's just fabulous. Isn't it, Marshall?"

"Fabulous."

"Thank you, Ms. Siegel, Mr. Pollack."

"What's the stuff on top, Belle, honey? It's so delicious. And *shiny*."

"It's dressing, Ms. Siegel—ketchup and mayonnaise mixed together. With a little pickle juice mixed in."

"Well, it's fabulous." Lois pushes more of the dressing off to the side.

"Thank you, Ms. Siegel." Belle disappears back into the kitchen.

"God, Mother. Why do you have to talk to Belle like that?"

"Like what?"

"Like that."

"Like what?"

"Like she's a child. Nobody likes to be treated like a child."

"What? I just said the shrimp was fabulous. Right, Bing? Am I going crazy here?"

Bingo holds a hand up in protest, always reluctant to get in the middle of the mother-daughter disagreements.

"I just said the shrimp was fabulous. It's a fabulous dish. Shrimp. With dressing. Right, Marshall?"

Marshall deposits more white wine into each glass and opens a second bottle.

"You know what I mean, Mother."

Marshall scratches up the remainder of the salad with the side of his fork, making a grating metallic sound. He stares at a single spot on the tablecloth and beats loudly with his fork at the last speck of dressing.

"For Christ sake, Marshall."

"What? What?"

Belle removes the salad plates and replaces each of them with a low bowl of gazpacho. The cool puree of tomato, green pepper, red onion, garlic, parsley, and white vinegar replenishes the room with tang and bite.

"Gazpacho, Mr. Pollack," Belle says proudly, placing the wide bowl gently in front of him, "your favorite."

Marshall breaks into song: "Me-chelle, my Belle . . ."

"My God, Marshall! Do we need to hear that?" Lois applies a new coat of lipstick. Lipstick for Lois is like sorbet, a cleanser between courses.

"Thank you very much, Isabelle, this looks lovely." Marshall gazes sharply across the table. "Why can't you make gazpacho like this, Lois?"

"Because," Lois rasps in a loud whisper, "Marshall, *gazpacho* is made *entirely of nightshade vegetables*. It literally *leaches* the calcium from your body. Gazpacho *leaches* calcium." She glares at him.

"I wasn't sure I had anything left to *leach*," Marshall says, quaffing up a full spoonful of the green and red liquid and smiling to the group.

Lois checks her lipstick in a compact. "I saw a fabulous Warhol show in Bar*th*elona." Lois pronounces the *c* like *th*. "The early drawings."

"Hi*th* Penile Period?" Jillian bites her teeth against the lip of the crystal glass, finding thanks on this holy day for the moment of personal entertainment.

"Warhol was not entirely"—the group waits patiently for Bingo's expert opinion—"penis-centric."

"You are so wrong, Bing!" Jillian raises her scotch glass to her uncle, forgetting for an instant that he is no longer who he once was. "Did you see the *Sticky Fingers* cover, Bing? You can literally reach in and *feel* Mick Jagger's dick! You unzip it and you stick your hand right in and you can *feel* it."

"Brava! Brava!" Bingo claps and smiles. Jillian is embarrassed of her outburst of animation.

"Can we please stop talking about Mick Jagger's *genitalia* at the Shabbat table." Lois whips her napkin back onto her lap. Bingo's laughing has now turned into a small coughing episode. "See what you did, Jill? Marshall, hand Bing some water."

"I'm fine, darling." Bingo wipes his mouth with a napkin.

Belle removes the soup bowls, leaving the cabbage leaf-shaped plates below them. And one by one, steaming platters of all shapes get placed on the table. Mounds of Belle's famous food, sweating underneath healthy sprinkles of salt and melting cubes of butter, fill the empty spaces. Marshall lifts up a saucer and inspects its bottom through his reading glasses. Jillian rests her head on her chin, alternating sips of scotch and wine. A nauseated body and a vacant mind are the best she can hope for tonight.

"Belle, honey, if it's no problem," Lois puts a her hand on the housekeeper's arm, "and only, only, if you have it around, could you steam up some fish, maybe a vegetable for me. Sole, if you have it. Broccoli, maybe. Or spinach. No salt. No butter. Steamed in lemon juice. No oil. No rice. Maybe a little salad. Dressing on the side. Honey, you are such a dear. Aren't you lucky, Bingo? To have such a dear in your life for this many years. Belle, you are simply a dear."

"Surely, Ms. Siegel." Belle walks back into the kitchen.

"Belle." Bingo's voice is as loud as it's been all night. Belle turns around to face her boss.

"Yes, Mr. Loevner?"

"My sister," the words take forever to come out of his mouth, "will be having the regular food tonight."

"Bing . . ." Lois wipes at the corners of her mouth. "I just was asking . . ."

"This is still my dinner table." Bingo takes a hearty sip of wine.

"Surely, Mr. Loevner." Belle disappears from the room. Jillian laughs into her napkin. Lois presses her lips together and lifts her hair back into shape. The room is quiet for a number of minutes as the food is served in silence and Lois fishes around her pocketbook for one thing or another.

"I think I should quit my job. It's a terrible job. A stupid job. I'm going nowhere." Jillian's words cascade out of her mouth.

"What, darling? What are you saying?" Lois is frozen, her date book poised in the air.

"Never quit a job without another one to go to, pussycat." Marshall punctuates the conversation.

"*Now* you want to quit your job? My God, Jilly."

"It's my stupid life." Jillian can feel the sedatives rocking her body back and forth. She would like to just crawl into the kitchen and spend the rest of the evening with Belle, eating dinner out of Tupperware.

"Every job has its good days . . . and its bad days." Marshall uses his utensils for emphasis.

"Thanks, Marsh."

"Did you tell the Bomb Agency about *it*?"

"Did I tell the Bomb Agency about *what*, Mother?"

"My God, Jilly, you know *what*, for God's sake."

"Shut your piehole, Lois. If Jilly doesn't want to tell them it's Bingo's store, she doesn't have to." Marshall tilts his head up at Lois—his eyes loom large through his thick glasses.

"*Was* Bingo's store." Bingo wipes the food from the corner of his mouth.

"Everyone in this family is insane." Lois straightens out her napkin and fixes her hair.

"Jillian can make up her own mind." Marshall takes off his reading glasses and points with them. "She's a grown woman."

"But I think if she just tells them who she is—"

"Will you stop!" Jillian pounds a fist beside her plate. "I don't give a *shit* about what all you people think." She stretches out her eyebrow, pulling the eye into an extended slit. Her elbow slips off the table and she nearly pokes herself in the nose, the alcohol and unmarked pills seeping deeply into the neurotransmitters.

"Don't swear, Jill. It's impolite."

"Jesus. Never mind I said anything, okay? It's a great job. I love it. I've never been happier. Happy, happy, happy!"

"They're just using you, Jilly, to get what they want." Lois waves her lipstick in the air. "You should use them right back while you still have some leverage." Lois closes the gold compact and puts it back in her purse. "Always stay one step ahead of people, darling. Look at me."

"Can you just all leave me alone?" Jillian chomps down on an ice cube; the pieces of it spill out onto the table.

Jillian draws circles in her potatoes with her fork. Her eyes begin to drift in no particular direction. Her fork is heavy—the cool metal of it stinging her fingers or maybe warming them, she's not sure. Bingo's dining room has gotten impossibly small.

A chunk of potato flies out of Jillian's mouth. "Oopsie." She licks it off her arm.

"Don't chew with your mouth open, honey." Lois's words seem to drip thickly from her face. Jillian looks down at the lipstick marks on Lois's napkin, they look, for a moment, like red snails crawling across her lap.

"Can I go to bed?" Jillian manages to whisper the smartest words of the day into Bingo's fleshy ear—saliva building up in her mouth.

She holds her cheek against his for a moment, feeling the shaking of his head as if it was her own. His skin is warm. She can still smell the lingering molecules of his familiar bouquet.

"Go on, honeydew." Bingo plants a feeble kiss on her forehead. "The Pink Room."

"Good night, Mommy. Good night, Marsh. Night, Belle. Night night." Her foot gets caught on the leg of the chair. "Shit."

"Where are you going, honey? You don't want to miss Belle's Baked Alaska. She made it especially for you," Lois says, holding the lipstick tube out in front of her.

Belle stands in the doorway and shoos Jillian away with a dish towel.

"I love you, Belly Belle." Jillian stomps her foot and twirls in a circle. "You love me always."

"You go on now, honeydew." Belle smiles.

"Too much to d-r-i-n-k," Lois mouths to the room.

"I can spell. I'm not a baby." Froth spatters from her mouth. "You fucking farts." The room is a drunken whirl of patterns and people. "You're all gonna miss me when I'm gone." She stumbles forward. "You're gonna miss me. I miss Jillian Siegel! I didn't mean to reject her from the organism! That's what you people are going to say." She turns around into the hallway and trips over Bingo's walker.

"Oh, honey, we're not *rejecting* you." Lois rubs at her teeth.

"You're just going to bed."

Jillian doesn't hear a word of it.

"You fart family."

5

JILLIAN'S been sleeping in the Pink Room off and on for nearly thirty years. Foreheads are stroked here. Shoulders are rubbed. Curtains are drawn. Cups of tea magically arrive and disappear. Clothes get folded. Sleep is peaceful and deep.

Mornings come later in the Pink Room.

The room, and everything in it, is feminine, flowery, and in variations of Bingo and Alain's mutual favorite color—pink. The sheets are covered with tiny roses that frill and curl at every edge. The bedside lamps turn on and off by long pink tassels. An antique mother-of-pearl comb and brush sit faceup on the pale rose dresser, as if an elegant woman might at any moment stroke her hair one hundred times before bed. A delicate pink plate holds six antique decanters of powdery eau de parfum. The faded pink-striped brocade wallpaper with the bamboo overlay is perhaps two decades past its prime, but the fine handmade cloth could never be replaced. Even the light bulbs in the room are Soft Rose GE Luminaires. Alain claimed the pink-tinted light "retouched the wrinkles away" and when he heard Soft Rose was about to be discontinued, he stocked up on them by the case and stored them in the basement.

A colorful picture of Bingo, taken in the Maldives by Alain, sits in a braided silver frame on the second shelf. Bingo is blazingly tan in the photo (as he was solidly for more than fifty years), and the effervescent smile on his face conveys everything anyone would need to know about their relationship. Bingo was, with Alain, both childlike and childish—the genius and the martini mixer. Alain was uncontainable, the pixie—never having a proper jacket to wear to the club, always starting the pillow fights, and just as happy with his mustard sandwiches at the side of the road as he was with the rack of lamb at "21."

Had he lived past the cancer; had he hung in there just a little bit longer; had she held her arms around him just a little tighter—everything, Jillian thinks, would be different.

If he just would have stayed . . . if they all would have stayed . . . all the world would still be pink.

Dog-eared paperback books live out their retirement on the heavy wooden bookshelves along the wall: *Elizabeth: Fifty Glorious Years; Lauren Bacall: By Myself; Debrett's Book of the Royal Wedding; Judy Garland: Beyond the Rainbow; Rebecca*, by Daphne du Maurier; *Lana: The Lady, the Legend, the Truth;* and *Good Times, Bad Times*, by Harold Evans, punctuate the bountiful collection of gossipy autobiographies, American classics, and steamy potboilers. His collection of page-turners once spent many a day on lounge chairs at the club or by the pool in Palm Beach and now spend their twilight years on these oak shelves.

Jillian picks up the black-and-white ad framed on the top of the shelf. The typography is dated, but the concept is still a classic. It is the same image she saw earlier in the day on the wall of the Loevner's war room at Bomb. Only here it feels more like family than ammunition.

Photographed by Mario Carnieri and designed by a young graphic designer named Richard Hauerbach, it is the most well-known image from the most well-known advertising campaign of its time.

Jillian remembers Bingo asking her to sit alongside him on top of the white piano for the nineteenth ad in the campaign series. She remembers not knowing who Briana Terrell was, the tall movie actress pretending to kiss Bingo on the cheek and wearing the floor-length satiny dress. She remembers looking down at her own white Mary Janes—the floor was so far away and she needed to go to the bathroom. She remembers the man who brushed her hair into pigtails, who thought she was nine even though she was seven, and the short bunny-fur coat and matching muff she got to keep after the photo shoot.

"Je t'adore Loevner's!"

The faux-French headline that ran across the top in the chic serif type caused quite a stir in its day. It was a phrase that Bingo, fluent in French, and of course, Alain, found queer. But, as Bingo used to say to Jillian, "Always hire the best and then trust them implicitly." And trusting the twenty-five-year-old Richard Hauerbach paid off. Queer or not, it was the headline of every one of the ads in the campaign for the illustrious department store and on everybody's lips in New York and, to some extent, the world.

Bumper stickers across the tristate area appropriated the popular headline, replacing the word "Loevner's" with a little silhouette of a Boston terrier or a toy poodle. Even Bridget Bardot repeated the phrase on Johnny Carson, blowing a kiss to the viewing audience, *"Je t'adore Loevner's et les Etats-Unis!"* The three-second exposure on the popular talk show caused an unparalleled spike in sales at Loevner's the next week.

It was Hauerbach's idea and breakthrough for its time—the first big campaign to feature a real person, the proprietor of an establishment as spokesman—Bingo, the smiling, podgy, accidental ambassador for the department store he founded.

And little Jillian was an afterthought for a layout that was just "a smidge too sparse," according to the collective opinions of those on the other side of the camera. *"What about zee little girl sitting on zee white piano?"* Mario Carnieri blurted out his stroke of brilliance. Richard Hauerbach agreed. *"Perfetto! Perfetto!"* cheered Mario as he snapped away.

The resulting image was the most beloved of a campaign that ran for nearly two decades. The identity of the young girl with the haunting eyes and the grown-up profile was never publicly released, but after its appearance in the *New York Times* and on a billboard on Madison Avenue, the store instantly sold out of every pint-sized bunny fur coat and muff, and every pair of white, black, and pink Mary Janes, and the mysterious little girl with the aquiline nose became the anonymous star.

The photo, this photo, framed and kept safe forever on the shelf, captures this halcyon time—before Alain went away, before Loevner's went away, the moment before the whole world became dull again.

Jillian kisses her fingertip and touches it to the glass. *"Je t'adore."*

She pries off her clothes letting them fall where they may. A particularly stubborn high heel gets thrown across the bed. Earrings and bracelets fall into a heap beside the table lamp. Tight jeans release from her ankles with multiple inelegant side kicks. She crawls into bed without removing the bedspread. Someone will do that later. Someone always does. She feels too full and swollen but doesn't have the energy to get up and relieve her stomach of dinner and the last of the scotch and wine. Her eyes glaze over and promptly shut into a dead sleep.

"Reach into my jacket, honeydew, but don't let me catch you." Bingo *pushed his hand further into his pocket then turned away, pretending to look up numbers in his telephone book.*

"Take the Treat" had become almost a weekly ritual now that Jillian was spending months at a time at her uncle's apartment. It was a game guaranteed by Bingo to put a smile on the face of even the most sullen little girl.

"What is it? What is it?" Jillian leaped around her uncle's desk, excited to get another one of her uncle's hand-picked goodies.

"Well, if I tell you, it wouldn't be a surprise, would it?" Bingo hummed to himself as he pointed his pocket toward his young niece.

Jillian tiptoed toward her uncle, holding her hands tightly over her mouth so as not to giggle.

"I hear you!" Bingo said into the air toward the phone. "Don't forget, if I catch you, you can't have it."

Jillian breathed deeply to quiet her laughter. Her mind raced for ways to get her hand into his jacket without his feeling it. She moved her body close to Bingo, leaned against his side, and acted as if the game was already over, or possibly forgotten about. Of course the game was not over, but it was the best way she could think of to keep playing it. "What are you doing?" she said nonchalantly, sincerely enough to fool him.

"Honeydew!" he said, not believing the girl's seemingly short attention span. "We're playing 'Take the Treat.' You know what I'm doing. I'm pretending to talk on the phone." He ruffled her bangs and pulled her ponytail.

"Ta da!" she said, her hand laid out flat in front of him—prize and all. "I fooled you!"

"You did, honeydew!" Bingo laughed and hugged the child close. "You're getting so good at our little game."

Jillian looked down at the object in her hand—a thin gold band with a square green gem gleaming in the center. "A grown-up ring!" It was the most beautiful thing she'd ever seen. Tears nearly leaked from her eyes as the green sparkled in her hand. "And I'm not even grown up yet!"

"Little girls should have special things that make them feel special." Bingo kissed her forehead. "Big girls too." He held her face toward his. "No one else needs to know when a girl feels lonely or sad. She can look at her special thing and feel happy again."

They both knew the secret he allowed her to keep from the rest of the world. They both knew that an emerald ring, snatched from a silk pocket, couldn't keep a child from missing a mommy or a daddy she never knew. But it could hold the feeling frozen for a moment—keeping it hidden in plain sight—locked away in a beautiful gem of one kind or another.

They both admired the ring on her finger. "Everyone deserves to find something special where they least expect it. It puts a smile on anyone's face. Never forget that, my sweet." He kissed her ring finger. "Always put a surprise in every 'pouche'! Everyone needs cheering up once in a while"

Jillian hugged her uncle tight around the neck. She never wanted to let go.

The knock at the door is quiet. Belle's knuckles are barely audible over the shifting of sheets and down.

"Honeydew?" Belle quietly enters.

Jillian presses her face into the pillow.

"I have some honey tea and lemon." She sets a dainty steaming cup beside the reading lamp and sits her body down on the edge of the bed. Jillian's hand is tucked into a tight fist against her open lips.

"My little baby girl." Belle strokes the stray hairs off her forehead. Jillian instinctively turns and curls her long body toward the housekeeper's lap.

"My baby girl."

Still thick with sleep, Jillian hears Belle's words, the whir of the air conditioner, and the antique French clock tick back and forth.

"You still six years old, honeydew." Belle wraps a loose hair behind Jillian's ear. "Your heart still missin' a piece."

Jillian grabs at Belle's lap and finally lets the tears come down.

6

JILLIAN tiptoes out of the apartment and noiselessly shuts the door behind her. Her head aches and her constitution on this Shabbat morning is in no condition to face Bingo or even Belle or much of anything else. Bingo is normally an early riser, but his current condition and variety of medications encourage sleeping in. Jillian is envious of his shorter days, wishing she too could abbreviate this morning or even eliminate it entirely.

"You're up early, Miss Siegel." The downstairs doorman, Mr. Bellacorsco, rubs his hands together and shifts his weight from one foot to the other.

"I am, Mr. B." Even the words hurt on their way out of her brain. She needs a coffee more than life itself.

"You want I should get you a cab?"

"I can get it, Mr. B." Jillian stretches her head around in a circle in an attempt to loosen the clogged muck. She raises her hand and a cab pulls over immediately. She climbs onto the bouncy seat.

"You take care now, Miss Siegel."

"I will, Mr. B." The cab rushes forward. "Downtown," she says to the driver, "Union Square." Even though she spent the majority of her childhood above Forty-second, it has never provided any comfort. *Escaping* always means heading downtown.

There is some sort of liquid on the floor of the cab. It moves back and forth in waves like a tiny black ocean. She balances her boots in the center, between the two puddles, and plants her heavy suede purse down beside her.

The streets pass by, and she gazes out at the familiar sights. Loevner's Department Store now has an Eastlake Cineplex on one side and a TGIF on the other. But even flanked by these banal establishments it's still as classically elegant as it always was—the colossal portico chandelier handblown in Venice is visible from the street. None of the nine new locations around the country can compare to the majesty of the original.

She passes Punjabi's Indian, Avenue Cakes & Cookies, and the Rite Aid where she stole silver hair clips and a box of hair color last year after a particularly challenging shrink session. As the cab rushes by Thirty-third, she remembers sitting in her old shrink's office. Actually, one of the eight shrinks she's had over the last ten years—Dr. Susan Weinberg or Shienberg, or Shoenberg, or something-berg. The cab stops at a red light and other cabs carrying other passengers surround her: old men, couples, businessmen, mothers with their children, children alone, women on cell phones.

Dr. Susan Steinberg. That was her name.

She was the one who nodded civilly, blew her nose into hankies she kept in her sleeve, frequently looked at the clock, and occasionally caught Jillian saying things like "I'm not ready for a normal man." Dr. Susan Steinberg would jump on these statements after weeks, even months of silence, and pry out lengthy definitions of *ready* and *normal.* Jillian's notorious line "I have a right to keep my own secrets" led to an entire month of questioning.

"You're hanging on to your secrets for dear life, Jill. You're getting something out of it," the doctor said one Wednesday between four and four forty-five P.M. "What are you getting out of it, Jill? What are you getting out of hanging on so hard?" These are the big-money questions.

"Misery," she said, defiantly staring Dr. Steinberg straight in the eye.

"You wouldn't work so hard just to be miserable. You're getting something out of it that you like—that protects you, Jill."

"What am I getting out of it? I don't know, Susan. You tell me. You're the professional. What am I getting out of it?"

"One thought is that you push people away before they leave you. One thought is you try to be funny rather than deal with a direct question. One thought is that you're afraid to tell me your secrets because you're afraid that even I will abandon you." The doctor blew her nose into a hanky. "That sharing your secrets means sharing the deepest part of you—the part that's afraid and feels ugly." The clock ticked very loudly at Dr. Susan Steinberg's office.

"What do you think about that, Jill?"

Dr. Susan Steinberg had a Matisse print on the wall—goldfish swimming in a bowl. There was a decorator box of Kleenex on her coffee table. Her office smelled like Chinese food from the takeout place downstairs.

Dr. Susan Steinberg was not happy at all when Jillian Siegel self-diagnosed the completion of her therapy by leaving a message on voice mail. "I really think this has been great for me, Susan. I have a really, really great new boyfriend and I'm really getting along with my mother now and I think I really have the skills to move forward now. You taught me how to fish for myself, as they say." Jillian wrote down the four key points and practiced the speech a few times before calling. She felt that leaving the message rather than simply vanishing into thin air could have been appreciated a little more by Dr. Susan Steinberg.

"Seventeenth is good for you." Jillian is not sure if the taxi driver has asked a question or made a statement. In any case, he is right:

Seventeenth is close enough to Union Square and is as fine a choice as any. It's below Twenty-third, and that's all that matters this morning.

Coffee. Coffee. Sugar. Carbs. Coffee. Jillian's cravings take over, and her mind fills with focus and determination—and not weak, burnt diner coffee in a blue-and-white Greek cup; this is a day for full-on name-brand coffee with hand-steamed milk in a large overpriced paper goblet—name-brand coffee and full-dose simple carbohydrates, an oatmeal scone, a corn muffin, a cinnamon coffee cake topped with chunks of walnuts and crumbled sugar.

She climbs the stairs two at a time to the Barnes & Noble café on the third floor and keeps her breath steady to cushion her achy body and ward away any negative thoughts that may creep in on the short climb. The open coffee bar is lively on a Saturday morning; the smell of overroasted, freshly ground three-dollar-and-twenty-nine-cent coffee permeates the air like a sweet, smoky fireplace.

"Can I get a blueberry scone and a Grande no-fat latte?" Jillian asks over the hissing sound of milk steaming. There is a dull ache at the crown of her head; the heaviness wanders to the frontal lobe and back again, the result of dead brain cells created yesterday settling into the lower strata of her cranium. "Thanks," she says as the extra-large cardboard cup gets passed her way. She could also use about a gallon of ice water and a pitcher of orange juice, but the shock of it all might be too great for the moment.

Her cell phone rings from the depths of her cavernous bag. She reaches past yesterday's underwear and the pair of stockings from La Petite Coquette and down in the depths of her pocketbook.

Jillian opens her phone and cups it against her shoulder. "Hi. It's me."

"Hi, *It's me.* It's me."

She takes a sip of latte and tries to figure out what she's going to tell Alex about yesterday.

"So?"

Jillian realizes she should give him something. He deserves *something*. "It went great, Alex, really, it went great. All a girl could hope for. Billy was eating out of the palm of my hand."

"And the outfit was perfect?"

"*Perfetto.*"

"That's great, J. I'm so proud of you. You really earned it."

"Yeah." Jillian takes another scorching sip. "I did."

"We should celebrate tonight."

"I don't know, Alex."

"Bernie's doing a party at Lotus, that new place down in the meatpacking district. He already put us on the list."

"Oh God, Allie, I'm just not in the mood for it."

"Well, I am. I am in the mood to celebrate my girlfriend and put her on a pedestal."

"I just think I should stay home and rent a video or something." Jillian sits down and leafs through *Paper* magazine left on the small café table. She's whining, but it's the only song she can seem to sing this morning. She's not the girl he thinks she is, and the feeling is not good. She's malignant and untreatable, and his limitless faith is driving her crazy. It's beginning, even, to feel pathetic.

"What's going on, Jill? Is there something you're not telling me? Did something bad happen?"

"Can we just get off the phone? I'm just in a crappy, shitty, crappy mood and talking on the cell phone ad infinitum isn't helping. My ear is hot. Literally. The right side of my head is metastasizing as we speak." She curls her shoulder into the phone—keeping the conversation as private as possible.

"Then come uptown right now and meet me at the hovel. I'll take you to the museum and we can grab an early Saturday pint at O'Leary's with the drunks."

"Alex. Please. I need to just walk around. Go shopping. Be by myself."

"An overpriced martini always cheers you up, J. We can have one drink, then we'll go home and I'll take compromising photographs of you in your knickers."

"You make it all sound wildly appealing, Alex." Jillian lays her face down on the open *Paper* magazine in front of her—she wonders if her cheek will absorb the David LaChapelle photo of Amanda Lepore like silly putty on a comic strip. Redundant, she thinks, as poor Amanda has already been stretched and pulled so much.

"Fine. I'll be down to your place at ten. We'll meet up with Bernie and Amy at Lotus after that."

"I can't, really."

"You can and you will, Siegel. You will put on something sexy, freshly laundered, and hung neatly on a hanger by the lovely Yolanda, and we will meet our friends and make a toast to you and then you can do whatever the hell you want."

"I'm not gonna be any fun."

"Well, you're gonna not be any fun with *me*, Jill. I'll pick you up at ten."

"*Oyyy.*"

"I'll see you at ten. Bye."

"Bye."

Jillian take another bite of scone—crumbling it into a thousand sugary pieces. She brushes them off the fluffy front of her sweater. Jillian tries to *feel what she's feeling*—a favorite Susan Steinberg technique, to use one of Susan's *ness* words, like *loneliness, sadness, emptiness.* But the best she can manage is *shit-ness, fuck-ness, piss-ness.*

She has lied to her boyfriend yet again. Staying "one step ahead," as Lois would say. But she's pushing him further and further away without meaning to. And he's letting her do it. Jillian wonders if it's all actually his fault. If he really loved her, he would know better than to believe her.

She tucks the phone back into her purse, puts the *Paper* back on the pile, heads through the café and into the book section. The coffee has cooled down a bit and soaks into her throat like a soppy warm broth—the burnt amber taste of it chasing down into the depths of her stomach. She makes her way up and down the rows and slurps up the milky brown liquid. Her stomach churns and gurgles. It takes concentration just to keep it all down.

The Fashion & Beauty section is a familiar escape. She has, in the past, lost herself to these coffee table books, leafing through—wanting and craving everything she sees. The spider-thin red pump on the cover of *Manolo Blahnik* looks poisonous. She lays her hand flat on it, allowing the glossy-coated picture to prick at her palm. *Shoes: Fashion and Fantasy* sits right next to it; the chunky rainbow-heeled Ferragamo like a psychedelic hippopotamus parked in the center of the stark page. It barks at her as the layers of colors undulate off the white background. She holds the side of the table, feeling seasick, as if she might vomit.

The model on the cover of *Bobbi Brown Beauty Evolution* glares out at her. She is a predictably pretty brunette with blue eyes and a retouched complexion.

"Hi, Jill," the model says from the cover with her husky, modulated voice, perfect nose, and flawless Bobbi-arched eyebrows. "How are you feeling?"

"Pardon me?"

"I said, how are you feeling?"

"How do you think I'm feeling?"

"I guess you got fired." She blinks her perfectly smoky eyes. "You must be very sad about it."

"Sad? I'm not sad about it. I'm angry."

"What do you feel angry about?"

"I feel *angry* I don't have a job. I feel *angry* that I lost said job and Brandon Pietro—a boy to whom *style* means pointing to a photo on page seventy-eight in *Men's Hairdo* magazine before the hairdresser begins to cut—did not. I also feel *angry* that Billy Baum—another boy, to whom *loyalty* means staring into his secretary's cleavage for days on end—ruined my fucking life."

"Well, it wasn't a very good campaign, Jill. You should have just stopped after the first board. Everyone knows that."

"Well, thanks to Billy, my life's turned to shit."

"Wasn't your life already in the crapper, Jill? Even before all that." The model's glossy lips remain perpetually smiling.

"What do you mean?"

"You know what I mean."

"No, I'm sorry, I don't."

"Well, you steal, for one. And that's a big one, Jill, as in 'Thou shalt not steal,' and for two, you are very messy, which is not a commandment, but still fairly annoying and certainly symptomatic of some of the larger issues going on here, and three, nobody knows you, and along those lines nobody loves you, and along those lines you don't let anyone in to even try."

"Alex loves me."

"He doesn't even know you."

"Screw you."

"You shouldn't swear. It's impolite." The model smiles.

Jillian sucks down a slurp from her cup. "What do you know anyway?"

"Nothing really, I'm just a picture."

Jillian turns the book over on the table, revealing a much smaller version of the picture on the back side of the book.

"If it's any consolation Jill, I'm just a facade too." The model smiles a smaller smile.

Jillian wants to buy the Bobbi Brown book just to throw it over the edge of the building, just to feed it through a shredder, just to hurl it into a garbage truck or donate it to the Salvation Army, destined to sit in a church basement for the next hundred years. *Who does she think she is, anyway? She's just two-dimensional.*

7

JILLIAN escapes Barnes & Noble as fast as she can, walks across Union Square, down Fifth, through the park, through the Village, past Bleecker, past Bruno's Bakery, across the wide canyon of Houston Street, and into the warm, familiar embrace of Soho shopping. The usual downtown girls stride up and down the streets in their sleek weekend boots and glossy lipstick. On a Saturday, most of the people are fakes—bridge-and-tunnel, cheap versions of the originals—but there are still enough of the real deal. The boys, like always, travel in packs and limit their wardrobe to crisp white work shirts, a dab of hair gel, the latest cell phones and gizmos, tight Levi's, and big black shoes from Tootsie Plohound.

They all seem especially ridiculous today, everyone pretending to have somewhere to go.

She breathes in and out for focus as she makes it past a few of her favorite stores without yielding to temptation. Today is about recovery, not shopping—a cleansing period, a meditation, a way to recompose and start fresh. She just needs to pass the time until the day just . . . passes.

Her cell phone rings from the bottom of her bag. Without taking it all the way out she glances at the caller ID: LOIS. MOBILE. Jillian opens the phone just a centimeter and clicks it shut again, effectively aborting the call. A call with Lois is not part of the cleanse.

I ♥ SOHO T-shirts dangle in front of a tiny sidewalk store at Prince and West Broadway. She never noticed this cozy tourist shop before with its baby Statues of Liberty, American Flag shot glasses, mini Chrysler Buildings, and fake Tag Heuer watches inside. The T-shirts hang above her head. They sway lightly in the breeze just inches from her eyes. She smiles at them and lets one brush the tip of her nose.

"Very nice, these shirts," a woman proclaims from behind the shirts, noting Jillian's expensive handbag and fine scarf.

"I'm just looking." Jillian smiles. She can see the sky beyond the shirts forming a majestic blue background to the red, white, and black designs. Only a few clouds today interrupt the flat blue. She feels peaceful in this setting for the first time in days. The T-shirts and trinkets in the store are so sweet really, simple mementos for people to take home to their coworkers or their children, souvenirs from their trip to the Big Apple.

The woman hangs up more shirts with a long rod she lifts above her head. The little store smells like pierogis and cooked cabbage. The woman's hair is bottle red with roots of grayish yellow. She wears a pavé diamond wedding ring and rose-patterned stretch pants.

There is a large box of fluffy socks on the floor. 2 PARES FOR $8. TAX INCLUDE, according to the handwritten sign. Jillian bends down to pet them. The tiny fuzzy balls are surprisingly soft and cuddly. Hundreds of pairs fill the box in a pleasing rainbow of colors: brick, putty, celadon, ocher. The gray pair is hardly gray at all. Lighter than charcoal, darker than light gray, this pair is slightly "heather"—on the cool of slate.

This is a superb color, truly. She remembers Vanya, one of the women who worked the perfume counter at Loevner's, and her slate-heather cashmere sweater set. It was impossibly luxe and soft-looking against Vanya's creamy skin. Jillian has committed the color to memory for more than fifteen years. According to Vanya, this particular shade of slate-heather, with nuances of both warm and cool tones, was impossible to re-create in American factories. "America never gets color right, my dear. Only France and Italy. If you want color—you must go to Europe," Vanya said, twirling her mother-of-pearl buttons. And now here it is, Vanya's celestial slate-heather, in this cardboard box on Prince and West Broadway.

"Very nice, these shirts." The redhaired woman greets another customer, barely looking down from her work on the racks above.

The sun catches the tender sock fuzz. Jillian wonders if they might be real cashmere. She's heard that many of these little stores get great deals on cashmere in bulk. She extends her hand over the length of the sock ball. It is palm-sized and fits neatly in her grasp, but instead of making it disappear as usual, the ball goes flying from her palm, as if propelled by its own will. Jillian's heart jumps. *Damn it.* Jillian scrambles to grab it again and settles back into place. She checks up and around her periphery again. *All still clear.* She must be off her game. Billy Baum has shaken her from her normally solid ground, but this is only a small thing from an easy store. All is certainly clear.

She clasps her fingertips around it. The redhaired woman is still adjusting the display, making sure the most popular designs face outward onto the street.

Jillian grips the sock ball hard. She squeezes every drop of air out, compressing it into the smallest shape possible. As tightly as she grasps with one hand, she releases and relaxes the rest of her body, seemingly not caring at all about the socks, but looking upward to get a better look at the red-and-white SOHO LIFEGUARD T-shirt. She drops the sock ball into her pocket briskly and stands back to look as if she's getting a better view at the shirt.

"This very nice shirt." The redhaired woman says as she pulls it off the rafter with her pole and swings it toward Jillian. "Beefy-T." She points at the label. Jillian looks and smiles as she pushes the fuzzy lump down hard into her pocket. "See?"

"Nice." Jillian looks at the dangling price tag. "I'll take it." She decides that the overpriced twenty-three-dollar shirt more than enough makes up for the store's loss on the cashmere socks. She is always fair about these things.

"Good. Nice color for you."

Twenty-three dollars is not cheap, but it really is a small price to pay for a T-shirt *and* a pair of cashmere socks in Vanya slate-heather gray. Jillian pulls out her wallet, keeping her elbow firmly planted against the lump of stolen socks on her right side.

"How much is it?" she asks the woman for no reason but to stall and assess the situation.

"Same as all. Twenty-three bucks."

"Oh. Okay. Lemme see what I have here." Jillian pulls out a ten and thirteen crinkled ones from the zippered change section of her wallet. She puts the wad on the counter. "Here you go." The redhaired woman counts out the bills slowly in a different language. Jillian watches the woman closely—focusing on her eyelashes as she counts.

Then, for the briefest instant, less than a millisecond, less than a nanosecond, or maybe not even at all, the redhaired woman glances down at the box of socks. Jillian's air passage nearly closes shut. *Shit.* She pushes hard against the fuzz ball, compressing it as tiny as possible, wishing it away. Her skin grows hot and red, and her breath turns instantly sour.

Jillian looks around. She could get rid of the socks in a bath-room trash, but there is no bathroom. It's too late to pull them out and sneak them back into the box. Besides, she's wrong. The redhaired woman was just blinking her eyes. A normal involun-tary reflex. The woman continues to count out the bills and smile. Jillian is sure she is definitely wrong, definitely; she didn't look up at all, and the box is too full to notice one pair of socks gone. And besides, why would anyone suspect her out of all the people milling around the stand? She just bought a twenty-three-dollar shirt, after all. The woman smiles again. Jillian was certainly wrong. Everything's fine. It is hers.

"Thanks." The word barely makes it out of her mouth. She smiles at the redhaired lady, their eyes locking together for an instant. She tries to remember if she said the mantra, but she can't recall. Getting out of there is all Jillian can think about. Getting out now. She takes the plastic handle bag from the woman. Redhair smiles again. Jillian's heart is beating furiously. She turns and walks out, holding the bag snugly against her lumpy right-hand pocket.

Jillian pushes her legs forward into long galloping strides. She uses every inch of her body, stretching and reaching every last tendon, to propel forward. Eight, nine, ten steps and she is halfway down the block toward Spring Street. She awakens all senses for something amiss, but nothing. Her legs begin to cramp so she slows down. She is nearly safely past Spring. Surely by then, by the time she reaches the patterned red bricks on the south side of the street, she will be free and clear.

"Excuse me." Jillian denies hearing the words at first.

"Excuse me! Lady!" Jillian looks back at Red speeding down the street, her hose-covered feet squeezed into high-heeled sandals. A large pasty-faced boy, perhaps nineteen or twenty, lumbers alongside her. "Excuse me, lady girl." *Stay relaxed. You bought the Beefy-T. You are an advertising executive.* "You come back to store." Jillian's blood blasts away from her limbs and into her core, causing her fingertips an instant stomach-churning prickle.

"Why? Did I leave something?" Her mind races for the proper thing to say, the thing a regular person would say.

"You come back to store right now." The pasty-faced boy stands there, yards wider than Jillian, his white face prickly red from the neck up.

"I'm sorry, but I have an appointment in Tribeca." Jillian turns south and begins to walk. *Maybe this will all just go away, get lost—like Nana's antique hair clip you misplaced in seventh grade or Bingo's gold fountain pen you left in a cab.*

"Ivor. Go." The big boy takes one lunge and then wraps his oversized hand around Jillian's upper arm and nearly lifts her off the ground. He turns her northward and the three began walking back toward the store, Jillian's toes nearly off the ground.

"Excuse me. He's hurting me. This is not legal. You can't just grab a woman off the street. Oh my God." Jillian is aware of the Soho people around her. She lets her hair fall in front of her face for cover. The boy's fingers dig deeply into her triceps, probably damaging some nerves or at least bruising the sinew.

"Ivor. Come," Red barks at the boy.

This sort of treatment cannot be legal. People have rights in New York City. This is completely unacceptable. Jillian should call Benjamin Fishbaum. She has rights. She should scream for help. *This is truly unbelievable.* Ivor leads Jillian into the store and behind the T-shirt display and into a back room, only big enough for a small metal desk, two chairs, a calculator, and four thousand pieces of paper.

"Are you junkie?" Red asks the appalling question of the century.

"Am I *what*?"

"Are you junkie? Junkies steal and sell on Wall Street."

"Excuse me?" The tiny room is clearly not meant for one person, much less three. The smell of cabbage and sweat is nauseating. *A junkie? Is she kidding? Do junkies own Gucci handbags? Real Gucci handbags?*

"You steal sock. You think I don't see?"

"What?" Jillian's air is thin, and the word comes out like a squeak. As the adrenaline shoots through her brain it's impossible to think or stall or remember any of her rehearsed and reasonable excuses. She pulls the sock ball out of her pocket and holds it out. *These Vanya gray socks?* "You mean the socks I just *bought*?!" This is the only maneuver that comes to her at the time.

"You buy Beefy-T. Not sock." Red pulls the socks away and slaps them down into the middle of the desk.

"What do you mean? I just bought these socks. You said twenty-three dollars for the T-shirt *and* the socks. I paid you. For both." Jillian is scrambling.

"You think I fell off truck today?" Red picks up a stapler and staples the end of a piece of paper with the slam of her fist. "Ivor. Call." Ivor opens a pink leather address book on the desk. Jillian's heart sinks. *Stupid.* She is so stupid. She knew. She knew. She is off her game completely. Billy Baum ruined everything. Even this.

"I bought these socks!" Jillian stares at the fuzzy ball on the desk.

"Junkie steal my business. You sell on Wall Street? You sell on Wall Street? Ivor, get camera." Red is looking around the tiny room, under papers, behind books.

Jillian's air runs out, and the words merely hiccup out from her throat. "I shop in Soho all the time . . ." Ivor pulls out at Polaroid camera from the desk. He points the camera in her face and presses the button.

"Heroin junkie." The camera whines and buzzes and a photo emerges at the bottom. Ivor pulls it out and waves it like a fan. Red spits a few phrases out at the large, doughy boy. Ivor nods and pulls out a clinking mass of metal from the bottom drawer of the tiny desk. In an instant Ivor handcuffs Jillian's wrist onto a bar fastened to the wall. Apparently the bar is there for no other reason than this.

"You can't handcuff me!"

"Citizen arrest!" Red turns and marches out of the tiny room and back through a sea of wavering T-shirts. "Junkie."

Jillian sits there in the tiny paper-filled room with the sock ball in the center of the desk and Ivor standing over her. The metal cuff digs into her skin. Her head is pounding. She is humiliated. This place and these people are disgusting. She doesn't belong in here.

She looks around at the papers—an array of meaningless numbers and forms tacked or taped to every surface, stacked high wherever possible. On the wall beside her is a gallery of criminals. A Hispanic man in his fifties with dark circles under his eyes, a skinny woman perhaps in her teens or twenties, a black teenage boy, a woman in her forties wearing a wig. Each is dated at the bottom—presumably the day he or she was caught by Red and Ivor. They all have the same expression on their face—guilty, regular criminals going about their daily business.

Ivor admires his newest portrait and staples it with a *pow* to the wall under the Hispanic man. He writes the date at the bottom in red. "Good one," he says.

It is safe to assume, she thinks, that this will all be over in a few minutes. They will keep her here until they grow bored of the charade or need to use the desk or decide to file some of these papers.

The clock on the desk reads two-forty. Ivor stands tall with his gargantuan forearms folded in front of him. His eyes move from the socks back to Jillian and back to the socks, as if at any moment the fluffy mound might scamper away. Twenty-two minutes pass. It's three-oh-two P.M. and Jillian has to pee and eat. The humiliation has worn down into just plain ridiculousness. She balances her chin on her free hand. Outside the room, Red continues her work. "Beefy-T. Good on you. Twenty-three dollar." Jillian stares at her plastic bag from the store and the fluffy ball of Vanya heather-slate socks on the desk.

The door finally opens at three fifty-seven. Red comes back in. Her voice is soft and sweet as she speaks to someone following her. "And how is your mother, Jerry?" Behind her, a policeman enters the already crowded room. He ducks his head and turns his body sideways through the undersized door. The sight of him, a mighty mass of blue polyester in this paper-filled cave, is more odd than intimidating.

"She's doing fine, Mrs. Yankelovitch. She's got that inflammation of the knee. What do you call it, bursitis?"

"Oh, yes. Bursitis. Very painful, Jerry."

"But other than that she's as healthy as a horse."

"Good. Is good, Jerry." Jillian is slumped down small into her chair. The discouraged look on her face is not much different than the others in the portrait gallery—worn down. Red has put on a fresh application of lipstick and rouge.

"So what can you tell me about what happened here today, Mrs. Yankelovitch?" The officer asks, careful not to make too much of the question.

"These," Red points an erect finger at the ceiling then down toward the center of the desk, "are stolen socks."

The officer picks up the fluffy round from the center of the desk. "These?" Jillian looks at his nametag—Officer Jerry Cannell. She wonders if Officer Jerry Cannell is buying Red's dramatics.

"Yes. Those are socks."

"How much are the socks, Mrs. Yankelovitch?"

"Two pair, eight dollar."

"So one pair, four dollars?"

"Yes. Four dollar, Jerry." The officer fills the doorway and helps himself to a big heap of air—the last of the oxygen in the room.

"I paid for them." Jillian's feeble words escape. She tries to tell her mind to believe her own story. If she believes then he will too. This is why the mantra works. Usually.

The officer looks at the handcuffs, silver toy handcuffs, around her wrist.

"Mrs. Yankelovitch, can you take the cuffs off the girl?" The officer is merciful. Jillian takes it as a good sign.

"Oh, yes, sure, Jerry. Ivor! Key!" Ivor produces the key and releases her. Jillian grabs at her reddened wrist and twists some life back into it.

"You paid for them?" The officer is clearly open-minded to the possibility.

"She pay for Beefy-T. No socks."

"Did you pay for the socks, ma'am? The officer smiles at Jillian.

"I did. I paid. I mean, I thought I paid."

"She did not pay for socks!" Some other words fly out of Red's mouth along with some spit.

"Mrs. Yankelovitch"—the officer puts a hand on Red's shoulder—"these are four-dollar socks. She said she thought she paid for them. She bought a nice shirt from you—"

"She did not pay for socks." Red summons a lower octave.

He looks back at Jillian. "You thought you bought the socks, ma'am? Is that what happened?" Jillian nods and rubs again at her wrist. She tries to look weary in a I'm-not-trying-to-look-anything kind of way. The officer is on her side. She'll be out of there in no time. "Mrs. Yankelovitch, do you realize the amount of paperwork involved in this sort of thing? Can we just call it a day?"

Yes, yes, yes. Jillian wills the words into Red's mouth.

"She did not pay for socks," Red insists.

"It is my personal recommendation to call it a day, Mrs. Yankelovitch. Honestly, if it weren't for my ma . . . well, it's New York City, Mrs. Yankelovitch." Jerry smiles again. "I'm busy catching the real bad guys, right?" He throws a fake punch at Ivor's belly.

"Okay, Jerry." Red backs down finally. "Whatever you say. You know best."

"Let's send the girl on her way." Officer Cannell winks at Red and reaches a hand out for Jillian. *Yes!*

"Thank you, Officer." Her legs are stiff from sitting in the cramped chair for so long. She shakes them out. She reaches down and grabs her purse and glares at Ivor one last time. *He certainly is a big ugly boy!* Jillian shakes her hair out, swings her purse around her shoulder, and picks up the bag with the T-shirt in it. She is glad to be getting free of this room, this smell, and these people. She is glad to be innocent again.

But then the smallest sound of metal hitting the floor breaks the moment.

And on the floor, directly below Jillian's hand, below the opening of her sleeve, a miniature Chrysler Building rolls back and forth on the ground.

8

OFFICER CANNELL'S precinct smells of urine and wet chalk. He holds Jillian by the elbow and walks her through the door. Their oddly formal coupling reminds Jillian of walking down the aisle with Lonny Sharpsman at Naomi Wecht's wedding. Lonny held her by the elbow and kept trying to cop a feel with his pinky as they walked. Jerry Cannell isn't trying anything of the sort, but Jillian still can't get Pachelbel's *Canon* out of her mind. Her immense pocketbook barely stays secure around the officer's broad, sloping shoulder. Jillian wonders if she'll ever laugh about this one day, if this too will get added to her album of amusing anecdotes.

"Do you have anyone you could call? Your father, perhaps."

"I don't have a father."

"A friend, then?" Jerry Cannell sits across from the table and pushes a phone toward her. Jillian wipes at the fingerprinting ink on her thumbs. She is exhausted and just wants to go home.

"I don't know."

Jillian has someone she could call for natural-looking, chunky highlights; she has someone she could call who would know all

the lyrics to *"Je T'aime . . . Moi Non Plus"* by heart; she has someone she could call who could get her into Balthazar at eight P.M.
on a Saturday night; but for this, she has no one. She stares va-
cantly at the officer's walkie-talkie.

"It's an FRS radio. It's basically just a fancy walkie-talkie." He
presses down on one of the buttons. "One-Adam-five, one-
Adam-five." He smiles at Jillian. "There's a buncha channels."
Officer Cannell pushes a few of the buttons.

"So if I knew what channel you were on . . ."

"And what subcode. There's a buncha subcodes too. And you
could unscramble the voice scrambler . . ." He looks at his own
toy proudly.

"I could hear the police?"

"Well, we switch channels and subcodes all the time so the bad
guys don't listen in." Officer Cannell winks. Jillian appreciates
the distinction he's implying. "But the bad guys use these things
too, y'know."

Officer Cannell puts the radio back in its holster. "I would rec-
ommend you find somebody to call, Miss Siegel. I can keep you
in holding for a while, but if you don't have your ID, we're gonna
have to check you in to housing until the judge is in and we can
clear you. And you don't want to go up to housing. Trust me on
this, Miss Siegel."

A flash of *Annie* goes through her mind—lots of little orphan
girls scrubbing the floors while Miss Hannigan splashes buckets
about.

"What does that mean?"

"It means you need your ID—license, passport, or government
card—here as soon as possible, or you get taken by paddy wagon
up to County." The officer pushes the phone closer.

She could call Alex. She's sure he'd be thrilled. "Sorry, honey, I
can't meet you at Lotus. I'm having sex with a gal named Big
Helen up in County, but maybe if you have a second, you could
pick up my ID from McKay's and pop on over and spring me
from the joint. Oh, and say hi to Bernie for me."

Or she could call Lois and tell her that instead of selling a screenplay in Hollywood like Linda Friedman's daughter, Lois's daughter's busted and maybe when she's back from Gstaad and done at the Liebermans' and after Pilates but before her manicure she could bake a cake with a really big file in it and come for a pleasant visit. She could add that mink is entirely appropriate when visiting an inmate.

She dials. It rings only once.

"Jill?" It's Alex on the other end of the line. His voice sounds sweet. She wants to call out to him, but she can't bring the words up from her throat. "Jilly?"

She quietly hangs up the phone with her index finger and dials another number.

One ring, two, three . . .

"Hello, Loevner residence." The voice is comforting and familiar.

"Hi. It's me."

"Honeydew?"

"Hey, Belle."

"What's a matter, honey?"

"I don't know, Belle. Nothing, I guess." Jillian picks off pieces of a sticker on the side of the phone. She wants to tell Belle. If there was anyone in the world she could tell, it would be her. But she can't. The words are just stuck down too deep.

"You sound funny, girl."

"It's nothing. I'm fine." Jillian cups her hand over the receiver trying to muffle the sounds of the precinct.

"I never believe your sugar, child."

Jillian's nail chips off against the sticky paper. "I'm just tired. I just need a good night's sleep."

"Mmm."

Jillian plucks off a piece of cuticle on her thumb. The long tendril of skin leaves a drop of blood in its wake. "How's he doing?" It feels as if she swallows a boulder every time she thinks of him.

"You saw him, child." Jillian holds back a wave of tears. "You know how he is. He never wanna be living a life like this. Things being outta his control just ain't his specialty."

"Down in Interview West," Officer Cannell speaks crisply into his radio.

"Where are you, honeydew?"

Jillian looks around at the cramped rust-colored room. "I'm in the subway station." She sniffles in the water dripping from her nose. "Union Square."

"The subway? You ain't taken the subway since we went downtown for Mr. Pelozzi's apple pies when you was just a girl."

"I like the subway."

"You hate the subway, child." Jillian feels itchy all over, as if she's breaking out in a rash.

"I'm another five minutes down here with the perp." The officer's voice echoes in the room.

"You in Union Square?"

"Uh-huh."

"Well, you find your way back home, honeydew. You find your way safe."

"I love you, Belle."

"God bless you, child."

Jillian hangs up the phone. She can hear her own breath as it folds in and out of her lungs. She could curl up in the Pink Room, but that place is a galaxy away.

"Did you call someone?"

"They weren't home. I just left a message." Officer Cannell knows this is not the truth, but it is a lie he will allow tonight.

"Well, we'll just set you up in holding and see what we can do. You think of anything or you need to make a call, go to the bathroom, just let us know." With an old-fashioned key he opens the metal door to the holding room. Inside there's a long stainless steel bench—a sleek piece of modern furniture under different circumstances, but in here it's just a place to sit and sleep. On the opposite wall is a thick Plexiglas window with a hole cut out at the bottom. Jillian's stomach goes flip-flop, as if she was being left on the first day of school. She curls up on the cold bench and pulls the sleeves of her fuzzy sweater down to her knuckles. She's cold, but they didn't let her keep her pashmina or even Nana's pinky ring. One never knows, she thinks, when a scarf and a rose gold cocktail ring could be used as dangerous weapons.

"I'll make sure they get a meal down to you right away. Good luck to you."

She shuts her eyes and tries to just push it all away.

"You can be such a troublemaker, Miss Calamity Jane." Has it been hours or minutes or days of sleep? Jillian can feel the big embrace of Bingo from behind her as if he was actually there and not a well-worn memory.

"Are you trying to win the drama queen award of the family?"

"You're the biggest queen in this family."

"That's true, as the world knows." Bingo continues smoothing down her hair until their breathing synchronized. "Of course, the world, if it were up to Mr. Allen and his splendid comb-over, wouldn't have any more queens in it, especially those running department stores, my dear. America, according to Mr. Allen, is no longer as fond of a good faggot as it once was." Jillian's forehead is damp and cool to the touch.

"You have a comb-over."

"A vice allemande, like myself, with a well-styled comb-over is urbane, darling. Mr. Allen's is merely splendid."

"Why don't you just tell Craig Allen to shove it?"

"Ah, honeydew, if only it were that simple." Bingo kisses the tip of her protruding nose. The chiffon curtain ripples against the window. The clock ticks quietly beside the bed. Bingo smooths out his niece's hair and looks out through the dark window. The central air-conditioning goes off, leaving an infinite quiet in its place.

"Bingo?"

"What, baby chick?"

"If you were going to commit suicide, how would you do it?"

"*That's a morbid question, honeydew. You don't need to be asking about that.*"

"*C'mon,*" she fights through a yawn, "*it's just a question. I'm grown up enough to just ask a question, Bing.*"

"*Well, I hear Jerzy Kosinski did it right. You know who Jerzy Kosinski is, darling?*"

"*I'm not a complete plebe. He wrote that Peter Sellers movie.*"

"Being There. *Oh sure. Fabulous.* Cockpit. *He was a magnificent jockey—a very small man. Five feet two or something like that. Tiny. Handsome man. Thick head of hair, but tiny.*"

"*Queer?*"

"*Oh, lord no . . . notorious Casanova.*"

Jillian hung on every word. "*So how'd Jerzy Sweater do it?*"

"*Well,*" Bingo flattens out both hands in front of him and opens his eyes wide, "*he poured a nice cognac for himself. Put on the sound track from* Out of Africa. *Gorgeous music. Perfect for this sort of thing. Got into the tub. Stuck a Baggie over his head and just . . . did it. Done. Finito. Au revoir, Jerzy. I hear it's the most civilized way to go.*"

"*Hmm, the Ziploc technique. Very interesting.*"

"*They say you just fall asleep peacefully.*" Bingo runs his hand up and down his neck.

"*Personally, I'd go for the pills.*"

"*But then they find you in a pool of your own vomit.*" Bingo makes light of it.

"*Well, whatever.*" Jillian does not mind the thought—Lois finding her in a pool of her own vomit. What could be more appropriate?

"*Honey, you gotta think about what you leave behind for people.*"

"*I'd be dead. Who would care?*"

"*You want people to see you at your most imprudent?*"

"*I think it would serve them right.*" The rumble and roar of the air-conditioning kicks back on.

"*Die young, leave a good-looking corpse.*" Bingo nods and takes another sip. The air-conditioning roars again and stumbles to a stop. "*Now get to sleep, honeydew. Belle will make you tea and toast in the morning.*" Bingo strokes her cheek. "*No one's getting in the tub with a*

Ziploc tonight." He circles a few strands of her tangled hair behind her ear. *"It's all chicken salad, my little girl. All chicken salad."*

"Night, Bing. I love you."

"I love you too, honey."

"You got a roommate in there, but she's no trouble."

Jillian forgets where she is for the moment until she hears the clink of the jail door being opened. *Has it been hours or minutes or days of sleep?*

"That's okay. I like the company," a girl's voice breaks in.

Jillian opens her eyes; they are sticky, and her neck is stiff. Her jeans feel crunchy.

"Did you get your meal?" Jillian looks up at an officer and another figure silhouetted in the doorway. She has to block the light with her hand. A girl smiles down on her. Jillian's hair is flattened against her forehead. She pulls the strands away and wipes them behind her ear.

"Pardon?"

"Did they give you any food yet?"

"What? No. No food." Jillian remembers where she is. It is not a comforting thought.

"I need two meals in Holding West." The female officer talks into her radio. Her uniform is tight, and her stomach protrudes out beyond her belt.

Jillian watches the girl sit down on the other side of the metal bench. "Hey." She offers a quick nod. "I'm Ashley Alvarez." The girl has difficulty pronouncing her own name but gives it a valiant try.

Ashley Alvarez? *It's a strange name*, Jillian thinks, *for a girl like this.* Clearly not Hispanic in any way, she's as white as they come—pale-skinned with a wide, turned-up nose and blonde hair with the faint remnants of blue Crazy Color in it. She seems happy to be here.

"How do you do?" she asks purposefully and politely.

"Fine, thanks." Unlike her guest, Jillian is not in the mood for company.

"We'll get you girls some food, a-sap."

"Is it turkey or baloney? I heard there'd be turkey or baloney." The new roommate is antsy and excited.

"I'm not sure. I believe it's baloney." The female officer wonders herself, as if she too could use a good sandwich.

"Shut up!" The girl is so excited now. She moves closer to Jillian and leans in like they're sharing the moment. "Turkey's good but baloney's my favorite." The girl smiles again—as if Jillian could care remotely.

Jillian clasps her knees tight against her chest. She stretches her sweater over her legs and looks at the girl from behind the fuzzy material. The girl's hair reminds Jillian of Alex's old Lacoste shirt, washed a thousand times. A pimple scabs over at the base of her chin and a spray of beige freckles coats her cheeks. Her eyes are clear blue, completely open and direct. She looks back from less than a foot away and smiles without blinking—seemingly waiting to offer or be offered something.

This girl is definitely not from New York.

Jillian works her legs back up to a fully seated position and pushes her body a few inches away from her roomie.

"Oh, shit. I can be such a dork sometimes. Sorry." The girl backs up a bit. "I need to 'acquire a more distinct sense of personal space.' " She works hard to enunciate the words. "That's what Poppy says. He's always saying I need to 'acquire a more distinct sense of personal space.' "

The girl is wearing a silk, floral-print dress two sizes too large. The fold marks are visible down the front of the skirt, as if it just came out of a package. On her feet, she wears an old pair of Keds with silver tape around the left toe. She looks like a poor man's Cameron Diaz—run through the rinse cycle a few hundred times, wearing her aunt's new dress, and without the high-priced team of makeup artists covering up the less-than-stellar skin issues.

Jillian watches as she takes a tiny embroidered pillow out of her dress pocket and plays with it absentmindedly. It's a curious thing—dyed crimson fabric on one side and burnt umber on the other with rows of gold beads sewn down the edge and plastic filaments poking off the top. The girl turns the odd thing in circles in her hands and stuffs it back in her pocket when she notices Jillian staring.

"Here you go, ladies." The officers hands over two brown paper bags.

The girl smiles politely at the officer and grabs her bag.

"Do you know when I'm getting out of here?" Jillian groans despondently from her place in the corner.

"There's only two ways outta here, hun: you either have someone bring down your ID so we can clear you, or you go up to housing by paddy wagon." The officer shuts the door and locks it. "So either way, I got no clue." The officer walks out of the rust-colored room and shuts the door behind her.

The blonde girl opens her bag, takes out the contents, and sets them on the bench neatly beside her: a sandwich on a bulky roll encased in plastic wrap, a pint carton of vitamin D milk, and an apple. It looks like a school lunch, or the cold snack on United Express.

The girl neatly spreads the bag out on her knees and removes the plastic from the sandwich. She takes a bite. "What's the deal with baloney, right? I mean, it always says *spices* on the label." She takes another bite of the sandwich and chews. "That's so weird, right? Like what kind of spices?" She continues chewing and pondering the meat product. "Like what kinda spices do you need in baloney?"

Jillian takes a bite of her own pale, mealy apple.

The two sit there chewing and thinking in silence.

Jillian peels away the plastic from the roll of white bread. Of course there's not a chance it could be French sourdough and *jamón ibérico* from Dean & DeLuca, with a little slice of melted Brie. She lifts up the top piece of the roll to reveal the reddish-beige fold of meat. She's so hungry her head is spinning, but the thought of the limp, fatty disc is repulsive.

"It's cool." The girl gulps down the milk. "It won't make you barf or anything. It's like Oscar Mayer or something. Name-brand baloney."

The meat specialist continues to eat her bag lunch. Jillian opens the milk and takes a sip of the mildly cool liquid. It's been a hundred years since she's had full-fat milk. It does not quench thirst, one could say it even *causes* thirst, but it does trickle down into Jillian's empty belly, coating it nicely with much-needed calories and milk fat.

The girl finishes her meal and places the plastic, empty milk carton, and apple core into the bag. She pushes down on the bag until it's flat and places it beside her. She exhales and slumps down an inch or two, staring at Jillian's sandwich.

Jillian looks at the girl's wide, pleading eyes. "You want it?"

"Me?" She looks hopeful.

"It's fine. Take it." Jillian wipes her chin with the back of her hand then smears it across her sweater. The soft filaments drag along with the wet liquid. The fine material no longer resembles the radiant object from her closet; it's more like a tabby cat left out in the rain. "I won't eat it. I don't eat food that isn't from an identifiable source." Jillian gestures for the girl to take the sandwich.

"I'm sure food from identifiable sources has to be better for you." She seems to agree without knowing what she's talking about. "You know, for your body and stuff." The girl stares at Jillian's sandwich as if she's talking to it. "Like Wendy's as opposed to the mystery meat stuff they sell on Fourteenth."

"Go ahead. It's fine. Really." Jillian hands the sandwich to the girl, hoping the chewing will give her some peace and quiet.

"Thanks." She hurries the sandwich into her mouth. The girl has pale, ruddy skin, and her nails are bitten to the core; even the cuticles are swollen and pink from abuse. "I'm in for petit larceny," she says happily. "Did you know it's actually not *petty* larceny? It's spelled *petit* like French. I always thought it was *petty*, like, you know, *petty—no big deal*, but it's not, it's *petit*, like French. My friend Gordo told me."

"Really?" Jillian's lack of any remote interest goes unnoticed.

"They tried to get me on burglary." She talks through Jillian's sandwich, disproving the theory that the chewing would stop the talking. "They always try to get you on burglary, 'cause it's a felony. They ask you, like, 'Did you bring that bag with you into the store? Do you have any cash on you?' They always try to get you on more shit, I mean, more stuff. I hate the bacon, man. Except that one who brought the sandwiches. She seems pretty cool." Her thumb flies toward her mouth, as if propelled by its own force. As quickly as she begins to gnaw on her cuticle, she forces the thing back down firmly into her lap.

"What about you? One of those white-collar crimes, right?"

"I was accused of shoplifting." Jillian tries to fluff her sweater back up and shake her hair into something presentable. "But I didn't do it."

"No shit? Me too!" The girl is excited now. Jillian regrets speaking at all. "But I did do it. I mean, I admit it, freely. I did it. I mean, what is there to hide, right?"

"Well, I didn't."

"Oh yeah, sure." She nods in agreement. "They make mistakes all the time." Her pity is annoying. "You got a record?"

"No! I don't have a record."

"I was just asking." She rolls her eye like a teenager. "Then why'd the cops bring you in? They usually just cite you out then you go on your merry way."

Jillian cannot believe she is having this conversation. "Because I left my fucking license at McKay's on Twelfth Street, okay? So I had no ID on me." Jillian rolls her eye at her own annoying story.

"That is so idiotic!" The girl tries to contain a laugh.

"I know." Jillian too, for the briefest moment, finds it funny. The girl smiles and Jillian face softens just a bit.

"You know what time it is?" The girl seems instantly anxious.

"I don't know. The middle of the night. The morning. Yesterday. Who the fuck knows."

The girl walks over to the Plexiglas and presses her face against it, trying to see the clock on the near wall. Jillian wonders what time it is too—without a view of the outside, it's impossible to tell.

"My friend Gordo's making bail for me."

"You're lucky to have such an understanding friend."

"Yeah." The girl's fingers go back up into her mouth. "Unless Claudia comes. But she's so busy, I can't imagine she would actually come herself." She rests her backside against the painted cement wall. Her pale printed dress contrasts the rust color nicely. She gnaws away at her cuticle and stares at the opposite wall.

Jillian looks out through the tiny holes in the door. She wonders how much new air circulates in the holding room.

"Ashley's not really my name," the girl confesses.

"Yeah?" She's curious but only in the smallest, tiniest possible way.

"It's Shelly."

Jillian counts the holes in the door. There are nine holes per line and ten rows of nine.

"Gordo got me this really gnarly ID. Some chick he knows makes 'em."

Only ninety air holes. That's not a lot of air for two people.

"So, hi." The girl, Shelly, pulls the cuticle away from her teeth and walks up to Jillian and shakes her hand again. "I'm Shelly."

"I'm Jillian. My name's really Jillian." Jillian shakes back.

"It's more, you know, professional to shake someone's hand rather than just waving, right? My friend Claudia's always trying to teach me that kinda stuff—stop me from being such a dufus. Claudia's really polite and stuff."

"Good manners are nice to know."

Shelly cracks her knuckles and paces the tiny room. "Is your boyfriend bringing down your ID?"

"My *boyfriend*? No."

"Oh yeah? That's cool." Shelly tries to glimpse the clock again. She reaches both hands into her dress and itches her breasts. "You know they'll stick you up in housing if you don't have no ID."

"I know. They told me." Jillian feels along the side of her jaw. A few pointy hairs emerge. She picks at one with her fingernails.

"You don't wanna go up to housing. They're like Satan worshippers up there. That's what Gordo says." She's pacing quickly now. "What do you call that? Satanists. Like, people who like being mean to you?"

Jillian assumes she means *sadists,* but you never know. "I'm trying not to think about it." Jillian scratches off the tiny scab next to a hair follicle on her chin. She blots off the drop of blood with her knuckle.

"They get all up in your face up there." She goes on as if telling a campfire story. "They look everywhere, like behind your ears, in your mouth, even in, you know, your *pirates.*" She points to her crotch for emphasis. "They look for any shit you could bring in. Hidden and stuff."

"What do you mean?"

"Like drugs, knives. That kinda stuff."

"What do you mean they look everywhere for it?"

"I mean they take a flashlight and look up your peehole and your butthole and that's exactly what I'm saying, exactly why you should try and get your boyfriend to come down and bring your ID!" Shelly is aggravated, worked up. Cuticles are being sacrificed for this conversation.

Shelly sits down on the far end of the bench. "I went up to housing once." She twirls the cuticle off in her teeth. "I burnt up my mom's basement, you know, by mistake." She bites at a piece of skin on her lower lip. "It was just my birthday, like the week before, so I was no longer a minor." Shelly smiles at Jillian. It's a sad, desperate sort of smile, where the edges of her mouth don't move too much. "Anyway, it seriously sucks up in housing, and they couldn't give a flying fuck about you or your private things." Shelly applies pressure to her chewed thumb. She too hugs her knees into her chest and rests her head there. "So that's why a person needs their ID before that kind of thing happens to them."

Jillian puts a finger in one of the tiny airholes and pulls. Her body slides across the metal bench toward the door and her finger gets cut on the metal. "Shit." Jillian sucks on her finger and puts her nose close to the holes and breathes. She doesn't want to think about housing and flashlights and the Satanists looking up your *pirates;* she just wants air, real live air, not the stagnant swamp that passes for breathing material in this tiny space. The oxygen is cooler on the outside. She sits down on the floor beside the door. "I'm just gonna try and figure it out myself. I'm sure something will come to me. It always does." Jillian takes little breaths of the cool exterior air.

"Hey, you know"—Shelly is excited now—"I could get your ID when my friend bails me out. I mean, I could get it and we could be friends. You know, outside the slammer."

"That's okay I'll think of something."

"Suit yourself." She seems offended.

"I think I'm just gonna figure it out myself." Jillian has no idea how she is going to figure it out, but the plan will definitely not feature the arsonist prominently.

"I mean, I'm not lookin' for you to pay me." A finger goes up to her teeth. "I got my own bank, y'know. Jeeze."

"I can take care of it myself."

Shelly slumps down lower on the bench. "Whatever." She makes a "W" sign with her thumb and forefingers then immediately begins chomping at them, yanking little bits of flesh away and staring at the bloodied grooves left behind. She dabs the injured skin against her dress then inspects her fingers again.

The room is quiet, except for the faint ticking of the clock, muted by bulletproof Plexiglas and metal.

"How did you burn down your mom's basement?" Jillian moves the hair off her face.

"It was completely retarded." Shelly responds quickly, as if she was thinking about it too. "I was trying to melt this plastic thread I was using, and it didn't turn out the way I thought it would. It was just stupid. So they kicked me out." Shelly smiles hopefully, like someone who just got knifed in the stomach but doesn't realize it yet.

"Where did you go?"

"First I went to my dad's place in Florida for a while, but that didn't work out because he has a new kid and they don't have enough bedrooms and everything. So then I went to my mom's friend's place in Ventura, but she got all weird on me. And then I went to this guy's house I know, but that kinda crap never works out. So, you know, then I came here. Times Square. *Total Request Live.*"

The room echoes with the sound of footsteps and clanking metal. The door is suddenly yanked away from Jillian's face.

"Ashley Alvarez." An officer looks over at the ruddy blonde girl. "Check-out time." The officer looks down at Jillian on the floor in front of the doorway. "You okay, missy?"

"Yeah. I was just breathing. It's hot in here."

"Hotter up in housing, I'll tell you what." The officer leads the girl out by the elbow.

Ashley/Shelly smooths the front of her dress and adjusts her hair. "I'm outta here." She smiles at Jillian.

Jillian smiles back. She is, for a moment, thankful to be rid of her prison roommate—the girl with a burnt basement and the bitten cuticles. But the sound of the door shutting and the tiny burst of cool wind it releases from the outside replace the thankfulness with an indescribable loneliness.

She curls into a ball, like a potato bug, she thinks, like the gray insects that crawl on the sidewalk and tighten into a protective knot anytime someone gets too close. She falls asleep on the floor hoping, like the bug, to unfurl and awaken, having rolled away to a new and safer place.

"Jillian, Jillian," a thousand tiny voices wake her, a million maybe. The Loevner's chandelier sparkles above her, illuminating the space around her with dazzling specks of light. She feels as if she's in a petri dish, the centriole of a gelatinous organism. Tiny fluffy sweater fila-ments move and sway over her skin, creep around her breasts, under her armpits, over her belly. "Jillian." They turn from burnt orange to Vanya slate-heather and back again in a perpetual autumnal cycle.

They sway like waves of grain, these stolen fibers. At the neck they reach up and caress her. "We love you, Jillian, we will keep you warm. We will never leave you."

"Your ID's here."

Jillian is startled awake. She has not, in fact, rolled away to someplace safer; she is still here, like Gregor Samsa, like the insect, metamorphic and cowering under the metal bench at the far end of the room. She rubs her eyes wondering if it's morning yet. Officer Jerry Cannell is standing at the doorway. Covered in dust from the floor, Jillian crawls out from under the bench.

"What?" She looks up at the officer's shape against the fluorescent light behind his head. "What?"

"Your friend left this at the front desk."

"My friend?"

She squints up at an envelope in the officer's hand. In fat, pink letters it reads: JILLIAN SEAGULL DRIVING LISENCE. "It's your license, right? Jillian Laurel Siegel. West Twelfth."

Jillian has never in her entire life met anyone who would spell her name like the bird. She has never known anyone who might write it out in a child's scrawl, misspelling the simplest of words. She has never met anyone who would do that—who would hike on up to McKay's, track down Melva, convince the gum-smacking salesgirl to part with said *lisence*, travel back down to the station, smile, and pull out her juiciest, pinkest pens and painstakingly write down each word. She had never met anyone who might do that. Not until last night. Not until Shelly. Ashley. Ashley Shelly.

"Yeah. That's me."

"No priors. You're clear."

"I can go home?"

"You're a free woman for the time being."

Jillian picks off some dirt from her hair. She is both spooked and thankful to have been saved by the arsonist.

"Stay outta my jail, Miss Siegel."

9

Message 1: Hi honey, it's your mother. *What? No, it's Jilly. I'm leaving a message.* That was Marshall. Marshall, say hello. That's Marshall saying hello. We're on our way to JFK. I wanted to call before we left. *What? That's not my Vuitton, Marshall. Use your noggin. Mine has the pink pom-pom. You know that, darling.* Anyway darling, talk to you later. I'll call from Roberto's.

Message 2: Hi honey, it's your mother. I just tried your cell phone again and I think it's broken. I called and then I heard a click and then I heard some noise like, shwsh, shwsh, shwsh, then it just went blank, completely blank. *What? It was a shwsh, Marshall.* Then when I called back no one answered. I just thought you should know. By the way, Marshall and I have decided to go do the Marrakech trip again next year. We'll simply have to stay at another hotel. You can't judge a whole country just by one hotel, right, darling? Isn't that fabulous? Bye, honey.

Message 3: Roberto is fixing a marvelous Negroni on the veranda. Anyway, it made me think about your job, darling. Call me at Roberto's. Bye, honey.

Message 4: Hi, hun. It's Carol from the office. I'm sorry to call you at home on the weekend, but I'm supposed to go over vacation pay and COBRA benefits on your date of termination, do an exit interview, and that other wonderful stuff. Of course nobody told me anything about it, so I just want you to know I'm around. Give me a call at the office. I'm here all weekend. Call me when you're feeling up to it.

Message 5: Why don't you ever put your cell phone on, Bubb? Don't forget about Lotus tonight. Wear something sexy. We're celebrating.

Message 6: I'm wondering if your phone is broken, honey. It's your mother.

Message 7: It's ten P.M. You didn't forget about tonight, did you? I'm in the cab. I can't wait to kiss you. Bye.

Message 8: I'm standing right outside your apartment. I didn't bring the key. I didn't think I'd need to bring the key. We can be late for this thing, no problem, but it doesn't look like you're there. I'm leaning in, fuck, ouch, fuck . . .

Message 9: Okay. I see no lights on. Are you at your mother's?

Message 10: Okay. No one's at your mother's; where the fuck are you?

Message 11: Darling, I really think your phone is broken. I heard that shwsh shwsh noise again. Marshall doesn't know what that noise was. *What? No, darling, she's not there. I'm leaving a message, what does it look like I'm doing? She's not at Bing's. She doesn't just go to Bing's anymore.* Anyway, darling, you can afford to pick up the phone and call me at Roberto's, darling.

Message 12: This is so typical, Jill. I'd actually prefer to be worried about you, which I would be, which I am, which I guess is completely stupid of me. Just meet me at Lotus if you decide to come home ever. Or don't. Whatever.

Message 13: I'm going to sleep now, darling. It's something like a billion hours ahead of New York time. But call as soon as possible. But in the morning, darling. And not too early.

Message 14: Did you just try to call me? The phone rang but then it cut off. Maybe I'm in a drop zone. Lotus. It's sort of near that store that you like—the one where you wanted to buy that really expensive shirt. You can't miss it. Tell them you're with Bernie. I've had two martinis already, which is incredibly stupid. I feel like an idiot, your boyfriend waiting for you at your own party, Jill.

Message 15: So I guess I can count on your not coming at this point? Great. Fabulous. The magnificent Jillian Siegel strikes again.

Message 16: So we're leaving. It's like three or three-thirty. I actually don't know what the fuck time it is. What time is it? Shit, I dropped the fucking phone. What?

Message 17: You know you can be such a bitch sometimes. And I can only say this, *Seventy-seventh and Park, please,* because, as you may have guessed, I've had way too many martinis, and then I had these blue marlins or martins or something. Anyway, you say you want to have this relationship and then it's like you're never there, you're never here, y'know. Self-absorbed, selfish Jillian Siegel. Selfish. Self-absorbed. And y'know, Jill, one of these days it's just not gonna just *be* here anymore. I'm not gonna be here. Y'know, I know it's hard, but could you work hard for something in your life just fucking once, Jill? Anyway, call me when you're done being wherever you are, whoever you are, and maybe I'll be home. Or don't. And I won't. Bye.

Message 18: And you think I don't know that something's been going on with you? You think you can just hide everything from me and pretend it's all perfect for everybody here? So you may think that I think it's all perfect with you, but I know it's not. So don't think that's what I think, Jill.

Message 19: Morning, darling, or afternoon, whatever it is there. That reminds me—maybe China is better in the spring than Marrakech, someplace with fabulous shopping. Hong Kong maybe. Remember that cute little doll we sent you from Hong Kong with the matching fan? Or maybe it was just Chinatown. Anyway, call your mother.

Message 20: I was calling to see if you ever came home. I guess not. Whatever.

Message 21: I was thinking about the Bomb, darling. Call me.

Message 22: It's Alex again. Just checking. This is just great. Just great.

Message 23: I was thinking how important it is, darling, for you to stay at the Bomb. It's your mother, Jill. At least until, Bing, you know, leaves us. I was thinking about how simply marvelous it would be for him if you won the old account. Marshall agrees. Think of someone other than yourself for once, sweetheart. Anyway, we'll be at the Ritz in Paris. Call me. Tell Michel at the front desk it's for me, darling. He'll put you right through.

10

JILLIAN SIEGEL showers for fifty-two minutes. She scrubs at her ankles, between her toes, behind her ears, down her crevices, she lathers under her armpits and shaves the dark layer of black that has accumulated; she massages her face with a bristly washcloth, working over every plane. She lets the scalding water fall and fall on her. She does this for fifty-two minutes, until she is clean, until every pore is expunged of its sin, until she is boiled back down to her unblemished nub.

That night Jillian does not return phone calls or watch videos or order Lemon Sauce Crispy Almond Chicken, Wok Wonton Soup, and Steamed Barbecue Pork Buns from Jennie Chen's; instead, she cleans her apartment.

She can change.

She can do this herself.

She throws out the murky water and soggy hydrangea from last month's farmer's market. She bundles the dirty clothes into a blue recycle bag and puts them to the left of the door—bound for

Frenchy's Laundromat on University. She tosses the dried-up bag of limes and washes the week-old wineglass. She turns over the top drawer in the kitchen and relieves it of its unidentified keys, empty matchboxes, scraps of paper, and dried-out pens—it is nearly empty when she is done, a packet of Kleenex, an unused notebook, and three sharp pencils rolling from back to front.

She matches socks and gloves and throws away the one-offs. She rids the closet of all unworn, too big, too small, too-*too* items and reduces the amount of opened shampoo samples on the ledge in the shower to her one favorite.

She clothes her body in nothing more than a sleeveless white undershirt and simple underwear and pulls her hair back into a taut, wet ponytail. She heats up water to a boil, pours it into a mug, tucks herself between the tight white sheets of her freshly made bed, takes one sip of the soothing, meaningless brew, and promptly goes to sleep.

"It's a long story, Lois, one that I really do not wish to elaborate on at the moment." Jillian gets the call over with—it has to happen sooner or later.

The Lois call is easier than the Alex call. She can invent something on the spot; she always does. But Alex will be more demanding. She'll wait until he's at work and leave him a message at home. He won't let her get away with that, she knows it, but it's all she can manage for the moment.

"My God, Jilly. Marshall and I thought you were dead in a ditch somewhere. Even Alex left a message at the apartment." Jillian can almost hear the eyebrow raise through the phone line. And right on cue, Lois continues, "You really have to treat that boy a little better, darling. He was beside himself, and very *schnockered*, I might add. I mean, my God, I barely understood a word he said. Do you think Alex has a problem with alcohol?"

"I'm not dead in a ditch somewhere, Lois. I'm alive and living on Twelfth Street. And no, Alex does not have a problem with alcohol."

"Okay, honey, it's up to you; it's your life. If you want to go on with your life letting everyone walk all over you, that's your choice." Lois crunches on an ice cube; the sound of it is amplified by the phone line.

Jillian admires her clean kitchen drawer. "I was on a sort of *retreat.*"

"A spa retreat?"

"Sort of like that."

"Well, honey, that sounds lovely. Meryl Berkman does the Golden Door twice a year. She builds incredible lean muscle mass every time, which wouldn't kill you, you know, Jilly. Plus she cleanses, which is wonderful to do. I'd cleanse except you're not suppose to with an irritable bowel. My bowel's been irritable since the whole India fiasco. Remember the India fiasco, darling?"

"Uh-huh."

"Jacqueline called from Madrid. She was so worried about Bingo and of course devastated that I couldn't get to Granada until next week."

"Uh-huh."

"She's going to wait until I get there to have the party. Isn't she a dear? The Alhambra is a fabulous place for a party, Jilly. If you ever have a chance to go to a party at the Alhambra, I highly suggest you jump on it. And Granada is lovely, if you don't actually stay in town."

"Uh-huh."

Jillian sorts through her mail: twelve pieces of junk, two bills, *New York* magazine, *Time Out,* and *Vanity Fair.*

"That's great, Mother." Jillian opens *Vanity Fair* to the cover story on Gwyneth Paltrow and the joys of motherhood, marriage, and all-around greatness in general. The caption reads, "Paltrow looks stylishly retro but hopelessly modern in Chloé's bohemian peasant blouse with flouncy sleeves and a delicate tie at the waist." She turns the magazine sideways to looks at the details. "Chloé Silk Peasant Blouse. $1,570." "*Just great.*"

"Well, honey, I'm sure you're off to work. But I just wanted to make sure you're alive before I go, since no one ever informs me about these things."

"I am alive, I am cleansed, and I am off."

"And check in on Bing while I'm gone."

"Uh-huh."

"Good-bye, my sweetie. Kiss kiss."

"Bye, Mother."

11

THE DOORBELL rings before she finishes drawing larger, hairier breasts on Gwyneth Paltrow on the cover of *Vanity Fair*. Jillian peers through the blinds. *Jesus.* It's the arsonist from the slammer, carrying a box of Krispy Kremes and an old plastic bag from Macy's. Shelly looks in the window and waves. "Hey, it's me. Shelly. From jail!" Shelly is smiling and knocking on the glass. "I brought doughnuts!"

Jillian runs to the front door before the girl yells to half the people on Twelfth Street. It's Monday morning, and thousands of people walk east or west past her apartment on their way to work. Jillian opens the front door just an inch.

"Remember me? From the jail cell!" Jillian pulls the girl into the foyer.

"Jesus, I know who you are," Jillian whispers. "What are you doing here?"

"I brought you your medicine." Shelly lifts the Macy's bag a few inches. "And doughnuts!" She opens the box to Jillian. "You wanna mack on one?"

"My medicine?"

"From that drugstore. You left it on the drugstore counter with your license. Gordo didn't want to leave it at the station, in case it was illegal or something." Shelly pulls the prescription bottle out of the giant plastic bag. She hands it to Jillian. The plastic bottle is entirely ensconced in a hand-knit cozy hanging from a long strand—like a necklace or a long purse.

Purple cashmere?

A purple cashmere prescription bottle cozy purse?

Jillian pulls the bottle out of its custom cashmere shell and inspects the brightly hued sleeve with beads dotting the bottom. She hasn't thought about her precious stash of pills since the other morning before Billy's. The bottle (and its contents) seems so banal compared to its fanciful little holster. "Did you make this?" She holds the material up to the light. The complicated array of knits and purls, beads and filaments are in complete disarray yet somehow perfectly harmonious. "It's really cool."

"And I knew your address 'cause of the license and all. Laurel's a cool middle name." Shelly disregards the question and holds the doughnut box up toward Jillian again. "Y'want?"

"I don't eat doughnuts." Jillian opens the childproof bottle and examines a pill. She decides to put it back rather than in its normal position, melting under her tongue. She puts the purple cozy on the counter next to her magazines.

"Oh, yeah, sure. That's right. You don't do food that isn't from an identifiable source and everything." Shelly looks at the box. "They're from D'Agostino's," she adds hopefully.

"I have to go to work." Jillian turns her back on the girl and walks toward her closet.

Shelly turns around, clutching her Krispy Kremes, and heads out the door. "Okay. That's cool." Shelly waves her gnawed fingers and walks out the door. "It's all good." She waves again. "See ya."

"Yeah. Okay."

Jillian closes the door behind her and looks out through the blinds. Shelly stands at the stoop and turns her head up and down the street for a minute. In the sunlight the girl looks different. Her eyes are clear, almost translucent; her skin is pale white with a sprinkle of beige freckles; and her hair, the part of her natural hair color that shows through, has fine gold filaments running through that sparkle in the sun. Shelly rings the bell again.

"I'm gonna seriously piss my pants." Shelly points at her abdomen and shifts from foot to foot.

Jillian opens the window a crack. "They have a bathroom at Tito's Burritos across the street."

"Oh. Okay." Disappointed, Shelly turns to walk down the front stairs, folds up the Macy's bag, and stuffs it in her pocket. She looks in each direction, curls her bluish blonde hair behind her ears, and heads down the street, directly in the opposite direction of Tito's.

"Wait." Jillian opens the door and yells after her. "You're going the wrong way. Just come on in and use my bathroom for a second. I don't have to go to work for another couple minutes."

Shelly turns around and nearly skips up the stairs. "Thanks. I *totally* have to pee." She walks straight into Jillian's apartment and vectors her way to the bathroom. She doesn't close the door. Instead she raises her voice over the sound of the flow. "Like where're you supposed to go when you're just walking around? Girls can't just whip it out, right?"

Jillian can hear Shelly's stream stop and start until it finally peters out. Shelly flushes and walks back into the living room pulling up her underwear and itching her behind. "You're gonna wear that to work?" Shelly looks down at Jillian's boxer shorts and undershirt.

"What are you, my mother?" Jillian takes the hot water off the stove and pours some into a mug.

"No, dude, you wear what you want." Shelly pulls out a doughnut. "I just thought you'd wear something that doesn't show your entire crotch to everyone."

Jillian looks down at the open fly in her boxer shorts. Embarrassed, she pulls the fly shut.

While Jillian is still wearing what she slept in, Shelly looks like she's ready to host a public access show for the well-dressed homeless. Her blue-blonde hair is sticking up everywhere, and she's wearing her old Keds and another oversized but oddly delicate dress.

"Hey, what's that Ativan stuff? Is that for an infection or something?" Shelly chews on another doughnut. "Or is that, like, too bogus to ask?"

Jillian just stares at Shelly in amazement.

"Sor-r-ry." Shelly looks closely at the photograph of Jillian on the wall—the Cigarette Picture taken by Alex at RISD. "Nice photo. Who took it?"

"Ativan is a benzodiazepine." Jillian changes the subject quickly. "It's for anxiety. It takes the edge off."

"The edge off what?" Shelly chews her second doughnut.

"I don't know, Shelly." *This girl is hopeless.* "The edge off . . . anxiety. I guess." Jillian takes a big slurp of the hot water and looks at the clock. Work has already started. She pictures everyone at Bomb gathered in the Loevner's war room discussing this and that—doing the things she should be doing.

"I like anxiety and stuff. It keeps me alert." Shelly plops down onto Jillian's couch and takes another bite of her sugary treat.

"Anxiety keeps you alert?"

Shelly's face flushes red. "I don't know. Anxiety? Bipolar? Manic something? One of those brain-mosh things keeps me alert."

"Like getting arrested and landing in jail?"

"You know what? Don't get all salty with me." Shelly fits her words out through the bite of doughnut. "High on your fucking horse. Miss I-didn't-do-it." Shelly chews. "You were in jail too, you know."

Much to Jillian's surprise, the arsonist wins a debate point. "Yeah, but that's different."

"What's so different about it?"

"I'm not a criminal. I'm an executive with a regular job, a great job, in fact, clothes that *fit*, a great boyfriend, and a normal life. I didn't belong in there." Jillian realizes what she's said as soon as she's said it. "I'm sorry, Shelly. I meant neither of us belonged in there. That place sucked." To her surprise again, Jillian is sorry—sorry that venomous words just seem to pour out of her mouth uncontrollably.

Shelly looks down at her dress and furrows her eyebrows. She shoves the remainder of the Krispy Kreme into her mouth and adjusts her skirt. The two sit there in silence. Jillian hovers over her steaming cup, feeling badly but not knowing how to fix it.

"Just because you have a regular apartment and fancy clothes and a regular job and your bottle of benzo-azepines doesn't mean you're all Miss Perfect." Shelly bites down hard on her cuticles.

"You shouldn't bite your nails. You could permanently stunt their growth."

Shelly pulls her fingers from her mouth, shoves them into her pocket, and cracks her knuckles against her thigh. "You sound like Poppy."

Jillian massages her temples. This conversation is giving her a headache. Why does she always want company but want to be left alone at the same time?

She fights the urge to hide under her bed and instead lifts her elbow up and smells her armpit. She can't remember if she put deodorant on—she doesn't sense a trace of the light citrus scent of Dr. Hauschka's Fresh Roll-on. Without a job to go to, the morning's lost its routine, and now she smells.

This is what it is to be rejected from the organism. This is what happens to *rejects;* they push everyone and everything away from them and then they sit around by themselves stewing in their juices; they let their eyebrows grow out and miss their Brazilian waxing appointments. First comes the isolation, then their entire being begins to rot from the eyebrows on down to their chipped pedicures, until one day (not too long from the day they stop wearing lipstick and deodorant) they can be found shouting obscenities on University and walking through the Village in their nightgown.

"I need to get a manicure," Jillian says with a guttural grunt. She smells her armpit again and stares into space. "If I don't get a manicure, I think I might die."

Shelly tries to follow Jillian's logic. "Okay . . ."

"And I think I need company." Jillian turns and looks at Shelly. It's the first time she's ever acknowledged a thing that has possibly been true for decades. "You wanna come?"

The wad of doughnut balances in Shelly's mouth. Flakes of fried doughnut spit out. "Like when someone else paints your nails?" Shelly brushes crumbs off her lap. "Shut up!"

Jillian slips off the counter and puts the mug in the sink. "Mondays are perfect days for manis." She's on a mani mission now, and nothing can stop her. "No waiting." Jillian runs into her closet and grabs a pair of Joe's wide-leg cords. "You could get a French manicure. Something, you know, nice."

Shelly extends her fingers to look at them—nothing but swollen pink stumps on the end of short, pale phalanges. "A French manicure! I'm so stoked."

"*I'm* so stoked." Jillian pulls the cords over her boxers and offers the girl a smile. She is thankful for the companionship, however bizarre it might be. A mani will kill an hour. An hour will be almost lunchtime. Lunchtime will be . . . time for lunch, and then with a fresh set of nails, the afternoon will fly by. She grabs her purse and her keys.

"What about work? Don't you need to get to work?"

"They won't miss me for just this morning."

12

"YOU gotta pick a color." Jillian and Shelly sit next to each other in the long row of seats at Kim Lee's Nail Salon.

"What color is French?" One by one Shelly picks up dozens of nail polishes, looking at the bottom of each bottle. The Korean ladies get their tools ready: bowls of soapy water, sanitized nail clippers, and filing stones. Both ladies are wearing blue hospital masks covering their mouths and noses.

"French is sort of almond or off-white."

"Raisin in the Sun. What color would you call that?" Shelly picks up a dark bottle and looks at the name.

"Definitely not French."

Shelly runs the wet brush along her short, stumpy fingernails. "What about In the Pink?" She strokes on another stripe of the color.

"That looks pretty good. That's sort of French." Jillian lifts up a bottle of red. "Little Red Corvette." She brushes a nail with the bright red hue. "What do you think?"

Shelly is mesmerized.

"Great, right?" Jillian admires the classic color and hands the bottle to the Korean lady.

"I wanna do that too. Little Red Corvette."

Both girls place their hands on the white towels in front of them. The Koreans lay their tools out in front of them, lift up their customers' hands, and begin to file.

Both girls relax as their nails are prodded, poked, and clipped. Jillian can feel the stress melt away even in the overly lit and gaudy environment. Both girls both stare into space as their hands and wrists are massaged with cheap, perfumed lotion, the strong Korean thumbs kneading every inch of muscle and tendon. Even this tackiest of environments cannot diminish the pure sense of gratification and escape.

"Seven dollar each." Shelly's manicurist's words are muffled behind her blue mask.

"We gotta pay before they polish." Jillian reaches in her purse for cash.

"It's on me." Shelly hands the manicurist two twenty-dollar bills. "For me and her." She articulates her words. "Thanks. Keep the change."

"You don't need to do that, Shelly. I've got money."

"I know you have money." Shelly doesn't look at her. "I got money too, you know."

"Thanks." Jillian can't remember the last time anyone besides Alex ever treated her to something. Even something cheap—like a manicure. "That's a big tip, y'know."

"How much are you supposed to tip?"

"Like, a couple bucks, maybe three?"

"So what?" Shelly looks like she's doing some quick addition in her head. "I'm a good tipper. Poppy says that's important. That way people remember you when you need them."

"What does your dad do exactly?"

"My dad? Poppy?" Shelly starts laughing hysterically. "Poppy's not my dad. My dad's just a guy." She wipes her eyes. "Poppy's like a president or something. He's Claudia and Gordo's boss.

He's in Japan this week. Or China." She inspects her nails, now smooth and moisturized. "Poppy and them kinda help me out when I need it." Shelly looks suddenly nervous, like she's said something she shouldn't have. Finally, both girls' nails are polished, and they stand, each with a fresh, shiny coat of Little Red Corvette. Shelly's—wide and stumpy, Jillian's—narrow and oval.

The Korean ladies pick up the girls' purses and move them over to the plump leather couch. Shelly and Jillian sit down, careful to hold their hands in front of the small fans and away from their bodies. "That looks good." Jillian admires her color. "Old school."

Shelly is blowing on her fingernails and shaking them in the air. "Yeah. Totally." Shelly holds a finger up close to her eyes until they go crossed. "Are you Jewish?" She delivers the question nonchalantly, looking at her fingertip, as if it's the least important question of the day but the one she couldn't wait to ask.

"Yeah. Why?"

"I just don't know a lot of Jewish people." Shelly points her fingers to Jillian and models the color. "I know mostly just regular people."

Jillian puts her own nails in front of the tiny fan. "I thought we were regular people." Jillian's joke goes over the radar.

"Your folks wear those big black coats?"

"No. That's a different kinda Jewish. We're more the shopping and eating Jews—if you get to go shop or eat for a holiday, we'll celebrate it."

"So you got to celebrate Christmas?" Shelly seems excited at the thought. She rolls her fingers back and forth in the light.

"Naw, we didn't celebrate Christmas." Jillian lightly touches the tip of her index finger to feel for tackiness.

"That blows."

"We used to have Hanukkah, though." Shelly nods. "You get a decent amount of stuff on Hanukkah," Jillian says without a lot of enthusiasm. The truth is Jillian got an indecent amount of stuff on Hanukkah. It was the time of year when Lois left a billion *fab-*

ulous presents from a billion *fabulous* places in front of the fire-place. Jillian, Bingo, Alain, and Belle opened the boxes and bags from Lois: rugs from Tibet, fan dancers from Madrid, posters from the Picasso Museum. And then there were the thousands of things from Alain and Bingo from Loevner's. Every silvery-wrapped item handpicked and put together by the seasonal girls in Loevner's professional wrapping service. The tower of boxes reached nearly to the top of the Hanukkah tree.

Bingo and Alain would sit back and consume caviar and "buckets of Grande Dame" as Jillian unfurled Matisse prints from Lois and modeled her new outfits from Loevner's. Then they'd settle down to a traditional Hanukkah dinner of steak tartare (which Alain swore was the same recipe used at the Georges V Hotel), Bingo's French fries (which took all day for him to make and caused a mess in the kitchen that Belle swore about for weeks), Belle's famous 7UP Chicken, and candy apples from Violet's for dessert.

Then Jillian had a whole second celebration on Christmas Day at Belle's house in Queens, with Belle, her husband, their children, and grandchildren racing around the living room. There the whole opening-presents thing happened again, with Bingo and Loevner's supplying the entire family with more lovely gifts.

"Yeah, we had Christmas too. At least we did after Randall and his little kid moved in with my mom. People like doing Christmas with little kids, right?" Shelly's eyes chase around the room and she has a tight, frozen smile on her face. "One Christmas, when I was thirteen, my dad sent me a watch he got in Florida." Her eyes light up when she tells the story. "A Timex Cavatina gold-tone dress watch with real pink crystals. It had its own case with a velvet cushion on the bottom. None a that bogus shit." She smiles. "I think he just sent me a card or something the next year. But the watch year was pretty cool."

Steeped in their own stories, they both just nod and leave it at that. Shelly blows on her nails and waves them in the air again.

"I did it, you know." Jillian stretches out her fingers and counts them. "I mean, I took that thing that they said I took. That little Chrysler Building."

"I know." Shelly leafs through *Vogue* with a flat middle finger.

"I mean, I didn't really want it. It was completely stupid."

"I know." She turns the page. "Holy shit, look at that necklace. David Yurman, dude." Shelly holds the page up to Jillian. "Poppy says David Yurman is totally e-class and really rich ladies wear David Yurman."

"David Yurman is totally nouveau riche, Shelly."

"Nouveau riche rocks."

Jillian signals Shelly to turn the page. "Did you hear what I just said?"

"Yeah. David Yurman is totally nouveau riche and you stole the little Chrysler Building. You're telling me because you know I couldn't give a shit. You wanna friggin' medal?" Shelly points her finger out to Jillian. "Dry?" Jillian smooths her finger over the small bit of red.

"Yeah. Dry." Jillian runs her own fingernails along her cheek. She pauses for a sniff of the fresh lacquer.

The two girls sink back into the cushy couch. They hold their nails out, all twenty of them, and wiggle them around as if they're playing a duet on an invisible piano.

Shelly picks up a candy bowl from the table. "I do it like this when I, you know, do it." She slips it beneath her jacket. "A sleight-of-hand thing, I guess you'd call it. Me and my friend use to steal stuff down at the tourist stores in Chula Vista. It was our *technique*." Shelly pulls the candy bowl out from her jacket and puts it back on the table. "We called it *cutting*, you know—our code word for what we did. We had a pretty good gig going." Shelly unwraps a peppermint and pops it into her mouth. "How do you do it? *Cut* stuff?"

"I don't want to talk about it." Jillian shakes her freshly painted nails in the air.

"C'mon, dude. I told you about my code word."

"Oh, big revelation. Let's go to the store and *cut* some seashell necklaces. Like no one would ever figure that one out." Jillian feels as if she's twelve talking to Shelly—forging a friendship in the school yard with childish banter and one-upsmanship.

"No one has yet, man." Full of herself, Shelly pulls the peppermint out of her mouth and licks it.

Jillian sprays some Qwik Dry onto her fingernails. "Here. They'll dry faster." Jillian sprays Shelly's fingernails as well. "I've got a mantra."

"Say what?"

"A mantra. A thing you recite for good luck." Jillian pulls her body into an upright posture and closes her eyes. "*It is mine.*" She says in a mystifying voice like a gypsy. "It's my mantra. When I, y'know, *cut* stuff." It actually feels good just to talk about it. Like it's not so terrible or depraved—like it's normal.

"It is yours?"

"*It is mine.* Like everything laid out before me is mine. Like I already own the place. *It is mine,*" Jillian emotes.

"No shit?" Shelly's eyes are wide.

"I didn't do my mantra that day. You know the day we met. It's like a thing that I do. A ritual." The confessions simply spill out of Jillian's mouth, and she doesn't do anything to stop them. "So I got caught. I think because of my not doing the mantra."

"Is it like a spell or something?" Shelly waves her hands around like an East Village clairvoyant.

"You can't just do it without a reason." Jillian pulls Shelly's hands down to her lap. "You can only do it under real circumstances."

"Can I do the mantra?" Shelly wipes a bluish tendril of hair off her forehead.

"I don't know." Jillian looks at the girl's wild, hopeful eyes. There's something pitiful but sweet in them. "But, Shelly, it's not like it's foolproof. It's more metaphorical." She is sure Shelly does not know the word. "C'mon. We're dry." Jillian helps Shelly up off the deep couch.

Shelly sprays another coat of Quik Dry onto her nails. "Let's motivate."

The air outside is crisp. It is a quintessential New York fall day—cool but sunny, the smell of winter not yet hovering in the air. Shelly holds her fingers out and admires them under the sunlight. "The Little Red Corvette looks awesome, right?"

"It does." It is a perfect New York day, and Jillian is sincere about the bright red polish being a good choice. She's been sincere all day, and the feeling is refreshing.

"Good." Shelly pulls out the nail polish bottle from her other pocket and dangles it in front of Jillian. "For touch-ups."

"Jesus, Shelly. You know you can buy that stuff. They'll sell you a bottle of nail polish for, like, a couple bucks."

"I know." Shelly jumps around with the bottle, flying the thing in the air like a children's airplane. "Around the same price as the Chrysler Building, right?"

"Jesus, Shelly."

"Shit. What time is it?"

"I think it's like around noon."

"I can't even head back to my place until later. My roommate's there, and I owe her rent." Shelly bites at her thumb. Her entire head shakes when she does this. Jillian is reminded of Bingo, but she flicks the thought from her head before it has the time to land. "Fuck." Shelly looks up and down the street. "C'mon, can't you just show me the mantra thing? Your work won't mind if you're gone a little while longer—right? It'll be like a lunch break or something."

"Yeah. Okay." Jillian has never told anybody about the mantra, much less shown it to someone in action. The feeling is crazy and exciting. Besides, she has nothing to do the whole day either. "It's gotta be something small, though."

"Just cut a couple little things." Shelly is hopping around now. "I'll be your *pawtna*. It'll be cool."

13

JEFFREY is in the meatpacking district—an area that just a few years back was home to only Florent, Hogs & Heifers, and transvestite hookers. Now, with Jeffrey, Stella McCartney, Soho House, Gansevoort, and an array of clubs, galleries, restaurants, and shops, the meatpacking district, despite the lingering scent of meat and the occasional tranny or two, is really one of the biggest draws in all of Manhattan.

They walk toward Jeffrey's facade. Jillian wraps her wool coat tightly around her—she gets chilly when she gets nervous, even on a beautiful autumn day like this one. "Jeffrey is the perfect place. They never put security tags on really expensive clothes." Jillian drags Shelly by the elbow toward the front door.

"It's big league." Shelly sniffs the fresh nail polish on her thumb and shifts her weight from one leg to another.

Jillian's heart is pumping. "You wanted to see the mantra in action, right?"

"Definitely, dude." There is a large man at the front door with an earpiece on. "That's the security guard," Shelly whispers, and cracks her knuckles.

Jillian eyes up the six-foot suit at the front door. His main job in a place like this is to smile to the ladies and hold the doors open for them. As long as she's smart about it, she'll be okay. Shelly, however, may be another story.

Shelly is picking pieces of skin off the corners of her thumb. "When do we do the mantra?"

Jillian looks toward the sky. She calls upon the magic that has always been at her fingertips. "First you gotta put everything else out of your mind." She feels like a witch or a yogi or a super-hero—powerful and extraordinary. "It's all about focus and really feeling it."

Shelly is bouncing on her feet, itching her shoulders, and biting at her knuckles. At this moment she seems more mongoose than human. Jillian considers how bad of an idea this really might be.

She grabs Shelly's fists out of her mouth. "Look, Shelly, I'll go in there with you, but if you get caught there is no way I even know you, okay?" Shelly's leg springs up and down shaking her whole body. "Stop that." Jillian braces her. "Take a breath. I'll do my mantra, and you can do it with me. You can be totally relaxed and confident after you do it. You'll completely have your act to-gether." Jillian reassures her like she usually reassures herself. She feels a sense of responsibility for the girl—getting her in, getting her out, without anybody getting caught.

Shelly eyes are wild. "I have to concentrate. Gordo's always telling me that. I have to concentrate on the thing I'm doing." Shelly peels off a corner of her fresh nail polish. "Shit. Oops. Shit."

Shelly's eyes dart up the street. Jillian wonders how many times Shelly's been arrested exactly. "So we'll just stand here and be quiet for a second." Jillian closes her eyes and shuts out the sounds of the street. "Repeat after me." Jillian takes a breath and looks right at Shelly. "And you've got to really believe it or else it doesn't work. Breathe."

"Shit." Shelly is still bouncing.

"It is mine." Jillian grabs Shelly's cold, hard fist and steadies it in her own. *"It is mine. It is mine."* Jillian whispers the words and looks out at the horizon, feeling them, as she has for many years, seep in and become real.

"It is mine." Shelly repeats the mantra and, like Jillian, makes the wish with all her heart.

"Now we'll go in separately and leave separately. That's the way you should always do it." Jillian has never done this with another person, but she knows that two people are more noticeable; they talk and chat, gesticulate and take up space. One person, however, glides through like a sylph, all-powerful yet nearly invisible. She watches as the security guard holds the door open for a well-dressed lady. "You look out for me. I look out for you. Deal?"

"Deal."

The game is beginning, and it is exciting.

Jillian goes first—striding confidently past the guard, disregarding his presence completely. Shelly follows behind, trying her best to look smooth.

While Jillian normally favors cramped, understaffed stores for this type of thing, on a Monday at noon, Jeffrey is just the opposite: bright, vast, devoid of the weekend tourists, and populated mainly by sales staff, lean bald mannequins, and colorful lights that hang from the ceiling and dot the space with pleasing shapes. The music, which, on a weekend, blares at club volume, is nonexistent—as if the whole store is recuperating from too many weekend lemon drops. She's has not been to a real store like this in days, and she finds it unspeakably comforting. In this world she is herself—all things are possible as she floats into the ample entryway and toward the lavishly filled racks. She inhales the perfume. Jeffrey smells like fresh-milled wood and chilled white tulips, a little bit like Loevner's old Men's Department.

"The fragrance of the dream. Any store should have it," Bingo used to tell Jillian when she was young. "Every store should be its own world—delighting all of the senses and inspiring the soul to imagine the possibilities."

She has never bought anything at Jeffrey—the "bank," so to speak, is empty, so anything she takes today is on pure credit. But to Jillian, it is a teaching assignment—a gift to Shelly—generous in its own way. Plus she'll make it a point to buy something expensive in the future—shoes maybe, something unstealable.

Unlike her student, Jillian looks as if she belongs here and was indeed honed in places just like this. Every inch of her body built for exclusivity: the long tennis club legs, the private school slouch, the downtown haircut, the narrow wrists and ballet neck, even the ample Loevner nose with all its implications. She belongs here at Jeffrey or anywhere in the same league. Saleswomen nod and mouth hellos, even the few other customers assume she belongs there. She was taught this department store dance long, long ago—on grand floors, under magnificent chandeliers, by well-perfumed teachers.

Shelly is another story. She's attractive enough, with her *shiksa* nose and sturdy frame, but her ill-fitting dress and decade-old Keds just do not scream Jeffrey material. A saleswoman walks past and gives Shelly the once-over.

Jillian touches Shelly's arm lightly and begins a simple conversation with her. It is her first lesson, and she figures that some of her own appropriateness might wear off on the girl, allowing Shelly's existence to make more sense. "The show was fabulous last night, don't you think, *Ashley*?" Jillian gracefully walks forward, lightly touching Shelly on the elbow.

"What?" Shelly's knuckle goes up to her mouth.

"The show?" Jillian gently guides Shelly's hand from her mouth, walking forward, careful to make only slow, poised movements. "Wasn't it great?" Jillian pulls out a shirt from the rack and lifts it to show Shelly. "This is gorgeous," she says to her. "Isn't it?"

"Right. Yes. Awesome." Shelly smiles and looks at the shirt. She breathes and breathes and smiles. "Right. Nice."

Jillian lifts up a dark blue Zac Posen pinstriped suit and eyes it, bottom to top, careful to look like a person who could buy this suit if she was so inclined. She knows exactly the look—wanting without needing, liking without requiring, eyeballing the details wherever they reside: a double-stitched lapel, an asymmetrical zipper, a dart at the waist. Jillian shakes her head no and looks at Shelly. "Terrible color. Too bad, really."

"Yes. That certainly sucks." Shelly has quieted down. The buzzing around her fades a bit. If you look at Shelly in this quieter moment, Jillian thinks, you can see the vague resemblance of someone appropriate at Jeffrey. She could, if you squint your eyes, seem like someone so well off, so wildly wealthy, that she has actually developed no sense of style or taste. These people exist and Jillian has seen them: walking through the Jewelry Department, meandering through Better Suits, even in Vendome Gowns on Loevner's uppermost floor—homespun people in cheap shoes who leave with a dozen fancy garment bags or a six-carat diamond-and-sapphire brooch.

"Never disregard the Farm Brigade," Bingo used to call to Vanya as he left the Perfume Department. "Even the discombobulated might have a legendary appetite for the sublime." Bingo would wave his hankie in the air as he held his niece by the hand. "You never know, Van."

"Why don't you take a look at some of the things over there." Jillian pushes Shelly gently away. It is time for them to split off and do their chores. "That way you can see if there's anything you *want*." Jillian talks in code, moves in code, smiles in code. "I might see if there's anything I *want* too."

Jillian is enchanted by the environment. Now she does want something, anything to gather up and bring home.

"Oh sure. Oh, yeah. Okay."

"And breathe."

"Oh yeah. Breathe. Yeah." Shelly breaks away from Jillian and glides to another part of the store. Jillian moves to the next rack like a dancer; she is edgy and stimulated but remembers her role.

"That's a beautiful suit. We just got the season in." A smartly appointed brunette saleswoman walks by and hangs up a sweater.

She too is familiar with the dance, appearing interested, but not too.

"Lovely." Jillian smiles without too much excitement and moves on. The store is not filled with customers. It is nearly empty up front. A dark-haired woman with a Pomeranian on her arm unfolds sweaters and puts them back on the shelf in whirled-up balls, and Shelly is on the other side of the room, holding gowns up to her chin and looking like an oddball.

Jillian surveys the room out of the corner of her eye. The smaller objects, the ones that would fit in the dark spaces of her handbag, are gathered in the center of the room closer to the check-out counter. Perched on Lucite shelves that hang from the ceiling like an art installation, gloves, handbags, shimmery chiffon scarves, furry hats, and collar pieces for winter are neatly displayed with their price tags carefully concealed.

Jillian squints to the far end of the room at Shelly. Shelly looks no stranger than the woman with the dog—no more or less deserving. *It is yours,* she shoots silently over toward Shelly.

"How are you today?" A dark-haired saleswoman in black plants, a short-sleeved cashmere sweater, with a white work shirt underneath, refolds a scarf on the see-through ledge. Her shoulder-length hair is neither an inch shorter nor an inch longer than it should be.

"I'm fine, how are you?" Jillian gives her a little extra, a tiny rise in the voice. "How have you been?" she adds for emphasis.

"Oh, fine. Great to see you. How have you been?" She too modulates deliberately.

"Selma? Right?" She thinks of this name because of the actress Selma Blair who favors this clean, downtown preppy look.

"No." She looks confused for a moment. "Sonia."

"Oh my God. Sonia. That's right! I'm so sorry." Jillian puts a feather-light hand on the salesgirl's shoulder. Sonia appreciates the gesture. "You look like the Selma who used to work here."

"Gorgeous coat. Whose is it?"

"I don't know. Can you believe that?" Jillian turns around and bends toward Sonia. It's an opportunity for intimate bonding.

Sonia thrusts a cool, tiny hand into the spot behind Jillian's neckline. "Ryan Roberts! He does fabulous little coats!"

"Roberts. That's right." Jillian puts a light grip on Sonia's forearm.

"It's wonderful." And Sonia places her fingertips on Jillian's sleeve, returning the gesture. "And, I'm so sorry, I've forgotten your name."

"Christie," Jillian says. "Christie Maguire."

"Right. Christie." Sonia nods enthusiastically. "How *are* you?" Sonia really wants to know. Really. Jillian then remembers that Christie is a Christ derivative and Maguire is as *goyisha* as it gets, not so believable with, as Bingo used to say, "a palatial protuberance" like hers, but the alias is already in play.

"Great. Everything looks so great today. Some new stuff, right?" Jillian looks directly at Sonia, but surveys the room in her periphery. The woman with the Pomeranian walks around talking on her cell phone, and Shelly is relatively calm in the Gucci section.

"Did you see Spring? We just got it in."

Spring means something different in a store like Jeffrey than it does in the rest of the world; it is the name of an *event*, a collection of *things*—not a season. And while spring is months and months away, in Jeffrey and stores like it, May flowers are just around the corner. This is why Jillian loves these places—the regular rules do not apply.

"I did! Spring looks fabulous! Great detail! Wonderful pieces!" Jillian chooses her words wisely.

"You've got to see the wools. They're *amazing.*" Sonia makes it all sound so edible. Jillian opens her eyes wide; the gesture invites more dialogue. "Let me show you." She follows Sonia to the front, grabbing an embroidered scarf as they turn. She crumples the material quickly into her hand and pushes it into her coat sleeve with one finger.

"Isn't it fabulous?" Sonia holds the suit up to her own chest, letting the thing drape out in front of her. She smooths over the material with the other hand, "The line is spectacular." Sonia doesn't even notice the missing rectangle of material.

Jillian touches the weave. The scarf, now a tiny ball of fabric, resides compactly under the forearm. A hundred dollars, maybe even more. Jillian can't remember the color of the thing, but she is sure it is lovely. "Graham would love that." Introducing the concept of a man-behind-the-woman, Jillian thinks, adds an additional element of believability.

"Well, it's gorgeous on. I'm sure Graham would love it." And indeed, Sonia is buying and expanding on the Graham concept.

"What about that new dress in the back?" Jillian complicates the moves, improvising choreography to take the two tangoing across the floor.

"The silk georgette?" Sonia lights up at the thought. "It's spectacular. Fabulous on." The two women swoop to the back, Sonia leading the way. Jillian deftly removes a pair of leather gloves off the shelf as she goes, folding them and slipping into her pocket.

Nothing has price sensors. She looks briefly at the front doors, double-checking that they are free of any sensor devices too. She looks above. No cameras, no black balls on the ceiling. Nothing. Only the big man at the front door. The feeling is blissful, hopeful, magical, sweet.

"Look at this color!" Sonia caresses the Balenciaga from underneath. So sheer, her hand is visible through it.

"Gorgeous." The dress drops and floats to the ground with the tiniest push. She can see the price tag: $4,800.

"Oops. Lemme just get that." Sonia hangs it back up and balances the precarious straps. Jillian wants to keep moving.

"Way too sheer though. Graham hates me in sheer." Jillian turns away from the dress to the front of the room. She knows it could be hers and the idea is too frightening. "What about shirts? I need shirts."

"We have a really fabulous tuxedo shirt with a wide collar. Very cute. It's a day-to-evening look. Let me show you." Jillian sits down in the ample chair by the dressing room, the air bursts out from the cushion as she settles in. "Can I get you a water? Tea? Espresso?"

"Thanks, a water would be great."

Jillian sits and drinks an Evian in Jeffrey's dark leather chairs. Sonia shows her four Jill Sander blouses, three Branquinho cocktail dresses, a hundred-and-eighty-dollar T-shirt, three pocketbooks, and a pair of eight-hundred-thirty-five-dollar Rene Caovilla silver Swarovski-crystal-pavé high-heeled sandals that would be just "stunning" with the Branquinho. Sonia even massages a little of Chantecaille's Le Jasmin body cream onto Jillian's hand.

For Jillian, it is like sitting in the sun.

The buzzing of the cell phone is undeniable. Sonia's dance politely stops while Jillian attends to it.

"Hi, it's me." Jillian says pleasantly, cupping the phone to her ear.

"Hello, darling. Paris is simply gorgeous this time of year but the Gypsies have gotten out of control. Thick as locusts, darling. It's dreadful."

"Fabulous. That's simply fabulous." Jillian smiles and gesticulates.

Lois seems perplexed. "It's your mother, darling."

"I know!" Jillian puts as much effervescence into these two words as possible.

"I was just calling to remind you to see your uncle this week."

"Okeydokey!" Jillian makes a funny face at Sonia who returns it with a wink.

"Are you going to Shabbat-at-Bingo's, darling?"

"Not sure." Jillian pretends to laugh and laugh.

"Are you okay, darling?"

"Fabulous. And you?"

"I'm fine, darling. Are you at work?" Lois is crunching on something.

"Yes indeedy."

Shelly walks by and smiles at Jillian. She gives the slightest nod to the front door and walks toward it.

"Gotta run. But lovely of you to call."

She watches as Shelly gets closer to the front; her heart pounds into a tight squeeze.

"All right, my darling. Just a little reminder to see Bing."

The security guard smiles and opens the door.

"Okay. See ya later." Jillian stares into the guard's eyes. *It is hers, it is hers, it is hers.* Shelly smiles and she exits to the left.

Jillian exhales.

"Oh my God. Is it two-thirty? *Oy.*" Jillian folds the phone shut and tries to backtrack the *"oy"* but can't. It will just have to sit there for now.

"Would you like to try anything on?" Sonia asks, holding up a number of outfits. The saleswoman can barely disguise her moment of hope.

"I'm so sorry, Sonia. Graham is going to kill me. I said I'd meet him for lunch an hour ago." Jillian gets up from the chair, careful to keep her hidden goods tight to her arm.

"That's okay. I can hold them for you," Sonia says optimistically.

"Sure. I can come back tomorrow with Graham at lunchtime."

"Oh great." Sonia gathers up a few of the things into her arms. "I'll put them under your name, in case I'm not here. Do we have you on file?"

"Yes, I'm sure you do." Jillian is certain they do not. "I'll be back tomorrow. Around the same time."

"Great. I'll be here."

"Good-bye, darling. It was great to see you again." Jillian reaches out for an air-kiss. After twenty-seven garments, the intimate gesture is appropriate.

"Good-bye, my dear." Sonia kisses back. "Tell your gorgeous husband I said hello."

Jillian smiles at the security guard and walks out the front door.

14

SHELLY is running down the street. "I am so stoked, dude!"

Jillian is scrambling down Washington to catch up to her partner. "Stop! C'mon, Shelly." Jillian is doubled over in front of Hogs & Heifers.

Shelly does a handful of jumping jacks and then bounces on the ground. "This is so slammin'!"

"Was I right, or what? Isn't it like you feel like it's your store? Like all the stuff in it is yours—whatever you want?" The invigoration is nearly unbearable.

Shelly's head is pointed downward between her legs. "I think I'm going be sick."

"Me too!" Jillian laughs. The smell of old beer lingers outside the bar.

"What d'you get?"

Jillian pulls out the gray-green scarf and looks at the price tag. "Two hundred and twenty dollars!" Shelly's mouth drops open. "Do you know how much shit I could be in right now?"

Shelly catches her breath and marvels at the tag. "Nothing *petit* about that." Shelly runs her fingers underneath the see-through fabric. "That's the coolest color I've ever seen in my life! Shit."

"What d'you get?"

"I got this!" Shelly pulls out a small wooden sign from her pocket. It reads: NEW FOR SPRING.

"The signage? You took the signage? You took the *signage* from Jeffrey? What are you gonna do with that?"

"Shut up!" Shelly looks at the placard and puts it back in her pocket. "I got all nervous and shit." Her hand flies up into her mouth, and she starts to bite away. "I'll find something to do with it."

"Oh my God." Jillian can't stop laughing. "This is so crazy. I've never done this with another person. It sorta ups the ante." Jillian looks up to catch her bearings. "We need to celebrate." Jillian looks over at the old honky-tonk bar beside them. The smell of dried-up beer and cigarette butts buzzes around them.

"This place is open." Shelly starts walking toward the bar

"I was thinking something with a little more ambience." Jillian takes Shelly by the arm and walks down Thirteenth.

Jillian catches her breath as they enter the foyer of the Hotel Gansevoort.

The Gansevoort's answer to Tokyo-fabulous, Garden of Ono is straight ahead. It's a Robatayaki and sushi bar with well-placed rocks, a centerpiece light fixture that looks like trickling water, beautiful people, and ambitiously priced food. Just the sight of it makes Jillian giddy; it's just what she was hoping for—low-calorie urban indulgence. The feng shui-ed entryway is lorded over by a tall Asian hostess with a taut smile.

"Two for tea!" Jillian bounces up to the mahogany hostess station.

The woman surveys the crowded room. "It's going to be a few moments." She gives Shelly a subtle once-over.

"How 'bout tea for two. Is that quicker?" Jillian starts to laugh.

Her laughter gives way to short, horsey snorts. The hostess offers a tiny smile.

"You retard. What is that?" Shelly pushes Jillian's shoulder away.

Jillian is doubled up, snorting and laughing uncontrollably. She tries, to no avail, to hide her face with her hands. It is the first time in years Jillian has laughed to the point of snorting. "Shut up." Jillian wipes tears from her eyes. "Shut up." She can't even remember what was so funny.

"That is the rudest thing I've ever heard." Even Shelly is embarrassed.

"I know." Jillian calms herself. "When I laugh really hard, I do this snorty thing. It's completely mortifying."

"Ah, yeah."

"I think I need my uvula removed or something." Jillian clears her throat and composes herself. Jillian pulls out the soft doeskin gloves from her purse and yanks off the price tag with her teeth. "You can have my gloves."

"You got the scarf *and* gloves!" Shelly is thoroughly impressed.

"Yeah. Pretty much. I got them while I was talking to the salesgirl. It's pretty easy when you keep them distracted. You want them?"

"But they're yours."

"They'll be nice with your manicure."

Shelly gingerly strokes her face with them. "I can't believe I own gloves like this!" Shelly rubs one of the gloves on Jillian's cheek. "Soft, right?"

The two girls stand at the hostess station cooing and trading feels of the exquisite material.

"Jilly?" A tiny, well-dressed woman walks up to the girls and puts a hand on Jillian's shoulder.

"What?" Jillian looks behind her and notices the undersized woman. "Oh. Linda!"

"Jilly! Hi, darling." Linda Friedman smiles and looks Shelly up and down. "I startled you." Linda is carrying an orange and black Louis Vuitton shopping bag, another from Stella McCartney, one from Comme des Garçons, and another from Destination. At less than five feet tall in heels with a helmet of silvery white hair, Linda Friedman looks like a small, well-coiffed bichon frise.

"No, Linda. Hi. We were just looking at my friend's new gloves." Jillian's face turns hot and red.

"Suki and I were just at Phillips de Pury for the auction. Suki won the most fabulous Bresson." Linda waves her hands around, her bags crunching and moving along with them.

A few feet behind Linda is her daughter, Suki Friedman, Jillian's ex-best friend—blow job, and now apparently screenwriting, queen. Never growing an inch taller than she was in seventh grade, Suki is also only five feet tall in heels. Both mother and daughter are wearing matching red lipstick and carrying the same array of shopping bags.

And, Jillian notices, peeking out from Suki's dark mink coat is the Chloé silk peasant blouse—the one from *Vanity Fair*.

"Jilly." Suki reaches in for an air-kiss.

"Suki." Jillian crouches down to her fashionably diminutive schoolmate and returns the touchless gesture.

"It's so great to see you." Suki says.

"You too." Jillian adds.

"I'm back from L.A. for a visit. The shopping in L.A. is totally lame."

The Spence girls volley hellos, each saying nothing more or nothing less than the usual obligatory blither.

"And you're so thin." Suki smiles. It is the compulsory remark, the thing every old friend is expected to say whether true or not.

"And you're so thin."

Shelly stands off to the side, smiling back and forth like she's watching a tennis match.

"So what are you doing with yourself, Jilly?" Suki flips back her glossy, chemically straightened hair.

"Well, you know. I was just buying some gloves, these gloves, with my friend"—Jillian grabs Shelly by the arm and pulls her toward them—"my friend, Shelly."

"Pleased to meet you, dear." Linda holds out a limp hand to Shelly. "I'm friendly with Jillian's mother, Lois, who is just as gorgeous as this little girl." Linda pinches Jillian's face into a fish shape.

Suki offers Shelly an identically lifeless handshake. "I meant with your life, Jill. What are you doing with your life?"

"Oh. You know. Advertising. Selling sugar water to the poor pathetic masses. Rape and pillage. The usual." Jillian doesn't want to give Suki much.

"Well, Suki sold a screenplay in Hollywood," Linda chimes in, finding the first appropriate moment to squeeze in the latest news.

"A screenplay? Great." Jillian tries to create a smile by opening her mouth and lifting her cheeks in an upward motion.

"Wow! Like a movie!" Shelly lights up at the thought. "Who's in it?"

"Oh, God, mother—please." Suki swats the thought away. "It's no big deal."

"No big deal, darling!" Linda leans in to the girls. "ICM sold it for in the high six figures." Linda raises her eyebrows.

"*Oy*, Linda." Suki's been calling her mother by her first name since she was eleven.

"High six figures and you're still wearing a *schmatta*." Linda yanks on the blouse and winks at Shelly.

"It's a Chloé, Linda. It's *supposed* to look like this."

"It's still a *schmatta*." Linda turns her attention away from the Chloé. "Did your mother tell you we were going to Prague in the spring?"

"She said Bangladesh or something."

"Bangladesh!" Linda raises her eyebrows at Shelly. "Who goes to Bangladesh anymore? Right, Shelly, darling?"

"Hardly anybody." Shelly smiles back. "Nowadays."

"Fabulous shopping in Prague, Jilly, honey. Jilly's uncle discovered Prague before *anybody*, Shelly dear. He was so fabulous. *Is* so fabulous, darling. God, I miss the old place. There's simply nowhere a girl can go for true style anymore. When Alain Crawford left us and Bing went into his little *funk*, nothing was ever the same! Nothing, darling." Linda is waving her free hand in the air. "But we can only go on mourning for so long. Right, honey?" Linda smiles at Jillian, waiting for some sort of response.

"It will just be another moment," the Asian hostess announces to the girls.

"Did Jilly tell you she was once a famous model?" Suki raises her eyebrows to Shelly. "And we knew her when."

"Jesus, Suki." Jillian shakes her head in disbelief.

"No she didn't tell me." Shelly glares wide-eyed at Jillian.

"Oh my God, Jilly!" Suki brings her index finger to her lips and laughs. "Is it all still so hush-hush, even after all these years? Who even cares now, anyway?"

"Wow. I'm best friends with a supermodel."

"It was not like that." Jillian is suddenly mortified.

"Oh, darling," Linda joins in. "Don't sell yourself short. You were practically on Carson, darling." Linda winks and changes the subject. "Those are gorgeous gloves, honey." She reaches out to touch them. "I saw these at Jeffrey! I love Jeffrey. Jeffrey is the new Barneys, darling." Jillian watches Linda's eyes closely, but Linda Friedman is always a hard read. "Do you girls shop there often?"

"Um. Once in a while." Shelly is cool and collected. "They gotta lotta good crap."

"They do. They do." Linda smiles at her daughter. "They do have a *lotta good crap*, darling. Don't they, Suki?"

"They do." Suki agrees.

"Next time you go to Jeffrey, you tell Sonia that Linda Friedman says hello. She's my girl over there. We're heading there now as a matter of fact. Would you like to join us?"

"Oh. Wow. Great. No. We can't." Jillian's palms grow wet. She tries to quickly compute the potential implications. "Yeah. We were there a while ago. A few days ago, really."

"*Years* ago," Shelly adds.

"We were just looking at the gloves now, though. Today. Now." *Shut up, Jilly.* "Yeah."

"The new-for-Spring suits are *ug-ly*." Shelly smiles and bats her eyelashes at Linda and Suki Friendman.

"Really?" Linda seems confused.

"Yeah. Absolutely gross."

"Really? That's odd for Jeffrey." Suki is confused now too.

"Yep. Disgusting. Too bad, really." Shelly smiles confidently.

"I can seat you now." The hostess pulls out two menus and walks toward the tables.

"It was nice—"

"It was nice. . . ." Jillian and Suki's words overlap.

"It was nice to see you."

"You too."

"You look great!"

"You too!"

"You should call me!"

"That'd be great."

"Yeah." Both girls sigh as the good-byes dwindle into nothingness.

"Well, it was a pleasure to meet you, Shelly darling." Linda reaches in for a kiss on Jillian's cheek. "And tell your gorgeous mamma I said hello when she gets back, darling."

"I was pleased to meet your acquaintance." Shelly enunciates the formal sentence and gives Linda and Suki's hands a good stiff shake.

"You too, dear." Linda makes her way out the door, holding her shopping bags in the crook of her elbow.

"Bye, Jill." Suki wiggles her fingers once again.

"Do you know who that was?" Jillian contains a snort as they sit down.

"I don't know. The queen of friggin' England?" Shelly lifts the giant bamboo menu in front of her and tries to make sense of it.

"My mother's best friend, Linda Friedman, and her daughter, Suki. Suki and I used to be friends a really, *really* long time ago. I can't believe I ran into Suki and Linda Friedman in the meat-packing district of all places. They had to be totally suspicious."

Shelly holds the menu an inch from her face.

"On their way to Jeffrey of all places," Jillian continues.

Shelly looks around the restaurant. She looks back at the menu and squints. "Eight ninety-five for a tea infusion? What the fuck is that?" She looks back at the pool in the center of the space. "Are you supposed to go swimming in there?"

Jillian disregards the question and looks back toward where Linda and Suki disappeared. "Do you think they know?"

"Know if you're supposed to go swimming in there?"

"Know about our *cutting* at Jeffrey."

"Quit being so bent. Why would they know? And who cares anyway?" Shelly squints at the menu. "What's *Robatayaki?*"

"If Linda Friedman knows the entire world knows. My mother, Marshall, my uncle, the entire Jewish population of the Upper East Side. And of course, Suki Friedman has the biggest mouth on the planet, so if Suki Friedman knows then everyone on earth is covered."

"So what?"

"What do you mean, so what?"

"So what if you're not Miss Perfect."

"Not perfect? I have," Jillian reduces her voice to a whisper, "a two-hundred-twenty-dollar scarf from Jeffrey stuffed in my purse."

The waitress comes over. "What can I get for you, ladies?"

"I'm gonna have this eight-dollar-and-ninety-five-cent green tea thing and this other thing I can't pronounce." Shelly points at her menu and smiles up at the waitress.

"The *Ono iwashi* appetizer?" The waitress offers a lesson in pronunciation.

"You got that right." Shelly shuts her menu loudly and hands it to the waitress.

"Okay. And what would you like?" The waitress holds on to her polite face.

"I'm also going to have the eight-dollar-and-ninety-five-cent green tea infusion and the *Ono-Sumi-Yaki-Kushi-Ya*. Whatever the hell that is." Jillian smiles and shuts her menu loudly too.

"Thanks, ladies." The waitress rolls her eye, takes the menus, and walks away.

Shelly eyes up the fancy room. "That's so cool you were on Carson Daly."

"It wasn't Carson Daly, Shelly. It was a really long time ago. Let's just drop it."

"Were you on TV?"

"It wasn't like that. It was something I did once for my uncle. It's nothing you would've seen." Jillian pulls out the gossamer scarf from her sleeve and folds it neatly in her palm. The fabric tickles her skin, and just the touch of it makes her feel safe and happy.

"Lemme see." Shelly pulls the scarf toward her. "Shit, that's a sweet color. Like the ocean or something. Did you see all the beadwork? Little beads like that are really hairy to sew on. It would be great for one of my Threadbags."

"For your what?"

"My Threadbags. They're sort of like this crap I make at my apartment. Janky shit." Shelly pours out a mound of sugar onto the table and pokes her finger into the center of it.

"Like prescription bottle cozies?"

"Yeah. Like that." Shelly holds up the scarf to the light and doubles over the translucent material.

"Shelly," Jillian leans into her new friend, "I gotta tell you something. It's serious."

"Okay." Shelly puts on a serious face.

"I don't have a job." A knot instantly forms in Jillian's stomach as the words come out. "I mean, I lost my job. I got fired." She bites at the inside of her cheek. "My boss is an asshole. He fired me."

"That's so cool!" Shelly slaps her hands on the table loudly. People at neighboring tables look their way. "That's the best news," Shelly whispers.

"What's so great about it?"

"We can hang, you know, be *peeps*. We can get manicures and cut stuff, y'know"—Shelly softens—"like real best friends." Shelly sprinkles some sugar from the table into her mouth.

"I can't really afford to get in trouble again."

"We won't get in trouble. We'll just do little shit. Like haircuts and junk like that. I was thinking of dyeing my mop. What d'you think?" She pulls at her faded locks.

"You can't *cut* a dye job, Shelly. You need to pay for that kinda thing."

"Yeah, but we could *cut* some cash. For hair jobs and those mani things." Shelly is thoroughly excited. "I know how to bank up."

"Like bank robbers or something?" Jillian is surprised that the thought actually crosses her mind and sounds imaginable at the moment.

"Nothing like that. Me and my friend use to do it back in Chula Vista. It's kind of like cutting but a little different." Shelly bites down on the corner of her pinky nail. "It'll be our beautification fund."

"Like for lipstick and Brazilian waxes?"

"Beauty junk."

"Beauty Cash!" Jillian blurts it out. The words sound good. All two of them.

Shelly nods. "Right on."

"We could go tomorrow if you wanna meet me at Macy's Department Store. Formulate a plan."

"How about today? We could just walk up to Macy's after tea." Jillian doesn't mention that she actually needs more of it today; that the feeling is flowing freely in her veins since Jeffrey, and she needs more of it before the day is over.

"I can't. I gotta go meet Claudia and Gordo at Vira's office. I got a lot a shit I need to do before Vira gets back." Shelly draws her finger around the pile of sugar, making a circle in the center of it.

"Who's Vira?"

"Vira's Poppy. His real name's Vira, but I call him Poppy because I think he's more like a Poppy than a Vira. I'm the only one who gets to call him that," she boasts.

The waitress brings over two steaming porcelain pots and places a tiny white cup in front of each girl. Shelly pinches up sugar between her fingers and drops it in the cup. She stirs the granules around with a spoon until they melt, then lets drops of sugar tea fall from the spoon onto her tongue.

"Vira? That's a weird name for a guy."

"It's short for something. I can't ever pronounce the whole thing. Viracourt, Virachoke, I don't know, some fancy-ass name. People just call him Vira, except me."

"What does Poppy—Vira—do exactly?"

"Oh . . ." Shelly's eyes dart around the room again. "Business stuff." Shelly sips her tea. "He's pretty much the only guy who's ever really watched out for me." She smiles. "You know, like a real dad."

Jillian smiles back.

"He's not making any moves on me, if that's what you're thinking." Shelly gets suddenly defensive.

"I wasn't thinking anything." Jillian doesn't feel much like probing anymore. Maybe it's better if she doesn't know much more about Vira than that.

"So tomorrow? Below the big Macy's clock? For Beauty Cash?" Shelly pushes open the heavy doors of Hotel Gansevoort.

"Below the clock. For Beauty Cash!" She truly can't wait. Shelly. Macy's. Beauty Cash. It feels like an adventure in a strange new land.

The rush of cool air hits Jillian's face. She peeks out as if Suki

Friedman might still be standing there, waiting for her with her Bresson print, six-figure screenplay, and Chloé blouse, but she's not.

"The store opens at ten. An hour will give it a chance to fill up. You should always wait until a store like that is filled up. It confuses them." Shelly is sucking on a lemon candy from the hostess station. "And don't be late. It's completely uncool to be late for an appointment. That's what Claudia says."

"Okay, Shelly. I won't be late for the appointment." Jillian laughs. "Eleven. At Macy's. Below the big clock." Jillian fastens the bone button on her coat. "Hey, Shelly?" Jillian pulls open the drawstring on her pocketbook. The gray-green scarf blooms out like a flower.

"Yeah?"

"You want the scarf too? You know, for your Threadbags. I'm not really a scarf person."

"The one from Jeffrey?"

"I don't really think I would wear it, I'm sure you could find something to do with it."

"Shut up! Are you kidding me?" Shelly gently holds the poof of material in her hands. "You want my sign?" Shelly pulls out the wooden placard and shrugs her shoulders. "I got another one from Loehmann's just like it."

"Yeah, sure. That's great." Jillian tucks the sign under her elbow. "Thanks." In a way, it's the nicest gift she's ever gotten.

Shelly puts on her new gloves and walks up the street toward the subway station. She swoops the scarf around her neck and lets the diaphanous ends fall behind her back. "I'm so Poppins right now!" Shelly yells as she walks backward toward the stairs. "Perfect in every way."

"Me too, Shell." Jillian holds up the sign and waves as Shelly descends into the station.

15

"CHRIST, Jill. What am I supposed to think?" Alex is pacing in front of Jillian's bathroom door, the keys to her apartment still in his hand. His body appears then disappears from in front of the door as he walks back and forth the entire length of the apartment. "You're gone for the whole weekend, I mean, the night, the day, no one knows where you are, not even your mother . . ." His worn suede coat and old, paint-stained Carhartts are a stark contrast to her white underwear and bare, lanky body.

She remembers Alex wearing these pants when she first met him standing behind her in line at Carr House on the RISD campus. It was almost a decade before their actual relationship started—before sex was swirled in the mix and a real future could even be contemplated. It was near the end of the school year, and he looked a little familiar—just another one of the many Brown students, going through an artsy phase, who took to hanging around Benefit Street and the classes the college had to offer. She was having a chai latte with soy milk before DeCredico's design class, and he was drinking a coffee with milk before heading back up the hill.

She remembers he was writing a note to himself with a ball-point pen on the knee of his pants above a splotch of white paint. "My phone number," he remarked, when she leaned over to take a look at what was so important it had to be written on a pair of pants. "I always forget it."

He didn't look like just another one of the frivolous Brown imports—he was intense and authentic even then. She could see it in his eyes when he read his paper and sipped from his cup. She noticed then, as she does now, all the seductive details about him: the thin wire of his glasses, framing his eyes, capturing the pools of blue within them; the crease, more a fold than a dimple beside his smile; the lanky legs and graceful ankles; the fair hair on his skin, surrounding him like a halo. And he had her number even then on that first day, as he wrinkled his nose at the soy milk in her chai and joked that she was a dairy snob.

She liked that he was not intimidated by her as most people were; that he saw through her aloof behavior and chain-smoking to the girl who could eat an entire sundae at Big Alice's or tap dance in the glass elevator at the Biltmore. She liked that he shared Diet Coke with her at the movies (even though he hated diet), that he never wore aftershave, and that he'd occasionally leave his beloved old Hasselblad at her apartment for a few days.

She remembers the friendship that grew between them in the darkroom as they were printing the notorious Cigarette Picture of Jillian. They hadn't even slept together yet and wouldn't, not for ten more years, but the photo captured how he saw her then and perhaps now. Like the swirling smoke, she was captivating but elusive.

They both saw it in the image. They both saw who she was—lovely and breakable. She saw it as she plunged the paper into the sweet-smelling chemicals and watched the grays and blacks emerge. He saw it as he hung them up, one after another, on the line in the RISD darkroom. The intimacy of the picture was electric. They kissed that night, in the dark, under the hanging photographs. Just once they kissed. Before the year ended and, like the smoke, whispered away as quickly as it emerged.

* * *

"I wasn't anywhere, Alex, okay? Can we leave it at that, please?"
She tries to stay one step ahead of him. "Plus Lois never knows
where I am. You should know that. I *screen*." Jillian sits on the toilet brushing her teeth. She has a sinking feeling in her stomach,
like she wants to tell him everything, like she wants to pack a
backpack with two T-shirts, a toothbrush, and a pair of girl's
Carhartts and run off to Mongolia or Vietnam or Darjeeling or
wherever he's off to next, like she wants to pour herself into him
and never leave, but instead she just sits and brushes and conjures
up excuses and defenses and watches him get smaller and smaller
in her periphery.

"Were you *screening* me?"

"I wasn't *screening* you. You know I don't *screen* you."

"How do I know that, Jill? How do I know anything about
you?" Alex is nearly out of breath. "Did you call me? Someone
called me and hung up."

"Why would I call you and hang up? That is completely
ridiculous." Jillian avoids his eyes. She thinks he should notice
her avoiding his eyes. *A good boyfriend would notice when his girlfriend is blatantly lying.* He should be all over this sort of thing.

"I don't know, Jill. You tell me. Why would someone call and
just hang up?" Alex has stopped pacing. He just stands there with
his palms faced outward toward her. His face is red, like he's
about to burst into tears.

"I don't, Alex. Why would someone call and just hang up?"
She spits the foamy glob into the bathtub and washes out her
toothbrush. It is his fault, she is sure. If he loved her, he should
be all over this. He should just shake it all out of her.

Alex's hard shoes march across the parquet floor. Jillian looks
in the mirror and inspects her pores. Maybe, she thinks, she can
just escape into these shallow crevices—float away with the
sebum and follicle and back to a place where Alex would just be
fine and everything would just be normal and she could just have

a regular life and a regular boyfriend who isn't about to say something hard and terrible. "And what is this?" his voice bellows from the kitchen. "Pears? From a regular store! And a bag of red beans? You never eat beans."

"Adzuki." Jillian yells back. "Organic."

The refrigerator door opens. "Sweet white miso, Jill?" She plucks errant hairs from underneath her brows, concentrating on each one like a meditation. Alex marches back to the doorway and holds up a green cellophane bag. "Komba? Are you fucking a vegetarian?"

"Kom*bu*." Jillian stands close to the bathroom mirror and plucks a hair from her chin, right in front of Alex. "I liked the package." She glides a thin black hair out from its socket under her chin. "And no, Alex, I'm not fucking a vegetarian. There was no food in this whole fucking place so I went to the store and bought some stuff. I thought it would be good for me to start eating cleaner—you know, only eat food from an identifiable source." She has the words rehearsed. She will not stray from her performance. She is who she is, and he can take it or leave it.

"So you bought clean food?" Alex's voice is so high now, it nearly squeaks. "Can't you see yourself, Jill? You always do this— buy *something*, get *something* that's supposed to fix you. Like somehow cleaner food is going to make you . . . cleaner."

"Yeah, Alex. News bulletin." *Keep on top of this, Jillian.* "Clean food makes people cleaner. Why is that so hard for you to understand?" She folds her arms underneath her breasts, grabbing at the layer of skin that covers her ribs and leaning on one hip. She turns toward the mirror so Alex doesn't see her eyes darting about. He is pacing again; his face is hot red.

"Jesus." He marches into the bathroom, opens his zipper, points his penis into the toilet, and begins to pee. She compresses the small mound of flesh on her chin to the mirror and plucks at it with tweezers. "What are you doing?"

"I'm plucking my chin hairs." The words squeeze out from the side of her mouth as she pulls.

"Your chin hairs?" Alex leans in to look, his urine stream moving beyond the bowl.

Jillian points down at Alex's penis. "Watch the pee." She pinches at her skin to slide another wiry hair out. "Yes, I have chin hairs, Alex." She points her tweezers toward his face. "Girls have chin hairs." She holds up another bit of chin skin and pokes at it with the pointy tweezers. "We girls don't tell our boyfriends and our husbands about our chin hairs. We pluck in private. It's the great secret we girls keep for one another."

"Okay. Girls have chin hairs and you're a girl and you have chin hairs. Great." Alex zips his penis back into his pants. "You can be such a *schmuck*, Jill." Alex flushes and begins to pace again. He runs a hand through his hair. "Do you think I give a shit about your chin hairs?"

"Yes, as a matter of fact, I think you do." Jillian sits on the corner of the sink. "I think you want me to be perfect."

"*You* want you to be perfect. I just want you to be honest." The annoying word slices through the entire apartment then just sits there like a lump.

Alex is so wrong for her. So wrong.

"Look," Jillian drops her hands in front of her for emphasis and sincerity, "I'm completely sorry about Saturday night. You don't even know how sorry I am." It sounds like someone else is speaking from her mouth; she feels distant from her own words.

"Tell me, Jill. Tell me how sorry you are." Alex backs up and sits on the couch, then stands up again, striding back toward the bathroom. "No wait. Let me tell you how sorry *I* am." Jillian stands there, her chin hairs still hanging from the tweezers. "Jill." Alex walks over to her, puts a hand on each shoulder, and steadies himself. "This bites. It's like I have this imaginary girlfriend in my head who confides in me, needs me, trusts me, but what I really have is this . . . big empty room. Where are you, Jillian? You left me in this big empty room. Now I'm just standing here all alone wondering how the fuck I got in this place." Jillian's arms are nearly numb from his grasp. "I went out to celebrate the woman I love and adore. Where was she?" He slaps his hands down on his legs. "I don't know. She doesn't know. And like usual, she doesn't want to talk about it. Well you know what, woman I love and adore, I'm sick of it." Alex releases his grasp and leans against the bookshelf.

He leans there with the Cigarette Picture hanging next to him—like they're the true couple: Alex, the man, and Jillian, the irrelevant old photograph.

Jillian wants to cry, but she is not sure if that compulsion is purely manipulative or actually real. *I'm a thief. I was in jail. I was fired. Billy Baum thinks I suck. I lost my one chance at the Loevner's account, the one thing that would make my family truly proud of me. My housekeeper left me, again. She hates me. My face is asymmetrical. Bingo is dying, and I can't even look him in the eye. I wanted to be there, or maybe I didn't, but I fucked up. I am a fuckup, Alex, and you're gonna leave me anyway so why should I give you anything?* The words are so loud in her head, but they can't come out. "So what are you saying?"

"I guess I'm saying that I'm sick of this shit. I'm sick of coming in last in your life. I'm sick of your hiding out in this relationship. I'm sick of being betrayed and lied to. I'm sick of your pretending to be somebody you're not."

The tears swell up behind her sinuses, causing her cheeks to ache. "Who am I pretending to be?"

"You're just pretending, period. Pretending to be somebody who cares about me."

"I am. Somebody who does all that." Jillian can hear the ping in her own voice as if she is trying to convince herself the words are true. "I am. I do."

"Where am I? Take a look." He swirls his arms around his head. "I'm here. I'm always here and available to you. And where are you, Jill Siegel?" Alex walks up to her and gently cups her chin in his hand. "I believe you're a good person with a good heart. I wouldn't have been here for two years if I didn't think that. But that's not enough for me. I deserve more than that."

"So what does that mean?" An unforced tear bursts through her duct and drops to the floor like a water balloon.

"It means I can't do this anymore."

"So you're leaving me? Like we always knew you would?"

"Don't be so sensational. This is exactly what I mean. It's all *my* fault. *I'm* leaving *you!*" He runs his hands through his hair. "I'm not your father." Alex picks up the wooden placard on Jillian's counter: NEW FOR SPRING. "What the fuck?" Perplexed, he puts it down again.

"But you *are* leaving me, and I'm not going anywhere." Jillian's face is contorted as she pleads. She is sure she looks ugly and swollen, and this is not helping any, but she can't seem to stop herself, her habits, her racketeering, her modus operandi.

"You were never here, Jillian." Alex grabs his blue Patagonia off the coat rack and his Hasselblad from the shelf. "I'll see you, J." He kisses the side of her cheek and walks out the front door, leaving the key on the counter

Jillian pulls everything off her hangers and from her closet shelves and sits on the floor of the tiny room. This dark place has always been her retreat—where to come and think about nothing, where to disappear into. She has no room in here to think about Alex and the palpable absence of him. She has no room to think about how predictable this all is—how everyone leaves in the end—fathers, mothers, uncles, boyfriends. She can't begin to think about the desperate loneliness. She can't begin to think about how she has no family, about how she has no job, about how she has nobody to call up or write to or be with. She has no room for any of that, so she just sits in her closet, folding and re-folding everything into little piles.

First she organizes by color. On the left-hand side she starts with blues and blue-greens, putting all the blouses and pants, sweaters and silks into neat columns that resemble the sea. She smells the clothes piece by piece, identifying how old or new a particular item is purely by the acridity or perfumey nature of the scent. Much of the whites and blacks smell warm and woodsy, while the less frequently worn brighter colors on the opposite end of the room still have the bitter smell of their previous environments.

The color-organizing principle gets confusing, especially when black takes up so much room, so she reorganizes by season. She creates a fall section on the left—light wools and canvas, luxurious weave and nubby fabrics. And in the middle, she creates a summer pile made up entirely of filmy silks, broad square scarves, and willowy dresses. Winter takes up the most room with its furry sleeves; thick, coarse wools; and down-filled puffiness.

But organizing by season seems too nebulous—one thing for fall is fine for summer, and summer for winter, and winter for spring. And of course shoes can hardly be brought into the schematic—summer shoes work all year round, and winter and fall shoes blend together. So she starts again with stolen on one side and purchased on the other. But this process is too messy and confrontational, so she stops after three pieces, all stolen, never worn.

Jillian organizes and reorganizes the things in her closet by every principle she can muster. She sits, unmedicated, on the floor of her dark and tiny room, in her 940-square-foot apartment, on the block between University and Fifth, across the street from Gotham Bar & Grill, across the street from Tito's Burritos, across the street from the rest of the world. She folds as beautiful people come and go, as girls are proposed to, broken up with, as they fly on airplanes, as they put on lipstick, giggle with friends, adjust bra straps, and take cell phone calls. She refolds and rehangs and thinks about what the rest of the people in the world might be doing: getting haircuts, making out in taxis, cheating on tests, shaving their legs, taking photos with their Hasselblads.

Jillian folds by herself in a walk-in closet on Twelfth Street. She folds and folds as the world floats by—not feeling a part of it, not feeling a part of anything.

16

JILLIAN wakes up on her couch at seven A.M. The weave of the wool has left dots on the side of her face and down her legs. Except for a slight case of itchiness, she feels alert and ready for the day ahead. There's an unidentifiable excitement in the air—like Christmas morning—it all feels cleaned out and ripe with possibility.

She doesn't have to meet Shelly for hours so she decides to walk rather than cab it up to Macy's. She's a free woman now. A single girl on the streets of New York. It's fun, romantic even, if she thinks about it just the right way and continues a brisk pace uptown.

Being an objective observer in New York is entertaining at this hour. Everyone looks so self-important, as if the world hinged on the call they need to make on the way to the office or the meeting they're racing to across town. This morning Jillian takes her time and enjoys the freedom. Maybe being on the outside of the organism is good after all.

She decides to take the long way so she can wander up Madison, past the familiar old surroundings. The doorway on her right leads into the building that always looked like a golden cave to her—shiny Art Deco stalagmites and stalactites closing in on a dark, open center. The bald man with the pencil mustache still sits at the front accepting packages and buzzing in visitors.

The old Violet's Chocolate Shoppe has been replaced by an Enya Shoes. Jillian remembers going to Violet's with Bingo for a chocolate-covered strawberry on Wednesdays after school. On Friday's, Mrs. Dell'Rosa, one of the perfume counter ladies, would bring her white chocolate pretzels from the little shop— the sweet velvety coating giving way to a surprisingly salty crunch. Jillian wonders how many years Violet's has been closed.

She craves a white-chocolate-covered pretzel from Violet's so badly her eyes begin to water. Her body feels raw and in desperate need of a candy-coated comforter to cushion things up.

She looks through the window at Enya Shoes. It's absurd that a store like Enya, with its beige comfortable pumps and bland chunky heels, has replaced the magical Violet's—dark, humid with cacao, the lingering breeze of fancy-lady smells, and filled to the brim with mysterious afternoon confections. She suddenly feels old.

And then the Citibank next door—a sleek, modernized version has taken the place of the old stone building. Jillian barely remembers the days when she and Bingo would take over a giant envelope of money to the special aisle at the bank every afternoon before they went back to the apartment—the days when Loevner's was just two rooms and on the second floor, and the entire day's worth of business could be stuffed into one manila envelope.

The Eastlake Cineplex is now on the southern side of the grand department store. This side was where the Children's Department once was, where Jillian's bunny-fur coat and muff came from. Children's was where mothers brought their children for light-wool Easter coats, or back-to-school ensembles in rich autumn umbers and brick reds, or maroon velvets and lace for the High Holidays. Literally hundreds of Jillian's dresses, matching coats and hats, party shoes, school shirts, festive handbags, and coordinated gloves were from Children's.

Jillian remembers Mr. Newman, with the rust-colored toupee,

who worked in Children's. The "red rug," as Lois called it, sat on the top of his head as if it might jump off and scamper away at any moment. Mr. Newman loved to lavish Jillian with treats of all kinds. "Honeydew!" Mr. Newman would raise his arms into the air as if surprised by her daily excursion into his domain and then dig into his pocket for a lollipop. "Why don't you surprise your uncle and wear this new Varlee petit point dress back upstairs? Mr. Loevner loves petit point." Jillian would try on the dress or the coat or an entire new plaid ensemble and twirl around for Mr. Newman and the Perfume Ladies in the next department next. "How's the 'twirl factor,' honeydew?"

"Look at it, Mr. Newman! All the way past my hands!"

"Look at our little star, Miss Leilani!" Mr. Newman would clap with the ladies. "We see. We see, Mr. Newman."

Jillian pushes open the grand doors of the old place. She hasn't been here since Bingo gave it up a million years ago. Too many memories pulse through these walls. But today she feels like walking headlong into it and letting them pummel her from all sides until she is raw and broken open.

Alain's magnificent chandelier still hangs down from above, dwarfing anything within its view. To Jillian it was, and still is, no less spectacular than the moon—with its giant revolving paillettes reflecting the morning sun onto the earth below. "Always have a great opening act, honeydew. The entrance should be the biggest moment of any store," Bingo would say as he walked through with his well-dressed niece. "It's the 'Once upon a time' part of the fairy tale—it puts you in the mood for the rest of the magic."

The foyer of Loevner's Department Store has not been altered in any significant way in decades. As grand and tall as a church, with the iconic chandelier dropping down from the ceiling, the entryway gives Jillian chills down her back each time she enters it.

In the past, at Christmastime, Alain and his team of art directors and set decorators would fill this giant space with a tree that, to Jillian, seemed almost as large and dazzling as the one at Rock-efeller Center. While Bingo, and most of the country club Jews like him, celebrated Hanukkah privately, publicly Christmas was the only holiday that existed. Christ babies, mangers, doves, angels, Santas, wise men, reindeer, Marys and Josephs were all fair game at the store, without even so much as a nod to the brethren during the season. "Menorahs depress people," Bingo would say. "Even Jews want some *goyishe* spectacle at Christmastime."

One Christmas Alain created an homage to Hans Christian Andersen throughout the store. The entire place was transformed into a winter wonderland. He even placed life-size, custom-made glass skating rinks on either side of the big tree in the foyer. Built in Germany to Alain's specifications, with six toy children ice-skating on the shimmery glass surface, the elaborate sets were the most spectacular thing Jillian had ever seen. She sat for hours looking down on them, dangling her feet from the second-floor balcony. "Are they real, Alain? Are the children real?"

"They are enchanted, honeydew." Alain said the word *enchanted* as if he himself was made of fairy dust.

"Enchanted?" Jillian asked, not sure what the word meant.

"A magic sorceress put a spell on real children, and now they skate and skate until she sets them free for one day a year on Christmas morning."

"She sets them free?"

"For only one day a year. On Christmas!"

Jillian remembers begging Alain and Bingo to take her back to the storefront early Christmas morning. She walked the whole way down Park in her new red-and-black camel-hair coat, skipping between the two men, hoping to catch the evil sorceress removing the curse so she could watch the children skate off their perpetual rink and into the real world for the day.

"It seems we have missed the children's yearly exodus," Alain said as Bingo opened the vast front door and shut off the alarm. Jillian smoothed her hand on the empty glass ice. The children, like Alain had said, were gone—not a trace of them left anywhere except for the six tiny pairs of golden skates placed beneath the tree.

The next day, Jillian watched as Alain's team packed away the rinks—the enchanted toy children back on the glass surface with their frozen smiles, pink cheeks, and warm woolen scarves. "I hope you had a wonderful day," Jillian whispered into one of the boys' ear before he was packed back away.

The following Christmas was the year Alain built Jillian's secret hideout behind the walls of the first floor of the department store. Not even Bingo knew about it. "To Narnia, *oui?*" Alain said, naming the passageway after the season's *The Lion, the Witch and the Wardrobe* theme. He showed Jillian the panel in the wall— right where the old wooden escalator let people off on the first floor, behind the perfume counter, and how it opened magically when you pushed it in just the right place. "It's your secret hiding spot, honeydew," Alain said as he winked and knocked against the clandestine entrance. "Your great escape, *cherie.*"

Jillian remembers pushing the Narnia panel open for the first time and walking back through the endless hallways and caverns behind the walls. It was the best secret she could imagine having. Once in a while Jillian would follow a secret hallway and find a new surprise from Alain: a room set up with dolls or a princess bed with a music box next to it. Her favorite surprise from Alain was the trunk filled with fancy grown-up clothes and shoes, jewelry, and hats—his favorite pieces saved from the racks. "You never know when a girl needs to dress up, *oui?*"

People come and go through the grand foyer, but unlike years ago when people wore gloves to a store like Loevner's, these people make their way chomping on gum, wearing old jeans, listening to iPods, talking at full volume, even stuffing the last of a sandwich into their mouths as they walk. Jillian knows that this is what people do now in stores—but here in the foyer of Loevner's, she expects things to be different. The modern hubbub just doesn't seem to fit.

Pierre and Gerhardt, the old Loevner's doormen, are still

there. Much more alive than the stick figures she had drawn for her campaign, their matching plaid coats have been replaced with zippier sports jackets, and they are as droll as they were two decades ago. The men are each about a hundred years old. Jillian smiles but doesn't say hello. Too many years have passed.

The burled wood walls are covered with backlit posters: WATCHES GALORE ON 5! DAZZLING CRYSTAL TATTOOS ON THE GROUND LEVEL! CELEBRATE YOUR FEET WITH 10% OFF ON SANDALS!" Jillian cringes when she sees them. Bingo didn't believe in signage like this. Modern "improvements" like indoor advertising, talking elevators, and expensive security systems didn't impress the store's proprietor much. "Honeydew," Bingo would lecture as he toured the floors with Jillian, "no one comes to Loevner's to be bombarded with bells and whistles—they come to be seduced." That's why he brought in Alain in the first place—to create "moments of *seduction*" in the store. "The key to selling is to create a universe in which people want to escape, my darling. Loevner's is an oasis from the real world," he would say. It was the same advice he gave the board years later, that obviously fell on deaf ears.

Jillian inhales the old smell, reminding her of the days years ago when she first learned about fragrance and personal signature from the Perfume Ladies—the tall Miss Leilani, the *zaftig* Mrs. Dell'Rosa with the husband who cooked ziti, and the cool Vanya, a "pansy without a stem" according to Bingo, the blonde who wore sweater sets and pearls and whom Bingo entrusted to pick out assorted items of clothing in the store for young Jillian. Lois called them the *Goy* Girls, perhaps because she was jealous, but to Jillian they were always the Perfume Ladies—elegant and all-knowing.

She follows the familiar wafts of Chanel No.5 back to the western half of the ground floor. The old escalator in the back is dark and out of service, but the up-lit glass perfume counters are as beautiful as always. She can almost see Vanya there, one hand on her hip, waiting for Jillian while holding a pile of colorful shirts or a new pair of pink Mary Janes from Mr. Newman.

"Can I help you, darling?" The saleswoman arranges shiny pink boxes on a shelf behind the counter. Jillian traces the outlines of the glass bottles on display.

"No thank you. I was just looking." Jillian smiles at the woman.

"You just let me know, honey." The woman's voice pierces into a deep space in Jillian's brain.

"Mrs. Dell'Rosa?"

"Yes?"

"It's me, Jillian. Bingo's Jillian!" Jillian can see the same face buried under twenty years of time, the big smile that gives way to the pointy incisor, the clear brown eyes, the beige face powder, the smooth, high forehead.

"Honeydew?"

"Mrs. Dell'Rosa!" Jillian's eyes fill then burst with tears. She ducks her head and rubs them away with her finger. "I'm sorry, Mrs. Dell'Rosa. I don't know why I'm . . . It's just that I didn't expect—"

"Oh, honey, you're gonna ruin your face." Mrs. Dell'Rosa whips a tissue from her sleeve and holds it up to Jillian. "Here. Blow, honey." Jillian grabs the tissues and wipes her nose. "Look at you! All grown up." Mrs. Dell'Rosa reaches over the counter and holds Jillian's hands.

"I am. I am *all grown up.*" Jillian sniffles in the last of the tears.

"What are you doing with yourself, honeydew? We lost track of you, you know, after the sale and . . . you know."

"Are the other ladies still here?"

"Oh no, honey. Just me. Beth-lynn, Miss Leilani, moved to Tallahassee with Mr. LaFollette from Shoes. Isn't that a hoot?" Mrs. Dell'Rosa laughs from deep in her belly. "And poor Vanya died a while back."

"Oh no. Vanya died?"

"She had some female cancer, honey. They caught it too late." Mrs. Dell'Rosa pulls out another tissue and hands it to Jillian. "But look at you. You look wonderful."

"My life's a mess, Mrs. Dell'Rosa. It's just a mess."

"Oh honey, I don't believe that for a second. You were always such a star child. That's what we used to say. Blessed, y'know. Beautiful, talented," she reaches out and rearranges Jillian's tangled hair, "smart as a whip."

"My uncle's sick."

"Yes, I heard about that. I'm so sorry, honey."

"And I lost my job. I got fired. And my boyfriend broke up with me. And things just really suck right now in general."

"This too shall pass." Mrs. Dell'Rosa curls her hand under Jillian's chin. "When you get to be my age, which happens quicker than you think, honey, you realize that the whole thing is just a big flimflam: an illusion, or what have you. The bad and the good. Just an illusion, honey." Mrs. Dell'Rosa smiles deep into Jillian's eyes. "Mr. Dell'Rosa had some cancer last year."

"Oh, I'm sorry."

"He's doing fine for now, but you never know when things could change. So we took a trip to Hawaii. The Big Island. And we bought a new couch, a real splurge. The kind that adjusts, honey, on both sides, so you can watch the television and be very comfortable." Mrs. Dell'Rosa shuts her eyes and smiles—the familiar pointy incisor pokes through past her bottom lip. "You just move through it all and hope you love who you can love. And if you're very lucky, honey, a few people love you back." She repositions the glass bottles on the counter, adjusting a few just a millimeter left or right.

Mrs. Dell'Rosa pulls a bottle out and mists it in front of her. "Joy, honey." Jillian leans in instinctively along with her old friend. Both women inhale the cloud of molecules floating down from the sky. "It was Simone Signoret's signature scent."

"It's beautiful."

"It is. Now you say hi to your uncle for me."

"I will." Jillian waves the mist onto her body and heads back toward the front door.

"You take care, honey."

17

"HEY. You're late. I thought you weren't gonna bag out."
Shelly taps Jillian on the shoulder below the big clock at Macy's.
She's wearing another one of her oddly fitting outfits, and her
bluish hair is wet and tangled—pulled back into an impromptu
ponytail and held in place with a few plastic barrettes. "Claudia
says you should never be late. People won't take you seriously."

"I know. I'm sorry. I just had to stop somewhere on the way
here."

"Hair 'a the dog?" Shelly holds out half of her Krispy Kreme
then quickly swipes it away. "Ah, I'm just messing with ya. I know
you don't do the doughnut." Shelly stuffs the pastry half into her
mouth and walks in through the revolving door. Jillian follows.
"Beauty Cash is so crazy cool you won't believe it."

As Jillian pushes on the glass, she feels the familiar rush of
blood and the cool film of sweat emerge on her palms. She has
not, not ever, taken anything from Macy's. But she has certainly
spent her fair share here over the years—emergency panty hose, a
pair of impulse Nikes, an umbrella here and there, sensible luggage. Everyone who lives in New York has at one time or another

bought something, even something stupid, from this store. Macy's owes everybody.

Halfway through the turnaround, the cell phone rings from the bottom of Jillian's pocketbook. She reaches in and opens the device. "Hi, it's me." Jillian presses her index finger in the other ear and wades through the spinning door, hoping to hear Alex's apologetic hello more clearly.

"How hard is it to check in on Bing once in a blue moon, darling?"

"I can't really talk now, Lois." Jillian stops and lets Shelly go on ahead down the escalator.

"Well, I can't very well just waltz over to the apartment from Europe. Obviously."

"C'mon." Shelly emerges back upward from the down escalator, walking two steps at a time against the flow. "C'mon!"

"One second!" Jillian holds her hand over the phone and watches Shelly disappear downward again.

"Are you at work, darling? What's that noise?"

"I've got to run, Lois. I've got stuff to do."

"Listen, darling, any day could be his last. I know you find the thought of checking in on him repulsive, darling—"

"I don't find the thought *repulsive*."

"And Belle has her hands full over there."

"Belle takes care of him fine, Mother."

"So you're saying you won't go?"

"I'm not saying I won't go. I'll go. It's fine. I'll go."

"Good."

"Look, I really have to run." Shelly is waving her arms up and down from below. Jillian wonders just how much more attention the two of them could create for themselves.

"And please don't let Bing eat so many carbohydrates, Jilly. He could die from that alone. It's called 'high glycemic index.' Google it, darling."

"C'mon, Jillian!" Shelly shouts from the lower level.

"I've got to go." Jillian follows Shelly down the escalator.

"So you'll check in on Bing?"

"Yes. Yes. Okay."

"Good, darling. Now maybe my migraine will go away. Dr. Chandra says it's my third eye backing up, but I think that's a load of manure."

"Good-bye, Lois."

"Good-bye, my darling."

Jillian hangs up and looks up at the black ball on the ceiling, the security camera—probably running at this moment. She looks straight into the dark sphere, wondering if it can read her thoughts as well as her movements; wondering if it knows how alone she is in this world; wondering if it knows that she can't stand the thought of being near her beloved uncle and his putrid smells and decaying body; wondering if it knows all about her.

"I'm not so sure this is a good idea." Jillian looks back at the white security columns by the front door. "We're not getting anything past those front doors, Shelly."

Shelly is still chewing on her doughnut. She points above to the black ball. "That's the only one they got running, probably. These stores can't afford to run all their eyeballs. Most of them are just blanks—*blind eyes.*"

"Oh yeah? How do you know?"

"I just do." Shelly chews as they walk off the escalator onto the bottom floor. Jillian smells the fatty, sugary scent of Mrs. Fields cookies baking. "Besides, Beauty Cash has nothing to do with taking anything out of the store."

Shelly and Jillian land in front of a display of bright ceramic mugs and pitchers. Bingo would have abhorred the prosaic display. "Don't just plop things in front of people, honeydew, and expect to inspire them. Use your imagination, my dear. Delight them at every corner."

"I'm telling you, it's unbelievably sweet. Just watch out for LP." Shelly chews while she talks.

actually has never left the floor, maybe a secret sign or something like that.

"Well, that's too bad." The saleswoman looks concerned and picks up the phone and makes a call. Jillian and Shelly look at each other. Jillian is sure this was a completely stupid plan. She watches the saleswoman's eyes and tries to read her lips on the phone. A handwritten sign next to the phone has the word SECU-RITY on it and an extension number.

They should never have gone to Macy's. It was a completely crazy plan. *Whose idea was this anyway? The saleswoman is now on the phone to Security and in minutes there are going to be handcuffed and taken down to Officer Cannell's place for baloney sandwiches and whole milk. This is completely stupid.*

Jillian notices the call ending. The saleswoman's voice grows louder. "Okay. I will. Sure. Thanks." The saleswoman looks at the girls as she hangs up the phone. *This is it. We're completely screwed. We're completely fucked. Never follow Shelly. Who is she anyway? What are you doing here? Get out.*

"Well, that's just too bad it didn't work out. It's a fabulous knife block. And all these beautiful knives! It's the best in the store." The saleswoman smiles at Shelly. "I can't give you a refund on a credit card here. You'll have to go up to ten." *This is it. This is where they walk away and right into the arms of Security, into a flurry of bullets and tear gas, and handcuffs, and . . .* "But if you don't mind cash, I can do that here." The saleswoman opens her cash register and points a wad of twenties at the girls.

"Cash is fine." Shelly rests her elbows on the counter and smiles.

18

"HELLO?" Jillian lets herself in and closes the door lightly behind her. "Belle?" Despite the fact that Bingo rarely makes it outside his bedroom nowadays, the apartment is immaculately clean and well appointed: the midcentury artwork glistens under the warm lighting; the Calder mobile stirs around in an easy circle; in the alcove, a dainty nosegay of rosebuds sits in a silver vase eager to unfurl its petals. Belle has recently rearranged the entrance room, though, the first time in decades, to allow for Bingo's walker to get through. The grand circular stone table has been moved off to the side. An elaborate bouquet in a crystal vase is set in the middle. She rarely spends a moment alone in this room and the quiet is unfamiliar, but, like the magnificent entryway of Loevner's, the room itself seems animated—full of life and song.

"Hello? Honeydew?" Belle is in the bathroom; the calm sound of splashing echoes through the rotunda, like she's washing a baby. "I'll be right out."

Jillian hangs up her coat and sets her purse down on the table.

She wishes Bingo was still like he used to be. He was her confessor, her savior. He would know what to do about Alex and Billy Baum and everything. She could even tell him about Shelly and Beauty Cash. She could put it all on pause and crawl beside him on the bed and sing French songs up at the ceiling. His imitation of Billy would be stupendous, dribbling tea down his chest and scratching his behind. He would wince exquisitely at the stories of Alex and his boorish obsessions and his lack of appreciation of style and scent. He would listen to Jillian like a girlfriend, not a mother or a shrink, nodding and agreeing and gently guiding her to a better place. She wouldn't even notice he was doing it. It just would happen.

She wishes for this man back. She needs him to be there for just a moment. Instead she is checking in on a dying stranger.

She shouldn't be here at all.

"We're just in the powder room, honey," Belle calls out as the water moves and shifts. "There we go. There we go," she says.

Jillian sits down on the monogrammed antique chair and stares out at the circular room waiting to face the inevitable. She feels alone, even here, separate and strange. The room looks bigger with the table moved out of the way, the floor underneath etched out in a large black-and-white checkerboard pattern, descending into long black and white diamonds back down the hallway by the bathroom toward the bedroom.

In the middle of the floor under where the table had been is a large clean square. It's not the same shape of the foot of the table—it extends farther out, like a pale scar left from something else. It is exactly, as Jillian remembers, the same shape and size of one of Bingo's old Henry Moore sculptures. One Jillian had not thought about for years.

In the years before the Parkinson's, Bingo (né Meyer) Loevner was an eminent Henry Moore collector. His hallways were filled with the dark stone figurines—positive and negative spaces framing the room in grand empty ovals. Mr. Meyer Loevner ("Bingo" for as long as anyone can remember) was one of the first on the Upper East Side to bring Moore into his home. While the rest of the Upper East Side was putting Rothko and Johns above their important couches, Bingo and his partner, Alain Crawford, brought Moore from large public galleries into their own intimate salon.

During her stays at Bingo's as a child, Jillian spent hundreds of hours aboard the various sculptures, turning each into a new creature of entertainment: a horse, a dog, a monster. There were no children in Bingo's building, so the priceless collection became her playmates. Her favorite Moore was named Bill, a large stone figure with a giant hole in the center. Its actual name was *Reclining Figure #12*, but Jillian preferred Bill. The morning hours at Bingo's were the most hectic and a time when Jillian was left to occupy herself. Uncle Bingo spent his time in his silk pajamas on the phone speaking French and German to people and jotting down notes onto a tiny pad of paper. Alain had already started his day at Loevner's. Belle rushed around the kitchen, putting things in the oven or taking them out or cleaning them up. Loud men burst through the front door wielding folded newspapers above Jillian's head, and fancy-smelling women in voluminous fur coats would come to kiss Bingo on both cheeks and show him their new dresses and jewelry.

No one had much need for little girls in the mornings. More often than not she went unnoticed her until she spilled a glass of juice or knocked over a chair by mistake.

So she and Bill made friends.

"Do you like my hat, Bill?" Jillian would ask politely, balancing a platter on her head. Bill usually did not like her hat until it became as elaborate and precarious as possible. She and Bill drank tea and had breakfast together and shared the news of the day. Jillian would even climb inside Bill's center hole, and if she tucked her knees under her nightgown and held them tightly to her chest, she could fit her entire body inside his. She could sit there for hours, in Bill's womb, and one time was not noticed until late into the morning when Belle came to clean.

When Jillian was seven, *Reclining Figure #12* was sold to Mr. and Mrs. Augusten Burke-Williams of Memphis, Tennessee. Jillian awoke to find Bill gone and the bright square on the floor where his base met the marble. "Where's Bill? Where's Bill? Where's Bill?" Jillian shouted up and down the hallways, her hair flying behind her in knotted tendrils, tears streaming down her face.

"Who's Bill, child? Who's Bill?" Belle asked, shaking the stiff little girl by the shoulders as she stood behind the satin curtains in Bingo's reading salon.

After a long stubborn silence, Belle gave up and walked back into the kitchen, leaving Jillian alone and unacknowledged.

Nothing ever stays, Jillian thought to herself. *This is the only thing you can count on.*

Jillian reaches a toe out to touch the clean square, the lingering evidence of a little girl's *folie à deux*.

"Here we come." Belle grunts and lifts, her voice strained by added weight. "Here we go," she adds quietly, almost to herself.

Jillian watches as the bathroom door opens. The squeaking of the hinge breaks the silence in the room. It's like a scary movie, Jillian thinks, where the tiny noise precedes the most frightening scene. Jillian's heart begins to beat loudly. She's nervous and scared, and it feels as if all the loneliness of her childhood gurgles up into her throat. There is a chilling and pervasive fear in her— one that she can't define—like that stiff little girl behind the satin curtain.

Belle and another foreign silhouette emerge. The waddling thing is small, hunched over, and draped in faded terry cloth. The sound of the walker adds a strange rhythm to the room. There is no hair on the head, at least the part of the head that one can see. The smells emerge with it—old breath, Bentadine, wet rug. It is Bingo, she knows it is, but it is also not Bingo. Where did he go?

She feels completely alone.

"Let's get ready now. Jillian is here." The words float away from Jillian and back down the hall. Belle leads the figure back into the bedroom. Her hands are clad in latex gloves, and her gold wig has shifted to the right.

Jillian feels dizzy. The room suddenly collapses into a small tight cage. She wants to stay. She wants to give the stranger in the robe a dose of tenderness and love, but he is not Bingo, he is not. She is frightened and she can't do it; she can't face it. *Where is he? Where has everyone gone?*

"I can't, Belle." Jillian manages to get out her quiet plea. "I can't stay." She yells louder, as loud as the small amount of air in her lungs will allow. "I'm sorry, Belle." Tears drop down from her chin and onto the black-and-white-checkerboard floor. Jillian grabs her coat and pocketbook and opens the door. "I'm sorry. I just can't stay."

19

JILLIAN and Shelly have been shoplifting for nearly a whole week straight. Jillian's closet is now filled with clothes she hasn't worn yet, *looks* she hasn't even perfected. Instead of refining everything down to one specific style, she has opted for *all* styles, *all* things, one for every day, every hour. Her pocketbook hasn't been cleaned out the entire time: it's filled with clothing tags, lipsticks, crushed envelopes, hair ornaments, scarves, and various beauty products. It weighs a ton, and Jillian's rotator cuff on that side has been bothering her for three days.

Her new highlights look great. The stylist recommended a few garnet chunks in front and a layering of middle tones in back. The wildly successful Beauty Cash plan has allowed for an eyebrow shaping, a facial, a massage, an extended bikini wax, and new hair color and cuts for both girls. "That skirt you got at Intermix kicks ass!" Shelly's own brand of compliments have been free-flowing for days.

And it does *kick ass.* Her entire wardrobe has been transformed, and the various pieces have added up to a perpetually refreshed feeling. There aren't enough days in the week to wear what has come home.

They have developed their own language—an encoded lingo that allows them to talk about nearly anything in front of nearly anyone. The words have tumbled out one by one—invention by necessity. After a day, they had a few; after a week, they had so many phrases to remember, they wrote them down on a piece of hotel stationery Shelly had in her pocket.

THE OFFICIAL CUTTING DICTIONARY

CUTTING, GETTING	Stealing, shoplifting
FAUX-PO	Faux Police, security guard, Loss Prevention (LP) agent
PIZZA	Stolen goods
DOOKIE	Electronic sensor device
DOOKIE DOOR	A door equipped with dookie alarms
EYEBALL	Video surveillance
FIRED UP	An entire store equipped with plentiful security
42	For two girls. Jillian and Shelly. "We should cut forty-two."
TOUCAN (OR PEACE SIGN)	Bad color for anyone
PULL A BUDDY	Vacate the premises— like Shelly's old boyfriend, Buddy
B.C.	Beauty Cash
WASTE-A	Waste of space, not worth cutting
U.A.S.	Ugly as shit, also not worth cutting
EMPTY	Safe, no security
CRICKETS	Safe, no security, "So empty, you can hear the crickets."
WATCH THE MANI	Stop biting nails (watch the manicure)
COSTA MESA	The coast is clear

H.Q.	Jillian's apartment
KICK IT	Dump the stolen item
OVER THE FENCE	Out the door with the stolen goods
A GOOD SALLY	A gullible saleswoman
OUTTIE-5000	Leaving the premises— outta here
A TOTAL PETE	A gullible salesman
WILL ROBINSON	Danger, Will Robinson. Seriously bad, get out

Jillian has done the math and it still makes sense: while she has not spent enough money at *every* store to justify all the damage that's been done, she has *cumulatively* supported these places over time—spending entire paychecks at various establishments along the same street month after month. While it seems like a bending of the rules, it makes sense on the whole—money spent in one place pays the sales force; the sales force in turn spends the money, probably nearby, probably on clothes, probably at the very boutiques that Jillian has ventured to.

It all still evens out in the end.

The girls sit side by side in the pedicure chairs at Bliss Spa. Jillian decided to spring for the sixty-five-dollar Hot Milk and Almond Pedicure and the twenty-three-dollar Hot Cream Manicure at the fancy designer spa instead of the regular mani-pedi with the Korean ladies. Shelly just nodded along. It's not that the resulting look of the Hot Milk is noticeably better than the regular mani in particular; it's just that with the overabundance of Beauty Cash, they decided to go extravagant.

Shelly's freshly dyed sienna-brown hair sets off her strikingly clear eyes and porcelain skin. The soapy smell still lingers around her head. The cut, a few inches lopped off the back and fringey layers in the front, emphasizes her natural curls and sturdy attractiveness. "Horse brown!" Shelly looks across the way into the mirror. "It's good, right?" Her creased, oversized outfits have been replaced with pieces attained mostly by Jillian's agile hand.

With Shelly's blunt, glossy curls and polished wardrobe, she looks little like the petit larcenist Jillian first met a week earlier.

Bliss Spa smells like lemon verbena, hot milk, and fruity-scented acetone. The nearly imperceptible chatter of designer manicures is low and hypnotic. The girls wiggle their toes in the soothing white footbath. "That boy-beater T at Big Drop would be good on you too. I should have done a forty-two." Jillian peers into her purse at the hot pink material. "It sucks that you pulled a Buddy before you got anything. The scene was pretty empty."

"I didn't see anything I really wanted."

Jillian watches as Shelly talks and looks at herself in the mirror. She's adorable, in a way, like a puppy—inelegant and unself-conscious.

"I was looking for some silver stuff. Y'know, something that reflects light." Shelly flips through a magazine.

Jillian smiles at her and relaxes back into her chair.

"What's that look for?"

Jillian laughs. "It's just funny, that's all."

"The pedicure?"

"It's just funny that we're girlfriends." Jillian is still smiling. "I hate girlfriends."

"Why would anybody hate friends?"

"I don't know," Jillian searches for an answer that would make sense to Shelly. "Friends are just nosy and they gossip about you and they think they know everything about you." Not saying the real reason out loud, Jillian just shrugs her shoulders. "I don't know. In the end I think they always betray you."

"I would never betray my friends." Shelly sucks on the button of her jacket.

"Yeah, but you're different." Jillian rests her chin on the heel of her hand and grieves for a moment, an emotion usually kept at bay, now frothing up to the surface.

When she was young, Jillian never had a lot of friends. Mostly she spent time around adults—at the store, at Bingo's, with Alain. Lois once tried to get Jillian to play with the little girl in the apartment down the hall from Nana's in Palm Beach, and a few times she invited Mrs. Mazur and her daughter from dancing school over, as if all little girls of the same age might naturally get along, have things in common.

Bingo and Alain's friends were movie stars, torch singers, models, writers, fashion designers, and such; they often brought over their dogs, their hairdressers, their new husbands—they even occasionally brought over their fortune-tellers and plastic surgeons—but they never brought over their children, if they even had any to bring.

Back then, Suki Friedman was the closest thing Jillian had to a real girlfriend. They were the well-appointed accessories to their mothers' lives, always there, yet never integral to the main activity. Their friendship developed out of their mutual no-man's-land.

But in eighth grade, the year after the two girls spent the summer rooming together at Andy Frommer's Professional Tennis Camp in Canada, Jillian started to mature physically: her body, her face, even her hair became womanly. At four feet nine and completely flat-chested, Suki still looked like a child. (Eventually, at sixteen, Suki Friedman more than made up for her shortcomings with a new sports car, breast implants—a gift from her mother—and a sexual enthusiasm that rivaled the seniors. But at thirteen, she was still a kid.)

By October of that year, Jillian was regularly invited out by the cool crowd. By December, Jillian was getting the attention of boys and men alike. By May, even though Jillian would have still called Suki her best friend, they had barely anything to talk about.

In early June, the two were seated at the same table at Cindy Steinbach's bat mitzvah. Willing to do anything to seem older, Suki was wearing a grown-up fur coat, a heavily padded bra under her designer dress, and her mother's four-inch heels to add to her height. Suki managed to sit as far away from Jillian as possible, but when the band came on and the rest of the girls dispersed to dance, Jillian tried to make conversation.

"I can't believe Cindy's stupid brother, like, *is* the band," Jillian said, referring to Nick Steinbach, Cindy's older brother and lead singer of Wham! Again, his cover band that played occasionally at school dances.

"I know. Nick Steinbach is so gay," Suki said.

"Yeah. Way gay."

Both girls looked over at their classmates—a gaggle of girls dancing with each other in the center of the floor. Jillian would have been welcome to join them but stayed back so that Suki wouldn't be the only one left at the giant table.

"God, they're all such fucking idiots." Suki pulled out a pack of Marlboro Lights and tapped them loudly on the table. "Jesus, I need a smoke."

"When did you start smoking?" Jillian asked, not recalling ever having seen Suki with a pack before.

"Oh my God, Jilly, I've smoked since I was, like, in sixth grade. I can't believe you didn't know that about me."

"I've never seen you smoke." Jillian sipped on her Diet Coke.

"Well, I do," Suki said indignantly.

They sat slumped in their chairs watching as a few of the girls paired off with the boys during a Wham! Again slow song.

"This is such a joke." Suki flipped back her hair and smoothed out the blown dry layers.

"You wanna dance, Jilly?" Bear Bouchez leaned over to Jillian and smiled. Bear Bouchez was a soccer player—cute and popular—and the son of one of New York's most prominent architects, Jean Bouchez. "Oh, no thanks, Bear. I'm just hangin'. Maybe later, okay?" Jillian smiled.

"Hey, Suki." Bear looked over and nodded. He pushed the flap of his hair away from his eyes. It would be two and a half years before Bear would be the recipient of one of Suki's famous blow jobs on the Concordia golf course, so all he had for her was the unenthusiastic greeting.

"Hey, Bear," she replied with equal indifference.

"See ya, Jilly." The boy smiled as he walked away.

"Bear Bouchez is so gross. I heard he's uncircumcised, y'know." Suki put on lipstick. "His parents are French. The French are so rude."

"I think Bear's father was Lois and my dad's architect," Jillian said, finishing her soda. "He did that apartment my mom had a long time ago on Sixty-sixth."

"Jean Bouchez was my father's architect before your father could even get his shit together enough to have an architect," Suki said, twirling the pack of cigarettes in her hand. "I'm not as stupid as you think, Jilly." She looked Jillian directly in the eye.

"How would you know?" Jillian had never heard Suki be so outwardly angry at her. "You didn't even know my father."

"Yeah," Suki crossed her legs and dangled her high heel out from the table, "and neither did you."

Jillian sat back, her heart pounding and her face growing flush. "I knew him for almost a year before the crash, Suki. I mean, I was just a baby, but—"

"Oh, right. The heroic plane crash. Right." She laughed.

Utterly confused, Jillian glared at Suki.

"Oh my God! I can't believe you're so gay you still believe that bullshit." Suki unwound the plastic thread at the top of the Marlboro Lights. "Why do you think there's no pictures of him with you, idiot?"

"Because my mother never takes pictures." Jillian was satisfied to have caught Suki with this one. Lois never *did* take pictures. "The plane crashed right before my first birthday, Suki. They were coming back from Mnemba Island in Zanzibar." Jillian's face was poker hot, and the noise of the band and the people faded away to nothing.

"That's not what Linda told me."

"Well, Linda doesn't know everything."

"Well, Linda *does* know everything, and your father didn't die in a plane crash over *Zanzibar*, Jilly. That's just some exotic bullshit you made up." Suki smoothed pink gloss over her lips.

"I didn't make it up," Jillian pleaded. "I wouldn't make that up." Jillian's body stiffened. She wanted to run, but she couldn't. She wanted to stop Suki, but she couldn't. She wanted her ears to seal up forever, just to avoid hearing the rest of what Suki had to say, but she couldn't. Somewhere inside she knew the story about Zanzibar wasn't true, but she never let the thought enter. She learned to seal everything up and never let any of it come in.

"He died because he killed himself before you were even born." Suki shut the tube of gloss and put it back into her small clutch. "He did it because he didn't want to have a kid. He didn't want to have you. That's what Lois told Linda."

Jillian sat there, the words she never wanted to hear landing like a brick on her head. She had the sudden desire to take the glass of Diet Coke and shove it into Suki's face or into her own. She wanted to disappear. She wanted everything to just go away. Jillian vowed at that moment never to have another friend, never to let one in again, never to invite one through the door. Jillian Siegel had no real immediate family—and now, no best friend.

It was fine with her. Just fine.

Suki put her cigarette pack back in her purse and buttoned the jacket of her petite ensemble. She stood up, all fifty-seven inches of her, and readied herself to leave. "I heard Lois was pissed. Y'know, because of all the mess and stuff. She had to move out of the Jean Bouchez apartment."

"This feels so good." Shelly makes circles in the milk with her feet.

Jillian looks over at Shelly—she is everything Suki was not—big, clunky, hopeful, open, dependable. Shelly would never betray a friend. Jillian is glad to have found her.

"Hot milk is better than cold milk," Shelly added.

"I'd have to agree." Jillian allows the rich warmth to crawl up her body. Both girls sit back as their toes are cracked and massaged in the soothing liquid.

"How long do you think I'll take to dry? Poppy's coming back today from his trip, and Claudia said I should come by the office at two." Shelly cracks her knuckles one by one.

"There's always Quik Dry in the worst-case scenario."

"Claudia says Poppy missed me. Isn't that cool?"

"I guess it's cool."

"I mean, he's a really important guy with a lot of people who work for him. Even in, like, Beverly Hills. He's the shit, y'know. I just think it's pretty cool for a person like that to miss someone like me."

Jillian keeps her mouth shut. Shelly's excited about it, and she decides to leave it at that. Some things are just better left unsaid.

"I know!" Shelly grabs Jillian's hand. "Why don't you come up to his office with me? It'd be cool if you met him, you know. He won't mind."

"*He* won't mind meeting *me?*" She doesn't even know him and she's already appalled by his audacity. "How nice."

"Well, yeah." Shelly seems to be careful about her words. "He just doesn't like meeting many people. I mean just regular people. People he doesn't do business with. But he's fine with meeting you."

"How generous."

The Bliss manicurists slather the girls' calves with a thick pink cream that smells like marzipan.

"How old is he anyway?" Jillian asks.

"I don't know how old he is." Shelly gnaws on her knuckle. "Older than Claudia. I don't know. Old, I guess. Jeez, what's the twenty-questions shit? He's just a businessman, that's all. He talks about money stuff when he's in town, and then he then flies different places and does more important stuff. Claudia stays here and takes care of his things here." Shelly wiggles her body defiantly. "Ow! Fuck!" Shelly brings up her foot to take a look at it. A small drop of blood trickles down. "Shit."

"Sorry, ma'am." The Bliss attendant presses down on the cut and applies a cotton pad with a drop of lavender oil.

"*Ma'am!* That's so funny." Shelly relaxes back into the chair like Jillian.

"Does Vira know about cutting?" Jillian continues the inquisition. She watches as Shelly's fingers go straight for her mouth. "He does, doesn't he? He does it too!"

"No way!" Shelly sits up in her chair. "Vira never cuts anything. Never!" Shelly relaxes back. "Well, not anymore." Shelly looks down at her toenails. "But I guess he knows about it. Sort of. He knows pretty much everything."

"Does he know that *we* cut together?" Jillian is staring right at Shelly.

"Yeah. Maybe."

"Jesus, Shelly! *Oy.*" The Bliss pedicurist looks up. "You told him that I cut with you! I can't believe you. That's my own private business," Jillian whispers loudly.

"He doesn't care, believe me. He's fine with it. He's not gonna bust you. He's not gonna bust anyone." Shelly and Jillian both stretch their necks around in a circle. "He's not exactly all clean himself."

"Great. Lovely." If Jillian's feet weren't freshly dipped in hot milk, she would just walk home right that second—jump in a cab and get away from Shelly and Vira and this whole creepy scene. She doesn't need this. She doesn't need a girl like this and a man like that.

"Lookit, Miss Priss, when I came to this city I didn't have no shit—no place to stay, no friends, no money, no nothing—and those people helped me out . . . more than my own family, that's for sure." Shelly itches her hair all over. "Gordo even saved me from going up to County. And he didn't even know who I was!"

Jillian watches Shelly closely as she talks. The girl's eyes are wild and passionate.

"I was pulling one a my old Chula Vista tricks at Loehmann's. Only you know something—that shit don't work here, dude." Shelly looks Jillian straight in the eye. "And Gordo was shopping for a Flik Flak to send home to his nephew in Peru and he saw me doing my thing. He came outta nowhere and put his arm around me!" She seems out of breath. "I didn't even know him and he didn't

even know me, but he put his friggin' arm right around me."
Shelly's face flushes red. "That's what a friend is, Jillian, in case you
need a definition—a friend is someone who keeps you safe."

Jillian feels suddenly sick—terrified that Shelly has something
she'll never have.

"I didn't even see the Faux Po. He was right there watching,
and I woulda gone up to County for sure because I had no ID
and I had the pea soup. Y'know. Grand larce'."

"Pea soup is grand larceny?"

"I brought the soup in with me. Premeditation. I was dropping
these earrings I needed into it."

"You put jewelry in your soup?"

"Yeah. We use to do that at the mall all the time in CV." Shelly
shakes her head, as if Jillian should have heard of this sort of
thing before. "So Gordo gets me to drop the soup in the can and
got me outta there. He takes me back to Vira's office, and I
thought they were gonna bust me—like they were narcs or something. But instead a busting me, they're all nice." Her voice
squeaks as if she might cry. "And so Claudia says they been looking for a white girl like me to be on their team." She smiles. "So I
started hangin' with them." She cracks her thumbs and checks
out her hair again in the mirror. "So I'm going up to his office at
two. You want to come or not?" Shelly crosses her arms in front
of her.

Jillian starts to laugh. She already knows her answer. Maybe
because she wants a piece of what Shelly's described, maybe she
feels jealous and competitive, and maybe she's just not ready to
get off the ride. "What the fuck." She shakes her head in disbelief. "I'll come." She wonders if it's a decision she may come to
regret.

20

"C'MON. I've got the key."

"Vira's office is here? At the *Pierre?*" Jillian follows Shelly as they walk into the lobby of the fancy hotel. She wonders if Shelly's made a mistake. "Are you sure, Shelly?"

"Yeah. The Presidential Suite."

"Vira's office is in the Presidential Suite of the Pierre?"

"Not always. He likes to hang in different places. Y'know, at different hotels and stuff, see what floats his boat." Her pants are still rolled up over her knees. "His office was at the Four Seasons before." She says it as if it's normal.

The Pierre is on Sixtieth and Fifth, past Bergdorf's, near Cipriani. Jillian doesn't know anyone, including any of Bingo's friends, who's ever had a full-time office in a hotel, much less in the Pierre or the Four Seasons.

The doorman holds the front doors open for the girls. The entryway is dazzling—bathed in golden light with elaborate European-style detail and impeccable craftsmanship, the room is as grand as New York gets. "I think Poppy likes to flash it up for the people he works with." Shelly twirls her hair into a knot. "Show them he's got the bank."

"It would seem so." Even Jillian is awed by palatial space.

The two girls walk through the regal foyer toward the elevators. Shelly's Keds flap against the smooth floor. The sweet smell of oriental lilies from the massive arrangement underneath the chandelier fills the room. The low shimmering light of the room is quieting and stunningly elegant.

"It's cool you're gonna meet Poppy." She cracks her knuckles as the elevator doors shut in front of them and swipes her card key into the slot marked PH. "He's way more cool than you'd think."

"I don't think anything," Jillian says, as she fixes her hair in the mirrored reflection of the elevator door.

The elevator goes up thirty-nine floors without stopping. A quiet "ding" marks their arrival at the penthouse. There are only two suites on the floor, one at either end of the hallway. Jillian follows Shelly to the left down the dimly lit corridor.

"*Eh, hola. Buenos días!*" A tanned, well-dressed woman with chestnut hair emerges from the door on the right and is suddenly standing beside the girls—her manicured hand is on Shelly's shoulder. "Look at you, *papayita! Jou* look gorgeous!" She kisses Shelly on each side of her face.

"Cool, right?" Shelly twirls her head around for the woman.

"I love!" The woman looks Jillian straight in the eye and smiles.

"And I brought a present for you." Shelly reaches in her pocket and pulls out a hot pink silk handbag topped by a long handle embroidered with beads. Rubber bands are threaded throughout the top and stick out in curly beige tendrils. It is not a bag that they stole, but it does look familiar. It looks like a shirt sleeve cut and trimmed and resewn into something new. Jillian recognizes the cuff at the bottom and the three buttons holding the side closed. "I know how you like purses."

"S'beautiful, *mamá.*" The woman takes the bag and tries it on over her shoulder. She kisses Shelly again on both cheeks.

"You're such an artist!" A rush of ruddiness forms on Shelly's cheeks like pink Rorschach tests.

"And this must be Jillian Siegel!" The woman's Cheshire smile is broad and moist, and her high cheekbones emerge like apples from the hollow beneath. "I am Claudia Monteagudo. Viracocha's business associate. You just call me Claudia." She pronounces the name slowly and deeply, like "Cloud," and wraps Jillian in a seductive embrace. Her whitened teeth shimmer brightly. "A real New York City woman, *sí?*"

Jillian smiles at the dark woman as she recovers from the intimate hug. "Born and bred." Claudia continues to hold her smile out widely, like a runner-up for Miss Universe watching the winner take her crown.

"Come." Claudia wraps her arm around Jillian and leads her to the door. "Vira will be so exciting to meet you. He just come back from Korea this morning." Claudia straightens Shelly's hair out—brushing it lightly with her fingernails, "It's so gorgeous. Sophisticated. He gonna love it." She opens the ebony door with the swipe of a key. "Go on, *mamá. Vámonos.*" Claudia gently pushes Jillian into a sumptuously appointed living room. "He don't bite."

Shelly hops in front of Jillian and leans against the plump arm of the luxurious couch. She grabs the TV clicker and points it toward the large television in an antique armoire at the corner of the room.

The room is lavishly decorated with paintings, vases of fresh flowers, elegant furniture, conference phones and fax machines. It is, Jillian thinks, what the private rooms of Buckingham Palace might look like—"*Goyisha-chichi,*" as Bingo would say.

Jillian sits down on an overstuffed armchair by the doorway to the other room. She should feel uncomfortable, but the center of this strange hive is oddly invigorating and festive. Shelly switches the TV to music videos.

"Look who in the house!" A short man with a broad face and marble-brown eyes enters the room and comes up to Shelly.

"Hey. Ho . . ." He sambas right up to Shelly, gyrating his Jell-O belly up to her. "How's my homes?" He pretends to punch Shelly in the shoulder.

She blushes. "I'm fly, G."

"He here yet?" The man goes over to the bar at the end of the room and rips open a bag of smokehouse almonds.

Shelly turns off the sound and flips the channels. "He's probably talking business with Manuel and Claudia in the office." Shelly points to the room beside Jillian.

"Whas with the hair, homie?"

"I dyed it." Shelly's eyes don't leave the TV.

"It look kinda Mexican." He pours some almonds into his mouth. "Like a beaner!" He laughs as he downs the snack. "Vira know you got company?" He points the bag at Jillian.

Through the French doors, Jillian can see a young man sitting at a table in the next room. Claudia is sitting next to him, and they both talk to an older man, probably Vira. He paces around the table. The door is slightly ajar, and Jillian can hear them talking in the next room. Claudia's voice is different than before. It is sharp and quick. Jillian pushes the hair back away from her ear.

Vira speaks in heavily accented English. Claudia and Manuel follow his lead:

Manuel: They got a profile on the team, and there's no way we can go in there with just the regulars. We have to break it up or we won't even get five minutes on the job without heat.

Claudia: Our plans are under way as Vira knows.

Vira: I can assure the two of you, I will not allow for a problem on the Red job. If this is taking too long, we move to plan B. Is that understood?

Claudia: Understood. We'll be ready.

Manuel: They shifting things around in there, Vira, and it's getting very hot.

Vira: If Claudia says we'll be ready, we will.

Claudia: We'll be ready.

Manuel looks up from the table and out toward Jillian. Jillian turns her head quickly back into the room.

"Vira knows she's here. Claudia said it was cool. She *wanted* me to bring Jillian up." Shelly clicks the channels back and forth as she talks.

"Oh. So that's her." The man raises his hand. "Hey, Jillian Siegel. You finally come for a visit."

"That's Gordo." Shelly points at him with the clicker. "They call him that, 'cause he's fat. Right, *Gordito?*"

"Hey. I no fat." He jiggles over to Jillian and punches himself in the stomach. "That's all muscle. Go ahead, punch me, man." Gordo is grimacing as he continues to punch himself harder and harder.

"So what's all that moving around in the middle?" Jillian laughs.

He pours another handful of nuts into his mouth. "Aw naw, you girls are baggin' on me. That's just my working name, man. That's all." Gordo walks back to the mini bar and opens a soda. "Coke?" He points a bottle toward Jillian.

"He won't tell no one his real name," Shelly says from the couch.

"No thanks." Jillian puts her hand up to stop him and turns to face Vira's room.

He opens the Coke and hands it to Jillian anyway. "It don't got germs. It's hotel Coke, man. It cost like five bucks or something." Gordo notices Jillian staring into the other room. "That's Vira you checkin' out." He takes a swig. "Don't let him catch you doin' that."

Jillian brushes her hair off her face and pretends she wasn't looking.

"He's de king here—De Beers. He's De Beers pretty much everywhere he goes." Gordo takes another sip of his Coke. "Ain't that right, *mamacita?*" He fake punches in the direction of Shelly.

"Whatever you say, *Gordito.*" Shelly breezes through the channels, one after another.

"Saks Fifth, Neiman's, Armani, Bergdorf, man. New York, Boston, London, England, Australia. You name it." Gordo belches into his fist. "Everyone know Vira."

Jillian glances through to the other room again. She sees the man stand up from his call and pull a plump plastic bag out from a giant box by the desk. The bag contains something made out of yellow material, and, from what Jillian can see, the box is full of hundreds of bags just like it.

He tosses the bag up in the air and catches it.

Shelly is flipping back and forth between stations. "You probably got some girl name or something," Shelly teases her friend as she flips through the stations a second and third time.

"I ain't got no girl's name, *mamá.*"

"Petunia, some shit like that."

"Hey, watch your behabor." Gordo points the Coke bottle at Shelly. "You better not let Vira hear you cuss and shit. He kill you, man." Gordo drinks down the rest of his Coke and belches in Shelly's face.

"And we don't appreciate bodily functions either, Mr. Palomino." The French doors open fully, and the small tanned man from the other room emerges carrying the plastic bag. He's wearing a well-pressed striped shirt with French cuffs and narrow pleated trousers. A thin eel-skin belt defines his slender waist. He leans over the couch and kisses Shelly on the head. "I missed you while I was away, *hija.*"

"Poppy!" Shelly bounces off the couch and wraps her arms around the man's neck.

He pulls up a piece of Shelly's hair and takes a whiff.

"I dyed it. Isn't it cool?" She searches for a look of approval, which he does not offer.

"I brought you a gift from my trip." He smiles at Jillian as he hands Shelly the bag.

"Poppy!" Shelly rips open the plastic and holds the contents up to her body. It's a yellow silk dress—too pale for Shelly's coloring, too dainty for her robust looks, and at least two sizes too big. "Awesome, Poppy! I love it!" She throws her arms around the man and drowns him in a hug.

"I thought it would be perfect for you."

Jillian peers behind him, back into the room and back at the box filled with hundreds of the same dress.

"Turn that rubbish off." He nods to the television. "American television rots your brain. Why do you think there are all these stupid people in this country? It's like crack, like *coca.*"

"Sorry, Poppy." Shelly lowers her head and immediately clicks off the television. "And I brought you a present too." Shelly jumps to her knees with excitement.

"Another one of your crazy trinkets?" He winks in Jillian's direction.

"No, silly. Her!" Shelly nods her head to the right. "Jillian!"

He looks up at Jillian. "Ah, you've brought me Miss Jillian Siegel. Just what I always wanted." Jillian does not like being referred to as a gift, nor does she like the idea that everyone has been expecting her, but for the moment she makes no outward objections. "Provide me with a proper introduction, *hija.*"

Shelly mechanically holds her hand out toward the slim, weathered man. "Viracho . . . Virachoke . . ."

"Viracocha."

"Vira*cocha* De La Puente, may I present Jillian Siegel." Shelly then points to Jillian. "Jillian Siegel, may I present Viracocha De La Puente."

Viracocha pats Shelly approvingly on the head. "That's my girl. Claudia is teaching you so well."

"Pleased to make your acquaintance." Viracocha reaches out for a handshake. His hand is surprisingly narrow and feminine. Jillian shakes firmly and professionally nonetheless. He is calculatedly refined and deliberately elegant, from the custom shirt to the freshly buffed fingernails to the handmade shoes. He is certainly not what she pictured, not in the least.

"Charmed, I'm sure." Jillian is acutely aware that her ironic sense of humor is lost on everyone in the room.

"You are much more beautiful than on your driver's license, Miss Siegel."

"Ah yes, the infamous driver's license." Jillian looks at Shelly and raises her eyebrows. "Well, that's not saying much, Mr. De La Puente."

"And you blush."

She is surprised to feel the warm heat building in her cheeks.

"This is a good trait in a person. It keeps you honest, *sí?*"

"It's just a little hot in here." Jillian feels her forehead with the back of her hand.

"Nonsense. It means I will always know when you're lying." He smiles and adjusts one cuff link. "Out, out, Mr. Palomino." Viracocha shoos away Gordo with the flick of a hand.

"Yeah," Shelly has her hands on her hips and wags her finger, "that means you, Petunia."

Viracocha De La Puente is at least forty-five, if not much older. The sharply carved wrinkles beside his eyes open and close as he smiles to reveal fine pale steaks against his skin. While Shelly and Gordo are strange blips on this elegant landscape, looking more like the help than the guests, Viracocha blends right into the atmosphere with his cappuccino skin, sharp blue eyes, European styling, and debonair confidence. As if at any moment the tango might begin.

"Why don't you go see if Claudia and Manuel need your help, *hija?* They're packing up the stock today." Viracocha takes Shelly's hand and pats it lightly.

"Oh, c'mon, I never get to stay. She's my peeps." Shelly sits up on her knees on the couch and pleads like a child at his shoulder. Jillian imagines that Viracocha never acquiesces to these sorts of requests. This one is no exception.

"I don't care whose *peep* she is; I would like to speak with Miss Siegel alone. Go on." Shelly gets off the couch and pouts until she reaches the front door.

"She's not some fancy lady, Poppy. You don't have to call her 'miss.' " Shelly is aggravated and acting childish.

Viracocha looks over to Jillian, cocks his head, raises his eyes. "Every woman is a fancy lady until she proves otherwise." He looks directly at Jillian, making a nonverbal connection above Shelly's head.

Jillian smiles back without playing her hand. Like shopping in an elegant store, this too is a dance with which she is familiar.

"Jill is fine, Mr. De La Puente."

"I told you." Shelly shuts the door behind her.

Viracocha walks to the bar at the far end of the room and opens a mini bottle of Evian. His gait is polished and graceful like a dancer or a figure skater.

"You ladies and your dungarees. Why do you girls want to look like men in this country?" He presses the bottle against his lips. "Would you like a dress like the one I gave your friend? Beautiful dresses. Expensive material." He runs his hand along his own sleeve. "Shelly loves these little presents."

"No, thank you." Jillian smooths the material of her slacks against her thighs. "I prefer my dungarees."

"Hmm." Viracocha leans in toward Jillian and then stirs the air up to his nose as if inhaling something sautéing on the stove. "Vetiver. My father wore Vetiver cologne every day that I knew him." His voice is thick and pebbly. "Odd that you should wear it too. They say Nefertiti bathed in Vetiver to perfume her blood." He sniffs it in again. "It smelled a little more *putrescent* on my father." He rolls the big English word around in his mouth and sits down again in the middle of fancy couch.

"My father was a tailor in Lima for most of his life. I used to watch him build suits." He takes a sip of water. "Manco Hidalgo was a client of my father's." Viracocha raises his Evian to Jillian. "All the top executives at PGE." He drinks to the thought of it. "Measuring and marking and pinning." He draws in the air with the small bottle. "My favorite part was seeing the jackets before he sewed the sleeves on. The padding stuck out at the shoulders and around the front of the chest, under the material. This formed the shape of the man. Made him broader, more defined." He cuts a triangle in the space in front of him. "He could make any man believe he was someone important. Just with a piece of clothing." He smooths his hand against his chest. "Have you ever known a man like that, Jill?"

Jillian thinks of Bingo instantly.

"I haven't, Mr. De La Puente." The mouthful of syllables does not fall easily out of her mouth.

Viracocha looks out of the window to a spot far away. "It's like architecture, really . . . did you know that a well-cut suit is like a great building?"

"I did not." Jillian remembers Bingo's theory that a well-cut suit should actually be inconspicuous—that the man makes the suit, not the other way around.

Viracocha stands and carefully rearranges the creases of his trousers and sits back down on the couch, his arms outstretched on both sides.

"Sit, Jill." He gestures toward the couch opposite him.

Jillian gets up and walks toward the couch. Her heart is pounding, and she is sure her face is pink.

"He wanted me to become one. A *sastre*. A tailor in Barranco." Viracocha raises up an inch as she sits down.

"And you didn't, I guess." She concentrates on cooling the pink from her skin.

"Tailors in Barranco don't have much to show for their work, Jill." He picks a small fiber off his pants and flings it with his finger.

"They have suits to show for their work." Jillian crosses her legs and puts her pocketbook on her lap.

"Suits are just suits, Jill." He waves his hand in the air again, making the whole thing disappear.

"I thought you said that suits are like great buildings."

He seems disappointed at her interpretation of the facts. "My father was an architect of small things, Jill. I am a bigger man than he." Viracocha smiles and settles into his posture, as if this is the only statement that truly relaxes him. "So." He takes a deep breath inward. "I'm sure you already know all about us from your friend Shelly. She does not keep secrets well, *la hija.*"

"Shelly didn't tell me anything, as a matter of fact." Jillian swings her arm around the back of the couch, trying to get into the pose of someone comfortable, someone with the upper hand. "But I am curious why your office is at the Pierre. Surely there are more economical places to go about your business."

"My office is at the Pierre because I appreciate beautiful things. And the Pierre is a beautiful hotel. Why not have your office in a beautiful place?"

A Manhattan postcard image flashes in Jillian's head—the kind that tourists have of carriage rides in the park, dinners at fine restaurants, Broadway shows, beautiful hotels. This is the image she prefers to keep and not the new one he is suggesting.

He rubs his palm along the arm of the couch. "I am a merchant of beautiful things, Jill. A middleman between the establishments and the people."

"A Robin Hood kind of thing?" Jillian's heart is beating loudly in her ears. She is being dangerously cheeky, and she knows it.

Viracocha laughs profusely. "Ah, Robin Hood. I like this Robin Hood." His laughter dies down. "But I steal from the rich and sell to the richer. A better business model for a thief, *sí?*"

He runs a finger down his starched collar. "You have to understand, Jill, we were very poor people. We learned to steal from the time we were *hijos.* We stole for *licor* and marijuana and sold it on the street when we were just babies. Whatever we could get. It is what we know. It is what we are good at." Viracocha speaks without any remorse or hesitation. "Being a thief is what I know. Stealing is what I am good at." He takes pride in his sins and makes no effort to keep them hidden. Strangely, Jillian finds this quality refreshing and admirable.

"And I can assume, from the looks of it, it is a lucrative occupation for you." Jillian does not gesture to the palatial surroundings, but they both know to what she is referring.

"And Jillian, working *for* me can be just as lucrative." He stares at Jillian, and there is an uncomfortably long silence. "If that indeed is what you're looking for. But as *remunerative* as working for me might be, I believe you and Shelly steal for different reasons," he goes on. "Of course, you are thieves nonetheless. You had a good home in this country. Your friends had good homes and clothes and shoes on their feet." He is pointing to her clothes now—swiping at her shoes, her jeans, her shirt with his hand, as if he was dealing cards from a deck.

"When we met your new friend, she was stealing jewelry she didn't even need. Small trinkets that would have sent her to jail if it weren't for the resourceful Mr. Palomino." He rubs his hand along his chin, as if smoothing a beard. "It was a fortuitous meeting for us both. We had been looking for an American for our team. We Latinos are too proud sometimes. We can be awfully prejudicial about whom we invite into our inner circle. I am just as much to blame." He laughs and smooths back his hair. "Maybe it is my *machismo, sí?* But I now know that our pride was our greatest weakness. So we were looking for an American, and Shelly was looking for a family." He smiles. "You and Shelly do not steal out of need like my people; you steal because your heart is empty. You steal because these *things,* as you say, give you a moment of love. Something you and your friend never truly got."

Jillian feels her neck become red and tense.

Viracocha leans in toward Jillian and puts his hand on her knee. "You see, Jill—you and I, we're not so different. We are both looking for lost love, *mi amor.*"

"I am not your *amor,* Mr. De La Puente."

Viracocha De La Puente empties the rest of the Evian into his mouth and crunches the plastic in his fist. "You are a funny girl." He laughs loudly. "And a Jewish girl," he adds.

Jillian is taken aback.

"The Jews are smart." Viracocha smiles as if he's delivering the highest possible compliment.

"Pardon me?"

"Look at the most powerful people in your country. Your president?" His hands fly up in the air in disbelief. "Well, yes, he is powerful. No one would say he isn't. But who are the ones who truly influence your people? Mr. Bloomberg, Mr. Greenspan, Mr. Spielberg, Mr. Houdini—et cetera, et cetera."

"Harry Houdini?"

"You don't think that Harry Houdini had influence over people?"

"I didn't think Harry Houdini was a Jew."

"Houdini could hold an audience in the palm of his hand." Viracocha seems agitated at Jillian or Harry Houdini or possibly all people in general. "My father greatly admired Houdini and became fascinated with the Jewish people in general."

"We're a fascinating group. In general."

"He always said that the Jews had the real power in this world. Not the *limeños*. We had nothing. We prayed too much and accomplished too little. The Jews had power and money." Viracocha rolls his hands as if performing a small magic trick. "The wherewithal to be resourceful and escape even the most perilous of circumstances. The ability to rise above their lot in life." He smiles. "Like Houdini!"

"Not every Jew is an escape artist, Mr. De La Puente." Jillian pictures the old rabbi from Rodef Shalom unchaining himself heroically from a Chinese water torture chamber. "But I understand the sentiment."

"Of course you do!" He slaps his knees. "And I hear you have been helping Shelly with her skills."

"Her *stealing* skills?" Jillian keeps her eyes on him as she delivers the dirty word.

He smiles. "But, of course." Viracocha locks his eyes on Jillian. "We have been hoping that Shelly can make a place for herself in our family, but, as you know, Shelly needs to make marked improvements in her confidence and technique in order to excel in our organization." He drums his fingers along his knee. "You have already been a very good teacher to your friend, and with a bit more confidence she can be assured a safe place with us."

"I haven't taught her anything. We've just been having a little fun, that's all."

"That's all?" Viracocha laughs. "The two *bandidos*. Butch Cassidy and the Sundance Kid—the two of you. You've seen that movie, yes?"

"Yes. I've seen that movie."

"Mr. Paul Newman. Mr. Robert *Redfert*."

"And I know how it ends, Mr. De La Puente. Not so *remunerative* for Butch or the Kid."

He rolls the Evian cap in his hands, breaking off the thin trail of white plastic on its end. "No cloud of bullets, Jill. That's not what we do." Viracocha aims an imaginary gun at her. "Pow."

She listens, not moving a muscle.

"We must diversify, Jill, if we are to survive. Our East Coast team is quite predictable . . . Limeños, Ecuadorians, a few Mexicans. We can no longer complete our work here without prejudice. Shelly offers us a wonderful addition to our team—an enthusiastic American girl. If she can progress with her skills." Viracocha pulls out a small device from his shirt pocket and puts it on the coffee table between them. "Do you know what this is?"

"That's an FRS radio." Jillian looks at the small radio on the table, remembering what Officer Cannell had to say about them—that the bad guys use them too.

"Fifty-six user-selectable frequencies. Thirty-eight analog and eighty-three digital interference eliminator codes. Three scramble modes. Five-mile range or twenty indoor floors. A high penetration through windows. Discreet, voice-activated microphone and earbud headset." Viracocha is turning the radio in the palm of his hand. "Do you know how to use it, Jill?"

Jillian picks up the device and pushes the buttons. "We Jews can figure out pretty much anything, Mr. De La Puente." She smiles broadly at Viracocha, not sure if he gets the joke.

"That's what I like." He slaps the couch beside him. "The *chootzpah*, that's how you say it, the *chootzpah*?" Viracocha crosses his legs and looks Jillian over. "I like a girl with this *chootzpah.*"

The front door bursts open and Claudia is shaking her hands in the air and shouting in Spanish. Her glossy smile is now constricted and tense. Jillian can make out a few of the words: *baboso, macho, ignorante, nada, nada!*

Behind her a wiry dark-skinned man yells back. Spit is flying from his mouth, his mop of black hair sticks to his forehead, *Ja, ja, ja.*

Shelly enters behind the two, scurrying after them. She has changed into her new oversized dress. "I'm sorry, Poppy. It's not my fault. I told them you were in here."

"Ms. Monteagudo!" Viracocha's voice interrupts the action without being any louder than it was a moment earlier. "Did you not remember that I have company?"

"*Baboso!*" Claudia's mouth forms a tight O. It is a stark contrast to her voluptuous warmth in the hallway. "Ricardo does not agree about diversifying for the Red job. . . ." Claudia's teeth are sharp as she speaks. "I told him he doesn't have a choice, Vira!"

"Ms. Monteagudo, do your ears not work this afternoon? Which part of 'I have company' did you not understand?" Viracocha raises his eyebrows. "I am in town for three hours and already I have to hear the two of you start?"

"Es'cuse me." Claudia bows her head.

Viracocha stands. "Jillian Siegel, may I present our associate, Señor Ricardo." He smiles as he makes the formal introduction. "And you already know Ms. Monteagudo. Shake Miss Siegel's hand, Ricardo."

The dark-skinned man obeys reluctantly. His hand is hot and faintly oily. A tattoo that wraps around his ropy biceps peaks out from a white undershirt; a gold chain dangles from his neck. Ricardo mumbles to himself as the two exit through the French doors, arguing in a whisper.

"I'm sorry, Poppy." Shelly bows her head to Viracocha. He kisses her hair.

"Miss Siegel is going to help you practice your new skills, *mi amor.*" He holds her by the chin.

"That is so cool." Shelly jumps up and down and hugs Jillian tightly. "We're gonna be real partners."

Jillian pries Shelly off her. "I'm sorry, Shelly." She looks back at Viracocha as she speaks. "I'm not going to help you practice anymore." She hands back the FRS radio. "I can't, Shelly. I'm sorry. It was a pleasure meeting you, Mr. De La Puente." The name does not glide off her lips easily.

"Suit yourself. Maybe you have found enough love for now." He smiles. "It was an honor to meet you, Miss Siegel." Viracocha walks back toward the French doors.

"Jillian!" Shelly mouths her discontent to her friend. "C'mon, please. I can't practice all by myself."

Viracocha puts a hand on Shelly's head. "Don't badger your friend, *hija*. It's not attractive." He walks away from them and opens a door to leave. "And Jill," he calls out before he disappears.

"Yes?" Both girls look back.

"If you change your mind about accepting our challenge, please feel free to call us here at the hotel. The room is registered under the name Claudia Monteagudo. We will make it worth your trouble. You can be assured of that."

Viracocha De La Puente shuts the doors behind him.

Jillian walks quickly past Shelly, out of the suite, and toward the elevator. Jillian wants to push the button and leave the Pierre as fast as she can, but Shelly races after her and slides into the elevator.

"C'mon. It's just for fun. Nobody gets hurt. It's a bogus game."

Jillian says nothing for the remainder of the trip downward. The doors open, and Jillian marches off into the lobby. "C'mon, please." Shelly reaches for Jillian's hand and tugs on it. "I *need* to do it. If I don't get this right, I'm out on my ass." Shelly is turning around in circles. "They take care of me, and they don't even have to. Vira, Claudia, and Gordo are the only people who've ever watched out for me, and if they want me to help them out, I will."

Jillian stops at the doorway and turns around to Shelly. "I didn't know everyone was going to know who I was. They obviously did, Shelly. They obviously knew a lot." Shelly bites down on the corner of her finger as Jillian finishes. "And nothing your little band of friends do up there is *just for fun.*" Jillian pulls Shelly's fingers out from her mouth. "Your friend, Vira, Poppy, whoever he is, and Gordito and the rest of the Peruvian cartel up there mean business, okay? That's the real shit. Whatever it is, it's the real shit, and you should kick it. Pull a Buddy, Shell."

Jillian reaches out and pulls on Shelly's dress. "And this thing . . . it's not perfect for you. It doesn't even fit you." Shelly looks down at the loose material and frowns like she never noticed until now. "And he's got a whole box of these stupid dresses."

Shelly looks like she's about to cry, but Jillian can't worry about that now.

"I'm not gonna do this. I don't need to. I don't want to." Jillian pushes the door open and holds it open for a second. "Cutting is something I do for fun. Like a hobby. Like model train building or knitting fucking prescription bottle cozies. It's a thing I do. It's not who I am." She marches out the door. "Find another klepto. This one has more important things to do."

"More important things? Like what?" Shelly yells out to Jillian as she walks away.

Jillian walks off without turning back.

21

AWAY. That's the only place Jillian wants to go.

Away from Shelly and Vira and the Pierre. Away from Loevner's and Bingo and the Bomb and Suki Friedman. This need to escape is a familiar feeling that has led her to many of the darker spots of the world: underneath beds, into the back of closets, the bathrooms of restaurants, into the secret caverns of Loevner's, into bite-sized chunks of Attivan and Zoloft, into all the alone places with no one but herself to face.

She closes her eyes and concentrates on the darkness inside them. She has nowhere to go so she just walks. With no particular destination in mind, she just moves forward. *Go straight, turn here, head across town one block.*

It is not so much of a lonely feeling as it is a meditation. She has not popped a pill for many days, and she has been cleansed of most things: her job, Loevner's, coffee, sugar, soon even Bingo will be gone from her. The raw feelings buzz through her system like caffeine.

Fifth Avenue turns into Forty-second, Forty-second turns into Tenth, Tenth turns into Fourteenth. The homeless men and women limp about, leaving their stringent smell behind them. The working masses click-clack their heels to and from lunches, to and from meetings, talking loudly into cell phones, using words like *caveat* and *end-of-day* and *drop-dead deadline*. Jillian recognizes the words—has used them herself even, but for now they have no meaning; she just gives in to the current of the street.

She walks along Fourteenth. The smell of burnt sugar cashews and cheap incense mixes into a sickly brew. She passes the discount stores, heading east, ignoring her sore insteps and tightening calves. Her head soaks in the heat from the sun, the honking of the taxicabs, the smog in the air. She can almost feel her new highlights on her head like a swarm of flies. She just wants to move forward and backward all day with the flotsam—think nothing, do nothing, feel nothing.

And then there it is.

Straight ahead. Like a billboard at eye level, a neon sign blinking inside the brain, a giant clarinet blown straight into the ear. What she knew was coming eventually.

Adweek.

Hundreds of *Adweeks*, lined up in organized rows in the window of Universal News.

Jillian stands in front of the glass—her eyes frozen straight ahead. Below, above, to the left and the right, surrounding her like a kaleidoscope is the same image repeated and repeated and repeated: Billy Baum and Brandon Pietro, standing side by side, arms crossed—Billy with his cockeyed grin, and Brandon with his unibrow and Oliver Peoples glasses and looking as content as he's ever been in his life.

"BOMB INCORPORATED AWARDED LOEVNER'S. ESTIMATED $180 MILLION ACCOUNT."

And in the corner, reduced to not much bigger than a postage stamp, is the old black-and-white ad featuring Bingo, the diminutive Jillian Siegel, and Briana Terrell in her fluffy pastel gown. The trio, frozen in the same pose they have been in for so many years. Jillian's face is no bigger than a few pixels. Under it, the caption sums up the charge at hand.

"Je t'adore, a tough act to follow.
Will Bomb be able to drop another one?"

Jillian reads on:

NEW YORK–MRVP Partners, Chicago has awarded the Loevner's Department Store account–worth an estimated $180 million–to Bomb Advertising Agency Incorporated, according to executives close to the companies.

The department store giant has not worked with an agency since the iconic campaign that launched the Richard Hauerbach Agency over forty years ago. Loevner's is synonymous with the campaign Hauerbach created and ran for nearly three decades. "Je t'adore Loevner's" featured founder and then-owner Bingo Loevner surrounded by a variety of Hollywood starlets– Briana Terrell, Shirley Mason, and Linda Mirran to name a few. The most provocative ad in the series featured an anonymous little model whose identity remains unknown today. Loevner has been famously tight-lipped about the girl, who is rumored to be now deceased.

"As our customer gets younger, so must our marketing. We need fresh, new thinking to reintroduce Loevner's to the daughters of our original customer," said Craig Allen, chairman and chief executive officer of the department store chain. "No one understands the pulse of our new audience better than Bill."

"We're delighted to be working with an American icon," said Billy Baum, CEO and executive creative director of Bomb Incorporated. "And MRVP was generous enough to align with us on their crowning jewel."

Mr. Allen declined to discuss rumors of an impending management shift, saying only, "Loevner's is a solid company with a strong future. Our relationship with Bomb Advertising is a long-term decision."

Jillian's head is all fuzzy again. Her stomach churns up inside and the smells of urine and decaying New York garbage float around her.

She remembers Craig Allen, the man with two first names, on the board of directors from years ago. She remembers when he came to Bingo's apartment one night in a big cashmere coat while she and Belle watched *An Affair to Remember* in the TV room. "That's the Republican from Chicago, isn't it, Belle?"

"Hush your face, child. They in your uncle's sitting room right next door."

She preferred Loevner's before Craig Allen came around. When she was just a little girl, it still felt as if it was hers. She remembers being so tiny she barely reached the door handles—but she can recall the feeling, even then, that they were all there for her to reach. And she's been told that she even learned to walk down the halls of the store, using giant empty water bottles tipped on their side to help her toddle along. Loevner's at that time was a fraction of the size, and Bingo's office was barely larger than a closet, but they had as much fun as ever—eating picnics on cashmere blankets on the floor or staying late to turn out the lights and say good night to the mannequins one by one.

But then Bingo got a visit from the man with two first names and a few others in suits and raincoats. After that, Bingo told Jillian he still owned the store but some other people would now have their say. And in return, Loevner's could get much bigger—open stores in faraway places like California and Japan, buy the building next door and remodel, support designers they couldn't before. Everyone was excited—except Jillian, who liked everything just the way it was.

And that's when Craig Allen started showing up now and again. She knew he came whenever there was real trouble—his face all squished up, his bald spot spreading over more and more of his head.

He came after an entire shipment of furs was ruined by the protestors working on the inside. He came when the new store manager was in the news for tax fraud. He came during troubles in the market or fluctuations in the price of oil. And he came that night in December, three weeks after Alain died, three weeks since Bingo had set foot in the store, to discuss personal matters.

Jillian assumed he was there, like all of Bingo's other friends, to wish him happy holidays, to offer condolences, to talk about how special Alain had been. She thought he possibly was there to encourage Bingo to get back to work, get his mind off things, get on with his life—the kinds of things Lois said.

But she remembers Craig Allen leaving without saying good-bye to anybody. She remembers he blew his nose into a hanky on his way out. She remembers eating fried chicken cutlets and corn bread and drinking strawberry milk on TV trays with Belle. She remembers Belle crying during *An Affair to Remember* even when it wasn't a sad part. She remembers that Lois was spending the winter in West Palm and hadn't been home in months and that she couldn't stop thinking about Alain and where people went when they died and that nobody answered her questions about whether Jews believed in heaven. She remembers Bingo not coming in to say good night to her after the man with two first names left.

"You get to bed now, girl. It's late."

"I want to wait for Bingo to tuck me in. He always tucks me in."

"He took his pill, honeydew. He already asleep. You just gonna have to be satisfied with my tuckin' in tonight."

Jillian sits on the stoop beside Pino Magazine and Smoke Shoppe, reaches into her pocketbook, and fishes out her phone. She pushes the numbers on the pad and watches as the animated waves move across the LED screen—sending her call out into the atmosphere. Jillian knows there is no one on the other line to answer, but she still craves his voice.

"Hi," his machine answers. "This is Alex." His name is so perfect, she thinks, short and direct with a sweet syllable at the beginning and a sexy one finishing it off. She wonders if he misses her too. "I'm not in right now, so leave me a message or try me on my cell."

"Hi." Jillian tries to sound happy and positive. "It's me, Jill." She holds the phone in both hands, cradling it away from the sounds of the people on the street. She can feel the electrical warmth of it against her cheek. "I didn't think you'd be home. I just wanted to, I just really wanted, I guess I don't know what I wanted." She feels instantly stupid to be leaving a message with no point whatsoever. "So I guess that's it. Um, bye." Jillian shuts the phone. How could she be so dumb? Maybe if she waited another day or two he would have called her first. But now she ruined everything. He may never call her back.

Jillian leans her head down on her knees. She wonders if people are looking at her, thinking they should throw a quarter in her cup or give her half a sandwich. The bottle of Ativan floats to the top of her pocketbook. Jillian opens it and breaks a pill into four even crumbs. She looks at the pieces in her palm and pushes them around. She contemplates taking one but instead just waits till they all melt there in her hand, mixing the pieces into a chalky paste and wiping away the white puddle.

She opens the phone again to call Lois. Even an annoying conversation with her mother would be welcome at the moment. Her finger rests in midair above the keypad, and it occurs to Jillian that she has absolutely no idea what number to call. She actually *wants* to have an annoying phone call with her mother, but she doesn't even know in what country to start looking.

Billy Baum and Brandon Pietro's photo hangs above and beside her, framing her face with their devilish grins.

She wonders why Brandon doesn't pluck his unibrow. Why would anyone pose for the cover of *Adweek* with an unplucked unibrow? One would think he could just pluck ten, maybe twenty hairs and the whole thing wouldn't be so annoying to look at. She has stood in front of Brandon Pietro many times, nearly cross-eyed, holding her hands behind her back to avoid lunging at his forehead and plucking the pointy hairs herself.

But then again, Brandon Pietro has Loevner's, and she doesn't. She has nothing: nowhere to go, no one to call, nothing to do. Her eyebrows are plucked impeccably, a few each morning, her chin, her armpits, her bikini line, her legs, even her toes have all been cured of the hairs that once infested them. And what has it gotten her?

"Thank you for calling. Please dial your password and press pound." Jillian dials her own mailbox. She punches in her code, already sure that there is nothing on the other end. *"You have one new message. To hear your messages, press one. . . ."*

Jillian pushes the button and braces herself to hear another message from Carol about health benefits or from Lois about Istanbul or Palm Beach or wherever.

"Hello, Jill. This is Claudia Monteagudo." It seems odd to hear her voice over her machine. Her accent is especially thick filtered through the various machines.

"I am hating to call you at home, Jill, but I want to extend a personal invitation from myself to continue with Shelly's education. No one has made Shelly to feel more confident about herself than you." She is using her more voluptuous voice. It is rich like truffles. *"I know Shelly would never ask for you herself. She knows that this would be rude and inconsiderate. Therefore I am asking you. I should add that Mr. De La Puente was quite impressed with you today and I know that he would be honored if you would accompany us. I am not expecting you to say yes, but I do know that we all would be exciting if you did. We will look for you at the suite at ten sharp tomorrow morning. If you cannot make it, we will certainly understand. But if you can make it, we will do everything in our power to look out for your well-bean."*

22

"YOU put the little *hear* bud in your *hear, mamá.*" Claudia holds the tiny device up to Shelly's ear. "Stand still, Shelly!" She sounds frustrated with her student. "*Mamá!*" Jillian walks in just as Claudia fits Shelly with the earbud.

"You came!" Shelly gallops over to her friend. "I told Claudia you would."

"Pfft!" Claudia is left holding Shelly's earpiece in her hand.

"I was in a walkie-talkie kind of mood today." Jillian puts down her pocketbook. As ridiculous as it is to admit, Jillian feels good being back in the sumptuously illicit suite and away from the real world and the feelings it conjures up.

"We're so exciting to see you, Jill." Claudia warms at the sight of Jillian and kisses her warmly on both cheeks, leaving the sticky residue of her lip gloss on both sides. "And as I said in my message, we will watch out for your well-*bean.*" She gets as close as possible. "I promise," she whispers in her ear. "I come out with you personally."

"Che-eck, che-eck." Shelly takes the earbud from Claudia and pushes it properly in place as she speaks. "This is so rad, you gotta try it."

"Finally, *mamá!*"

Claudia pulls out another radio from her pocket and hands it to Jillian. "And then this little part goes here." She gently pushes the bud into Jillian's ear. Claudia is careful to be precise.

"Can you hear me?" Shelly's voice comes over clearly into Jillian's ear. "How 'bout now?" She walks into the closet and shuts the door. "How 'bout now." She walks out of the closet and into the bathroom and closes the door again. "How 'bout now?"

"I hear you, Shelly!"

"You remember to keep the channel on seven and the subchannel on fourteen." Claudia turns the two dials at the bottom of the radio. "Are you paying attention, Shelly?"

"Check!"

"You always keep to this station unless we tell you otherwise, Jillian." She looks sternly into Jillian's eyes for recognition.

Claudia puts her palm over Jillian's hand. "My team"—Claudia raises her eyebrows—"always listens to me and always keeps to this station. I know how to keep the team safe." She looks again. "Trust. *Sí?*"

"*Sí.*" Jillian nods. Jillian understands that this pronouncement should be taken seriously. "*Sí.*"

"Is Gordo coming?" Shelly asks hopefully.

"No, *mamá*. Not today." Claudia puts her own earbud in and smiles one of her gracious smiles. "We ready to go?" Shelly looks disappointed and momentarily lost.

"As ready as we'll ever be." Jillian and Shelly grab their coats and head out the door.

"I have another little treat for you, honeydew."

Jillian remembers the excitement and anticipation of finding Bingo's hidden surprises—like a treasure hunt—a bit of danger and a big reward in the end.

"What is it?"

"I'll never tell."

Jillian walked behind her uncle and wrapped her arms around him. By this time, she was as tall as he was—her legs, long and skinny, and her torso, growing like a weed, and *Take the Treat*, a weekly expectation for the developing young woman.

"I just love you to pieces, you know that, right?" She kissed him on his cheek, leaving a trace of Watermelon Lip Smackers near his ear.

"Ah yes, but can you acquire the goodies?"

"What goodies?" Jillian faked ignorance and kissed him on the other cheek. One hand made its way into his pocket at the same time the kiss was planted. By this time, she was as adept as she was beguiling—whether sneaking a hand into his pocket or the bottom drawer of his desk or any one of her uncle's top-secret hiding places.

"How coy can one be?"

"This coy, perhaps?" Jillian dangled her prize in front of his face—effortlessly removed from his pocket, not even a molecule disturbed. "Hermès!" Jillian held out the scarf in a big square in front of both their faces. "A surprise in every 'poche'!"

"Puts a smile on every 'bouche.' Happy Friday, honeydew."

"Can you hear me now?" This is the only sentence Shelly has managed to get out since donning the device in Barneys. Shelly is wandering through the pricey juniors department on the mezzanine floor.

"Roger that." Jillian has adopted a *Hawaii Five-O* approach to speaking on the radios.

The challenge feels more like fun than anything else—like a good game of hide-and-seek at Loevner's when she was little.

"Can you hear me now?" Shelly is standing in the corner with her face pressed against the wall talking as softly as she can muster.

"Ten-Four."

"I will meet you outside after you're practicing." Claudia is keeping a lookout on the ground floor, and her voice comes over loud and clear. From the sound of it, she could be two inches away. "Keep your concentration, *mamá*."

"Roger that."

Jillian meanders through the crowded store. Nothing at Barneys is under a hundred dollars, except maybe socks. Midmorning on a weekday, Barneys is filled with women who shop instead of work. Jillian can spot them all in an instant: the St. Bart's tans; the freshly painted highlights and uptown manicures; the Tod's driving shoes, made for driving (or being driven) not walking.

"Only chauffeured women can wear shoes with no thickness in Manhattan," Bingo used to say to Jillian in the gown department of Loevner's. "The thinner the soles, the bigger the ball gown you show them."

"Will you lead us in the mantra today?" Jillian says into the air as she circles a rack of reconstructed T's. She's having fun, and her body shivers with adrenaline.

"*It is mine*," Shelly says.

"*It is mine. It is mine. It is mine*," both girls say in unison over the FRS radio into the airwaves. They are each careful not to move their mouths too much, but still the words are clearly audible.

Jillian mentally adds up how much money she's spent at Barneys. Not a lot, but enough, enough for a lesson in walkie-talkies. "Where are you exactly?" Jillian runs her fingers down the faux ripped collar of a shirt with a bunch of letters on it. The shirt is lightly stretchy and tough. A good combination.

"Bling counter." Shelly's words sound crystal clear. Jillian even hears the jingling of precious metal.

"Focus, Shelly. Don't cut any jewelry, okay? You'll be up in County in no time." Shelly could be an excellent thief if she didn't get distracted so quickly. She sensed Claudia's frustration earlier and assumes it wasn't the first time.

"I'm doing *surveillance*, okay?"

"You see anything?"

"Yeah and I'm spying one up right now as we speak."

"A Faux Po?"

"Live and in person. He's not even up my grill—must be the new hair. He's following some chick with a Fendi bag." Jillian can hear Shelly's breath as she speaks. "I'm right behind him now. I'm doing that move you showed me, y'know, holding stuff up like I think it's nice and then putting it back like I think it's not so nice after all."

"Don't do anything stupid with the guy right there, 'kay?" Jillian stands there quietly, hoping Shelly doesn't mess things up. "Why don't you come up to the second floor? There's some cool things up here. Nothing's dooked."

"No dookies hanging off anything?" Shelly is walking. Jillian can hear her breath quicken.

"Not a dookie in sight." Jillian runs her hand along the inside seam of a jacket, confirming that there are no security tags on anything except possibly leather.

"This is a crazy shirt. It's all torn up." Shelly is out of breath. Jillian hears the light wind rush in and out against her ear.

"Oh yeah, I saw that shirt. Reconstructivist stuff is very big at the moment. I read it on *Daily Candy*. I liked it." Jillian opens a scarf and peers over it. "I see you." Jillian wiggles her fingers over it. Considering the alternatives, Jillian thinks, this is a pretty fun way to spend the morning.

"Any Faux Po around?" Shelly wiggles her fingers back at Jillian from across the room.

"It's Costa Mesa, sista. Just you, me, and hundreds of people with nothing better to do in the middle of the day."

"No eyeballs either?"

Jillian looks up and around for a sign of the black security camera domes. "Not that I can see." Both girls are talking in a whisper. Jillian watches as Shelly balls up the deconstructed shirt in her hand and tucks it into her bag.

"For you!"

"A present? For me!" Jillian eyeballs the entire circumference of the room—no one is even paying attention to them. "You shouldn't have!"

Shelly's smile is visible from a few racks away. "I did my challenge! I'm, like, so psyched." She seems surprised.

"Congratulations." Jillian wanders into the next room, drawn in by the mass of muted colors and fabrics.

"Plus," Shelly adds, "it was a present. Kinda like a good deed."

"Check this room out." Jillian looks out into the colorful alcove of clothes and accessories.

"You wanna pull a Buddy?" Shelly is twenty feet behind Jillian. She follows Jillian into the next room—a more sophisticated, more expensive version of the last one.

"Not yet." Jillian is driven to see more of what the store has to offer. Maybe she could take advantage of the radios as well and get something really great. "Check this out!" Jillian holds up a sheer Miu Miu blouse with sequins on it as if she's looking at it; instead, she shows it to Shelly, who is now only a few feet down the rack. "It's nice, right? Five hundred and sixteen."

"Five hundred dollars is serious cash. For that thing?"

"What's it look like behind me?" Jillian glides the shirt off the hanger and folds it into a palm-sized square.

"There's some girls behind you, but they're not even looking this way. I think it's crickets." Shelly holds up a suit just to look occupied. Jillian pushes the sheer shirt into her sleeve and then releases it into the main compartment of her handbag.

"Can we just leave now? We did our challenge." Shelly looks around. She sounds nervous and ansty.

"Let's check it out upstairs." Jillian is determined now. She walks confidently out of the room and up the wide staircase to another winding staircase and up to the next floor.

The floor greets them with a start. Impossibly empty and graphic—the entire floor has fewer than a hundred pieces on it. The first sight is an intimidating, nearly incomprehensible item of conceptual clothing hanging from a thick maple hanger. Above it, a small crystal disco balls turn in the air.

"Is this leather?" Shelly moves deep into the floor's elegant atmosphere. Her new look—sleek, dark hair and simple, form-fitting outfits—fits right in at Barneys.

"I guess." Jillian arrives at the piece. The impossibly thin material has been cut like a beehive into a thousand tiny slivers of fabric hung together. Jillian opens up the fabric and peers through the thousand holes. "It's three thousand dollars!" Jillian struggles to keep her voice low, despite the fact that the number alone gets her heart beating wildly.

Shelly jumps in quickly over the radio. "Incoming."

"Can I help you?" A chilly, raven-haired saleswoman smiles at Jillian. She is wearing a long black skirt and, like Suki and Gwyneth, *the* shirt of the season, apparently.

The Chloé, Jillian says to herself. "Oh, hi." Jillian puts her hand on the woman's arm. The fine silk is warm to the touch. "How *are* you? It's me. Remember?"

"Oh, hi, hey, I didn't recognize you." The saleswoman immediately softens. "You look fabulous." It is clear she has no idea who Jillian is—but neither of them let on.

"Thanks so much. You look fabulous too. Are you still doing Pilates?" Jillian takes a guess.

"I am! Can you tell?" The saleswoman puts her hands on her waist and rocks back and forth. Her neat flap of glossy black hair shines under the lights.

"I'm so sorry, I've forgotten your name." Jillian looks at the woman with an appropriate mix of concern and regret.

"Vampira." Shelly interrupts the conversation through Jillian's ear bud. "Queen of the dead."

"Bettina," the woman says.

"Bettina! That's right." Jillian pushes the ear bud deeper into her ear and tries not to crack a smile, or worse—a snort.

"Bettina sleeps in a coffin," Shelly adds. It is hard to concentrate with Shelly's audible yet invisible color commentary.

"Can I show you anything today? We have some great new pieces in."

"I'm just looking around right now, Bettina," Jillian purrs out the casual sentence. "Everything looks just fabulous on the floor." The in-store lingo falls so easily off her tongue. "The season looks fabulous."

"Well, darling, you let me know if you need anything." Bettina smiles and touches Jillian's shoulder before she walks off.

"What was that?" Shelly is leafing through sweaters in the back.

"*That*, I'll have you know, was the new Chloé shirt. It's the must-have shirt for the season."

"Well then, you must have it."

"I can't exactly take it off Bettina's back, Shelly. There's a wait list for that shirt."

"Well, I'm looking at it right here on the hanger."

"The *Chloé*! It's fifteen hundred bucks."

"And it's right here where I'm standing. A buttload a benjis for a shirt, man." Shelly walks back toward the stairs to head up to five.

"You're not kidding me, right? The Chloé's right there?"

"Shit." Shelly drops to the floor on her hands and knees. "The earbud thingy popped out."

Jillian keeps her cool as she watches Shelly crawl around—her hands slapping at the floor. Bettina rushes to Shelly's side across the room, as does another customer coming up the stairs. "I lost my contact lens," Shelly says convincingly, and Bettina drops as well. "I'm like totally bumming." Jillian watches as both women crawl around on their hands and knees. "Was it a colored contact lens? You can find those more easily." The customer's voice is clear over the radio.

Jillian slides her body to the spot where Shelly was. She spots the billowy silk blouse from a few feet away. She tries to work the math; she's definitely not spent fifteen hundred at Barney's. Maybe hundreds—maybe five, maybe six, but definitely not fifteen. Not enough to even it all out.

But it's right there and it seems so simple and the moment's fleeting and it's the Chloé peasant and . . . *that counts for something, right?*

"I think I found it!" Shelly pushes the earpiece back in her ear—while still holding her other hand out in a pantomime of holding a contact lens. Jillian is dually impressed at Shelly's coordinated efforts.

"It's practically invisible," Bettina says.

Jillian watches from afar as the saleswoman's head dips in the direction of Shelly's hand.

"They're the new kind. You almost can't even see them."
Shelly holds up her finger. "They're the really expensive ones."

While the small audience watches Shelly pretend to put the invisible contact lens in her eye, Jillian coaxes the Chloé blouse off the hanger and toward her. She allows it to fold into a small package that falls easily into her jacket pocket. Her heart is racing as she surveys the room. This is definitely not cool, but it feels magnificent.

Everyone is watching Shelly and the invisible contact. It couldn't have worked out better. While Shelly may not be the world's best thief, at the moment, she's certainly the world's best distraction.

And now, believe it or not, Jillian is the owner of the most fabulous piece of the season. Gwyneth Paltrow has this shirt. And so does Suki Friedman. And now—Jillian Siegel.

"I got the Chloé, Shelly! Stylishly retro but hopelessly modern." Jillian follows Shelly up to five.

"Say what?" There is the audible crunch of fabric on Shelly's end.

"Never mind. We gotta pull a Buddy, Shelly." Jillian's adrenaline is now rushing into her veins. Her hands are quivering; her palms, dripping sweat. "Now! Okay?"

"Wait till you see these groovy hats." Shelly is making crunching sounds into the microphone. "This looks like a birdcage—for your head! Weirdo."

"C'mon. Let's go. I just cut a really huge thing." Jillian sees Shelly across the store and up the staircase. Below her on three, she can see Claudia traipsing the floor. She has no idea if she's still listening or not.

"You gotta try one of these things on."

Jillian's palms are sweaty. She pushes the shirt down beneath her elbow and keeps a calm face as she nods to Bettina. She fights the urge to run out on Shelly with the Chloé and makes her way up to the final floor of the store.

The top floor is like a gallery. Single gowns hang on the wall—maybe only seven or eight on the whole floor. The lighting is lower than the rest of the store, and there's a grand double door at either end of the space. It reminds Jillian of a room that Alain might have created—spare and subtle to let the magic of the individual pieces take over—as if each gown was standing in the wings, ready to make an entrance onto the stage. The only thing not hanging on the walls in the entire room is the fanciful hat stand in the middle of the floor. The space is perfectly choreographed—just few people drifting in and out like dancers on a stage.

Jillian walks over and smiles politely at Shelly. They pretend not to know each other as they look at the hats. Shelly picks up one of the strange little accessories and puts it on her head. It looks like a cockeyed tower of woven fabric. Jillian picks one up that has an aviary quality. She put it on her head as well. It looks like birds are swirling around her like a halo.

Shelly smiles, hat still on her head, and begins to walk away from the display.

"Where are you going?" Jillian whispers as Shelly heads down the stairs.

"I'm working on my concentration." Shelly keeps walking down another flight. Jillian chases after her with a quick walk. "Claudia says I should work on my concentration."

"Stop, Shelly. What are you doing?"

"I'm going over the fence."

"With the leaning tower of Pisa on your head?"

"Yep. With the pizza on my head. I'm setting the hat free. *It is mine.* Right? Isn't that the mantra?" Shelly walks down past the mezzanine.

"It's not yours, Shelly. You can't just walk over the fence with the Pisa right on your head. Stuff it in your purse or something or kick it."

"Do you see any Faux Po?" Shelly is walking forward with no hesitation.

"I don't think so." Jillian quickly follows her downstairs, whispering nervously into the unseen microphone, overwhelmed with the thought of the things in her bag and the hat on her head. "Shit, Shelly." Jillian fights to keep her own pace controlled and innocent.

"Costa Mesa?"

"I don't know. I don't know. Slow down." Jillian's eyes dart around the room for signs of security.

"I'm outtie-5000! See ya."

Jillian watches Shelly at the front door as she turns back and waves. "What are you waiting for?" Shelly disappears out the front door of Barneys.

For a moment Jillian feels completely alone—abandoned. She looks around for Claudia, her chest compressing the air out from her lungs.

But then Shelly's voice comes through again as if she were standing right there beside her. "C'mon, Jillian. I'm hangin here on the corner. You can make it. I'm here for you, dude."

Jillian stands up straight and marches forward. She fights to keep her body calm (cool slouch, relaxed shoulders, soft face). She can't even remember all that is stuffed in her purse and pocket. "*It is mine. It is mine. It is mine,*" she whispers as she adjusts the fanciful hat on her head and swaggers forward in long strides, the doorway within her sight.

She walks the long gauntlet ahead, allows the sweat to accumulate on the tip of her nose. She visualizes the outside. She visualizes Gwyneth Paltrow looking calm and cool in the Chloé. She visualizes Shelly, Claudia, Gordo, and Vira waiting for her in the *goyisha-chichi* lobby of the Pierre.

"Have a nice day, miss." The doorman smiles and nods to her, never even glancing at her hat or her bulging purse. "Come back and see us soon."

23

"OH MY GOD, oh my God, oh my God, oh my God!"
Jillian wiggles her way down the street, excited and walking as
fast as she can. "Oh my God, oh my God." She talks into the invisible microphone.

"Can you fucking believe it?" Shelly is walking blocks ahead of
her, her breath as loud as her voice.

"We got the Chloé!" Jillian does a jumping jack on the middle
of the sidewalk going up Fifth. The people on the sidewalk slip
onto the street to avoid her. She couldn't care less.

"And the torn-up T!"

"And the see-through thing! And the hats!"

"And the disco ball!"

"The disco ball?"

"Yeah. The disco ball hanging in front of that mannequin. I've
been looking for something to reflect light for a while."

"Shelly, you can buy those for like a dollar at Canal Plastics."

"Yell, well. I got it for nothing! Fuckin'-A-noodle."

"Congratulations." Jillian does nothing more to spoil the moment for Shelly. "And thanks for the shirt." She watches Shelly
disappear down the street ahead of her.

"The cut-up thing's pretty cool."

"I mean the Chloé."

"But I didn't cut it."

"Yeah, but I couldn't have done it without you."

"Your own personal mule at your service."

"My mule?" Jillian can hear the street noise mixed in with Shelly's voice.

"A mule is basically a distraction, dude. Usually they do it by cutting something and getting busted by the Faux Po. That way the real team can go about their business. I just did it with the contact lens thing."

"Well, you're a good mule then."

"A mule's like the lowest form of life on the team." Shelly sounds instantly disappointed.

"Well, you aren't the lowest life-form on our team. You were great." Jillian says whatever she can think of to make Shelly feel better. "Vira would have been really impressed." Jillian is bounding down the street, balancing the elaborate hat on her head. "And, *and*, we walked out of Barneys with, like, *birdcages* on our heads. The security guard even held the door open for me!" Jillian is skipping down the street by herself. Shelly is nearly out of sight. These are not small, contained steps, but large obvious skips and leaps. It has been a perfect morning, and her whole body is excited. "Shell, *you* are a crazy motherfucka!"

"No, *you* are a crazy motherfucka!"

"No, *you* are a crazy motherfucka!"

Jillian and Shelly repeat the phrase again and again into each other's ears. Jillian gallops down the street to the happy music of the words, alternating karate punches and kicks. She doesn't care that people are staring, she doesn't even think about it. It's all ecstatically fun. "Crazy motherfucka! Crazy motherfucka!"

"Hey. Whoa there." Jillian nearly kicks Brandon Pietro in the groin. "Jill? Jill?"

"Oopsie, sorry. Hey, oops, Brandon. Sorry." Jillian organizes her body back into an upright position.

"What?" Shelly's voice buzzes into Jillian's ear.

"Nothing," Jillian says aloud.

"What?" Brandon looks confused.

"Nothing. I was just rehearsing for this thing I'm doing. A speech thing." Jillian tries to cover up her tracks. "For the Ad Club." She kicks her foot up in the air. "With movements. Aerobic stuff." She smiles, not caring how stupid she sounds. Jillian does a little jumping jack and smiles at her old coworker.

"Hello?" Shelly keeps calling her. "Are you still there? Yo? You switch channels?" Jillian wonders how she can get the earbud and Shelly's voice out of her ear without looking any more strange than she already looks.

"You just left Bomb without saying good-bye to anyone." Brandon smiles, his unibrow lifting and lowering with his words. "We didn't even get to grab a good-bye brewsky at McSorley's."

"Yeah, well. I did. That's what I did. What can I say?" Jillian pushes the bud against her ear with her knuckle.

"Jillian Laurel Siegel. Jillian Laurel Siegel. Come in." Shelly repeats the phrase over and over. "Hello? Hello?"

"Billy said you resigned, but he always says that shit. Billy is such a dickwad sometimes. So what's the big scoop, Ms. Siegel?" Brandon holds his hand out to her face like a microphone. "What dark sinister plans lurk in the shadows for Jill Siegel?"

"Who's that?" Shelly's voice is nasal and sharp in her ear.

"Nobody. Shut up," Jillian whispers out. Brandon looks at her oddly. "No sinister plans, Brandon. I just left. Let's just say that's the big scoop. I was there one day and the next day I wasn't. I'm like advertising herpes. Apply a little salve and I disappear pretty quick."

"Is that on the record, Ms. Siegel?" Brandon's thumb gets close enough to Jillian's mouth for her to consider biting it. Instead she pushes his microphone hand away from her face.

"Not in the mood today, Brandon."

"Okay. Coolio. The big burnout. Happens to the best of us, right?" Brandon bobs his head up and down, waiting for Jillian to say something. "Hey, groovy hat."

"Thanks." Jillian puts her hand on her head and straightens the birdcage out.

"Sort of Fellini meets Tweety Bird."

Jillian holds herself back from lunging at his eyebrow hairs. One in particular is notably annoying—gray on the tip and poking straight out from between his eyes.

"I thought you were gonna stay and work on the Loevner's pitch. We won it, y'know."

"Testing, testing. Where are you? Who's that dude talking?" Shelly's questions fire into Jillian's ear. She twitches and holds her shoulder up in an attempt to quiet them.

"Are you okay, Jill?" Brandon looks at her oddly.

"I'm fine." Jillian pretends to cough, and rips the earbud out of her ear in one inelegant sweep then pushes it into her pocket. "Yeah, I know you won Loevner's. The world knows you won Loevner's. I saw the *Adweek*. Nice photo."

"You think? I wasn't sure whether to wear the specs." Brandon pulls his Oliver Peoples off his face and puts them on again. "But Levinson told me that glasses add a thousand bucks to your day rate. So I left them on."

"Uh-huh." Jillian looks down the street for any sign of Claudia or Shelly.

"I was gonna split, you know, had it up to here with Billy and his shit, but then, you know, I figured Loevner's would be pretty cool. Plus Billy coughed up some more coin, so I stayed. Good thing, right?" Brandon bobs up and down as he speaks.

"Yeah. Uh-huh." Jillian looks up the street. She wishes she could spot them somewhere.

Brandon punches Jillian's shoulder. "And they bought my campaign! Can you believe that shit?" He pushes his frames against his nose. "I mean we studied Hauerbach at Art Center, man, y'know? Righteous shit." Brandon's bobbing and smiling, bobbing and smiling. Only the calming thought of the Chloé in her pocket keeps Jillian from throttling him.

"Yeah. Righteous." She smiles.

"I did a referential thing," he continues, "a sort of revamp of the whole Hauerbach, midcentury shit. We took that old ad with that weird little girl in it, and, y'know, made it fresh. Used real models who weren't so old news. Pretty happenin'."

Jillian feels her stomach squeeze into her throat. She hears nothing of what he's saying.

"Jillian Laurel Siegel, please come in." Shelly's questions buzz out of Jillian's pocket.

"What's that noise?" Brandon looks strangely at Jillian's pocket.

"It's nothing, Brandon. I gotta run." Jillian looks up and down the street again. "I was in the middle of stealing some shit and now I need to rendezvous with the getaway team." Jillian offers Brandon a small salute, "*Hasta luego*, dude!" She pushes hard into the passing crowd to find Shelly or Claudia.

"Oh, yeah. Hey, cool man. That's cool. Good talking to ya." Brandon yells down the street at her. "Catch you on the flip-flop."

Jillian runs and runs down the street toward anywhere. The pounding of her boots on the cement make her knee sockets grind together. "Fuck Brandon Pietro. Fuck Billy Baum." She talks to herself as she moves forward until she can't go anymore.

Jilly, Jilly, Jilly. Jillian looks up at the buildings—each one covered in Brandon Pietro's revamped Loevner's ads. The rows of windows seem to outline the giant Didot letters. The bricks and archways of these once-solid structures explode outward like loose black pixels to create shades of darks and lights across the landscape. Even the sky itself billows and sways with the delusion.

Je t'adore. Je t'adore.

She shuts one eye to see if she can shake the mirage from her head, but it doesn't move; the skyline is completely gone, leaving the dramatic imagery in its place. The doe-eyed girl on the white piano stares down at her from all sides. But it is not the girl she remembers—it is some other girl and some other uncle and some other movie star. The originals have vanished, melted away. They no longer exist.

Jillian's breath feels cold and sharp as it surges in and out of her lungs. She is not sure which girl she is—old or young, rejected or adored, the one up there or the one down here.

Her cell phone rings, and she answers it automatically in the hopes it might be Alex. She needs his voice right now; she can taste his words in her mouth. He would know who she is, he would tell her.

"Allie?" The word barely makes it off her lips.

"Oh, thank God, sweetheart. How was Bing? Belle said you were barely there, darling."

Jillian shuts the phone at once against her chest. She lets out a wail that comes from the sidewalk and shivers its way up to her lungs. Her muscles are so tight she instantly feels a burning cramp in her neck and calf. With one ungainly thrust she catapults the phone toward the ground in front of her. She watches as it bursts apart in flying black shreds—the batteries, the mouthpiece, the back panel. It sits there splayed out, less satisfying than one might think, all dead and exposed. She crouches down to the ground and picks up the tiny shards, wondering what she's done. Not just about the phone, but about everything—her life, splattered too into ugly, unidentifiable pieces.

The pedestrians walk by as they do in Manhattan, neither stopping nor noticing anything out of the ordinary about a girl crouched and crying on the street in front of her broken mess.

"*Mamá?*" Claudia puts a hand on Jillian's shoulder. "Are you okay? What happened to you?" Claudia pulls Jillian up off the street.

Jillian looks at her with swollen red eyes. "I don't know." She doesn't trust the woman, but at the moment Claudia is all she has. Jillian starts crying into Claudia's shoulder. "I don't know what happened to me."

"We don't know where you were, Jill." Claudia wraps an arm around her and pats her on the back. "Is okay. Is okay, *mamá*." Claudia strokes her hair with her fingernails. Jillian can smell her Cristalle—sharp and familiar.

"Where's Shelly?"

"She okay. You no need to worry about Shelly. She okay."

"I need to get outta here." Jillian looks up from Claudia's shoulder out at the people and the stores and the traffic. "Can you get me outta here?"

"Whatever you want. Claudia take care of you." She smiles.

24

THE MUSIC is peacefully benign, and the heated table, comforting. Jillian is glad to be in the dark treatment room of Dominique's Salon on the lower level of the Pierre. It is, like the rest of the hotel, an elegantly calmative environment. There is actually no place on earth she'd rather be at this moment—it is a seductive escape into the heavenly underground.

She is alone except for the quiet masseuse and Claudia's voice over the FRS radio earbud. Claudia is in the next room getting one of her weekly facials. The spa services are courtesy of Claudia, which means they are courtesy of Vira, which in turn means, she imagines, they are courtesy of Barneys or Bergdorf's or Harvey Nichols or Takashimaya or David Jones or Louis Boston or any one of a number of other department stores around the world that Vira's teams have probably hit over the years or even months.

"Do you have family?" Claudia's voice has relaxed into her low chocolaty hum. It too is lusciously calming.

"I do. Uptown. But I guess they're sort of dwindling away." Jillian speaks to Claudia softly into the voice-activated microphone

as the masseuse runs her oiled hands up and down her back. She
clutches the device next to her on the table. She can feel the buzz
of it in her fingertips. "What about you?"

"I have not seen my mother for many years. She is still in
Peru, and I cannot go back to there. And my sister, she is dead.
My older brother died when we were very young. I only have one
brother left, and he is a troublemaker. He is alive, but his heart
died long ago." The words spread and fold as the facialist kneads
Claudia's skin.

"I'm so sorry." The room smells vaguely of lavender, clean
sheets, and cider vinegar.

"Is okay. It was a long time from now. Is nothing to me." Claudia's voice sounds softer without her face attached to it. Jillian
tries to picture Claudia as a girl playing with her sister or her
older brother, soccer maybe, barefoot on the streets of Peru.

"Claudia," Jillian takes a risk and asks a personal question of
the woman she barely knows and doesn't trust, "why do you
think . . . you know, you do what you do? At the stores and everything." Jillian holds the radio tight to her cheek.

"People take from me and I take from them. It is how the
world works, Jill." Even though Claudia is in the next room, she
sounds like she's inches away. "What about you?"

Jillian breathes out into the mouthpiece. "Vira said I have a
hole in my heart." She feels the blood inside her muscles being
kneaded toward her neck and face. The masseuse goes about her
work, not paying attention to Jillian's soft mutterings. "That I
don't have enough love."

"Don't listen to him, Jill. He's just an old man who thinks he
knows everything."

"I've been thinking about what he said." Jillian breathes deeply
as the masseuse works out a tight knot under her ribs. "I think
there's some truth to it. I mean, I know there's some truth to it."
She talks to herself as much as to anyone on the other end of the
radio. "I don't really have anything in my life that makes me feel
better than this. Y'know, what Shelly and I do. Is that weird? I

mean, it's a really bad thing and I know it's wrong, but it makes me feel so excited and hopeful. Like everything else in the world just falls away."

The masseuse tucks the sheet into the top of Jillian's underwear. She feels the warmth of the heated table beneath her and the silky feeling of the clean sheet on her back. "Then I feel relieved when it's over." Jillian talks into the air, forgetting that it's Claudia, forgetting that she's talking at all. "Then I'm just happy I have all this nice new stuff. Sometimes I come home and I put everything out on the bed and I look at it and for a moment I feel truly happy. Then I want to go back out right then and do it all again. Like fill up the hole again."

"To me is just what I was trained to do. Is all I know. Is all I know, Jill."

Jillian absorbs the words. "I mean this morning, at Barneys, walking around, getting that shirt, walking out of the store with those hats on our heads"—she looks up at the intricate stenciling on the walls—"that was like the best moment of my life." She lets the tension out with the words. "Am I stupid?"

"You are not stupid, Jill. Far from it. You can outsmart the system. You can outsmart *any* system. This is not a stupid woman who does this."

"And I think I'm really good at it."

"But you could even be better, *mamá*. Beyond your imaginations."

"By working for you and Vira?" Jillian knew the suggestion would come sometime.

"Training, Jill. You could never work for Vira without training." Claudia's words squeeze and shift as the sebum is extracted from her pores.

"Training? Is that what Shelly is doing?"

"Her challenges?" Claudia laughs. "That's just for fun, *mamá*. For Shelly, this is all just play. The training is serious. It's like learning magic."

Jillian likes the word. She always has.

"We have a teacher who trains you to be a master of your craft." Claudia chooses the most enticing words. "You learn how to play in a much bigger game. Ten times bigger, a thousand times."

"A bigger game than today?"

"Ah, *sí*. And with mastery comes risk. Only you can decide if you're up for that, Jill. No one is trying to push you into that. But we would welcome you into our family with open arms."

"And Shelly?"

"You and Shelly are not the same." There is a silent pause. "Shelly is more difficult to train than we thought. But Gordo has made his promises."

"So she could train too."

It takes Claudia a moment to respond. "If you like. We can give it another try."

Jillian lets the moment of peace warm her. Her eyes feel heavy. She could fall asleep on the table. Even Claudia's words, despite their content, calm and soothe.

"Just think about it."

Jillian lets the thought roll and tumble in her head.

25

SHELLY'S rented room is ten floors up directly over an Indian restaurant. There's an elevator in the building, but it's not working and, according to Shelly, has never worked since she started subletting the room a few months ago. The smell of Garam Masala and spicy lamb is nauseating on the impossibly long walk up the back stairs. "Do you do this all the time?"

"Yeah. It blows." Shelly seems distracted.

"You must have great quads." Jillian can feel the front of her thighs burn as they ascend.

"I guess." Her apartment is down a long hallway. The smells of meat cooking and kitty litter mingle with the Indian spices and make the surrounding aroma overbearing. She fishes for her keys and unlocks the damaged metal door. "My roommate's not here. I think she's bonkin' her skeevy boyfriend at his place." She opens the door.

Shelly pushes past a wall of glass beads hanging in strands at the front door.

"These are pretty." Jillian holds a string of beads up. There are literally thousands of colored beads glistening on thin strings hanging in front of the door.

"I strung them on dental floss I cut from Rite Aid a few months ago. I bought the beads in Hoboken."

Jillian remembers the beads dangling from the prescription bottle cozy and the handle on Claudia's handmade purse. "You strung these all yourself?" Jillian marvels at the hundreds and hundreds of strands—each one strung with uncountable beads. The undulating wall reminds Jillian of a brilliantly hued waterfall.

"Yeah." Shelly bites her nails and looks into Jillian's eyes for approval. "Kinda crazy, right?"

"Jesus, Shell." Jillian admires what must have been weeks and weeks of work. She runs her fingers through the mesmerizing strands. "This must have taken a while."

Shelly flips on the light in the room. It takes Jillian a moment to look up and register the sight.

Hanging from every conceivable spot on the wall and draped across every possible surface are a myriad of handmade objects: purses, bags, stuffed pillows, small dolls, large totes, tiny pocketbooks, cavernous baskets, minuscule holders. Some are identifiable, quantifiable—and some, unexplainable with no recognizable purpose or reason for being. Each one is meticulously handmade, cut from a thousand other things and remade into these wondrous, spectacular sewn pieces.

A surprise in every poche!

"It took me a while to figure out how to get that stuff to melt together without burning everything up." Shelly picks up one of the objects, a tiny, beaded bag on a neck-length chain, and runs her finger along the edge. "One fire's enough to set me straight." The fabric has seemingly melted into another fabric, an irregular strip of silver holding the edges together like a scar. "Mom and Randall would be so proud!" she says sarcastically.

"Did you make all these things yourself?" Jillian has barely caught her breath. The sight is truly mesmerizing. She walks over to a round bag. It's covered entirely with square mirrored pieces.

"The disco ball." Shelly turns the bag around. It catches the light and sparkles around the room.

"From Barneys," Jillian whispers to herself.

Jillian picks up a palm-sized pillow. It's pink cashmere on one side and aquamarine on the other. The translucent material has been folded and stitched so that it floats like a tiny sea.

"The scarf from Jeffrey."

Shelly nods.

"I ruined it, right?" Shelly walks over to the kitchenette against the far wall. She wipes off two glasses on her shirt and fills them up with water.

"You didn't ruin it." Jillian spins around the room, eyeing the millions of details. "Are you kidding? This is the coolest thing I've ever seen." The pieces of stolen shirts and jackets, fur collars and gowns are all reinvented into something new and mysterious, "I like them a lot." Jillian breathes for the first time since entering the room. "I mean, I *really* like them a lot."

"You want some water?"

Jillian takes the glass and wanders more though the room. A NEW FOR WINTER sign like the sign Shelly gave to her from Jeffrey spins upside down from the ceiling—a hundred plastic Christmas icicles surround it, tinkling quietly as she walks by. The effect is whimsical and bewitching.

"Is this what you do with the stuff that you cut?" Jillian kneels down to look at another bag hanging from the ceiling from a seven-foot crocheted band.

"Most of it. Some stuff I keep if all my clothes are all janky. But most of it goes into my Threadbags."

"They're beautiful, Shelly." Jillian takes a sip of water—the New York taste of it is satisfying.

"You think Gordo would think they're dumb?" Shelly is shy about asking.

"I don't know why anyone would think that, Shell." Jillian picks up a diaphanous sewn envelope held together with a bronze button. "These are wonderful, and you're an artist, Shelly." The piece could be an elegant evening bag or a beautiful object to admire and hold. "You could sell these. Easy."

"I dunno who'd wanna pay for this crap." Shelly twirls a pillow around in her hand absentmindedly.

"Yeah, well, maybe I know more about that than you think."

"They're just stupid gimcrack." Shelly finishes her water and drops the glass into the small sink. "That's what Randall used to say." Shelly replaces a bead that's fallen off one of the tassels on a purse. She seems to have disappeared into the task—tying a tiny knot with her pink, swollen fingers.

"Well, Randall doesn't live in New York." Jillian watches Shelly's fingers race around the beads.

"So Gordo says Claudia's gonna send you to training." She's concentrating on her task rather than looking directly at Jillian.

"I'm not going without my *pawtna*." Jillian sits down on a stool—the only piece of furniture in the room not being used for one of Shelly's Threadbags.

"Claudia and Vira don't think I'm *professional* enough for training." Shelly's threading more and more beads onto the purse.

"That's ridiculous. We did the Barneys thing together."

"We both know the difference between us. You're the real deal. I'm just a mule." Shelly aims another bead at the tiny thread.

"You're not just a mule, Shell." Jillian watches as she picks out more beads from a Tupperware container. "And anyway, I'm not doing it alone."

"I would really get a ton better with training, y'know." Shelly looks up at Jillian hopefully. "Gordo says they really teach you how to do it. How to be professional about it and everything."

"I know you would." Jillian takes another sip of her water. "If Claudia and Vira want me to train, you're gonna train too. We're a team." Jillian puts her glass down. "And you're my best friend."

Jillian looks up at Shelly. She is sparkling next the disco ball purse. Her eyes are clear, and she suddenly looks as happy as Jillian has ever seen her.

26

"THIS thing is nasty, man." Shelly's scratching under the waistband of her girdle. "I'm gonna get skank rank if I wear this thing one more day."

Jillian and Shelly are sitting in a darkened nondescript hotel suite in midtown. The room is a makeshift training center, set up like a classroom. They've been there most of the week. "You need to get used to them, homes." Gordo pushes Shelly's shoulder. He is the only other English-speaking person in the room. "You can't just sit there and scratch during a job, man."

"I know, but it's itchy." Shelly pushes him back.

A few clothing racks are set up on the one side, and each chair has items of clothing next to it: a man's suit, a silk shirt, a leather coat. About twenty students sit in the middle and take notes. Most of them have the round Peruvian faces and marble-black eyes of Claudia and Gordo. A few are average height but all are brown and Spanish speaking.

Jillian wonders if these people, like Claudia and Vira, were predestined for this path. If they left behind broken childhoods and broken families to come to this country and to this training center. She wonders if this is their last hope—the best thing in their lives. For a moment this thought makes her feel superior, but then she remembers that she found her way here too.

Despite Jillian's insistence, Claudia was reluctant to let Shelly into training. Even though Shelly was showing signs of potential, Jillian sensed that neither Claudia nor Vira ever took her all that seriously. The job was only days away, and it seemed like they were using her only for the grunt work. But Gordo vouched for Shelly, like always, and promised to stay with her throughout the intensive week. And besides, Jillian—the girl the cat dragged home—was a totally different story.

And so Gordo begat Shelly and Shelly begat Jillian and as long as they kept them close together, Vira thought, he could get his American booster after all.

The teacher, Mrs. Jarquín, and the students stare at the white girls off and on suspiciously. Jillian assumes that *gringas* rarely, if ever, make an appearance in these sessions. Had Gordo not made the introduction in Spanish and mentioned the name Viracocha many times to the men standing at the door of the room, the girls would not have made it through their guard.

The uniform is nearly identical: all the women *and* the men wear girdles that were properly fitted earlier in the week by Mrs. Zapata, the team's seamstress. The women wear long black draw-string skirts and the men wear slacks, also custom-fitted by Mrs. Zapata, with drawstring closures where zippers once were. There was some protest yesterday by one of the men in training, something to do with urinating and drawstring closures. Gordo didn't even try to interpret, he just laughed along, slapping the man on the back. Mrs. Jarquín, presumably having heard it all over the years, did not find it entertaining.

Mrs. Jarquín stands at the front of the room, folding items tightly into neat squares and sliding them down her own draw-string skirt and into her girdle. Gordo translates as best he can in a loud whisper beside them. Shelly watches him with bated breath. "You folding the material pieces over here and over here," Gordo repeats her hand motions, "like a tamale to put down your pants for bed." The room erupts in laughter—a joke the girls find less funny filtered through Gordo's English than the rest of the group. But indeed, after being slipped under the tight-fitting girdle by Mrs. Jarquín's agile hands, the "tamale" has no dimension whatsoever. No one would ever suspect.

"You trying." Mrs. Jarquín gestures to the room. Her strained English, Jillian assumes, is for the girls' sake. Every student gets up from his or her chair and carefully folds the piece of clothing beside them. Jillian has no problem. Making big pieces of clothing into small ones is a technique she has employed before. She pulls her girdle outward, slides the material down, and smooths it out along her hip. Shelly concentrates on folding the shirt exactly as the Mrs. Jarquín specified. Gordo helps her out with it but they both look at each other nervously when it comes time to stuff it down. After a quick pause, she plunges the item herself and smiles proudly as it slips easily under her drawstring—barely noticeable to the untrained eye.

Mrs. Jarquín repeats the process many times using a stopwatch. Eventually, after eighty or ninety attempts, most of the students in the room could be an opening act in Vegas—making shirts and sweaters disappear with the flick of the wrist. Jillian's hands ache and cramp. She wonders if the incidence of carpal tunnel is high among career shoplifters.

"Good, good." The trainer walks around the room feeling the various bumps and bulges. She has no problem correcting those whose clothing bulge is too big by thrusting her arm, elbow deep, down into the caverns of the student's pants. The girls giggle with each other as her arm disappears down the front of a male student's crotch. He stares in front of him, careful not to react too much to her direct touches. *Machismo* is not tolerated with Mrs. Jarquín at the helm.

"See, this pokes out too far in the front, make a big bump."

Gordo whispers the words in English to the girls as the trainer does her work. "Maybe he want to impress the *chiquitas.*" He laughs quietly with Shelly. They punch each other teasingly as they have been all day.

Mrs. Jarquín moves on to the more complicated items. She goes to the front of the room and lifts an entire men's suit in front of her on a hefty wooden hanger. Jillian whispers into Shelly's ear, "Is that a suit in your pants or are you just happy to see me?"

"Ladies!" The trainer raises her voice at the girls. The room of students turns around to look at the smiling white girls. "Pay attention or I send you home." She pronounces the words perfectly. The whole scene makes Jillian think of AP History.

Mrs. Jarquín folds the arms of the suit inward and rolls the entire suit around the hanger. She slips the triangular mass down against her inner thigh, hanger and all. She is not modest with this part of her body. It is her main instructional tool. The swell of her stomach hangs over the girdle, sucking in and expanding as if it has a life of its own. "You never leave the hanger. Remember that," Gordo editorializes into Shelly's ear. "Taking the hanger out, it fucks you up." She pays close attention and nods as he speaks, filing away his advice.

The group practices the suit and hanger disappearance for twice as long as the simpler items. Hours later, Jillian's hands are numb, her thighs are chafed, and at least two of the students in the room have required minor treatment for hanger injuries. But by four o'clock the collective inner-thigh-bulge caused by multiple suits and their hangers is minimal.

After suits, Mrs. Jarquín moves on to hand signals. She demonstrates many of them by carrying on a silent conversation with Gordo, relaying instructions that he follows precisely. The hand signals, she explains, are the same in Spanish or English. The unspoken language of shoplifters—accepted, apparently, the world over.

Mrs. Jarquín walks around the rack of clothes and touches a

silk shirt on the seam. "One finger touches the clothes, and that means it's good." Gordo continues to translate the words. Jillian absorbs the information easily—the hand signals seem fairly obvious, natural even. Shelly looks less confident. Jillian will review them with her. Claudia, she is sure, will not tolerate even the slightest slip.

"Two finger mean no good." Mrs. Jarquín fires the various signals off. "One finger to your mouth—quiet. One finger pointing up—security camera. One finger going round and round, pointing up—video tape running. Two finger pointing in direction—exit. Five finger pointing in direction—time to go." Gordo repeats everything in English. He shows Shelly the signals again until she nods in recognition. Jillian absorbs the new language swiftly. This kind of memorization is no different than learning the periodic table, a quick page of Chaucer, or a short round of French verbs.

Late into the last evening the students break into teams and review the use of the FRS radios. The room is filled with the murmurs of the team members talking to one another through the headsets.

"How am I supposed to remember all this stuff, man?" Shelly sounds worried over the radio. Even at this distance, Jillian can see her biting her nails.

"Watch the mani."

"Dang it. Oops."

"We always on channel seven and subchannel fourteen." Gordo's voice is audible over the radio too. "Claudia will kill you, homes, if you don't know that tomorrow."

"Tomorrow?" both girls say at once.

"What you training for, *mamá?* Yeah, tomorrow." Gordo walks around when he talks. Like everyone else, he moves slowly around the room counterclockwise, like a skating rink. "We do a practice job. Nothing big. That ain't for a few days."

"I can't do all this tomorrow, Gordo." Shelly's nervous, her eyes, wild.

"You riding high, *mamá*. You got nothing to worry about." Gordo catches up to her and rubs her shoulder up and down. "I watch out for my homies."

Shelly continues to bite her nails.

"You in too, *mamá*." Gordo gives his usual one-two punch to Jillian's shoulder. "Vira's personal request."

Shelly continues to bite and gnaw.

"We post up at four-thirty A.M."

"In the morning?" Jillian can't believe what she's hearing.

"Bloomingdale's. Bloomingdale's. *Oh yeah!*" He sings a little song and wiggles his belly at Shelly.

"Four-thirty—just to go to Fifty-ninth?" Jillian needs a cappuccino already.

"Chestnut Hill, man."

"Massachusetts?" Jillian is shocked at the sound of it.

"We take a little ride in the van." He puts his arms around the girls. "Keep our powder dry in the city."

27

THEY meet at dawn in the courtyard of the Palace Hotel, the location of Vira's new office, and ride for the first hour in the dark. The last time Jillian was up this early was to go to overnight camp when she was eight. Like she did back then, she feels sick to her stomach, nervous, and sorry she ever agreed, even wanted, to come. The van smells like air freshener and, she thinks, Ricardo's spicy body odor. No one seems happy to be there; even the van itself chugs along reluctantly toward New England.

Claudia drinks coffee out of a Citibank mug as she drives. Even at this early hour, her makeup is full and glossy, although her charm has not yet been turned up full throttle. Ricardo sits next to her in the front, his leather jacket rolled into a makeshift pillow and pressed against the window.

Shelly runs over the hand signals in the backseat of the van. "One touch—good. Finger in a circle—videotape is running. Five fingers pointing—we leave." Shelly repeats them over and over to herself.

"I keep thinking about Miss Zapata's *Cau Cau*." Gordo sucks his fingers. "Just like my mama's." He smiles back at Shelly.

"How can you think about *Cau Cau* at this fucking shit hour, *culazo?*" Ricardo's voice is muffled by his jacket.

"Just a little drive to Massachusetts, homes, then *boom, bam, boom,* then a little drive back to Brooklyn, then Mrs. Zapata's *Cau Cau.* Hey, Vira coming, right?" Gordo's perkier than everyone in the car. He bounces on his seat as he calls to Claudia in the front.

"Even Vira's gonna come?" Shelly seems nervous at the thought.

"If you don't fuck it up, *gringa.*" Ricardo mumbles to himself and pulls his wet black hair off from his forehead.

"*Hssh!*" Claudia snaps at him.

Jillian leans her palm against the cold window and presses her cheek against the back of her hand. *What's she doing here?* She feels suddenly isolated—completely alone and surrounded by strangers. The feeling is both claustrophobic and empty. Even the sight of Shelly isn't comforting this morning.

"You gonna love Miss Zapata's *Cau Cau* tonight. Is so good." Gordo pulls on Jillian's drawstring black skirt and sucks his fingers at her.

"I don't eat cow." Jillian watches out the window as the dark of the city releases into the pale blue sky and auburn trees along the highway.

"Is no cow, *mamá.* Is the stomach lining." Gordo circles his own stomach to demonstrate. "Stomach lining and potatoes."

Jillian just looks out the window, trying not to register his words.

"I can't believe you eat that stuff, homes." Shelly stops mumbling to herself and kicks the side of Gordo's seat.

"You gonna eat it tonight too, homes." He yanks on a chunk of her hair.

The team rides in silence as the van makes its way up north, each one lost in his or her thoughts, concentrating on the various tasks at hand.

Jillian opted not to wear the brash Tommy Bahama shirt Claudia gave her for the job; instead, she's wearing the Chloé peasant, like a badge of honor. Designer clothes are like armor, she thinks—protection from the masses. And the more expensive they are, the more protection they provide. Plus she thinks topping the ordinary shoplifter's skirt and girdle with a few yards of fifteen-hundred-dollar silk is appropriate for the occasion.

"You team with me today, Jill." Claudia looks at the girls in the rearview mirror. She is not smiling. "Shelly will go with Ricardo. Gordo on surveillance."

Jillian's heart drops into her throat and Shelly's face turns white.

"What?" Shelly's knuckles go right for her mouth. "I can't. Jillian's my partner!" Shelly leans forward toward the front seat and pleads with Claudia. "You never break up a team. You never leave your partner. Right? You told me that, Claudia." Shelly's nails are bitten to the quick.

Ricardo slaps the dashboard. "Fucking shit." He agrees with Shelly for once. "Why is the white girl on the number one team?" The veins in Ricardo's neck engorge and tighten; the look of it is obscene and phallic.

"It is personally from Vira," she whispers loudly to Ricardo. "We have to practice to break things up. We profiled all over the city, Ricardo. We need to mix up the regulars for the Red job. And now we all to practice, not just the Americans."

"Fuck that shit." Ricardo twirls the gold cross around his neck. Jillian watches as the slender piece of gold catches the sunlight against his oily skin. He slumps back into his seat. *"Chúpame la pinga."*

"It's no discussion." Claudia says the last word on the subject.

After nearly three hours on the road, the van pulls off the highway in Chestnut Hill and down the frontage road toward the mall. Jillian can feel the collective tension reach a crescendo as the team eyes up the building. Even though this is just a practice, a test run before Vira's big job, there is as much risk here as anywhere. And without the months of research Manuel normally does for Claudia and Vira before a job and the days of personal reconnaissance, the risk may even be greater than usual.

Claudia drives the van under the overhang and into the mall parking lot.

"I gotta team with Retardo?" Shelly says to Jillian. "He's such an A-hole," she whispers. Jillian looks in the front at Ricardo. He too is biting a nail and spitting the remnants out in front of him. "A-hole." Shelly's cuticles are bleeding, and her left thumb is swollen past the nail.

Claudia parks a hundred yards over from the Bloomingdale's entrance.

"You'll be fine, Shell. You know this stuff. And Gordo will be all over you in there. He won't let you get busted." They both look over at Gordo. He's gathering his tools and unloading the headsets from the van. He looks especially composed and ready, like a fireman or a paramedic on the scene of an accident.

Jillian watches Shelly stare over at him—her usual feigned disinterest morphing into a look of adult curiosity.

Jillian grabs Shelly's hand. "Hey, let's do our mantra." Shelly snaps out of it and both girls squeeze their eyes shut.

Claudia and Ricardo get out of the van and slide the side door open with a loud *fwop*.

They hold their hands together tightly. *"It is mine. It is mine. It is mine,"* they say, sharing their deepest unsaid fear and fearlessness.

"Tell the *lesbeens* we waiting for them when they done kissing." Ricardo slams the front door of the van and heads for the Bloomingdale's entrance. His hands are thrust down into his pockets, and he shakes out his hair as he marches headlong into the store.

"Manuel says it's a slow day in the house." Gordo is loud and clear over the radio in Bloomingdale's despite being a few floors away. The team's researcher, Manuel, knows every LP agent on the East Coast, the comings and goings of the local police, each security system's particular strengths and weakness; he is the least visible but possibly the most valuable member of the team. Manuel's job is to evaluate and exploit the weakness in each store until the place catches on and the team moves on to the next establishment. "Catching on," unfortunately, usually means somebody on the team is sacrificed, sometimes even the entire team.

Bloomingdale's in the city "caught on" a few months ago, busted a team Claudia knows from Brazil, and started tagging every item in the store—even the designer clothes. But Bloomingdale's in Chestnut Hill is a little behind the times, trusting the Boston housewives and debutantes a bit more and still tagging only leather.

"Don't get all cocky, homes," Gordo advises Jillian as they walk. "Working a job is just a gamble, man. Eventually you lose your hand."

Jillian adjusts her earpiece to fit more snugly as she moves into position in the Armani area. She makes a point of making no eye contact with Shelly as they go their separate ways. Claudia walks swiftly forward. She gives the signal for video surveillance up ahead. It's not too crowded in their area, just a few women walking around doing the usual. Nothing suspicious.

The floor and its contents are similar to Bloomingdale's in the city—a mix of loud junior items—short skirts, strapless shirts, warm-up suits, and real designer clothes with hefty price tags set apart from the rest of the store in pristine boutique spaces. All these stores—Bloomingdale's, Macy's, Jeffrey, DKNY, Big Drop, Institute, Scoop—and the items on their shelves have started blurring together in Jillian's mind lately. A fifty-dollar shirt doesn't look that much different from a five-hundred-dollar one. They're all just more of less pieces of material—their particular weight, depth and foldability are the only qualities she has to consider.

The math is impossible to do today, and besides, she thinks, what's the point? Today it's a job—nothing fair or equitable about it. She's here for Shelly mostly, and that's the only thing that feels remotely excusable about it.

she sat in the van earlier, sitting on a thick padding of stolen clothes stuffed underneath and around her lower half.

"I don't know." Shelly sucks on a tendril of hair. "He's just an asshole."

"*Pendejo? Pendejo?*" Ricardo yells from the front. His temples flex and throb.

"*Cállate la boca!*" Claudia slaps a hand on the steering wheel and continues to chastise in Spanish.

Gordo pulls items from his pants and puts them in a pile in the center of the floor: Armani pants, Tommy Hilfiger, Nike top—everything still neatly on the hanger.

Ricardo is spitting back at her and sulking in his seat.

"Check this out." Gordo holds a shirt up to Shelly. "Sean John! Nice." He disregards the yelling entirely, as if he doesn't even hear it.

"Cool." Shelly offers the best response she can, given the arguing.

Jillian pulls pieces out from her girdle. Her pile of stolen clothes grows in front of her.

"Let's just get the van out of here." Claudia is angry but focused. She drives the van calmly onto the highway going south.

"The lesbeens fuck everything." He continues to talk. "She," Ricardo points a hand at Shelly, "don't even know the signals. And she," he moves his accusations toward Jillian, pointing and staring his dark eyes into hers, "don't know when to shut her face." Ricardo points at her again. "How you do your job while you fucking chatting and squawking? You think this is fun, ass fuck?"

"You don't know shit," Jillian says quietly from the backseat as she pulls more pieces from between her legs. The guilt she feels about doing now a *second* job without the math adding up is surpassed only by the need to one-up Ricardo.

Claudia eyes her from the rearview mirror as she continues to remove items from beneath her skirt. Jillian's pile of clothes would overflow a lawn and leaf bag.

"What you got there?" Claudia notices the enormous pile of clothes at Jillian's feet.

"Donna Karan, Armani, Armani, Miu Miu, Dries Van Noten, Jacobs, D&G, Moschino . . ."

"When you get the Armani?" Claudia tries to keep her eyes on the road.

"During the chatting and squawking." Jillian glares at Ricardo. *They have no idea how good she is at this—how much she can get away with because of who she is.*

"Three fifty, four fifty, eight hundred, two, three, three," Jillian rifles off the price tags. "I got probably six or seven things while I was talking to her. She didn't notice a thing. They never do if you know how to work it."

"What's your total?" Ricardo is looking enviously at the impressive pile as well.

"I don't know. Eight, eight, seven, three . . . seven grand, give or take." The math is out the window.

"Homes!" Gordo gives Jillian a high five.

"*Mamacita!*" Claudia's mouth drops open. She starts laughing and drumming the steering wheel as if she herself just scored the goal.

"I got this DKNY miniskirt!" Shelly holds up the neon orange skirt. "It's cute, right?"

"That's great, *mamá.* Good job." Gordo gives Shelly a high five too.

"You got seven thousand dollars' worth of clothes?" Claudia turns around to Jillian for a moment.

"Give or take."

"*Cau Cau*, here we come!"

28

MRS. ZAPATA'S kitchen table is filled with food. *Ocopa, Aji de Gallina, Arroz con Pollo, Papa Rellena, Rocoto Relleno,* and the infamous *Cau Cau* release the steam of unfamiliar spices throughout the space. The room is small and plain: an old wooden table, a painting of Jesus on one wall above a pink clock, a painting of Mary on the other wall over the stove, a television on a cart to the side—but the noises of the street flow in lavishly through the windows and backdoor screen. Mrs. Zapata's grandchildren run and play throughout the house, occasionally swiping cookies from the counter. Two of them carry bright yellow play rifles and shoot at each other. One little boy enters the room wearing nothing but a paper bag over his head, his twiggy legs nearly the same color brown. He is quickly shooed away in Spanish by the old seamstress.

The ride back from Chestnut Hill was endless. Ricardo was angry, Shelly was jealous, Gordo was hungry, and, despite her enviable take, Jillian felt *nothing*.

The scene at Mrs. Zapata's reminds Jillian of Christmas at Belle's—loud, festive, and unfamiliar. Her hefty harvest is the talk of the evening, and she's its undeniable hero, but even though this has been her most bountiful haul to date, she still feels an indefinable craving.

Jillian stands in the hallway close to the kitchen. She's tired and raw and there's only one voice she wants to hear. She clutches Mrs. Zapata's rotary phone and tries to reach him. She thought she'd just be leaving another one of her futile messages, but, to her surprise, he picks up.

"I just thought we could meet for coffee or tea or something," she whispers to Alex, her lips grazing the receiver. He has barely said a word past *hello*. "I just have so much I need to talk to you about, Alex. I just really need a friend right now. If you can't be my boyfriend, at least you can be my friend because I really could use one."

Jillian listens to the painful silence on the other end. "Are you there?"

"I'm here."

"We could go to Serendipity. We could have a Sand Tart Sundae. You love their Sand Tarts, right?" Jillian tries to sound easy, despite her desperation.

"I meant what I said, Jill."

"But I miss you"—she chokes on the words—"I just really need to . . . I don't know . . . tell you what's going on."

There is a long silence. Jillian can hear him breathing. She holds the phone close, as if she might feel the warmth of it on her ear. If she could only see him, if she could only look into his eyes, she thinks she could finally tell him everything—about Shelly and work, about Vira and Claudia and everything. She could be completely honest with him, and he'd be there to catch her. "I miss you so much, Allie."

"But that doesn't change anything for me, Jill. I deserve more."

"Please, Alex. Please. I'm really ready to be who you need me to be." She'll say anything to keep him on the line for just a moment longer.

"I don't need you to be anything, Jill."

The front door opens, and she can hear Vira's voice and Shelly running to greet him. Jillian pulls the phone away as far as it will go and twists herself around into a guarded knot. "I just need to see you. Please, Alex. I just need this one thing from you."

She holds her breath and waits for him to speak.

"For just a coffee, Jill. No coming over here after."

"I got it."

"No me going over there."

"Just coffee."

"*Mamacita!*" Shelly sambas over to Jillian and bumps hips. "Poppy's in the house!" Shelly pulls on her elbow. Jillian turns around once more and pushes her face toward the wall.

"Look, Jill, I gotta go." Alex is sure and direct on the phone.

Jillian pushes Shelly back into the kitchen. "Oh. Yeah, me too. Sure." She ends the sentence an octave higher than she should and hopes the whole thing won't end just yet.

"Bye." His voice is quick.

Jillian listens as the phone clicks off on the other end. She knew he would hang up first and he does, but she still listens with morbid curiosity to the sound of the phone without him on it—the buzz of silence lingering on the line after the click. Like picking off a scab or scratching something too hard, she knows it will sting, and yet she does it anyway. She hangs there until the quiet turns into a toxic beeping, then unfurls herself and lets the phone fall back into its cradle.

"Welcome back from your little lover's quarrel." Claudia pours herself a cup of water and glares at Jillian suspiciously.

Jillian manages a smile and finds a place at the crowded table.

"*Buenas noches! Buenas noches, amigos!*" Viracocha enters the small, plain kitchen. He takes over the room with his gestures, his charisma, his festive proclamations. He kisses Mrs. Zapata on both cheeks and dramatically looks into the many pots still bubbling on the stove. Mrs. Zapata blushes as Viracocha then kisses her loudly, right on the lips.

"*Bravísimo! Bravísimo!*" Viracocha kisses everyone in the room on the cheek.

"I got a DKNY, Poppy!" Shelly smiles ear to ear.

"I heard, I heard." Viracocha moves toward Jillian and puts his arms around her. "Congratulations, *mi amor,*" he whispers in her ear, "you had quite an auspicious day."

Behind Viracocha is Manuel, the team's researcher. He follows, kisses Mrs. Zapata, and shakes Ricardo's and Gordo's hands before he sits down at the table.

Viracocha sits at the end near the sink. The ambience is a far cry from his usual dinners at Cipriani or Alain Ducasse, but he seems thankful to be sitting on an old wooden chair at the plain table. He seems to appreciate the simplicity of a simple Peruvian meal served at the family table. For him, this warm space is as aspirational as a three-thousand-dollar-a-night penthouse suite, but harder to come by. He looks like a man who, despite his money, still fits in nowhere. For a moment Jillian feels sorry for him.

He slaps the seat of folding chair next to him and looks at her. "Come, *mi amor.* Sit."

Mrs. Zapata serves the food mostly out of pastel-hued glass storage containers, except for the rice, which overflows an aluminum pie tin. The old woman sits on a step stool by the back door, eating sunny-side-up eggs on rice with fried plantains on the side. Manuel sits next to Gordo. His long ponytail is tucked into his collar, and his gold front tooth gleams as he laughs and chews. Claudia and Ricardo sit at the opposite end of the table from their boss. More sullen than usual, Ricardo drinks beer and slouches on his chair, while Claudia drinks enough red wine to stain a rim around her lips. Her eyes dart around the room, sizing everyone up. Jillian watches closely as Claudia's sharp eyelashes point and flap as each person speaks or changes position.

"Is that the cow-cow, G?" Shelly picks up a skewer of meat and takes a bite.

"*Anticuchos,*" Mrs. Zapata replies proudly from her stool. It is the first word she has uttered to the table.

"Umm." Shelly chews. "S'good."

"Beef heart, *mi amor.*" Viracocha reaches across the table and wiggles Shelly's nose with his finger.

"The heart of the bull!" Ricardo thumps his chest and slams down his empty bottle. In this light, drinking his beers and smoking his cigarettes, he seems more "tortured bohemian" tonight and less "gangster greasy."

"Care to try, Jill?" Viracocha holds a hot skewer up to Jillian's mouth. It smells sweet and woody. She tries to smile even though the food just seems to float in and out of her thoughts.

"Taste like my *chico.*" Ricardo mumbles and opens another bottle of beer.

Jillian ignores Ricardo and inhales. "Beef heart? Really?"

"It's Peruvian, *mamá.*" Gordo drumrolls two fingers on the table.

"When in Peru . . ." Viracocha raises his glass to Jillian.

The group watches as Jillian reluctantly takes a bite from the skewer and chews. She contemplates the flavor as the rest of the team awaits the verdict. "It's okay, I guess. Sort of." She smiles and takes another bite of the pungent meat. "Yeah, it's okay." The room erupts in cheers. Even Mrs. Zapata claps and drinks down another gulp of wine. Claudia looks on from the end of the table.

"I would like to make a toast." Viracocha stands and holds up a cup. "To the lovely Ms. Monteagudo, who has put together a group of people who, together, can do anything."

The group applauds. Gordo adds a whistle and puts his arm around Shelly. She pretends not to notice but leans toward him just a centimeter.

"To our new member, Miss Jillian Siegel, who proved today

that even our friends in America can act professionally and accomplish great tasks."

"Yeah, Jillian!" Shelly stomps her feet. Ricardo adds a few loud claps, staring directly in Jillian's direction.

"To Gordo and Ricardo, Manuel and Mrs. Zapata. And to this wonderful collection of people who, I have no doubt, will accomplish our upcoming mission with great success."

The team applauds and shouts. Even Mrs. Zapata's grandchildren have gathered at the doorway excitedly. The ruckus lasts for a good few minutes.

"What about me, Poppy?" Shelly looks up at Viracocha, who is still standing and now drinking out of his cup.

"And of course to Shelly too." Viracocha lifts his glass again. "*Salud.*" The room drinks to his words.

Claudia stands at the table holding up her cup of wine. Her lipstick lines the rim of the plastic like a shiny garland. "And *I* would like to make a toast. To myself, Ms. Claudia Monteagudo," Jillian is reminded how beautiful the name sounds coming out of the owner's mouth, "a loyal *limeña*, who had the good sense to find us some American blood." She raises her cup to her boss. "Because we cannot afford"—she looks down at Ricardo—"*none of us can afford* to have anything go wrong with this job." Claudia's words come out loose and angry. It is a side of the woman that Jillian has never seen before.

The room quiets down as she takes her sip.

"*Siéntate, mi amor.* Not tonight." Vira puts a finger to his lips and then points it like a gun toward Claudia. "Next week is a big week for the team. Our friend Manuel has been preparing for a long time for this, Ms. Monteagudo. Tonight is for celebrating."

Jillian excuses herself from the ongoing festivities, walks into the powder room and presses the door behind her until she hears it click into place. She closes her eyes and holds her face against the cool wall. She wants out of this place, out of this room and into

Alex's. She would crawl out of her skin to find him and slither beside him for just a moment.

The small room reeks of the heavy scent of cheap hand soap. The walls are thin; the noises of the kitchen and the street echo through them. Instinctively she opens the medicine cabinet, hoping to find the answer to her unasked question—an antidote to her nameless affliction. This one holds very little actually: a few Q-tips, a dirty juice glass with Band-Aids in it, a dusty old soap shaped like a lemon, a handful of change, and a prescription bottle with a Spanish label.

She pulls the bottle off the shelf and opens it. Eight plump red pills spill into her hand. She watches as the crimson spreads out along her palm in little kisses.

Jillian funnels the pills back into the bottle and shuts the cabinet.

Her face stares out at her from the mirror as it always does. The fluorescent overhead light casts a subtle green tinge to her skin. "What the fuck is your problem?" she says aloud as she points at her own reflection. "Get your fucking shit together, Jillian."

It sounds like something Alex might say.

"Jillian." Shelly knocks loudly at the door.

"I'm coming." Jillian turns on the water and runs her hands under—washing the sticky sins from her skin.

"C'mon. What are you doing in there? Everybody's leaving."

"*Ciao. Ciao. Ciao.*" They're all already saying their good-byes and thank-yous at the front door. "*Gracias, ciao.*" Shelly is hugging Mrs. Zapata and Manuel like the bride in a receiving line.

Jillian leans against the wall in the living room looking out and thinking about Alex and falling into his arms.

"You think you so fucking smart, *chucha?*" Ricardo comes up behind Jillian and pulls her by the sleeve toward him.

He's so close she can smell the sour digested yeast and hops on his breath.

"You not so fucking smart, Miss Jewish American Princess." He yanks again at her sleeve. "You don't even fucking go to church."

Jillian stands tall, towering a few inches over him. His hand is hard against her arm. She thinks he might punch her in the face.

"Fucking church, man. Everybody go to fucking church."

She looks him directly in the eye, determined not to budge an inch.

"You think you on the team? You think you and the *puta* over there are on the team?" He points to the front door. "You no on the team. You never be on the team."

She would like to disregard what he's saying but can't help but swallow every word.

"You just a mule to us." His mouth looks like a giant anus puckering, forming the round words and spewing them out.

Jillian can feel her head pump with blood.

Ricardo's body sways from left to right. "You like being my mule, *maruca?*" He grabs Jillian hard by the hair, pushes her head into his, and invades her mouth with his fat, wet tongue. He pushes it farther and farther toward her throat, filling the cavity entirely.

Jillian can taste the *adobo* and salt, beef heart and chicken gizzard fresh on its surface. She lets it take hold in there, just a moment, tasting it, just a moment, until it dissolves and wiggles away. "Get off of me." She pushes his head back, but he grabs her by the hips and thrusts his hard crotch in and out toward her like he's riding a rodeo horse. She rubs her eyelid, hoping to appear indifferent, and searches for something to say. "You fuck like a girl, Ricardo." Jillian grabs him by the backside and pushes his groin even closer toward her, right into the peak below her pelvis. "We Jewish girls like it a little harder." She gyrates her body onto his. "Oh yeah. Like that. Oh yeah." She pretends not to feel it against her. She pretends not to grind harder. She pretends not to let her body rise and fall with the pressure of him against her.

Ricardo's face turns sour.

"And," she puts her lips to his ear and lets the heat of her breath fall onto its thin lobe, "we request that our men, particularly our men who have just eaten a lot of *menudo,* brush their teeth before bedding us. And that they use deodorant."

Ricardo pushes Jillian off of him and nearly falls backward in the process. *"Vete a la mierda!"*

"Come with me, Ricardo." Claudia walks into the room at exactly the right moment and gracefully intercepts the action. She wraps her arm around his. "Let me get my brother another beer in the kitchen."

As he walks off with his older sister, Ricardo looks back at Jillian and swirls his finger around in the air—giving the proper hand signal for videotape running above.

Jillian assumes he means that, like twenty-four-hour department store surveillance, God sees all too.

29

"I LOVE this place." Jillian sips at her Caffe Vesuvius and tries to be light and airy under the garish light of the pseudo-Tiffany lamps at Serendipity. It is her first lie of the day, as the ice cream shop is too noisy and too filled with children in uniforms, running around, amped up on their after-school sugar. She once *did* love this place—it was kitschy and charming, romantic in its own brassy way, but now it seems to hurt—poke at her from all directions. She can smell the bleach rising up from the basement floor, hear the buzz of the Tiffanies, and feel the stick of the Naugahyde banquette on her legs.

Alex drinks a glass of water. His skin is tan except for the pale circles around his eyes and the bridge of his nose where his Oakleys fit. Jillian mourns for the adventures that brown his skin—his escapes to the exalted places, standing shoulder to shoulder with the people he finds there: ice fishermen in Alaska, bullfighters in San Miguel, falconers in Mongolia. These unaccompanied experiences grace his cheeks and freckle his lip.

He has not taken off his jacket nor is he sitting entirely on his chair. Instead, one foot pushes out, as if at any moment he might jump up from the table to go. He looks around between sips. His eyes have yet to land on her.

"Look, I just really needed to see you." Jillian huddles in close the table. She extends her hand outward toward him, hoping that her wishful body language might will him to her. "I've got some stuff I need to tell you."

Alex rubs his face with his hands and sits upright. He takes a long sip of water and signals to the waitress for a refill.

Jillian tries to land on him, land in his eyes. But she can't; he won't let her. "I lost my job."

The waitress fills his glass quickly and leaves.

"Yeah. I heard that."

The tension between them is palpable, even for a passerby.

"Billy fired me. But my presentation really sucked." It is the first time she's said it aloud to anyone other than Shelly. She is surprised that it feels good to acknowledge how terribly it all went. Like a giant breath released. The words sound funny to her now—not devastating. The adrenaline pumps through her, and she begins to giggle. It just went *bad*—simple as that. That's how some things go once in a while. The epiphany is refreshing and provides more than a modicum of relief. "It wasn't a *Big Bomb Idea*." She laughs harder when she says it—the words sounding insignificant and silly.

"I'm sorry about that, Jill." He looks around and taps on the table with his knuckle. The whole thing doesn't seem as funny to him. She stops laughing, and his eyes land on her for a moment. They're full with moisture, like cups ready to spill forward. He blinks it away and looks around again nervously.

Jillian wishes it could all just go back to the way it was before with Alex, but at the same time she wants to be different. She wants to let herself down with him, be honest and easy with him, like she is with Shelly. She wants all the confessions to sound funny instead of devastating.

She starts to shiver uncontrollably. Her breath comes out like chatter. She knows what there is left to say and it sticks like a ball in her throat. She feels the sweat drip down to her elbows and her heart clobber away in her chest.

"I steal things, Alex." She launches the words like an arrow with no thought of their direction. The blood pumps throughout her body, and her airway clutches in on itself. She's excited, excited and as afraid as she's ever been. "I think people do some pretty stupid shit to try and make themselves feel better . . . and I'm one of those people, and, well . . . I steal things." She says it again, just to feel the weight of it release some more.

"Jesus, Jill. What are you telling me here?" Alex breathes in deeply and lets the air come out in a giant huff. In three large breaths he goes from aggravated to angry to completely irate. He seems to explode—as if hearing her say *anything* would have made him erupt, but this has just put him completely over the edge.

Alex pushes back from the table, stands up, and runs his hands through his hair. He looks so tall from where she sits, far away. "I'm sorry, Jill. I can't do this. One day you have a million secrets from me, and the next you're telling me . . . well, I don't even know what you're telling me." His face turns red and swollen, and he stares at her as if something's just occurred to him. "How am I supposed to believe anything you say, Jill?"

"I don't know," she says back with a grimace. "You just should." It comes out like a plea more than a statement—frail and unbelievable.

The words do not sound funny anymore, and the modicum of relief she felt a moment ago is lost completely. She wishes she had kept her mouth shut.

"Alex?" Jillian watches as he turns to leave.

"I'm sorry, Jill." He raises one hand as he walks to the front door. "I just can't take this right now."

He leaves her there with her undrunk Caffe Vesuvius—the mound of whipped cream deflated into a fatty white pool floating on top. He leaves her there at Serendipity to deal with her puddle alone.

* * *

Jillian groans on her couch, pressing the coarse wool pillow flat against her face. She holds the Cigarette Picture against her forehead and rolls it back and forth until the glass cools her skin. She looks into it as if to find an answer. She used to see something beautiful there—a faraway maiden looking off into another galaxy. But now she just sees the old little girl: abandoned, self-protected, lonely, isolated, friendless, loveless, and swirling into the elusive ether as time creeps by. She doesn't know whether to hold it in her arms for safekeeping or hurl it across the room and watch it break into a thousand pieces. She runs her hand along the frame and holds it close to her cheek. "I'm sorry, Allie."

"Jillian! Jillian!" Shelly's tapping at the living room window breaks the silence.

She covers her face with a Max Mara skirt on the couch, tags still on.

"Go away, Shelly." Jillian's voice is muffled through Italian wool.

"I made you a present." Shelly raps on the window again, her voice audible through the old pane.

Jillian walks over to the door, opens it, then flops back onto the couch underneath the skirt.

Shelly shuts Jillian's door. "Whaddya doing?"

"I'm hibernating for the winter."

"Cool." Shelly crawls next to Jillian on the couch and rests her head on a balled-up pair of Hussein Chalayan sailor pants.

"You got a doughnut?" Jillian pulls the skirt off of her face to speak.

"Here. Have mine." Shelly hands Jillian a half-eaten Krispy Kreme. Jillian bites down on it. The sweet crunch is nauseating, and the fatty aftertaste is worse.

"Your place looks like shit." Shelly looks around at the new clothes and Chinese food containers still strewn about the living room.

"No! Really?" Jillian gulps down the wads of sweet dough.

"It's like you're living inside your purse." Shelly seems happy about her analogy.

"That's great. Thanks. That really makes me feel better." Jillian covers her face entirely with the Gucci silk. She breathes the material in and out and feels the humidity puff up under the cloth and then suck in and stick to her lips. "I made you something." Shelly pulls out the sewn figurine from her pocket. "It's a damn-it doll." Shelly pulls the cloth away from Jillian's face, like a magician performing a trick. "Ta da!"

Jillian stares at the beautiful object in Shelly's hands. Shelly dances it back and forth and hands it to Jillian. Sewn from patch-worked silk, corduroy, T-shirt material, linen, cotton, and probably a hundred other things the girls have stolen over the last weeks, it's shaped like an androgynous dolly with arms sticking straight out to the sides, bobbly eyes, and wildly uneven paillette sequin hair.

Jillian shakes it lightly and watches the eyes wiggle up and down. She shakes it again and smiles as the doll's pupils settle back into place. The thing hardly has any real features at all, but it's filled with a personality all its own. To Jillian, it seems both happy and sad, lost and found. It is pathetic and ugly and yet utterly happy in its own skin. "I love it, Shelly." She shakes her present up and down again.

Shelly holds the doll by the protruding arms. "When you're feeling sad and blue, like you could really slam it, take this dolly by the arms, and damn it, damn it, damn it." She slaps the thing against Jillian's face.

They both laugh.

Jillian takes the doll and smells it. It smells like all her favorite things mixed in together—new clothes, candy apples, toast, and dry cleaning. "It's a really nice gift." Jillian adjusts her body down onto the couch and holds the doll close against her chest.

She remembers Alain and the gifts he used to give her. She remembers her secret passageway and the beautiful place he built for her to escape into. She remembers the small things in her life that have been given to her and made for her, and she is truly thankful for all of those things. "I really love it, Shell." Both girls sink farther into the mess and look up at the ceiling.

"Are you all stressed out about the big job?" Shelly talks into the air; her voice is sweet and girly.

"I don't know. I guess I haven't been thinking about it."

"Well, I'm stoked." Shelly holds up a silk T-shirt and yanks off the tags hanging from the armhole. "I'm gonna make Poppy so proud of me."

Jillian thinks about what Ricardo said, about the two of them just being mules for the team. Jillian looks at Shelly nervously.

"I think it'll be the first time in my life I'll really get to do something important." Shelly is lost in her words.

"This is important Shelly." Jillian holds the doll up. "You make beautiful things, and you're a generous and honest person. That's about as important as it gets." Jillian hugs the doll again.

"I'm not important." Shelly curls on her side and smiles. "I'm just a booster."

The two of them sit there quietly through the whole afternoon. Jillian holds her doll, and Shelly bites her nails and pulls tags off clothes. They sit there as the sunlight slides from hard, hot angles through the blinds to cool, muted stripes running down toward the door. They sit and watch and listen to their own uneasy heartbeats.

30

"SHABBAT SHALOM!" Benjamin Fishbaum comes out from behind his desk and gives Jillian a big hug. She presses her head into his chest and wraps her arms tightly around his considerable shoulders. The feeling is completely safe and familiar.

"To what do I owe this good fortune, this *naches*?" Benjamin Fishbaum is well turned out in a fine double-breasted suit. His curly gray hair groomed neatly to his head serves as a sharp contrast to his black caterpillar eyebrows that shift and dart as if yearning to escape from their landing. "Look at you! What a gorgeous girl. A *shaineh maidel*. You know this phrase, *shaineh maidel*?" He cups her head in his ample hand.

"Shabbat shalom, Uncle Fish." Jillian inhales the brisk smell at the base of his pressed collar.

"You always had such pizzazz." He throws his head back with a snap. "Even when you were just a little *maideleh*." Jillian is wearing a trim velvet jacket and matching A-line skirt and a pair of pointy high heels from Florenie on Fifth. An oversized felt flower from Julian's is pinned jauntily on her lapel. *Pizzazz* might be one way of calling it. "Look at this girl! What a *punim!*" He pinches Jillian's cheek and looks into her eyes. "A tired *punim*," he adds, "and your uncle Fish knows a tired *punim* when he sees one." He raises his messy brows and lifts her face toward him for inspection.

"I am a little tired, Fish."

"And you look thin." Benjamin Fishbaum pats Jillian on the hand and sits her down on his squishy leather couch. "So, how's your mother? *Oy*, that one!"

"She's fabulous. You know Lois, Fish. She's never there, but she's always fabulous."

"A real *meshuggeneh*, that one. Do you take after your crazy mother, Jilly?

"I take after Bingo and Alain, Fish."

"Well, of course, we all know that. That Frenchman was more of a mama bear to you than the woman herself." Benjamin leans back into the seat and shoos away the bad thoughts that have just entered the mind. "Oy. Poor Meyer. *Ech.* It's terrible, just terrible. Bingo never wanted to go this way, my darling. He would have wanted something more dramatic. Like a movie. Or a book. Not this."

He composes himself again. "So what can I do you for, my darling?" He slaps his hands on the armrest to change the subject.

"I think a friend of mine might be in a little trouble, Fish. A little *ahf tsores.*"

"Very good with the Yiddish. You remember what Uncle Fish taught you."

"I want to give my friend, this guy, some advice, but I'm not really sure what to say." Jillian reaches out and twirls her hair— an old habit that accompanies white lies.

"And what's going on with this friend?" Benjamin pinches at his nose and furrows his brow. He looks like a rabbi on Yom Kippur contemplating the meaning of atonement for the congregation.

"Well, I'm not clear on all the details, but he, my friend, might be in over his head." Jillian twirls and twirls.

"Something illegal?" Benjamin seems surprised. "Is he a murderer, your friend?"

"He's not a murderer, Fish." *Not yet, at least.* "But I think he feels like one on the inside." Jillian thinks about her damn-it doll. She wishes she had it to hold close and keep forever in a safe place. "I think what started out as fun for my friend"—the words pour out easily now—"is not so fun anymore." The thoughts congeal as she speaks. "I mean, he used to have rules about everything—like a sense of what was right and wrong. I mean, right and wrong according to his own stupid brain." She laughs at the thought. "Rules like trying to be fair and people not getting hurt, but then he started breaking his rules . . . and they were idiotic rules to begin with . . . so now he's just lost."

Benjamin nods and listens—like a shrink without the notepad.

"Plus I think it may be getting dangerous. More dangerous than he realizes. Other people are in jeopardy. Good people whom he's actually grown to care about quite a lot."

"You know, my darling, it's not easy for a person to change. A person needs to know what he wants very clearly, have a very clear direction and path in order to get out of the messes he's made."

"I know." Jillian twirls a tendril of hair into a knot. And she does know.

"Do you think he's ready for that?"

Jillian rubs the ball of twisted hair. "It's just not who he is anymore." She looks at Benjamin and his fuzzy eyebrows. "It's not who he is at all."

"Well"—he slaps his knees—"it's good to know he has a head on his shoulders. And if your friend's a good *pisher:* smart, good family, a real good kid . . ." Jillian looks out over the room and through the window to the view of Park Avenue rooftops outside. She thinks about Bingo and his smoking jackets and the smell of his aftershave that lingered in his clothes. "Then he'll cook up a good scheme." He says abruptly. It was not the end of the sentence Jillian was expecting to hear.

"What do you mean, *he'll cook up a good scheme?*"

"A good *pisher* always has a good exit strategy." Benjamin gets up from the couch and rummages around his desk. "And exit strategies can be brilliant, my darling. A plan that protects the good, ensnares the bad, and saves the soul in the process." Benjamin pulls a pen and a yellow legal pad from his desk. "Sometimes saving the soul requires a little self-sacrificing here and there, as we all know." He hands over the pen and pad. "And make it smart. I hope he's smart, your friend."

An idea—an exit strategy—instantly occurs to her. It's a taste of power and control she hasn't felt in months. "Oh, I think he's a real smart *pisher*, Fish." Jillian puts the yellow pad and pen in her purse and senses a wave of excitement hit her.

Benjamin pulls Jillian up from the couch. "Up and at 'em, my darling. There's lots of work to do."

"Thanks, Fish." Jillian wraps her arms around his neck. He smells of shaving cream and dry cleaning. She lingers there as long as possible.

"You know, my darling, your *tsores* is my *tsores.*" Benjamin brushes her hair away from her face and squeezes lightly against her cheeks. "I'm here to help. I'm always here for the family. In good days and in bad. This is my lot in life, my darling."

Jillian kisses his smooth cheek. "You're a true *mensch*, Benj."

He walks Jillian to the door and puts his ample hand on her head. "Sometimes people need help from their friends to get out of their messes. You know the song, right?" He hums a few bars and squeezes her cheek again.

She laughs. "Perpetually avuncular, Fish."

"What can I say? I've got a severe case of avunculitis." Jillian offers her face up once again to the big *macher* before she waves good-bye.

31

IT'S FRIDAY and Vira has agreed to meet Jillian at the Round Bar in the Royalton Hotel. A chic Ian Schrager spectacle, the Royalton is now home to Vira's fourth penthouse office in three weeks. After a quick stint at the Plaza Athénée, Vira has opted for something more stylish, less "dusty" as he put it. Jillian had asked to meet Vira alone, and he obliged, offering to host her for "an afternoon aperitif" in the sleek bar rather than in his busy upstairs suite. She will give him one chance before she puts her plan in motion.

Packed from cocktail hour on, the Round Bar is strangely empty during the day, but the interior of the tiny room with its quilted walls, low lighting, and up-lit bar gives the effect of perpetual night.

"*Mi amor.*" Viracocha stands from his table and reaches both arms out to Jillian. "You look lovely." He kisses Jillian on each cheek. "May I get you something?"

"No, thank you, Vira. I'm fine." Jillian sits down on the steel chair. It's as pointy and uncomfortable as much of the custommade furniture in the hotel.

"I'm having a Campari and soda. It's a wonderful afternoon beverage." His narrow glass is backlit, the bubbles like tiny round bugs cling to the sides, and the red viscous liquid dangles at the bottom.

"No thanks. I'm fine."

"By the way, happy Shabbat, Jillian. Just a few hours away. Friday night after sundown, correct?"

"Yes." Jillian laughs at his religious naïveté. "Happy Shabbat to you, Vira."

"Do you go to your temple on the Shabbat?"

"No. Usually I go to my uncle's for dinner. I haven't gone in a while, but I think I'll be there tonight."

"Well, wish your family a happy Shabbat from your new friend, Viracocha." Vira takes pride in pronouncing his name.

"I will. Thank you very much." Jillian wants to get through the pleasantries.

"I have brought you a gift." He reaches under the table and pulls out a flat box with a bow. This is not a stuffed plastic bag of surplus product like he usually gives Shelly, and she already feels sorry for Shelly about what may be inside. "Open it, *mi amor.*"

Jillian pulls the ribbon off and opens the box. Inside is a David Yurman necklace like the one Shelly and Jillian saw in the magazine the day they got their first manicure. It's blandly ostentatious—a thick gold and silver rope, as fat as a noose, with violet gems dangling from either end—and as tacky as it looked in the magazine, only bigger and more real. "It's lovely, Vira."

"It is a David Yurman," he clarifies, in case Jillian couldn't read the forty-eight-point type on the inside of the box. While it is possibly the most expensive gift anyone has ever given her, she doesn't want it. Not only because it's another horrific example of why people without taste should not be allowed to have money, but because she doesn't want anything from this man. She's already stayed too long.

"Thank you." She puts the package underneath her chair.

He reaches out and holds Jillian's hand. "Now if this is about

Ricardo the other night at dinner, I want you to know I will take care of it. He will be punished appropriately. I can assure you personally."

"No, Vira. Please don't punish Ricardo. He was drunk. He didn't mean anything by it." Jillian doesn't want anything bad to happen to Ricardo or anyone on the team.

"That's no excuse for a man to behave like a boor."

"We were all drunk. It was a long day for everyone. Please don't punish him." She leans her head against her hand and lets her elbow rest on the table. She wishes she could just fall asleep and let this all pass on without her.

"As you wish." He swirls his glass on the table.

Jillian bites at the skin on her bottom lip and cracks her knuckles against her face. "I can't do this anymore, Vira. I can't do the big job with the team." Jillian can feel her teeth begin to chatter with adrenaline. "I need to do something different with my life."

Viracocha picks up his glass and holds the straw to his mouth. He takes a small sip and puts the drink back down. "I was once like you, Jillian, denying who I really was." He shakes his glass in little circles, stirring the heavy red liquid into a florid cloud toward the top. "But then I grew to be more comfortable with it. To accept who I was. You just don't want to admit it, but it's been you for as long as you can remember—always breaking the rules, challenging convention. Like me, you always believed you should have more in this world—what was rightfully yours had been taken away." He looks into his glass, remembering his own misfortunes. "I know you because I know myself."

Viracocha De La Puente suddenly looks old and shriveled— like an empty body in expensive clothes. Jillian doesn't like the sight of it. She does not want to be compared to him, ever—fancy but fossilizing.

"You don't know me, Vira. You don't know me at all." Jillian rubs the sweat from her palms onto her pants.

"But I do know you, Jillian, and, more importantly, I know Shelly." He stops and raises his eyebrows at her. "And I know

Shelly *very* well, Jillian, and I know she would be *very* disappointed if you weren't accompanying us on our upcoming job. Very disappointed indeed."

"Shelly's a big girl. I think Shelly will get along just fine without me."

Viracocha takes another sip of his Campari. Jillian can see the twitch above his jawbone.

"I don't, Jill." He puts down the drink again and leans his head into hers. "I don't think Shelly will get along just fine without you. As a matter of fact, I think Shelly will get herself into a lot of trouble without you." He flattens his brow with his pinky. "Do you think we keep Shelly around for our *entertainment*? Shelly is here because she provides a service for our team. We trained her for many weeks. We made an *investment* in her. Just because she did not turn out to be the answer we had hoped for ourselves doesn't mean her particular talents should be wasted."

He taps his fingers against the table and ponders his next point. "After the hunt, Jill, an animal is used for food—the prime pieces going to the most powerful of the hunters, but the fur, the bones, the innards, and even the scrap can still be used. This is how nature shows her respect for the beast." He turns his fingernails to look at them. "So even if all that is left of our investment in Shelly is the scrap, we will still respect the beast." He buffs them against his jacket. "And we have made an investment in you as well—our prime piece. Without you, Jill, without our American, our team is not whole." Viracocha sips his drink and leans back again. "What do you think, I just train you and I bring you into my family, Claudia protects you, watches out for you, I feed you with the food from my own people; and then when I need you, when it is time for you to feed me, I just let you walk away? Do you think that's the kind of man I am, Jillian?"

"I don't know what kind of man you are, Mr. De La Puente."

"I am the kind of man, Miss Siegel"—Viracocha crosses his legs—"who embraces his fate." He finishes his drink and gets up to leave the small room.

She is prepared to bring this man down, even if it means making personal sacrifices. She has never been more prepared for anything in her life.

"You will be there for the job," he asserts. "We are all counting on you. Shelly is counting on you. You don't want to let your friend down, do you?" He walks to the narrow exit in the corner of the hivelike space. "So we will see you promptly at nine A.M. for the Loevner's job, and you will follow Miss Monteagudo's orders implicitly."

The word falls like a brick. *Loevner's?* Her Loevner's? The big job is Loevner's? This was not figured into the scheme—not jotted down on Benjamin Fishbaum's yellow legal pad. She suddenly wants to choke him and watch the Campari and soda gurgle from his *boca.* Loevner's is not for the taking. It is hers, not his.

But in almost the same instant a new exit strategy emerges.

No one knows that store better than she.

It is mine. It is mine. It is mine.

Jillian keeps her smile hidden and this one last card to herself.

"Nine A.M. Is that understood?" Viracocha raises a hand as he disappears out of the room. "*Ciao,* Miss Siegel."

32

"HONEYDEW, c'mon in. You a sight for sore eyes, child." Belle opens the door and wipes her hands on a dish towel. Jillian nearly falls into Belle for a hug. The housekeeper wraps her arms around the girl, not understanding the depth to which she needs it.

"You want some casserole? I have some hot already." Belle's eyes are red, and her wig is askew and uncombed.

"Hi, Belly Belle." Jillian walks in, puts her purse down on the table, and hangs up her coat. "Is anybody else here?" Jillian takes comfort in the familiarity of the moment. Shabbat-at-Bingos's—just like always.

"You the only one here, child."

"Where's Bing?" Jillian looks back toward the bedroom. Her heart sinks.

"Oh, he still in there." Belle pulls out a tissue from her sleeve and pats at her eyes. "Mr. Loevner's still in this world." Belle points down the hall to his bedroom door. "But he ain't got much time, child."

"What do you mean, he's doesn't have much time, Belle?" Jillian stands with her back against the wall. She inches closer to it, like she could dissolve into it. "He was fine. He was fine when I was here." She feels frantic, like there's something she should be doing—someone she should be calling. The air in the room is thin, and she gulps at it. "Right?"

"These things happen so quick, honey." Belle is wringing the dry dish towel in her hands.

"Did you call my mother?" Jillian's eyes and ears chase around the room, as if everyone could just be hiding in the living room, getting ready to yell "Surprise." "Did you call Lois?"

"Ms. Siegel's on her safari or something. I don't even know what country she in." Belle waves the air with her towel. "C'mon in the kitchen. Belle get you something to eat."

"Please tell me what's going on, Belle." Jillian follows the housekeeper and sits down at the breakfast table. "I don't want any food." She pushes away the dish of mandarin oranges Belle puts in front of her.

"You need to eat somethin'. Everybody need to eat somethin'." Belle puts the kettle on and makes up a small plate of braised pork, boiled greens, and bread pudding—heaping spoonfuls out of large Tupperware bowls. Confused and distraught, she puts more and more food on the plate, as if it's all she can think of to do. "I cooked all this damn food." She looks angrily at the plate, like everything would just be fine if it weren't for the damn plate.

"Please Belle, I can't eat that. Some tea is fine." Jillian rubs her temple, trying to soothe the knot that has formed there. "What's going on with Bing?"

"I get you some pudding." Belle takes a casserole dish out from the refrigerator.

"I don't need pudding, Belle. Just stop and tell me what's going on?"

"He was coughing his food up this week, and then he got a high fever, child." She peels off the layer of plastic wrap on top of a dish. "He was just burning up on Wednesday. I called those hospice people. They say he wasn't sick enough for them to come. But he hardly moved since then."

Belle places a dainty cup, "a fairy cup" as Alain used to call the small cabbage leaf tea set he brought from France, on a delicate matching saucer. "I guess you gotta be dead for those people to come." Belle is talking to herself now. She is as busy in the kitchen as she possibly can be, moving things around, straightening them out. "So I called that doctor, that Chinese one down on Madison Mr. Loevner go to."

Belle scoops up a hefty teaspoon of honey and adds it to the cup. "So what's happening? Is he in pain?"

"They giving him some of these antibiotics through a bag that the nurse set up. And now they think we should get some food in him." Belle pours the hot water into the cup and dunks the tea bag only once. She carries the cup over to Jillian and places it in front of her. "Here you go, honeydew."

"Thanks, Belle." Jillian holds the warm cup in her hands without drinking from it. "What do you mean they want to get some food in him? You mean through a feeding tube?"

"I don't know, child." Belle pulls out her crinkled tissue and blows her nose. "Poor Mr. Loevner."

"That's not what Bing would want." Jillian feels a well of tears puffing out into her face. "He wants . . . *Out of Africa*, not feeding tubes."

Belle straightens out a box of tiny pencils by the phone, puts the lids on the Tupperware, and stores the containers back in the refrigerator. "I known that man for fifty years." A tiny hum is barely audible from her, like she is singing to a baby. "Hospice said they'll come back when the *process* begun." Belle spoons out squares of Jell-O into two glass bowls. She takes a spoonful of it into her mouth and puts the other in front of Jillian. "Oh, that man." Belle laughs a little and shoos her hand in the air as if Bingo tracked mud in the house or forgot to take his umbrella in the rain. "May the Lord have mercy and he go quick here in his own bed." Belle washes off the plate full of food.

"May the Lord have mercy," Jillian repeats Belle's words and takes a sip of her tea. Belle dries off the already dry table and sits down on the opposite side.

"Eat your Jell-O, child."

Jillian looks down onto the shimmering red surface. She pushes at the side of the bowl and watches it wiggle back and forth. She remembers the nights she sat at this table as a girl, her feet barely touching the ground, eating Jell-O with Belle as Bingo and the grown-ups had their parties. And now here she sits hoping for that man to die, if the Lord has mercy.

The kettle heats up; the whir of the molecules fills the room with tension and impending release.

"Why did Bing give up the store, Belle?"

"Give up the store?" Belle laughs and pours the water and dunks another tea bag in just once. "Mr. Loevner didn't give nothing up, that's for damn sure, child. They force his hand. That's what I know." Belle's nostrils are flaring. Jillian is not the only one for whom the old memories fester and rot. "The board forced his hand because a who he is—he and Mr. Alain—and that still get me angry today." Belle folds and unfolds her dish towel. "Mr. Loevner never make any pretense about who he is. He make no excuses. And no one, I mean no one, had a problem with that. Eat your Jell-O."

Jillian spoons a bite into her mouth.

"Before that, nobody much thought about it." She wraps the towel over the refrigerator handle. "And then those damn board of trustees come and tell him what to do."

"Craig Allen? Asked him to step down?"

Belle takes the half-empty bowl away from Jillian and puts it in the sink. "Mr. Loevner and Mr. Alain never made no secret about what they was. But that sorta thing wasn't all that popular at that time. Not like it is now, child, with the television shows and everything." Belle's as worked up as Jillian's ever seen her. "Well, they didn't exactly think that sort of thing was the proper image for the store—now that they owned their piece of it."

"So they asked Bingo to step down?"

"That'd be the way you say it in polite company." Belle cleans Jillian's bowl and puts it next to the sink. "I don't believe in sinning against God, child—but I believe that God is forgiving and that all men on this earth are forgiven in the eyes of the Lord. I, for one, think a man like your uncle run a fine store."

"Me too, Belle."

Jillian walks into Bingo's bedroom. It's dark except for the light beside his bed. Bingo is propped upright against a pillow, but his eyes are closed and his breath is shallow. She climbs onto the giant bed, a bed she has longed to climb into again for so many years—her clothes, slippery against the satin coverlet. She puts a light hand on his chest and feels it rise and fall. "Chicken shit, huh, Bing?"

She curls up beside him and nuzzles her face onto his shoulder. His smells are incorrect—sour where they should be sweet, bitter where they should be clean. She pushes the foul bouquet out of her mind. "I've been so bad, Bing." She wraps her arm all the way around him. He's smaller than he once was and she's able to hold on tightly. "I lie about everything." She balances herself up on her elbow. "Remember when I was thirteen and I told you I didn't have a camel-hair coat?" She wipes her nose against her hand. "Well, I did. I had the one that Alain gave me at the store, but I wanted two." She laughs to herself. "I lied because I wanted two *fucking* camel-hair coats! What thirteen-year-old needs two identical camel-hair coats?" She laughs again.

"And now the math doesn't add up, Bing. It hasn't added up for so long." She rubs her face in her hands. "Jesus, I'm such an idiot."

Jillian traces the paisley on his smoking jacket. The swirls of the pattern draw around, gently protecting him with their caresses. "I've got a plan, though, Bing." She nods to assure herself. "Fish helped me. Of course I lied to him too." Jillian smiles and wipes her nose again. "I was gonna ask you to help me," she cuddles close to her uncle, "but it looks like I'm on my own." She listens to the familiar roar of the air conditioning end with a quiet sputter. "May the Lord have mercy."

33

"RICARDO is such an ass. I can't believe he got in your shit like that." Shelly inspects each piece of clothing at the boutique the way Jillian taught her—from a place of confidence and rightfulness.

"He's okay. He's just a kid and he's scared. It's no big deal."

The girls move within the little boutique in Soho as one—Shelly pulls out a shirt for a look; Jillian does the same and tries to hide any of her inner thoughts. It's a small, crowded boutique, easy game for these seasoned veterans. Jillian thought an outing like this would make perfect sense to Shelly—a quick, easy fix, a warm-up before the job at Loevner's tomorrow.

"Well, he's a *pendejo*." Shelly sucks on the ends of her hair, wetting them into a point between her fingers. "I'm pretty psyched Vira wants me do the gig. It's like he really thinks I can do it."

Jillian stops and smiles at her friend. "He totally does, Shell." She is careful to sound enthusiastic but not overly so. "Why else would he have trained you like that? I mean, that was a big deal, right? Training the American girl. He's a businessman, right, and he invested in you because he thought you were worth it. Everybody believes in you."

"You think?" She's biting her nails. They're all bitten down to the quick, and the surrounding area is swollen and red. "Gordo too, right?" Shelly pulls a shirt out from the rack, wraps it into a casual ball, and slips it into the side of her coat.

"I know Gordo does." Jillian's assurances sound true enough as she looks at the clothes on the rack—running her fingers up and down the seams, palpating for the hard plastic attachment. She's never wanted to find a security device *on* something before; now it's the only thing she wants.

"Besides, Shelly, you're worth it. You're a genuine and creative person. That's pretty rare in the world."

Shelly twirls her hair into her mouth again. She bites at a dry spot on her lip and pulls at it with her lower front teeth. "You don't think they're gonna make me the mule on the job, do you?" She itches the side of her face. "I mean, they wouldn't do that to me, right?"

"I know for a fact they won't."

"I mean, they'd send me to County for a big job like this."

"You're not going up to County, Shelly. I promise you. I won't let that happen. I'm your *pawtna.*"

Shelly rips a cuticle off her thumb and looks around toward the front door. "Hey, wait. This place is fired up. Check out the dookie door. We can't cut here."

Jillian looks at the tall security stands on either side of the front door. "I think it's just for show. I've been feeling for dookies. Only a couple things have them. Just the small expensive stuff and leather."

"That shirt I took? That didn't have one, right?"

"It didn't. It definitely didn't."

"That'd be so bogus right now." Shelly fishes nervously around her coat for the hidden shirt ball. She pulls it out and lets it unfurl.

"See. No sensor." Jillian looks calm and sure even though her heart is pounding and she feels like crying. She is careful not to let any of it show.

"Yeah. Shit." Shelly seems relieved. "Claudia would be so pissed if we got busted right now. We couldn't do the gig."

They continue to meander through the circular racks. Jillian walks her fingers up and down every piece, frantically looking for something metal and hard, something pocket-sized.

"Aren't you nervous?" Shelly dabs at a bloodied bit on her thumb. "I can't stand it—I feel like I'm gonna crawl out of my skin."

"About the job?" Jillian spots a small cashmere scarf on the counter behind Shelly and tries to keep the conversation going as she grabs it.

"Yeah—about the job!" Shelly pulls another T-shirt off the hanger and crumples it into her purse. "What else is there?"

Jillian rolls the cashmere scarf into her hand and pushes it up her sleeve. She feels the rigid sensor against her skin. She can feel the metal button in the middle and the plastic clasp along the side. She's both thankful for what she has in her hand and terrified of it. The thing hangs off the lightweight scarf like a broken limb. Her hands are sticky with sweat, and her head aches.

"Shit." Shelly grabs Jillian by the arm. "We didn't do the mantra. We gotta put all this stuff back!" Shelly pulls out balls of fabric from beneath her jacket. She doesn't notice that Jillian hasn't taken anything else.

"Jesus, Shelly. Relax, okay . . . ?" Jillian holds her friend steady under the elbow.

Shelly rids her person of anything and everything she didn't come in with. "It's just bad luck not to do the mantra." Shelly is panic-stricken.

"It's just a goof, Shell, just words. It's not real."

"It's not just words!" Shelly assures herself. "It's not."

"Let's just forget it, Shell. I think I need to go home." Jillian glides the cashmere scarf back down to the bottom of her sleeve—just a millimeter away from her fingers. "Rest up."

"Oh. Yeah. Okay." Shelly seems to agree. "I'm just all freaked. I'll be okay." She curls her hair around her ears and chews at the edge of her pinky nail. "You don't want to get one of those hot milk manis? Maybe a massage or something?" She seems disappointed, lost.

"Not today. I just need to go home." Jillian pulls the scarf down from her sleeve and keeps a firm grip on it with her hand. She is careful not to let Shelly see the material peek from between her fingers.

Jillian hugs Shelly tightly. It is the first time she's pressed her skin up against her friend's. She smells of lollipops, baby powder, and the clean, astringent smell of brightly colored shampoo. It is a wonderful perfume, the opposite of her own.

Jillian presses her nose deep into her friend's hair. "You smell so good, Shelly." Jillian reaches her hand around to Shelly's purse and presses the ball of cashmere and plastic deep enough into it for it to drop to the bottom.

"I do? I'm not wearing anything." Shelly holds her arms out and smells her own sleeve, hoping to uncover what Jillian senses.

"You do. You smell so great." Jillian wants to let the tears fall down her face, but she doesn't. She smiles and hugs Shelly tightly again.

"You put back your stuff?" Shelly points her nose at Jillian's pockets.

"Yeah. Everything's where it belongs."

"You wanna go over the fence first?" Shelly points to the front door.

"No, you go. I'll make sure you get out safe." Jillian watches as Shelly walks toward the front door.

Shelly waves hard as she backs out the door. Her brown hair is showing its golden roots at the part; her feet clomp along the floor ungracefully; her fingers wiggle like spiders as she cracks her fingers one by one. "Outtie-5000!"

The sound of the alarm is quick and penetrating. It buzzes in and out, and orange lights swirl overhead. Jillian feels the noise in the floor vibrating her toes. She doesn't look at Shelly's face. Instead she watches the security guards as they approach her friend on either side. Jillian holds her head down and continues for a moment to rifle through the racks.

"May we see in your bag, miss?" The security guard holds out his badge to Shelly and moves her away from the entryway. Jillian walks slowly and purposefully toward the door, looking down at the floor. Her heart is beating loudly. She can hear the blood rush in and out in currents behind her ears.

Shelly's eyes catch Jillian's. She's holding out the poof of airy fabric. It's hardly a thing at all, barely even a square of material. The plastic sensor dangles heavily below her fingers. Her face is bright red and contorted into one big question mark. Jillian pretends not to notice her and walks steadily through the front door. "It's not mine. I didn't do it. I'm not a mule. I'm not."

The sound of Shelly's voice quiets as Jillian lets the glass door close behind her. She holds up her hand for the next taxi north.

34

LAST NIGHT I dreamt I went to Manderley again. It seemed to me I stood by the iron gate leading to the drive, and for a while I could not enter, for the way was barred to me. There was a padlock and a chain upon the gate. I called in my dream to the lodge-keeper, and had no answer, and peering closer through the rusted spokes of the gate I saw the lodge was uninhabited.

No smoke came from the chimney, and the little lattice windows gaped forlorn. Then, like all dreamers, I was possessed of a sudden with supernatural powers and passed like a spirit through the barrier before me. The drive wound away in front of me, twisting and turning as it had always done, but as I advanced I was aware that a change had come upon it; it was narrow and unkept, not the drive that we had known.

Jillian lets the words from the musty old book fall quietly out of her mouth and onto the pillow of Bingo's ear. These opening moments of *Rebecca* were always Bingo's favorite—mysterious, romantic, beckoning—and Daphne du Maurier, Jillian feels, is a fetching piper for his journey. The *process*, as the woman from

Hospice explained it, had begun, and Bingo's breaths were strained and numbered. Jillian was determined to give him the last thing she could—a moment of drama and *beauté*, during this, his otherwise unexceptional ending.

On and on, now east, now west, wound the poor thread that once had been our drive. Sometimes I thought it was lost, but it appeared again, beneath a fallen tree perhaps or struggling on the other side of a muddied ditch created by the winter rains. I had not thought the way so long. Surely the miles had multiplied, even as the trees had done, and this path led but to a labyrinth, some choked wilderness, and not to the house at all. I came upon it suddenly; the approach masked by the unnatural growth of a vast shrub that spread in all directions, and I stood, my heart thumping in my breast, the strange prick of tears behind my eyes.

There was Manderley, our Manderley, secretive and silent as it had always been, the grey stone shining in the moonlight of my dream, the mullioned windows reflecting the green lawns and the terrace. Time could not wreck the perfect symmetry of those walls, not the site itself, a jewel in a hollow hand.

Meyer Loevner gasps for air in his slumber, hoping to find little pieces of what was needed to hold on a bit longer. The body instinctively fights to stay, as Alain's too must have done, on that warm spring night amidst the French lavender and the blooming yellow mustard, the tumor grown inside enough finally to seize the body. She holds his cheek in her hand and breathes him out onto the moonlit labyrinth.

Jillian lets the door close softly behind her. Belle sleeps on a small chair in the guest room opposite Bingo's bedroom; her head is slumped and her arms clutch the needlepoint pillow usually found on top of the coverlet on the guest bed. *A friend is someone who knows you and loves you anyway* is stitched in blue letters against the gold background. Belle is not wearing her wig. Her gray hair is frizzed, and her scalp shows through in rows.

"Belle. Belle." Jillian kneels beside the sleeping woman and gently shakes her knee. "Belly Belle."

"Oh, what, honey? I must have nodded off." Belle looks around the room, gathering her wits.

"Bingo's gone, Belly." Jillian rests her head in her old friend's lap. "He's just gone."

"Oh no, child. Oh no." Belle smooths Jillian's hair away from her forehead. One hand brushes downward and then is followed by the other. The motion is soothing in a way that Jillian cannot describe. It's been so long since she felt cared for and in this simple motion of hands against hair, warmth against scalp, she feels all the love she has ever felt. Jillian hears the drops fall against her ear, Belle's tears, as big as elephants, pouring down onto her neck and mixing with her own.

"Belle?"

"Yes, child?"

Jillian lifts her wet face from Belle's lap. "I need you to do me a favor, Belle. Can you remember?"

Belle wipes away her own tears and focuses on Jillian.

Jillian pulls a folded sheet of yellow legal paper out of her pocket. "It's important."

"Sure, honey." Belle feels for her wig and seems momentarily embarrassed not to find it on her head. "What is it, child?"

"I need you to call Craig Allen."

"From Mr. Loevner's store?" It must seem like a strange request to her.

"I need you to call Craig Allen first thing in the morning. First thing, Belle."

"Okay, honey."

"He's in Bingo's address book. And you tell his secretary"— Jillian hands Belle the piece of paper—"you tell his secretary you have an important message from Mr. Loevner. An urgent message. That way she'll put you through."

Belle takes the piece of paper from Jillian. She's concentrating intently on Jillian's words.

"You read what's on this paper to Craig Allen, Belle."

Belle looks at the yellow sheet.

Jillian holds onto Belle's knees and stares right into her eyes. She is as clear as she's ever been with the woman. "It's very important that you read it exactly, Belle."

"Okay, honey. Okay."

Jillian gets up and kisses Belle on the side of the cheek and then once on the top of her head. She brushes Belle's hair back too, hand after hand. "Call Hospice after I leave. They'll come over and help you. I love you, Belle." Jillian puts Belle's palm against her own cheek. The feeling of it is always sweet and good. "And don't forget to call Craig Allen in the morning."

"I won't. I love you too, child."

Jillian walks down the hallway toward the front door. Her shoes click-clack in the quiet along the marble floor. Belle peeks out from behind the guest room door.

"Child?"

"What, Belle?"

"You have some trouble, child?"

Jillian opens the front door and walks halfway out. "What I have, Belle, is an exit strategy."

35

MANUEL drives the van up Madison and goes over the final briefing for the team. Jillian sits next to Gordo in the back, and Claudia and Ricardo sit quietly in the middle seat. Gordo sings a quiet song to himself in Spanish. It sounds, Jillian thinks, like a children's lullaby. The only other noise is Claudia sipping her morning coffee, leaving her shiny trail of copper lipstick on the edge of the cup.

Jillian looks out through the tinted windows onto the New York streets. It is a vast, unending place with no horizon line in sight. She's always amazed to walk down the same streets over and over again, day after day, year after year, and never really see the same person twice. The city is an infinite wave of people rushing in and rushing back out again. And yet with all that current and undertow, with the thousands and thousands who crowd alongside you, it still can be the loneliest place in the world.

Manuel reviews the highlights of the job. According to his most recent reports, there will be exactly six Loevner's LP agents on today, four starting at nine and two more at eleven. One is a woman, five are married, four of them have children, one has grandchildren, and one is a "live beaner," according to Manuel. Gordo, of course, finds this fact amusing. He comes on at eleven and "he'll be hungry for a stop," so everyone is to be out by ten-thirty sharp. They will have less than eighteen minutes to complete the job—an enormous order from Vira's most powerful Mexico City buyer, who has been very specific and who will accept nothing less than every item on his list.

There isn't one millimeter of the old place Jillian doesn't know by heart, but the layout is reviewed again from top to bottom during the briefing. She feigned as much ignorance as anyone else, counting the details on her fingers as if to memorize them. There's an exit on Fifty-sixth, one on Madison, two employee exits in the back of the store, four elevators, two escalators, four bathrooms, and one ancient wooden escalator that goes down from the second to the first floor but doesn't run anymore.

Each member of the team has his or her assigned exit, but all have memorized the whereabouts of the other three just in case. Two cameras run on each floor, but the ones on the north side aren't working because of an electrical problem. They haven't been working for over a year, after the uptown blackout, and nobody bothered to fix them. The working ones run live at scrambled times throughout the day but are rarely monitored. They keep no videotape, but that's likely to change once the new management takes over.

There are two security guards at the front exit, both of whom have been there since the fifties: one is nearly blind, and the other can barely walk, much less run after anyone. "No-dicks," as Manuel called them, who are there for show and to greet the ladies. Jillian smiles to herself as she thinks about her campaign—Pierre and Gerhardt tipping their hats to the thieves as they walk out the door with laundry bags of loot. "Come back real soon!"

According to Manuel, the store hasn't been hit in any significant way since 1983, when a Hispanic crew pulled a few dozen furs from the storage basement two weeks before Christmas.

Their van was eventually seized on Forty-eighth. An inside job, most likely. To date, Loevner's is the cleanest store in the city.

None of the clothes have sensors, including leather and suede, which is unusual for a store this size, but nonetheless an oversight, says Manuel, on management's part. Instead they have always focused on an overabundance of sales associates—one to every handful of customers, or "guests" as management likes to refer to them. The old-fashioned service, the *oversight*, to which Manuel refers, has kept the store running smoothly over the years, but that is likely to change drastically.

Jillian knows it was no oversight, just a commitment made long ago to purity and personal attention above technology and paranoia. Bingo always thought the cost of fear was greater than the cost of a few things walking out the door un-paid for.

Once in the store, the team is impeccably focused and organized. Not a spare word has been uttered, not a movement wasted. Jillian and Claudia are stationed on the third floor; Gordo and Ricardo are on five. While Claudia feigned disappointment in Shelly's absence, and told Jillian she'd have to do twice the work, Jillian didn't believe a word she said. The only thing Claudia was disappointed about, Jillian thought, was the fact that her mule was now gone. The woman had no intention of making sure Shelly got out of the store safely.

Gordo and Ricardo are in charge of "sweets"—leather and suede coats—and "pasta"—men's Italian suits: Armani, Hugo Boss, Brioni, etc. Gordo is also in charge of "toys"—big-name sporty gear for the under-twenty set: Hilfiger, Nike, Phat Farm, Sean John. Jillian and Claudia will hit the usual designer clothes: Prada, YSL, Chloé, Chanel, and the other usual suspects, as well as Loevner's unique selection of "undiscovereds": young Belgians, Japanese, Italians, and homegrown talent.

Delight in every corner.

This list was long, and the savvy client hadn't missed a beat.

* * *

The selected items were marked yesterday by a reconnaissance team with an inconspicuous tag—a small plastic orange square on the shoulder of the item stuck on with removable adhesive. Up to twenty percent of the items lose their tagging, so the list still needed to be memorized. Jillian knew what she was responsible for, and, if taken, it would be her biggest haul yet.

"Gordo? Clear?" Gordo is the "threepoint" on the team. Claudia will check in on him every minute to gain information on his whereabouts and any LP sightings. Claudia's voice is straight and purposeful; even over the radio her intensity and single-mindedness come across.

"Clear." Gordo too is not his usual cowboy self, and it sounds as if he's moving swiftly, getting the job done. Gordo expects nothing less than to get every item on his list. According to what he told Shelly, he never comes up shy.

Jillian watches Claudia from across the floor. She looks completely credible and comfortable—a casual shopper, an office worker with some money to spare, a rich wife planning her outfit for the evening. She does nothing to call attention to herself—she neither smiles nor looks suspicious in any way. Jillian observes closely and sees Claudia's hands moving at the speed of light—stuffing, folding, stuffing, folding—yet she just floats above the entire action as if the top and bottom of her body was disconnected from the middle. Jillian is reminded of Harry Houdini calmly dislocating his shoulders to wriggle from his suspended cage. Claudia is a truly skilled professional and her deceit is both impressive and sickening to watch.

Jillian is in position on the south side, tending to her work and checking quickly for rolling cameras or a glimpse of LP in order to give Claudia the appropriate hand signals. Each second that it sinks in further and further what she is there to do, Jillian's heart pounds harder and harder. Her nipples grow so erect they chafe under her sweater. Sweat pours down from her armpits and soaks the material along her sides. She concentrates on keeping her cool, keeping her cheeks from burning off her face.

"Ricardo?"

"Still clear."

Jillian pulls shirts and dresses by the handful and folds them into the tight little packages she's learned how to make. She isolates the back stairwell in her periphery while she works. The sight of it causes a near dizzying rush of adrenaline into her system. Hopefully, if Belle completed her job correctly, there will be only a few more minutes of this left. She will then have the tiniest chance and just a few milliseconds to leap for the stairwell, fly down three flights of stairs, and make it to the spot behind the perfume counter. Once there, her chances are about five percent. If the area is clear and the door is still there after all these years, she might make it; if not, if any one of a hundred remodels has removed the imperfection, sealed over the crack in the wall, she'll go down with the ship, plead her case, and take what she understandably deserves.

It's a risk she is willing to take. Like Gordo, she will not come up shy on this job.

"We moving to subchannel twelve." Claudia's direct proclamation slices through. Jillian's heart drops in her chest. Claudia has suddenly decided to take the team off their customary FRS frequency and move them to a less predictable one. This would ruin the plan entirely and render Belle's call pointless. Jillian sees Claudia begin to adjust her radio.

"Wait!" Jillian responds out of turn. It is not her place to disagree with the leader, and certainly not here, but she has to keep everyone on the original channel or everything will be blown. "I was having trouble with my signal. My radio must be having problems. Twelve isn't working."

"I get twelve. I'll take it." Ricardo is quick to add his opinion. He has no particular emotion in his voice, but the implication is there: lose the white girl with the bad radio. He'll move onto three.

Jillian holds her breath, watches the back hallway, and waits for Claudia's response. Ricardo's suggestion would certainly make sense—lose the girl and let someone take her place, although if Claudia takes him up on it, the entire plan will be blown. The team is still for a brief moment, awaiting Claudia's decision. Everyone will abide by what she says. "Keep on seven and the subchannel on fourteen. We need the American for the haul."

Jillian exhales and the team continues the work, their hands swirling, the endless seconds passing. The plan is that she and Claudia will complete their haul in eleven minutes and head for their exit. Her hands grow numb against the fabrics, but all she can do is wait and work as the minutes pass and hope it all comes to an end soon—one way or another. "Are Ricardo and Gordo in place on the fifth floor?"

"*Sí!*" Claudia makes a face at her from across the floor. "You know where they are." Jillian wishes she could have helped Gordo get out just like she did for Shelly, before any real harm was done, but the risk was too great. He's been nothing but good to her, and she wishes he could have a better life than this. Gordo is good at what he does. He could be good at anything.

"I just wanted to see if Ricardo and Gordo were still on the fifth floor and if we should stay here on three."

"Tell the *gringa* to shut her *boca!*" Ricardo's voice comes over the radio, the sound of movement and rustling along with it.

"Quiet!" Claudia adds with no small amount of suspicion. Then her attention moves toward the ceiling. She rolls her finger up in the air and points to the black ball on the wall, giving the hand signal to indicate that the security device is activated. She's careful not to look up, but Jillian does, her face clearly in view.

She looks down at her watch. Jillian knows that Belle has called already and given Craig Allen the team's radio frequency. She knows LP is watching now and waiting for the right moment to strike.

Claudia gives the signal to complete the haul and exit. It's the most unfortunate of all the hand signals—a slice across the neck, the death sign or "out of air." She watches as her finger glides along her neck, imagining all its implications.

"You know your exit." Claudia glares at Jillian and walks forward toward the front. Jillian spies Gordo walking smoothly down the stairs, clearly weighed down by dozens of items folded tightly into him.

Gordo turns to give a last look at Jillian. He raises his eyebrows to check on her. She gives him the complete signal across the room, finger across neck. Even though she is not complete, it is the only sign that will cause him to leave the store and perhaps get out in time. He is ahead of Claudia and Ricardo by at least a few seconds. *He might make it.*

"*ChuchaPussy!*" Ricardo's voice is muffled by the sound of running and his mouthpiece moving back and forth.

"*Rechucha!*" Claudia's breath is quick and loud. Jillian turns toward the front but can't see Claudia or her brother.

The reverberations over the earpiece are abstract and chaotic. It's like, she thinks, a video camera has tumbled onto the floor in an earthquake, revealing only the sounds of escape and bedlam, not the sights. The stereophonic pandemonium makes her dizzy. Her heart quickens, and she takes the moment of chaos to pull herself together and carry through with her plan.

She is prepared for this, but the whole thing happens quicker than she imagines. From her spot near the dark back stairwell she can see a man and a woman, decidedly LP in their beige pants, white shirts, and soft-soled shoes, marching toward the front stairs. She walks slowly, careful not to look obvious or in a hurry. Her heart is beating so wildly her vision blurs and the sweat pours down her palms. She turns right to look toward the front and the woman spots her—Jillian—the *gringa*, the one who didn't fit the profile. The one whom no one was expecting to be there.

With her chances dwindling by the second, she races suddenly for the stairwell. Awkward, stuffed full of clothes, with an earpiece taped onto her head, she rips off the headset and throws it behind her. The female LP races after her. The other agent presumably races after the rest of the team. Gordo either made it or he didn't by now. Jillian crosses her fingers.

The sound of the agent running behind her is swift but barely audible—the agent's sensible shoes do their job well, and Jillian can concentrate on nothing but leaping forward as quickly as possible. Even one mistake, one shift of balance, and her small chance will be eradicated.

Jillian blasts down the stairwell and out onto the second floor. Her feet know exactly where to land as the muscle memory takes over.

> . . . 1, 2, 3, 4, 5, 6, 7 steps, swing around, hold on to the railing, make the curve, gather momentum, bounce off the other wall, spring forward, leap through . . .

Instead of turning right toward the escalator or the front stairwell, as most would think was the only alternative toward an exit, she turns sharply to the left into the darkness. No one knows this store better than Jillian Laurel Siegel, and she's counting on it; this girl's been racing up and down these paths for the better part of a lifetime and every inch of it is in her blood.

> . . . Miss Mary Mack, Mack, Mack, all dressed in black, black, black, with silver buttons, button, buttons, all down her back, back, back. Ready or not, here I come . . .

Jillian leaps ten paces ahead of the woman and heads down the old wooden escalator in the corner. Most people wouldn't even remember it was there. It's been silenced for so many years. She listens carefully for footsteps behind her but hears nothing but her own lungs filling and collapsing, the hum of fluorescent lights, and the dull thumps of her feet hitting the wooden grates. There was a time when all the escalators in the store were narrow and wooden—their clippity-clap, clippity-clap taking customers up or down single file; now this is the only one left, permanently frozen in time, waiting for Jillian to bound over it once again.

The first floor is visible up ahead. The lightness of it emerges from the darkness of the old quieted escalator shaft. Jillian can see a large rectangular banner hanging from one end of the store to the other. It eclipses the view of the giant chandelier up ahead in the distance.

"Je t'adore Loevner's"

The black and white characters from the new ad shine down on her: the dashing new Bingo—as charming and flamboyant as the old one; the *au courant* Briana Terrell—taller and more buxom than the original but still elegantly poised off center, ready to spread her glossy wings and flutter away; and the contemporary Jillian—doe-eyed, multiethnic, and still hopeful.

The new image, Jillian must admit, is achingly beautiful and exactly what it should be. Loevner's still is what it always was—an enchanted forest, an elegant moment frozen in time, a tempting delight in every *pouche*. Even at the hands of Billy Baum and Brandon Pietro, the noble iconography has not been destroyed.

Perhaps their touch was not so clumsy after all.

Jillian stops to look as the three of them smile out at her, but then she hears the footsteps behind her gaining in volume. She flies down to the bottom of the old escalator and toward the brightly lit expanse of the ground floor. Just ahead, the predicable hustle and bustle and the piped-in music growing louder signals that she is an inch closer to freedom. The sight and sound seem otherworldly.

The driving thump of soft shoes on wood is again audible behind her. Jillian surveys the area and spots the perfume counter and the mahogany panels on the wall in the back. With one giant *grand jeté* Jillian leaps behind the opulent glass counter and squats behind it. Out of breath, she huddles there like a crumpled toadstool and waits for the LP agent to pass.

"Honeydew?"

Jillian looks up. Mrs. Dell'Rosa is smiling down at her, looking confused. The woman looks tall from this vantage point. Her head seems a mile away.

"Hi, Mrs. Dell'Rosa," Jillian whispers from her compacted position. Jillian tries to convey a million things with just one look, but at this point her fate rests in the hands of a woman who's specialty is *eau de toilet*, not reading minds.

Mrs. Dell'Rosa looks up and around. Jillian can hear the agent's voice drawing close. "Damn it." She hears the agent take a moment to catch her breath and survey the area. "Did you see that girl, ma'am?" The agent is right there, within inches of her view. "She had a long black skirt on. She was a white girl."

Jillian doesn't dare look up, instead she sits tightly in a ball at Mrs. Dell'Rosa's feet; the heat swirls around her body and evaporates off her in a mist.

"Did she need perfume?" Mrs. Dell'Rosa asks innocently.

"She wasn't a *guest* . . . she was . . . Oh shit, forget it."

Mrs. Dell'Rosa switches some boxes around and fidgets with a few things at the counter until the agent leaves. She kneels down to face Jillian. "Now, this is a familiar old scene, honeydew! It's been twenty years since we've played hide-and-seek around here!" Her pointy incisor pokes out from behind her smile. It is a welcome sight. "As far as I'm concerned," she rubs Jillian on her shoulders, "this place is still your playground. Yours and Mr. Loevner's," she adds defiantly. "You do what you want here, honey." Mrs. Dell'Rosa grabs an elegant bottle from the counter and mists it around Jillian's head. "You need it."

"Thanks, Mrs. Dell'Rosa." Jillian backs up toward the mahogany wall.

"Sure, hun." Mrs. Dell'Rosa pushes a pencil into her smooth gray bun and looks the other way.

From this vantage point, inches from the old panels, Jillian can see Claudia and Ricardo being walked toward the back of the department store by a half-dozen LP agents. Claudia's glossy smile has been etched off her face, leaving only a silent grimace in its place. Ricardo's arms flail out in caustic jerks. She has just a few seconds before they'll pass her again, and this time one of them will surely spot her. She doesn't see Gordo. She wonders again if he made it out.

Jillian is out of breath and her heart is beating out of its shell. The old wall is not much different than the old days—the wood grain identical to the way she remembers it, dark and cherry-toned, with brown swirls coursing through it. She puts her hand flat against the mahogany panel and pushes it to the left. It is still warm to the touch, as it always was, but it doesn't budge. She pushes it again. Nothing. She watches as the LP agents lead Claudia and Ricardo closer toward her. *C'mon.* She tries to be gentler, pushing it lightly left then right. *C'mon. C'mon.* Jillian sees the team and the agents nearing the counter. "C'mon. Please."

"Narnia's that one, honey." Mrs. Dell'Rosa's pointy-toed shoe taps the panel to the left. "I keep my smokes in there."

Jillian pushes lightly on the panel to the left and the tiny door slides open. The space, designed originally for a much smaller girl without a truckload of clothes stuffed in her girdle, is just big enough for her to fit in. Jillian crawls all the way through and pulls the panel shut just in time for the team to walk by.

She hears Ricardo's voice muffled through the wood. "I ain't talking to none of you people. Fuckass shitwads."

36

IT IS exactly how she remembers it. The smell of the unfinished wood like a fresh-baked loaf of bread cracked open and toasted. The perfume counter is distant—the pungent aroma mingles and softens with the sawdust. The perky music pulses through like an undercurrent and the voices are filtered through the two-by-fours.

Mrs. Dell'Rosa's cigarettes are here, a whole carton of them perched on a railing. A lighter and ashtray sit right next to it. A dozen cigarette butts sit smashed in the bowl, Mrs. Dell'Rosa's lipstick lining the ends in glossy red flower buds. A hand-painted fluorescent sign marks the entrance:

* *Narnia* *

It's spelled out in Alain's fancy cursive writing. No more or less ornate than the notes he once left in her lunchbox, *"A peach for my Peach,"* or in lipstick on her bathroom mirror, *"Have another glorious day in the kingdom, Princess!"*

Jillian can't stand up like she used to in the miniature space, so she crouches down and makes her way toward the makeshift salon. *Mademoiselle's Palace*, as Jillian and Alain christened it years ago with a can of Tab and a mustard sandwich shared between them, is at the epicenter of the passageway, the only area of Narnia that is not a hallway.

The stolen clothes seem stuck to her body, sucked in like a vacuum. She pries them off of her one by one, pulling them out like splinters from her skin-tight girdle. The back of her legs burn from the nylon material, and her body and mind ache from exhaustion. She crawls up onto Mademoiselle's Divan and tucks her knees under her chin.

She remembers the bed bigger and more glamorous, the height and girth of the bed in *The Princess and the Pea* perhaps, but now it's just a plain old piece of foam covered with an old throw, probably the same as it always was, in the center of a dank, musty oasis.

Jillian turns over and presses her face into the foam. In this cocoon she allows herself to grieve again for Alain—the long-ago loss so tangible in this room. And she grieves for Bingo—these feelings fresh and raw. She imagines the two of them soaring above the paillete chandelier: Bingo's smoking jacket tied high and elegantly around his waist, Alain's jeans shirt buttoned up the wrong way—the two sipping "buckets of Grande Dame," floating away to another shore. She grieves for her father, a man she never knew, a man who abandoned her for his own journey to Narnia.

And she aches for Alex: for his body, his smell, the way his skin is always moist but never oily, the way his eyes are clearer the closer he gets, the way he makes up nicknames for her—a new one every time he sees her, all too private and some too sappy to share. She laughs and runs a finger along her lips. She imagines he will age well, getting only a few well-placed wrinkles, his hair turning silver like his father's, his eyes staying clear and ready.

She longs for him on this pitiful old bed. She longs for him to make love to her through this piercing, bottomless sadness.

This place had always been a place for her to call her own, to think, to yearn, to compose herself—and here she is again composing herself and yearning. As she falls asleep she wonders how many times in her life she will find herself again in this dark cave, hoping to transform into something new.

In the morning all is quiet. The hum of vacuum cleaners penetrates the space. Right on schedule, Jillian wakes up from her mildewy repose and moves on to the last few steps. She opens the old dress-up trunk, Alain's secret gift, for the first time in twenty years and looks inside to see what remains.

She pulls out a mound of dresses, dozens of scarves and hats, gloves and shoes. The trunk is a vintage find; its contents would be the envy of a store like Decades: a place that specializes in untouched couture, discarded and forgotten in just this kind of way. These are crème de la crème vintage pieces from Alain's collection of personal favorites. Pieces he picked out personally for his own amusement, never to be sold in the store, only to be kept for one unimaginable day when they might be cherished in just this way: Jean Muir, Rudi Gernreich, Balenciaga, Madame Grès, Dior, Balmain, Saint Laurent, Nina Ricci, Cardin. Each one an artifact of magnificence.

Jillian trades her booster clothes for a Balenciaga from a hundred seasons ago. The wool dress, once ten sizes too big, zips up perfectly along Jillian's spine. She wonders if Alain had this in mind. The waist nips in perfectly and then swells out again along her hip. It is as if the piece were made for her escape.

She checks herself in the mirror Alain hung for her—a tiny heart-shaped trifle with a broken gilded frame around it. Alain never had much reverence for the thing. *"One should never spend too much time with mirrors, cherie. The mirror has ruined many a life,"* Alain said as he nailed it up at face height for the young little lady.

Crouching down on her knees, Jillian is able to see her body only one square at a time. She wraps a scarf around her hair and ties it all into a neat bun in the back. A fat pearl necklace doubles round her wrist, and a pair of size seven-and-a-half pumps slip on perfectly. Without really knowing for sure, she can say she looks great; she certainly feels it. A long night on a dank old piece of foam has done wonders.

Jillian pushes the scarf off her neck and with a dainty vintage pocketbook on her wrist and a pair of Jackie-O sunglasses, she pushes open the secret door and emerges onto the floor while no one's looking. She stops at the perfume counter and dabs some Fracas behind her ears. The scent of fresh gardenia blossoms fills her nose.

Jillian walks happily toward the front of the store. She takes one last look above her at the new ad. The three new characters look down at her and smile.

Je t'adore.

Jillian nods to the two old doormen as they open the grand exit for her. "Pierre. Gerhardt." She throws her scarf over her shoulder and walks through the door into the sunshine.

"Have a lovely day." They both tip their heads to her in unison. "Come back and see us soon." The magnificent chandelier sparkles behind their backs as she walks out through the front door.

37

Message 1: Hi honey, it's your mother. *What? No, it's Jilly. I'm leaving a message for her.* So anyway, I'm simply beside myself, darling. Marshall and I are at Charles de Gaulle. They wouldn't upgrade me, which is simply unbelievable. I fly enough with these people. Anyway, darling, I'm beside myself. I only thank God that you were there for him, during the, you know, passing. God! No one loved that man more than I did. *What? No, I can't do the aisle, darling, I get sick if I don't have a window.* Anyway, darling, I'll be home by midnight, and we can do the whole sitting shiva thing. Beverly has generously offered us her lovely apartment for the event, darling. I love you, honey.

Message 2: Hi honey, it's your mother again. I'm still at the airport. Listen, darling, can you call Zabar's and have them send over food to Beverly's for the wake, something lovely, maybe see if they can send some sturgeon and smoked salmon and maybe some of those feta triangles they do. A Jewish brunch but not too Jewish, darling. Or really anything lovely that you can think of. I love you, honey.

Message 3: And Dr. Brown's Cel-Ray, darling. It was Bing's favorite. I love you, honey.

Message 4: Hi. It's me. I knew you wouldn't be home. I was just calling to hear your voice. There. I heard it. That's all I guess. It's a good voice, Jill. I like the sound of it. It's me. Alex.

Message 5: It's your mother, Jillian. I'm calling from the plane. Can you hear me? Hello? Jillian, can you hear me? *Is this thing working? Stewardess. Stewardess. Ring the call button, Marshall, will you please?*

Message 6: Jillian darling, it's Benjamin Fishbaum . . . Uncle Fish. Can you come up to my office as soon as you get this message? I'm going through the will and apparently your dear Uncle Bingo, my darling, was a little more *meshuga* than we anticipated.

38

SHELLY walks into the common room to meet the man who called to volunteer his services. It's not the public defender she met yesterday with his crumpled suit and cheap shoes. This is a big, elegant guy in custom duds from head to toe.

"You want a *nosh?*" The gray-haired lawyer offers Shelly a Krispy Kreme, her favorite kind: plain glazed, right from the box.

She takes the doughnut and relishes the sugary crunch and the buttery aftertaste. She likes him already.

"You like?"

"Ummm. Krispy Kreme rocks." Shelly breaks the thing in half and hands a piece to the man. "You want some?"

"No, my darling, you eat. You have a healthy appetite, *kine-hora.*"

Shelly keeps chewing. She has no idea what his funny words mean, but it doesn't matter when there's doughnuts.

"So I hear you're quite the little artist."

"I'm not an artist." Shelly twists her dyed hair into a knot.

"That's not what I heard from the little birdies." He wiggles his fingers in the air by his ear.

"Well, I ain't."

"It's good to have a craft you can do that you're proud of. It's a *mazel,* and you should keep it up."

Shelly swallows the last bite of Krispy Kreme and surveys the locked cement room. "Yo, dude, take a look. How exactly am I supposed to do anything *artistic* in this friggin' place?"

"You'll be out of here in no time, dear. I'm not as much of a *nudnik* as I look." The lawyer clicks open his briefcase and pulls out a pile of papers. "One prior. Some property damage." He talks to himself as he reads. "A little gar*bage* here and there to clean up."

"Where's my other lawyer? The homey with the brown tie?"

"I'm your lawyer now. And you don't have to worry about a thing, my darling. I eat cases like this for breakfast. With the statement we have in your defense from someone named . . ." —he checks through his papers—"*Socrates . . .* we'll get you'll out of here, no problem."

"Socrates?"

He checks his papers again. "Socrates Palomino, I believe. A.k.a. 'Gordo,' a.k.a. 'Gordito,' a.k.a. 'G.' "

Shelly laughs. "Gordito. Right." She tries to look cool, brushing the hair off her face. "How is he? *Socrates?*" She crosses her fingers at her side.

"Well, your friend's given the court quite a bit of information about the ring and its operation, and he had a lot of helpful things to say about you. I believe he'll do just fine for himself." The man holds his hand out to his client. "But the other *goniffs*— the brother and sister, now that's a different story. They'll be deported and dealt with in their own country."

"And Vira? Vira . . . choke . . . a?"

He pats her hand. "Don't you worry about him, my darling. Let's just get you out of here."

She bites at the corner of her thumb. "I don't got no money, y'know. What's this gonna cost me?"

"Don't bite your cuticles, dear." The lawyer takes her hand out of her mouth and puts it in his own. "Nothing, my dear." He smiles at her, a warm, burly smile. His fat black eyebrows soften into two brackets above his eyes. "It's all taken care of."

"What do you mean nothing? Don't you people get about a billion dollars an hour?"

"What can I say, my darling? I'm a Park Avenue *mensch*."

39

IT'S the middle of the day, and the Miami airport is crowded. A mother walks by pushing a baby carriage and yelling for the boy behind her to pay attention and watch where he's going. A group of flight attendants marches through, smiling to one another and pulling their neat black suitcases on wheels. An airport worker pushes an old woman in a wheelchair to another gate.

The line at United is long, but the wait for First Class is only one deep. He has no luggage, only the clothes on his back, and he's holding the ticket to Venezuela tightly in his hand.

He's not nervous; why should he be? This is the risk he takes. It's always been a gamble—you just need to know when it's time to fold your cards and leave the game.

It is not hard to spot him—the dark slender man in the expensive shoes, the Piaget watch, and the custom-tailored dress shirt.

"Viracocha De La Puente?" Two agents approach from either side of him and grip to his elbows.

He looks up and around. A dozen armed men encircle the balcony above, their rifles aimed right for him. He takes his hand out of his pocket and shows them all his palm is clear. He smooths back his hair into place. It looks neat and glossy.

"Yes"—he smiles—"I am he."

40

"WE'RE just pleased as punch with the work you and your people have been doing for us, Bill." Craig Allen sits in the low designer couch across the table from the chairman and CEO in Bomb's executive office. He smiles widely as always, revealing a collection of bright white teeth. It's been only a few days since the incident at the store over which he presides, but the seasoned executive has learned to handle all sorts of situations with a good set of dentures and a cheery outward appearance.

"Par for the course, my man." Billy Baum is also grinning as hard as he can at his biggest client, trying to disguise his impatience for this type of interaction. He's wearing the taupe Armani jacket he keeps in the office for surprise visits such as this. This morning's latte dribble was more noticeable than usual, according to the agency's new junior public relations executive, Mandy Mandel. The jacket, she said, is a good distraction from the stain.

"And we're pleased as punch you're pleased as punch." Creative director Brandon Pietro is sitting beside Billy Baum, simulating unanimous glee. He's wearing the Paul Smith suit he bought yesterday at Bergdorf's on the way back from the gym. It was a week's paycheck, but he didn't blink—he just put half on one credit card and half on another and paid the tax with cash. (Brandon understands the importance of a good ensemble in a position like his, and so his suit collection far outweighs his apartment in both value and size.) He scratches between his brows, recently waxed into two separate entities for sixty-five dollars by the eyebrow groomer at the John Barrett salon—another recommendation from Mandy Mandel. "So what are you gonna do with yourself, Mr. Allen? You know, now that you're . . . you know, done." Brandon Pietro picks between his brows.

"Well, I have a few things up my sleeve. I need to socialize the plans around the family, see what sticks to the window. Maybe some independent consulting. Maybe a little fly-fishing at our place in Idaho. Some golf at Ocho Rancho, that sort of thing." Craig Allen looks at his watch.

Brandon puts his cowboy boots up on the desk, right over left, but Billy pushes them quickly away.

"We heard your people had some trouble up at the store earlier this week," Billy says, with a proper mixture of concern and disbelief.

"Oh sure, a very big thing," Craig Allen shares the scoop. "One of those international crime rings. Shoplifters." He seems as surprised as anyone about the news. "Apparently these folks hit stores all over the world. There was some special on *20/20* about these groups—a real organized bunch. They'd been studying our security folks for a few months." Craig Allen shakes his head. "We had a tip. It was the craziest thing. Just a bunch of numbers. The radio frequency these guys were using." He still looks confused by it all. "The oddest thing. Anyway, that's not why I'm here today." He shifts gears—going in for the kill.

"We can only assume it's about your new management team up there." Billy twists a pencil around and around in his hand nervously. "And what that means for Bomb."

"*Fuck*," Brandon mutters under his breath.

"This decision was out of my hands, Bill." Craig Allen has not stopped smiling. He always smiles, no matter what he's delivering. This is either a practiced habit or true sadistic joy—no one's quite sure. "It's a contractual thing, effective a few days ago. Legal, not personal." He spontaneously stands up and practices his golf swing with an invisible club. "I'm sure the account will stabilize after the transition, Bill."

"Sure, sure. Absolutely. It always does. Always does." Billy wipes the sweat from above his lip. He knows that accounts never stabilize after a thing like this. They simply disappear. He mentally cancels his vacation at Hotel du Cap.

Billy opens the door to his new humidor. "Cigar?" Billy points one out to Craig Allen.

"Oh, no thanks, Bill. Very kind of you, though. None for me anymore, I'm sorry to say." Craig Allen laughs and adjusts his slacks. He refocuses the subject to the matter at hand. "She's a great gal, really. I wanted you to meet her before she starts next week. I think you folks are going to like her." He smiles. "She's very . . . *creative*, as you people say." He makes a flamboyant gesture in the air.

"And, you say, she's related to the old owner?"

"Well, there's a bit more to it."

Billy Baum counts up the billings in his head minus the account. The number is about fifty percent less than it should be. Maybe more. He'll have to lay off a few dozen people, possibly even take a cut himself. He could kick himself for buying the house in Southampton before the quarter's end. It was a mistake—a big mistake.

"She should be here in just a few minutes." Craig Allen looks at his watch.

"Brittney!" Billy Baum yells for his executive assistant.

"Yes, Billy?" The buxom blonde pokes her head in through the door. She's holding a pile of paper towels just in case.

"Can you see that Mr. Allen's lady friend is shown back here immediately?"

"Sure, Billy." Brittney disappears back out the door.

"Mr. Loevner, *Bingo,* as those of us knew him called him, was a really marvelous man. I had the pleasure of counting him among my friends." Craig Allen repositions the front of his hair. "He was a real class act. A very . . . *creative* person."

"But you say she isn't related to him?" Billy clips the end off a cigar, trying not to sound too desperate.

"Oh, she is. She's his niece. I've known her since she was a tyke." He swallows some spit that's built up in his mouth.

"The niece of the old owner?" Brandon itches between his brows; the area is pink and swollen.

"Well, actually, she is the old owner, Brian."

"Brandon."

Craig Allen spreads his arms along the back of the couch and crosses his legs. "Bingo Loevner gave the department store to his niece when she was born. Right there in her birthday suit, she owns a department store!" He chuckles to himself in amazement. "Fifty-one percent." He snaps his fingers loudly. "She's the majority shareholder. Has been for years." Craig Allen blows his nose into a monogrammed hanky from his jacket pocket. "When he stepped down as chairman after his partner passed away, the girl was too young. But from what I understand, he really groomed her for this position for many years. Since she was a child. She was the apple of her uncle's eye."

Billy and Brandon nod and smile, smile and nod.

Brandon wonders if he can still return the suit.

"Ironically, this was the little gal in the old ads." Craig Allen points at the old photograph taped to a board leaning against Billy's wall. "The girl with the dark eyes."

"*The* girl?" Brandon raises his swollen eyebrows. "I thought she died in that Tylenol poisoning incident or one of those kinda things."

"Just urban legend. This little girl's big now, and she's alive and kicking."

The door slides open; the sound of metal pressing against metal interrupts the room. "And here she is now." Craig Allen stands up and adjusts his waistband.

The tall woman glides smoothly into the room. Her simple vintage Dior suit hugs her figure elegantly.

"Bill, Brian, I'd like you to meet Jillian Siegel."

"Hi, Billy." Jillian towers over the three men.

"Hey, Jill." Brandon Pietro starts frantically picking at a blemish on his chin.

"Well, well, if it isn't the infamous Jillian Siegel." Billy turns toward his new humidor and retrieves another cigar. He holds it out to Jillian. "Cigar?"

"No, thanks, Billy. I don't do cigars this early in the morning."

Brandon laughs into his sleeve and wipes the sweat from his forehead.

"This must be a pretty good day for you, Jill." Billy lets the moisture accumulate on his lip without wiping it away.

"Yeah. You could say that." She must admit, it does feel good.

"It looks like you two have met before." Craig Allen clasps his hands together excitedly.

"I recently fired Ms. Siegel." Billy glances over at Craig Allen.

"Oh my." Craig Allen sits back down.

Jillian continues Billy's explanation. "I didn't have the big idea. 'Rejected from the organism . . . blah, de blah, blah, blah." Jillian pulls a lip balm out of her diminutive baguette handbag. "New secretary, Billy?" She points her elbow out at the bosomy employee as she smooths on a layer of the lavender-flavored balm.

"You know me, Jill. I like to ship 'em in, ship 'em out." He smiles and lights his cigar. He takes a big puff and blows it up to the ceiling. "What about you, Jill? You like to ship 'em in, ship 'em out?"

"I'm not firing Bomb, if that's what you're trying to ask. The campaign I did was terrible. You were right. It just wasn't what I was built to do. Your campaign was the big idea. The B.B.I. As my uncle Bingo used to say, 'Hire the best and then trust them implicitly.' You're staying as the agency of record—it's my first official decree."

Brandon's "phew" is audible.

"Who knows, maybe after three or four years, we'll grow sick of each other; I'll fire Bomb and hire Joel Levinson's shop. Everybody does in the end, right, Billy?"

"So they say." Billy looks at the end of his cigar.

"We'll keep everything the way it is now—the team, the billings, the deliverables. But let's just say that I'm rearranging the power dynamic. Like it's my organism now." Jillian smiles.

"Well, that's darn good news." Craig Allen pushes up from the low, modern couch. He seems eager to shake everyone's hand and head off into the sunset. "Darn good."

"So it looks like I'll be seeing everyone on my first official day of work. Monday at nine—weekly status meeting up at my place." Jillian rubs her lips together, gloating in the tiniest details.

"We usually do the status meeting down here, Jill." Brandon plucks another stray hair from the bridge of his nose. "In the large conference room. Without the client. At nine-thirty. On Tuesdays." He crosses his legs the other way around, fidgets, then crosses them back again.

"Well, we're gonna have the status meetings up at the store from now on. At nine. Monday. *With* the client—me." Jillian tries not to smile too hard. "Your first assignment—help us introduce a new talent we'll be promoting up at the store. She's a self-taught designer with a brilliant line called Cut Threadbags. I'm sure you men'll do a great job. See ya then."

Jillian adjusts her Dior along her hips and walks out the sliding-glass door. She yells back from beside Brittney's desk, "The eyebrows look good . . . Brian."

41

"BEVERLY'S place looks fabulous, darling, doesn't it?" Lois kisses Jillian's cheek and wipes away the mark with her thumb. "She had Emelio Pinto go completely all out. Emelio does the most fabulous shivas. And look!" Lois points to the chandelier. "Bing's pink light bulbs!" Every bulb has been replaced with Soft Rose Luminaires.

Lois is wearing a pebbly black Chanel suit, the same one she wore to Moira Goldman's funeral, Len Fireman's funeral, and the lavish wedding at the Plaza, where Lana Seligman's daughter married, as Lois called him, "the bald *shvartze* with the earrings." "Isn't Bev a dear, Jilly?"

"I don't want to hear another word of it, darling, not another word." Beverly Berman blows an air-kiss to Lois as she waltzes across the floor with a plate of chopped liver from Zabar's. "If I was sitting shiva, darling, I know you would open your lovely home to me. And look at your daughter, the big *macher*, doesn't she look gorgeous, Lo?"

Beverly blows another kiss to her friend as she disappears into the crowd.

"You do look fabulous, Jilly. And look"—Lois's eyes land on the bottom of Jillian's trim, sophisticated dress—"no dungarees! Who'd 'a thunk it?" Lois spins Jillian around to the back and then to the front again. "Doesn't she look gorgeous, Marshall?"

"What? Of course she looks gorgeous." Marshall takes out his reading glasses and puts them on. "She's a gorgeous girl." Marshall eyes up Jillian in the vintage suit. "Gorgeous," he adds again.

Jillian smiles and strikes a pose for them. The material feels wonderful against her skin.

"And where's that gorgeous boy of yours?" Lois looks around the room. "I just need a little pinch of that *tush*, darling. Just a little pinch."

"I don't think he's coming, mother."

"Of course he is, honey." She continues to look. "Belle. Darling," Lois reaches out and places a gentle arm on the housekeeper walking by, "if it's not too much trouble could you get me a plain bagel and a *schmear* from the kitchen? The ones on the platter are all sesame. Sesame is simply ghastly for the colon."

"Surely, Ms. Siegel." Belle's new straight auburn wig frames her face in a sweet circle. Her crisp pink suit is a warm dedication to her beloved old employer's favorite color.

"Stay, Belle. I'll get it, Mother. Belle's not working today."

"She's not?" Lois looks completely confused.

"She's here with Mr. Wilson."

"Mr. Wilson?" Lois waves hello to another friend passing by.

"Her husband. Belle Wilson's husband. Belle's married, Lois."

Jillian smiles at the big man behind Belle. His cropped Afro and wide mustache have turned gray since she last saw him at Christmas in Queens over twenty years ago.

Jillian holds her old friend by the hand then shoos her off toward her husband. "I'll get my mother a bagel, Belly Belle." The retired housekeeper joins her husband of fifty-five years, their fingers lacing up together.

Jillian turns back to Lois, kisses her on the cheek, and wipes away the residue. "You really are a pain in the ass, Lois. You do know this about yourself?" She kisses her again and strokes her face.

Lois Siegel brushes back a strand of her daughter's hair and looks her eye to eye. "I love you too, honey."

Jillian is surprised to see him there in the kitchen, wearing a navy blue jacket, nursing a Cel-Ray soda, standing beside a platter of H&H bagels. He must have snuck in before she arrived.

"Alex?"

He wipes his mouth on his sleeve. His hair is neatly combed back, and his shirt is freshly pressed. He looks like a beautiful boy.

"Hi. Hey." Alex puts his soda down on the counter.

"Thanks for coming." Jillian's face flushes pink.

The caterers walk between them to pick up the blintzes.

"Your mom called me. From Italy or somewhere. She told me it was today. I wanted to be here."

"That was sweet of her." She cuts a plain bagel in half and spreads a layer of cream cheese on it. "And of you."

"I'm sorry about Bingo. I know how important he was to you."

"Yeah." She shrugs her shoulders and puts the bagel on a paper plate. "I miss him."

"You look nice. Really beautiful, Jill."

"Thanks." She looks down at herself, also amazed she looks this pretty, this feminine.

A caterer walks in between them and picks up a loaf of pumpernickel.

"I got a new job." Jillian makes conversation, the paper plate still in her hand. "Thanks to Bing."

"I heard. That's really great, Jilly. Pretty crazy stuff."

"A surprise in every *poche*, as Bingo always said." Jillian comes in close and looks him in the eye. "I sent the stuff back, Alex." It is a statement she is proud of—more proud than just about anything in her life up to now. "I sent all the stuff back. To every store. Even the stuff from five and ten years ago. I cleaned out my whole closet." Even now, Jillian can barely believe it, but it's true, and she's happy. "I sent them all gift certificates to Loevner's. On me. My version of an apology, I guess."

"Apologies are not your forte, historically speaking."

"No." She thinks about all the fumbled ones over the years. "Not my strongest suit." She smiles.

The two stand there together in the kitchen. The salty smells of sour cream and feta cheese, the sweet aromas of baking raisins and simmering coffee waft around them.

"I completely screwed up, Allie, and I'm sorry." She fills her chest with air and releases it. It's a small but monumental release. "I was a complete idiot."

"You were. I won't deny it." He puts his hand on hers. His palm feels warm and familiar.

She starts to laugh at the ridiculousness of it all. "I'm so messed up." She laughs so hard at herself she chortles. It is a low, warbled sound accompanied by snorts and heaves. It trickles down into a simple giggle.

He runs his finger down her hair. "And that's really a horrible, disgusting sound you make. It's like a snort or something."

"I know." Her giggling trails off.

"Isn't there plastic surgery you can get for that? Like have your uvula removed? It's all really very horrible, Jilly. Terrible." He holds her hand tightly.

"You think you could be seen with a girl who laughs like that?" She wipes a tear from her eye. "You think you could love a girl who's all messed up?"

A caterer comes between them and pulls out a tray of filo triangles from the refrigerator.

"Excuse me. Sorry." The woman shuts the refrigerator door.

Alex brushes his knuckles against Jillian's temple. "I don't know, Jilly. I'm just not sure." He kisses her hand. "Maybe I can." He takes a giant breath, smiles, and looks down at the paper plate still in Jillian's hand. "Are you gonna eat that bagel?"

"Oops, I forgot. It's for Lois and her irritable colon. Do you want to bring it out to her? She said something about needing to pinch your ass."

"I would love nothing more." He bows and takes the plate from her. "You know I can never turn down a little *tush* torture from your mother." He walks toward the kitchen doorway and looks back at her.

He's so handsome standing there and she loves him—no matter what. She holds her hands up in a square and blinks at him. "Taking a picture. So I remember."

He looks back at her through an imaginary viewfinder and blinks back. "Me too." He smiles again before he leaves.

Jillian wipes the wetness from her eyes and smooths her hair behind her ears. In the other room, past the Balthus and the bagels, almost everyone she knows is celebrating the life of a person she loved like no other. Lois and Marshall, Belle and Alex, Fish and Bev, Linda, even Suki, Si, Noreen, Adelaide, Mike, Henry, Phoebe, the Sachses, the Loevners, the Lasners, the Broidos, and the hundreds of other people who grew up and grew old alongside her family are here.

Her life is still enchanted. And the pieces of her heart, once thought mislaid, are not lost at all. The world is still pink, and the Grande Dame is still flowing.

Jillian laughs to herself and adjusts her dress along her hips.

ACKNOWLEDGMENTS

After rehearsing this speech for more than three decades in front of the mirror with a hairbrush as a microphone, I find myself finally at the podium, clumsy and unprepared. While I'm tempted to thank all the people who have ever been nice to me, from Miss Levine, my elementary school teacher, to Taylor Sinclair, my boyfriend in eighth grade, I will spare you of all but the ones I have scribbled on my cocktail napkin.

To Jennifer Joel, Greer Hendricks, Judith Curr, Marcy Engleman, Dana Gidney, David Brown, Alyson Mazzarelli, Jade Dressler, Suzanne O'Neill and Katie Sigelman—a group of monumentally impressive people whom I am ridiculously lucky to know.

To Griffin and Tallulah, Nan and Donald Solow, Jordan and David Sweeting, Janellen Radoff, Hannah and Herman Solow, Adelaide and Mike Sachs, Miriam, Ethan and Damon Jacoby, Sue and Steve Chainey, Lauren and Justin Skoble, Jeff and Rebecca Musser, Karen Goldberg, Sharon Reidbord, Juditta Musette—a wonderful family that fills my heart every day and gives me a home no matter where I am. And to Tommy Jacoby, to whom this book is dedicated—I wouldn't have done it without you.

To Ann Peterson, Alison Lurie, Matthew Iribarne, Greg Blatman, Augusten Burroughs, Suzanne Finnamore, Terry Richardson, Richard Avedon, Arianne Phillips, Calliope Jones, Donny Deutsch and Richard Kirshenbaum—my teachers, mentors, cheerleaders, advisers, and inspiration. You've kept my fire warm and my pen flowing.

To the people who made this story come alive: Sheriff Bob Doyle, Detective Matt Lethin, the Marin County Sheriff's Department, Daniel Adam Smith, Daniel P. Richardson, Richard Alvarez, Terry Shulman, Neiman Marcus, Whole Foods, "Sir Veillance," "B.P," and "Joseph Stalin."

My heartfelt thanks also to those who would not or could not be named.

A portion of the author's proceeds will go to support the National Resources Defense Council (www.nrdc.org).